High Gloss

PETER ENGEL

ST. MARTIN'S PRESS • NEW YORK

Library of Congress Cataloging in Publication Data

Engel, Peter H
    High gloss.

    I. Title.
PZ4.E576Hi   [PS3555.N39]   813'.5'4   78-21359
ISBN 0-312-37232-9

To my friend Sam
and my wife Patricia,
with love.

Chapter 1

O ne o'clock at night in New York is the time of those gray, faceless people who keep the dirty underpinnings of the great city more or less in working order. In the subway yards and bus garages, maintenance crews try to repair tired machinery for yet another struggle with the rush-hour crowds. In the factories, cleanup men haul out rank garbage. In the office buildings, which in daytime pulse with the incredible vitality of America's business, the only light is the glow of the emergency exit signs.

But the six people in the boardroom of Associated Products, Incorporated, had no thought of abandoning their offices. Admittedly each of them was exhausted from days of trying to stave off the financial disaster which faced the giant company and its major subsidiary, the Regina Cosmetic Company. Some were even more tired from days of jockeying for the best position from which to survive the disaster if it came. And each, except Frances Duke, the only woman in the group, looked haggard. But they all understood that if a solution of API's problems could not be found before morning, then tomorrow the forces leading inevitably to bankruptcy would be unleashed.

Associated Products, Incorporated, ranked seventieth on

Fortune Magazine's list of America's five hundred largest companies. Sales of its products, including those of Regina's cosmetics, were in excess of two billion dollars. Half of all households in Europe and North America used some API product at least once a year. The corporation had eighty-six factories in forty-eight countries, making everything from snacks to toiletries, from soaps to gourmet meals. It employed more than one hundred thousand men and women. In addition, API had huge real-estate holdings. Hundreds of middle income houses were under construction in new cities in the Midwest and in Australia. Almost eight hundred other houses in various developments in North America and Europe were completed but empty, victims of a worldwide economic downturn. An enormous entertainment development, of a size matched only by Disney World, was half-completed but stalled by lack of funds.

It was API's real-estate ventures, in fact, that threatened to break the corporation; for though on paper its property was worth a great deal more than its purchase price, under present economic conditions buyers were scarce. And the cash drain from the real estate continued, straining terribly the ability of the rest of the corporation to generate needed money. If a huge infusion of cash could not be found fast, Associated Products, Inc. would doubtless go under, a business catastrophe almost without equal in modern times.

Alex Petersen, president and chief executive officer of the Regina Cosmetic Company, leaned over the boardroom table and beat passionately on its shiny surface to emphasize his point. His determination to convince his listeners was almost violent. From boyhood, Petersen's stubbornness—his friends called it determination, his enemies, arrogance—had been a primary characteristic. It had led him from working-class origins to Princeton and eventually to the head of a huge cosmetics company. It had also broken his marriage and destroyed the chances for several others. Now it was causing him to fight tenaciously to save a company almost certainly lost.

"We've got to find a way to *make* it work," he said. "It's the only plan that makes sense. Otherwise, API will be broke within a month and Regina won't be far behind." He felt his anger and frustration mount. "It *can* work," he insisted. "Both companies are innately sound. API's consumer products sales can be rebuilt with a reasonable investment, and Regina's are strong. The whole problem is API's real estate. We're overextended. The interest we're paying is destroying us. But listen—even there, the land and the buildings are basically sound. Maybe they can't be sold in today's economy; I realize they're borrowed up to the hilt. But in a year or two we'll be able to liquidate most of them at a profit. API and Regina *can* make money. All we need is the cash to ride it out."

"All you need is a hundred million dollars," Jimmy Leonetti interrupted bitterly from the other end of the table. "I can't raise twenty percent of that in the next few weeks. No one could, not with the lousy press we've been getting."

Leonetti lounged in his chair, his tie loose, his shirt sleeves half-rolled over his forearms. He was a powerful man with enormous fists and the shoulders of a football player. Starting as a truck driver, Jimmy had built a reputation for toughness and speed. It was rumored that early in his career his competitors, annoyed at his fast schedules, tried to stop him; but he defended himself so well that several of them ended up with broken bones. No one ever tried to intimidate him again.

Eventually Jimmy Leonetti founded Interland Trucks, building it from a one-rig outfit to a giant fleet. At the age of forty-two he suffered a heart attack, and, for the first time, felt fear. Here, it seemed, was something he could not conquer. He recovered completely but no longer felt invincible, and decided to sell his company. Associated Products was the highest bidder. Jimmy took his thirty-plus million dollars and retired to a cattle ranch.

The retirement lasted only two years. He became bored with life on the ranch. His heart attack had become a bad memory, and his fear dissipated.

One of Leonetti's first moves when he decided to return to business was to persuade General Tobias, then president of Associated Products, that his experience—and his shares—entitled him to a seat on the board. At first Tobias was reluctant, but after he received a number of almost idolatrous references from a surprising variety of businessmen—and one especially impressive recommendation from a member of the Cabinet of the United States—he invited Jimmy to join the board. In the years since, Leonetti had become involved in countless ventures other than API. At only forty-eight, he was said to be worth more than fifty million dollars and was one of the biggest deal-makers on Wall Street. His friends ranged from a cardinal who oversaw the largest archdiocese in America to a Mafia chieftain. The money he raised for his deals was often anonymous.

Leonetti desperately wanted to find a solution to API's problem. If he couldn't, he would lose enormous sums of his own and his clients' money. But he knew when he was beaten. In view of the alarming waves of adverse publicity about the company, he knew that he could not possibly raise enough money to save it.

"I couldn't raise even half that much," said Horace Bronsky, his solid, almost round body at ease, but his voice emphatic. Coming from one of the most powerful bankers in the world, the statement was startling. "None of my clients would put money into an enterprise which Pamela Maarten says 'is fast asleep at every switch on their board.'" His usually cherubic face was grim. "If her *Business World* story had been the only one, I could have found the money. But you all know that there have been dozens of others, almost all negative."

"Except for those on Regina," Alex Petersen interjected, his hair falling across his forehead as he resisted thumping the table again. I can't admit defeat now, he thought. Not after all the effort of this last year. For a fleeting moment his old doubt returned about whether all the effort was worthwhile. Quickly he pushed it away.

"That's not enough," Horace Bronsky said tersely.

There was no doubt that Horace Bronsky was the most powerful member of Associated Products' board of directors. His father had been a barrow trader on New York's Lower East Side, and from as early as he could remember young Horace had been part of a violently competitive struggle. Like Mike Todd—whom he had known as a kid and financed, it was said, in later life—he started at eight years old, shining shoes. By thirteen he was hawking his father's wares, fighting a hundred other urchins for customers. When he was fifteen, his father died of cancer and overwork, and Horace took over the business. In six years he built it into a thriving discount center. He bought everything from cosmetic rejects to army surplus, and sold everything fast and furiously, usually making a profit but not afraid to take a loss on merchandise which didn't sell rapidly enough. "Make it fast or get out fast" was his motto.

By twenty-one he had enough money to retire his mother to an apartment in midtown Manhattan, send his younger brothers to school, and enter New York University. He took his undergraduate degree in less than three years, graduating *summa cum laude,* and entered Harvard Law School. At twenty-six he graduated second in his class and joined a prestigious Wall Street investment-banking firm.

From junior member to partner took him eight years, and from partner to senior partner only another five. By the time he was forty, he was one of the more influential bankers on Wall Street. Now, at fifty-five, he was one of the most influential in the world. His manner, cultivated over the years, was gentle and grandfatherly. He never seemed to hurry, and he tried to make people forget his quick, aggressive brilliance by behaving like a smalltown college professor. Yet no one in the boardroom doubted that he was just as much a fighter as Leonetti. He had not risen to the pinnacle of the banking world without being supremely tough. It was common for Horace Bronsky to raise tens, even hundreds of millions of dollars. Only a few months earlier, almost alone, he had resolved one of New York City's most difficult financial crises. Even more recently, he had merged the two largest private investment banks in the world into a commercial banking empire to rival Chase Manhattan or First National City Bank.

But like Leonetti, Bronsky knew when to quit. He too doubted if he could raise the hundred million dollars they needed. He was not even sure he wanted to. Many of his clients would lose fortunes if the company went broke, which would be bad enough for his reputation, he knew. But he had no intention of risking even more of that reputation by bringing in new money. "Sorry," he said, "but it looks over."

"I just can't believe—" Alex Petersen persisted. "There must be a way." He looked at the blank faces of Horace Bronsky and Jimmy Leonetti with a mixture of anger and mounting hopelessness. "Roger," he said desperately, turning to the quiet young man next to Leonetti, "can't you see some solution?"

Roger Knight III was Jimmy Leonetti's assistant, a brilliant financier whose New England reserve, Ivy League background, and Boston accent contrasted dramatically with his boss's rough trucker's vitality. It was hard to realize that this shy, almost effete man had been an Olympic ski champion and later a rising star on the Grand Prix auto-racing circuit. Few could understand why, in spite of his family's wealth, he had chosen to serve Jimmy Leonetti almost slavishly. No one knew that there were emotions in Roger Knight which sometimes threatened to overwhelm him, nor realized the depth to which his depressions sometimes pushed him. On those occasions he clung to Leonetti's vitality as to a life raft. As a very young man he had lost himself in the excitement of speed and danger when his depressions hit; now, in his thirties, he tried to lose himself instead in the frenzy of activity which always surrounded "Tough Jimmy." For his part, Jimmy Leonetti simply accepted Roger's devotion as his due.

Watching Alex Petersen fight on stubbornly while Horace Bronsky and even Leonetti admitted defeat, Roger felt deeply sad. If even these business giants can't rescue a company like Associated Products, he reflected, perhaps business has gotten completely out of control; perhaps it has a life of its own, which no one can direct. Then, relating to this more practically, he worried as he had for days about Barbara and her children. Barbara, whom he had known for only a few months but who seemed to be the first person in the world who really understood and felt for him, had all her money tied up in API stock. What an irony, he thought. For years he had helped Jimmy make deals for people he cared nothing about, and they had almost all succeeded. Now, when he cared so deeply, there seemed to be nothing he could do.

"I'm very sorry," he answered quietly, "I can't see any solutions either."

Darwin Kellogg, the calm and kind-mannered consultant who had helped Alex so consistently in his struggle to save Regina, was also deeply concerned about Barbara. He felt like a father to her. She had always aroused protective feelings in him. She did in most men, he thought wryly. He remembered how upset he was when she decided to marry that admittedly smart but tough and cynical Marty Cohen, then a sales manager for Regina.

"Are you sure he would love you as much if you weren't the owner's granddaughter?" he had asked her, as gently as he could.

She had bristled immediately. "Of course he would. He

loves me and he needs me." From the day she first met Marty, she had felt a sense of need in him which no amount of tough exterior could fully hide. Not for a moment would she admit, to Kellogg or to herself, that any other motive could be involved.

Now the marriage was coming to an end. About time, Kellogg thought. But things would be different if API, and with it Regina, collapsed. He feared the effect on Barbara would be severe. Admittedly, she would not be impoverished, because the family had outside investments; but she would no longer be rich, either. The servants, the yacht, the summer house—all those would have to go. Much worse would be the emotional impact. Her whole life was interwoven with Regina: her grandfather founded the company, her father ran it, and now her husband ran its international division.

Will she be able to leave Cohen once she knows that Regina's collapsing? Darwin wondered. He doubted it. Ever since he had first known Barbara, when she was a little girl, she had had an almost compulsive sense of responsibility.

If only I could show her that staying with Cohen is not necessarily her duty, he thought. But he was skeptical. She'll never leave him if he gets into real difficulties. What a shame. . . .

There was silence in the boardroom at last. They had reached an impasse. Alex Petersen sank back into his chair, his face seeming to lengthen with fatigue.

Frances Duke had hardly moved during the hours of discussion, argument, struggle, and now submission. She was an impeccably groomed elderly lady who from Regina's inception had been its administrative head. Sir Reginald, the company's almost legendary founder, had created the glamour, the publicity, the excitement, that fueled Regina's success; Frances Duke had made sure that the machinery to implement that success ran smoothly. In the three years since Sir Reginald's death she had retired somewhat, but she still supervised the development of new products and participated in company policy.

Sometime during the long years of success, Frances Duke had emerged as the queen of the cosmetics industry; admired by department-store chieftains, magazine beauty editors, even competitors. Only Estée Lauder and Mala Rubinstein had been as widely honored. The employees of Regina adored her for her kindness and her remarkable sense of calm and dignity.

But today Frances Duke's serenity hid an agitation more violent than that of anyone else in the room. The thought of Regina foundering was more than she could bear. All her adult life had been tied to Regina and devoted to Sir Reginald. Now the company was all she had left.

"Keep it going, love," Reg had said as almost his last words to her. "Remember, there's always a way." Then, with just a shadow of his jaunty old smile, he had added his favorite slogan: "If you can't fix it, fake it."

Frances Duke first met Reg Rand just as he was about to found Regina. She was hardly more than a girl, nineteen and full of romantic notions of becoming a painter. She had left her home in Cincinnati to study art in Paris, over the near-hysterical protests of her mother who was convinced that Paris was the very depth of sinfulness.

For nine months Frances had studied at L'Ecole des Beaux Arts. Day after day, she painted the street scenes and great monuments of the city. Yet the more she painted, the more she realized that her work had only picture-postcard quality. Gradually she came to hate it. Moreover, she found that the Left Bank was full of fakes, bearded young men with groping hands whose main creativity seemed to consist of finding reasons why she should go to bed with them. For all her ridicule of her mother's views, she was far too inhibited to do so. Rapidly, therefore, she found herself dissatisfied and friendless. It was a relief when the first summer vacation came. Packing her knapsack with clothes and painting equipment, she fled Paris and went, first by bus and then on foot, into the Loire Valley. She slept in country inns, ate fruit from the trees and bread and sausage from tiny stores, and drank wine or chilled stream water.

For days she walked through the fields and villages, smelling the warmth of the sun, watching the bees so heavy with nectar they could barely fly, staring at the wrinkled old men and the black-clad, gnarled old women. The light of the countryside seemed soft compared to the harshness of Paris. She saw with a new freshness. And at last she felt ready to paint—ready for the first time in her life. But she hesitated, afraid of what would happen to her if she failed again.

Eventually she steeled herself to set up her easel in a bend of the peacefully flowing river. She labored for several hours. Then she stood back to survey what she had painted—and knew she had failed. In her soul there was completeness and understanding, a sense of her oneness with the world, with the fruit, with the river which flowed as she flowed. But on the canvas there was only another picture postcard. She was heartbroken.

She did not know Reginald Rand was there, so silent was his approach, until he talked to her.

"It's hard when you don't have the means to express what you feel" were the first words she ever heard him say.

"Oh, yes," she said tearfully.

"Come and have a drink." They went back to his château overlooking the river and drank wine all afternoon until her sadness had evaporated.

She never really left him after that. Almost the next day she started working on his new cosmetics business, a business already fully developed in his head. She used her knowledge of colors to help him develop the right lipstick and makeup shades, sharing his enthusiasm as they wrote the first mail-order copy together. Frances served as model when they experimented with the new creams he had had concocted by a local chemist. But it was not until much later that fall, when the weather became cold, that Reg initiated an intimacy which left her with a love for him so deep that it survived his other women, his brief marriage, his arrogance, the vicissitudes of his business life—even his death. She could still feel clearly the splendor of that first night, decades before.

"Tonight our butterfly summer is over," Reg had said in a voice he reserved for recitation. "The wind whistles, the air is chill—"

"And you feel poetic," she said, laughing. "I can always tell; your speech becomes sententious. What you mean is, there's a storm outside, it's damn drafty, and we need a fire."

"Yes, that's true. But I also mean that the air is chill and our funny, frivolous, flirtatious summer is about to turn into a long, warm winter together."

She looked at him with surprise. He was smiling at her, but his eyes were serious. "Come," he said, "we'll fetch firewood."

They carried the wood across the grand hall to the smaller, cozier living room. Their footsteps echoed and, as they walked past the lamp in the corner, their shadows lengthened dramatically across the opposite wall. Then they rummaged in the butler's pantry for cheese, sausage and two bottles of a superb Bordeaux that Reginald loved. On most evenings Madeleine, a healthy, buxom woman from the neighborhood, cooked for them. But tonight was Saturday, the day they fended for themselves. Usually they dined at one of the excellent inns along the Loire, but today they had worked late on Reg's latest mail-order idea and he had decided on supper at home.

"I feel like an interloper," Frances said. "The wind makes the place seem especially empty. I'm glad you're here."

"It *is* empty," he said, making his voice sound funereal. "And we are alone in the midst of a real-life gothic romance."

She felt a shiver of excitement. "Shut up," she said. "You'll scare me."

"Come into my parlor," he beckoned, "and listen to the door clang behind you."

She carried her tray into the living room and placed it onto the heavy, somewhat battered, but beautifully polished table. Behind her Reginald swung shut the studded oak door with a crash so that she jumped in spite of herself. "See," he said, "I told you the door would clang and echo." He smiled at her fondly. "Our winter night begins."

The laid the fire and, sitting on the thick fur rug in front of the fireplace, watched the logs start to flame. She placed their trays on the floor next to them and turned out the central chandelier. Immediately the room turned a warm and flickering gold which illuminated only the antique picture frames so that they circumscribed nothing but ghostly black vacancies. The bronze studs in the table and in the door glowed. Reginald saw her looking at them.

"They look like the opals I used to find," he said, "before I lost the mines."

But it was not in his nature to feel regret. On the contrary, he felt almost constant pleasure in what he did; his life overflowed with the excitement of the moment. His heart brimmed with the love of whatever woman he was committed to, whether that commitment was for a week or a year or forever. He was a romantic whose ardor either so overwhelmed his lovers that they ran away, frightened for their souls, or, if they were strong enough to accept him fully, caused in them an extraordinary depth and length of response.

As she sat next to him in front of the now extravagant fire, Frances knew that this evening was to be her initiation not only into her own body, and into his, but into a spirit of love and romance which for years she had dreamed and daydreamed about.

Reginald laid the large velvet pillow from the armchair onto the fur rug; and then gently, as if she were exceedingly fragile, lowered her onto it. He lay beside her so that her body was between him and the fire. Shadows of flames danced over her simple cardigan and white blouse and played their visual music over the plain black skirt which lay tight on her flat stomach and molded itself in gentle swells over her legs.

Reginald's hand, almost as gentle as the shadows, touched her cheek and slowly, softly moved to her breasts, then her stomach, finally pausing, palpitating almost imperceptibly—as gentle, she thought, as the butterflies of the summer—on the hollow between her legs. If only he doesn't spoil it by saying something mushy, she thought. The boys in Paris who had tried to touch her were forever declaring their undying passion.

"Would you like to sin on a tiger skin? Or would you prefer to err on some other fur?" he said, grinning at her. She laughed back at him with sheer relief and, relaxing suddenly, felt a wave of desire so strong it made her body shudder.

Reginald, feeling totally filled with his love and desire for her, raised himself onto his elbow and, without his hand stopping its gentle caress, kissed her forehead and her eyes, then lingered for minutes on her neck and finally, even more gently, kissed her lips. She kept her eyes closed after he kissed them, feeling as though she had the whole warmth and beauty of the room trapped inside, afraid to open them lest some escape.

Reginald's hands, his lips, his whole body loved her and felt liquid with tenderness. It was an adoration he had often felt, but at the same time it was totally new, totally amazing. His lips played with hers, kissing, touching, sometimes nipping until she could stand it no more and opened her mouth to his, pushing her tongue into him instinctively, while her body started to press toward him and, unconsciously, she let her legs ease apart so that the hollow between them deepened and his hand had more space to flutter.

Very slowly, so slowly that her sense of loss brought tears to her eyes, his lips parted from hers and he moved his mouth down to her breasts. His face nuzzled them, and she helped him undo the buttons of her cardigan and then her blouse. Suddenly in a hurry, she sat up and undid the strings of her bodice, desperate to be free.

When she was naked from the waist up, she lay back on her pillow and drew his face toward her, feeling its rough texture with a longing that was almost unbearable, while he, filled with awe at her beauty, let out a groan that was almost a sob. When he took her nipple into his mouth, sucking her in more deeply than she had imagined possible, she started to flood; and when he flicked at her with his tongue, she was suffused with such warmth and longing that she dug her hands into his skin and pulled him toward her with all her strength.

She knew what it was to touch herself until she brimmed with warmth and wetness and then overflowed; but this was immensely more. Now she was as deep as an ocean and the fullness suffused her entire body.

Still his free hand played on her like the dancing flames, but more insistently now, until she all at once felt the excessive constraint of her skirt and petticoat. He started to loosen the buttons at her waist, then, and without a word, but with perfect understanding, to undress her. When he was done, he looked down at her as she lay before the fire, warm and innocent. She could feel her desire rise under his eyes. Then he bent down and kissed her whole body, caressing every inch of it, until her ocean started to toss and she knew that at any moment it must break through her barriers and drown her.

"I must see you too," she said. "I am so full. I want to drown in you."

Without a word he knelt beside her, feeling unbelievably strong, and removed his clothes, putting them behind him piece by piece. What dignity he has, she thought. She longed to touch him, and her hands moved toward his chest.

"In a moment," he said. "In a moment."

He would not let her touch him until he had removed all his clothes and she could look at his body entirely. And when she saw him, his muscled chest, his strong, sculptured thighs, his incredibly beautiful manhood standing erect amid the bush of hair, umber in the firelight, she felt such a burst of exultation that she could feel her whole body swell and sway.

"You are like Neptune," she said, incorporating him into her fantasy of an ocean.

"You are my queen," he said, and never called her anything else from that day on.

When finally he entered her, the waves engulfed her, carrying her higher and higher, until they crested into a huge tidal wave which lifted her into the sky and then deposited her slowly, so incredibly slowly, back onto the warm shore of his arms. . . .

Frances Duke forced her mind back to the present. To remember Reginald amid all this failure and defeat seemed almost sacrilegious. He would not have let failure overwhelm him. Only Alex seems to have any spunk left, she thought, and he's fading. So she sat, straight and dignified, a total contrast to the five tired and beaten men in the boardroom, her clothes as tidy, her face as composed, as if her day were just beginning. The men would have been amazed to know the turmoil of concern she felt. They would have been astounded to know of her mounting conviction that there *was* a way to help this new young president of Regina do what he wanted—and that she held the key.

In fact, it was a mystery to the men why Frances Duke was even present. "I shall attend your meeting tomorrow," she had told Alex Petersen the day before. "I believe it will be important."

Alex, not wishing to offend her, had agreed somewhat reluctantly; her presence could do no harm, he supposed.

The silence in the boardroom lengthened, merging with the greater silence of the office building and of the city itself. With an effort, Alex Petersen started to collect his papers. After a year of effort and crisis, it was all over.

None of the men were looking at Frances Duke when she broke the silence. Such was their lethargy that it took them a few seconds to realize what she had said. She had to begin again to make sure they had all heard her. When they did, the mood in the room changed drastically. Each man leaned forward, his attention galvanized.

"I have a solution," she began. . . .

Chapter 2

Alex Johann Petersen had first become involved with the Regina Cosmetics Company some fifteen months earlier when he had been unexpectedly summoned to the office of Herman Cosgrove, president and chief executive officer of API. It would be an exaggeration to say that the elevator ride to the executive offices on the thirtieth floor of their main office in Manhattan was terrifying to Alex. But it was certainly unnerving. In spite of the many times he had made the trip, in spite of his doubts in recent months that he wanted to stay at API—or in business at all, for that matter—he still felt apprehensive. The more so today, as he speculated what Cosgrove might want.

Generally, Alex was self-assured, at ease in social situations, a persuasive public speaker, fast with figures, imaginative with new products, tasteful in evaluating advertising and packaging. Still, he could not quite shake the apprehension of visiting the president's office. Ridiculous, he thought ruefully.

Walking through the long, empty corridors of the executive offices was even worse. The silence coupled with the perpetual newness of the carpet made the corridors eerie. The pictures borrowed from the Museum of Modern Art, each a brilliant patch of color stark against the wood paneling, somehow added to the coldness. He paused for a second before a particularly aggressive Dubuffet painting of a cockerel with full feathers ruffled. Instinctively he straightened his tie.

In an anteroom office, guarding the president's privacy, sat his secretary, a middle-aged lady with a thin mouth and cold eyes.

"Good morning, Jane," said Alex.

"Good morning, Mr. Petersen. You may enter. The president is expecting you." She spoke flatly. In the old days she used to try to establish some personal contact with these dynamic young men. She used to long for them. But her disappoinments had been too frequent and now, despite an occasional physical stirring she could not control, she maintained an icy distance. Alex smiled at her anyway and entered the enormous office of API's president and chief executive officer.

Herman Cosgrove sat stooped behind his giant desk as if he were some long-bodied sea creature perched on a piling behind a rock. Between him and Alex there stretched the endless carpet.

Alex hesitated.

"Good morning, Alex." The president had to call quite loudly to cover the distance. He rose cordially from behind the desk. Standing, he seemed smaller, dwarfed by the distance. "Come, sit over here," he called, pointing to a settee and cluster of chairs in the far corner. "Make yourself comfortable."

In spite of Cosgrove's friendliness, Alex's anxiety mounted as he walked across the room. The concentrated power of this office was tremendous. Throughout the world, eight thousand people sold API products. Its factories employed over sixty thousand men and women. Its research facilities spent thirty million dollars a year to develop new products, new materials, new processes. Its trucks delivered its merchandise over millions of miles each year and its fleet of planes carried its executives around the world. Over all this empire the president seemed to hold total sway. If his position, to which he had been elected only months ago, was already in jeopardy, that was certainly not apparent. From Alex Petersen's vantage point, Herman Cosgrove, as the corporation's chief executive, was its absolute dictator. He could not help but feel a sense of awe.

The contrast between Alex Petersen and Herman Cosgrove was ironic. For all his power, the president remained unprepossessing, almost ill at ease, as if he were a visitor awaiting the return of the real chief executive. Alex, with his suntanned, slightly aquiline face and well-tailored suit, looked fully appropriate to the giant office—a young patrician, born to power. His confident walk gave no hint of his nervousness. Yet just as he looked his most secure, Alex was actually remembering how far he had risen. Perhaps too far, he reflected, for a boy whose dad had hammered in roofs and only put on a shirt on Sundays, straining to fasten his collar around his tanned bull neck with the bluish vein down the right side. . . .

". . . understand you've been doing an excellent job on your products," the president was saying.

Alex realized that he had almost daydreamed away the first sentence. "Oh," he said, slightly startled, "thank you, sir."

"I think a man of your experience and calibre has a great deal to offer this company," Cosgrove continued. "The reason I asked you to stop up here was to discuss a new and vast opportunity." He paused for emphasis. He's ideal, he thought. He *looks* the part; the board will love him. And if the damned thing can't be run; he can always get another job. . . .

Alex looked expectant and relaxed, but his heart pounded.

"As you know, we have long been in the business of acquiring concerns, some of major importance. You will recall, for example, that our acquisition of National Snack Company was a major step forward."

"Yes, I know," said Alex politely, although he couldn't help remembering that National Snacks was having a lot of trouble.

"Today we are announcing another major acquisition."

I wonder if he remembers it's just me, Alex thought.

"We have determined to move aggressively into the fashion industry. It is one of the areas we have not yet touched. So I am happy to tell you that we have almost completed the acquisition of the large and highly prestigious Regina Cosmetics Company." He paused, evidently waiting for some sort of applause.

"I'm delighted to hear that, sir. A world-wide company, a well-known name." Alex's words showed no hint of his surprise. He had heard rumors that API was negotiating with Regina. But a few weeks ago, when API's stock fell, Regina was said to have backed out. Evidently, API had made a better offer. But why Regina? When the original rumor had spread, it had been widely suggested that Regina was heading for trouble. Perhaps API was in worse difficulties than he had realized. Could the critical magazine articles be more right than he had imagined?

The president's satisfied smile hid a jumble of similar thoughts. He was still angry that the Board was forcing him to buy Regina. On the other hand, the last weeks had shown no real improvement in API's position. Fortunately, the immediate cash shortage had been eased as the company's large, half-completed amusement complex had unexpectedly been sold for forty-two million dollars. Seymour Asquith, the company's chief financial officer, estimated that at the present rate of cash outflow, this would last almost six months. On the other hand, National Snacks which, contrary to Cosgrove's statements, had never been a good acquisition, was finding even stronger competition than expected and was doing badly; and API's pharmaceutical business was running into ever stronger government regulation and resultant costs. Cosgrove had to admit that the Regina acquisition would help API's figures greatly—*if* it could be run. If not—the president hardly dared to think. He looked out one of the room's fourteen windows at tiers of other buildings with more office windows, where other executives faced more problems. . . .

Suddenly Cosgrove realized that the silence had become too extended. He hurried on. "We need somebody with experience and class to run Regina," he said. "I have decided to appoint you."

For the first time, Alex looked shocked. "Good Lord!" he said. "Really? That's—that's amazing!"

"I think you're the right man for the job," said the president, pleased at Alex's surprise and ever quick with the appropriate cliché. He entirely misunderstood Alex's reaction, taking it for delight. In fact, Alex's main reaction was consternation. Did he want more responsibility? Four years ago, perhaps even two, this opportunity would have made him ecstatic; now he wasn't even sure whether he should accept. "I have one question," Alex started hesitantly. He wondered whether he would be considered impertinent, and realized he would. Then, on the spur of the moment, he decided to ask anyway. "Do I have a choice?" He smiled to avoid seeming too rude.

It was the president's turn to be startled. For a second he was as still as a terrified hare, belly flat to the ground, uncovered in its nest. Tough young son-of-a-bitch, he thought. He felt the acidity in his stomach and wished he could take a Tums. If he doesn't accept, Leonetti will have another chance to bid for the job. He wondered whether pushing Alex to the board had been a mistake. Not that he had much alternative. Looking straight at Alex, he said,

"No, I don't think you do." His smile was cold.

"How about a contract?" In his present uncertainty the last thing Alex wanted was to be tied down. Yet for a job of this size, a contract was normal.

To Alex's surprise, Cosgrove responded promptly, almost angrily. "Certainly not."

"What happens if things go wrong?" Alex asked, partly from his surprise, mostly to gain some time to think. "After all, the company is said to have been in some difficulties."

"I would hardly ask you to run Regina if the job were impossible." The president's voice sounded gritty. "If you are doubting your ability, you shouldn't take the job." He continued to stare at Alex. "There will be no contract."

Suddenly Alex understood. He wants a scapegoat if things go wrong, he thought. What a shitty business. At that moment, he almost walked out on Herman Cosgrove, on API, on the whole business world.

"There will be a substantial salary—a base of $150,000 plus a performance bonus which we'd guarantee at fifty thousand for the first year and which could go higher later. Plus car and driver, club membership, the normal perks." He hardly seems to be listening, Cosgrove thought angrily. Rich bastard, no idea of the value of money.

But again the president was wrong. Of course the money was tempting. Alex reveled in his ability to buy what he wanted without having to worry; but his concern now was different. Did he want the job, the hassle . . . ?

For another moment he hesitated. Then his fight for success reasserted itself. Oh, what the hell, he thought. I might as well give it a chance. If it goes wrong, so what? "I am honored," he said formally. "I would be delighted to accept the presidency of the Regina Cosmetics Company. I appreciate your confidence in me." He paused and then added, "And thank you for reassuring me that the job can be done. I would hate to be the scapegoat in an impossible situation."

Cosgrove was mortified that Alex evidently sensed the duplicity. Well, at least he had taken the job. He barely stifled a sigh of relief.

"Good," he blurted finally. "Good." He could think of no other word. "Good, good."

"When do I start?" Alex inquired. His credo had always been action, and his response to even such surprising and equivocal news was a desire to get moving.

"We've completed a preliminary agreement," said the president, relieved to be back to ordinary business. "The next step is to prepare the final documents for the closing. Most of the work has already been completed."

"I gather we almost made a deal some time ago."

"We did. But they backed out. And some members of our Board started having second thoughts." The president smiled avuncularly. "In the end I got my way."

"So the closing should be soon?" Alex prompted.

"Plan to take over a month from today."

"Yes, sir." Alex rose to leave. "And thank you." He wondered whether he would mean those thanks in the end or not.

As the door closed, the president rose abruptly and strode to his center window. Its view was a city-scape of grandeur. He stood there, legs apart, head bent forward as if it were slightly loose on his shoulders, arms folded over his vulnerable accountant's belly, and looked across at the hundreds of other windows which impersonally returned his stare. Sometimes he felt as if all those windows were glaring—glaring angrily just at him.

Could he have avoided acquiring Regina, he wondered, if he had made an impassioned speech against it? He wasn't sure. "But they don't like people who disagree," he said, and the words, spoken aloud in that impersonal office, seemed to give him a sense of self, almost of courage—the courage to believe that he wasn't licked yet. There must be a way to improve our profits, he thought. Somewhere there's bound to be some money to save.

Turning with renewed determination, he walked back to his desk and picked up the phone. "Jane, get me Cecil Rand," he said so aggressively that it sounded almost like a bark.

After a few moments the sere voice of his secretary came through. "I have Mr. Rand now, Sir."

"Cecil, listen—I've just given Petersen the job. I think he'll handle himself fairly well, but I doubt in the long run . . ." He left the sentence unfinished. "He asked for a contract."

"You didn't give it to him, did you? I mean, that might not be . . ."

"Hell, no!"

"Lovely," said Cecil Rand in his high voice. "Super. I'm not unhappy he has the job."

"Yes," said the president, "I think we have him just where we need him."

But the president's satisfaction did not last long. Goddamn board, he thought again. Why did they have to push Regina down my throat? He felt his anger surge as he remembered that meeting.

Chapter 3

T he day the board of directors had met in emergency session,
the tension in the formal boardroom was almost palpable.
Some of the twelve board members had feared merely for their
reputation, others for their investment, and a few knew that their
careers were at stake.

Herman Cosgrove always hated board meetings. They made
him feel subservient. It made him angry that even after all these
years he still felt the need to display the same obsequious dignity so that he could be inoffensive without seeming weak. Worst
of all, he hated board meetings because he could not quite conquer his nervousness. But today was particularly nerve-wracking.
Within a few months, Blake Richards, chairman and chief executive officer of API and Cosgrove's boss—his slave-driver it sometimes felt like—would be retiring, and finally, he, Herman Cosgrove, would become the chief executive officer. He could almost
taste the relief. But it wouldn't happen if the board became too
upset with the figures he was about to present. After all, he
could not abrogate responsibility for the company's performance.
He had held the title of president for almost two years now,

even if Richards had kept all the power to himself; responsibility without authority, he reflected cynically. When things were wrong, it was his fault; when they went right, Blake Richards took the credit.

Cosgrove yawned. He had worked half the night with Asquith trying to polish the figures. In the old days, when the company's profits were up, he had been able to set aside large reserves which he could use to cover any profit problems. But there were no reserves left; they had all been used up to make the last two years' profits, or to finance Richards' real-estate ventures.

And God knows, those ventures needed financing. When Blake Richards had first started the real-estate department—not for the good of the company, but just to get himself the presidency, Cosgrove thought bitterly—everything had gone perfectly. The world economy helped him; almost everywhere housing prices boomed. Even when he made a mistake, the market tended to correct it. And so he got the top job he so craved, even though he was sixty at the time, older than normal for the job. . . .

No, Cosgrove reflected, there were certainly no reserves left in API now. When the real-estate market softened, everything went wrong. Before either Richards or he had fully comprehended what was happening, they had found themselves in the midst of a violent business maelstrom from which there seemed no relief. As the world economy weakened, harmed by rising Arab oil prices and a recession in America, world real-estate activity declined and prices dropped.

In England prices fell so drastically that Gilbert Slatterly, the huge and flamboyant British real-estate entrepreneur, suddenly went bankrupt, pulling with him several smaller speculators and three construction companies. API sustained substantial losses but managed to cover most of them by paper profits on other deals completed with Slatterly just before his collapse. Nevertheless, the company's cash reserves were reduced severely.

In large segments of Florida the longtime shortage of resort housing suddenly turned to a glut as tourists stayed away and the land bought by Richards became unsaleable. In northern Italy, where Richards had started a huge housing complex, the falling value of the lira put a damper on investments, so that

API had to use up more of its own cash than expected to complete the venture.

Already Cosgrove had been forced to tell the board that profits would drop below forecast. Soon he would have to declare further reductions, probably drastic ones.

If only I can hold off a little longer, he thought. And if only no one looks too closely at those Liechtenstein transactions. His stomach knotted as it always did when he considered the accounting entries that had been necessary on that deal made with one of the surviving directors of the Slatterly empire. It was all perfectly legal, he kept reassuring himself; we had to make the entries to avoid declaring a huge loss. Nevertheless . . . He yawned again, partly from fatigue, partly from nerves, and coughed to cover his yawn. Better not to let these bastards see his tiredness, he thought, and turned to get himself a cup of coffee. As he did so, he noticed with surprise that Blake Richards was standing by the coffee urn, studying him. Cosgrove had learned to recognize that look. He'd seen it often enough before, when Richards was evaluating some opponent in a real-estate negotiation, wondering how far he could push.

With a flash of intuition as sudden and certain as a physical blow, Herman Cosgrove understood why Richards was so insistent on the Regina acquisition. He's not going to retire, he thought; the son-of-a-bitch is planning to stay put! Cosgrove knew that for ten years before his apopintment, Richards—craggy, black-haired, intense (his enemies had nicknamed him Blackhead) —had lusted after the top job at API. He had got it finally, less than five years ago, by embarking API on a huge and daring new real-estate venture. Now he wants to stay on instead of retiring, Cosgrove realized. And he's planning to repeat what he did by getting us into real estate, but this time with Regina. He figures they'll have to keep him on if he moves API into an entirely new field.

Cosgrove's determination to thwart old Blackhead's plan became, at that moment, implacable.

The oldest member of the board of directors, Cy Baldwin, had reached the age of eighty the previous year. The mandatory retirement age for directors had been waived by unanimous board action—in spite of the fact that he was clearly senile—

because he was API's largest shareholder, owning about ten percent of the company's stock. He was seated now in his customary chair at the board table; his rheumy eyes viewing his colleagues with concern. He sensed that something was amiss, although he was not sure what.

In addition to Richards and Cosgrove, the other member of the operating management of Associated Products who was also a board member was Leonard Abrams, the company's chief counsel, a lawyer of unquestionable credentials but no charisma, who had negotiated the acquisition agreement with Regina. Today he was as worried as Cosgrove. He felt finally confident that the company's international operations, run by Marty Cohen, a tough executive married to Cecil Rand's daughter, were in good shape. But its U.S. operation, run by Rand personally, seemed poorly managed and showed significant weaknesses and possible discrepancies in its financial data.

In any acquisition contract, the selling company warrants the correctness of its data. Theoretically, if the information and figures later prove incorrect, the deal can be nullified. But Abrams knew that any such attempt to unwind the deal after it had been completed would lead inevitably to a lawsuit so expensive and time-consuming it might well destroy both companies. So he continued to be doubtful about the safety and wisdom of buying Regina.

Jimmy Leonetti, with his flashy suit and long sideburns, was an anomaly in this group of conservative businessmen. But his giant's head was impressive, and his command of what was happening at API was broad. He knew everything about the operation of the Interland Trucks division. But he knew a great deal more and frequently voiced his concern about the progress of the company. It was never quite clear to the other directors how he gathered his information. Blake Richards was wary of Leonetti, whom he considered dangerous, and Herman Cosgrove detested him. But Horace Bronsky evidently thought highly of him, having invited him to join the board of another of his bank's large customers.

Leonetti was worried both because API was showing such obvious signs of trouble, and because Blake Richards was getting so damned arrogant.

"The whole art of real-estate dealing is to admit when you're wrong and get out fast," Leonetti had said to his assistant, Roger Knight. "Old Blackhead refuses to admit he's ever wrong. He'll fuck up that company for sure if he keeps it up."

"He's almost at retirement."

"Yeah, but you know that if we let him buy that flaky cosmetics company, he'll pitch to stay on. Probably convince my patsy colleagues on the board to let him. Particularly with no one but that poor fish Cosgrove as our white hope to replace him." Angrily he hurled a wad of paper at the wastebasket. "Shit. I should take over myself," he said, pretending it was an idea that had just hit him.

"When were you planning to run it?" Roger asked. "Between four and five in the morning?"

Leonetti laughed. "Well, maybe it's not practical," he said reluctantly. Nevertheless, he wasn't about to allow the Regina acquisition if he could stop it. Whether it meant having to keep Richards on or having to watch Cosgrove take over and fuck things up, he wanted no part of it. Roger Knight was right that he had no time to run API right now, but things could change. . . .

Darwin Kellogg had joined the board only recently and was therefore something of an unknown quantity to the members. He was president and chief executive officer of Marketing Management Corporation, a prestigious management consultant firm, and a contact man who knew everyone and was therefore a superb business-getter. His voice was extraordinarily soft—not weak, simply mellifluous—and, although he was only fifty, his hair was snow white. Up to now he had had little impact on API's board of directors, partly because he was a newcomer and partly because, wanting to please all, he had managed to balance himself dexterously between opposing commitments.

The only member of the board of directors who was not a businessman was Dr. Martin Brittainy, chancellor of Carson University. He carried a series of exalted titles, many honorary, and sported a superb academic manner. The remaining two members were longtime golfing companions of Blake Richards'. One was the president of a large industrial concern; the other, Marshall Lyddon, was the senior partner of a prestigious New York law firm. None of these three wished to be associated with any business failures, and each was startled by the sudden drop of API's stock. Marshall Lyddon was almost seventy and therefore, much to his annoyance, would soon have to resign from the board. He certainly did not want to seem to be running for cover. Selfishly he hoped that the problems at API were only temporary.

Underlying each director's concern was the recognition that if something went drastically wrong with Associated Products, Inc., each man might be held personally liable. Each would be faced with lawsuits brought by annoyed shareholders; each would be subject to enormous harassment. Until the last few years, outside directors were expected to be no more than wise men whose advice and counsel could be helpful. They were not expected to take responsibility for the companies they served, and they generally knew little of what was going on, viewing the whole matter as purely honorary. But recent court decisions required a director to take responsibility for the progress of his company. The touble was that most of these directors, like those on the boards of many major companies, although they were enormously shrewd and experienced, had time-consuming businesses of their own to run and could not devote the additional time needed to understand clearly what was really happening at API. Occasionally, if they smelled a major problem, they could be demanding and even disagreeable, but generally they were forced to take the carefully camouflaged word of the operating management on the company's progress.

Many business writers, Richards knew, most notably the influential Peter Drucker, had inveighed against outside directorships. But API, like most major firms, continued to believe that outside directors added prestige and possibly wisdom. And such directors also felt honored. Now, suddenly, they felt only worried; the honor might backfire.

Horace Bronsky, the last of the directors to arrive, entered the boardroom at exactly 9:30. There was no point, he felt, in wasting time by being early. He had already made several successful phone calls to raise money for a new wing of the hospital which he served as chairman of the trustees.

It was Bronsky who had brought Regina and API together. Several of his clients, and in fact he himself, had major investments in the Regina Company. They had realized some time ago that, with no powerful leadership, Regina was becoming shaky.

After Sir Reginald died, his son, Cecil Rand, though acknowledged to be shrewd, lacked the drive to keep the giant company moving. Regina was forecasting a substantial profit increase this year, but Bronsky worried how solid that forecast was. He feared Regina's performance might slip if aggressive new programs were not implemented promptly.

At the same time, Bronsky had been aware that API needed an immediate boost to its own profits while it got its cash problems under control. The merger between the two companies had seemed ideal. In his view, it still did. For in spite of his success, Horace Bronsky was worried that his own reputation could be seriously hurt if one or both of the companies ran into real difficulties. Even a Horace Bronsky could find himself suddenly ignored if a major mistake of his became public knowledge.

"Well, let's get started," said Blake Richards cheerfully. "We're all here." He felt the old gambler's thrill. The game was about to commence, the stakes were high, and he had in him, as he usually did, the premonition of victory. "This is a special meeting," he continued. "The only subject before us is whether we should proceed with the Regina acquisition, as approved at our last regular board meeting, and, in that context, whether API's performance without Regina would be satisfactory." He looked at Cosgrove. "Okay, Herman, let's get at it."

Herman Cosgrove tried desperately to maintain the same easy tone, but the figures he was about to show were awful. He felt thoroughly frightened, the more so now that he realized that Blake Richards would be no ally. The worse I look, the happier he'll be, he thought. With an enormous effort he managed to look calm as he moved towards an easel on which rested a beautifully rendered chart with the words *Associated Products Incorporated—Progress*. He removed the chart carefully, almost tenderly, unconsciously trying to delay the moment when he would have to show the board the performance figures. "This first chart shows clearly that our sales growth continued until recently, when there was a temporary reversal directly attributable to the sad state of the economy," he started.

Tall, lanky, emaciated—carrying, nevertheless, a small but protuberant belly—Cosgrove looked permanently unkempt. His suits hung limply on his thin frame; shoulders speckled with dandruff; his meager, cross-brushed hair never quite covered his balding pate. He was no great business leader, but rather a shrewd, tenacious, occasionally devious accountant who, after thirty years of service, had reached his present position through competence and sensitivity to company politics as well as through longevity. "He never makes a mistake" was the word about him. "He never does anything that hasn't been done ten thousand times before" was the popular response.

But the scuttlebutt missed the point. Certainly Cosgrove avoided all decisions which could later be held against him. But on those occasions when he saw no alternative to making a commitment, he could be decisive indeed.

In front of these commercial giants, Herman Cosgrove seemed even more bowed than usual; and none of the giants seemed much impressed, either by his explanations or by him.

The charts he showed, although presented optimistically, left the board thoroughly concerned. Profits were edging down, prevented from more rapid decline only by some rather debatable real-estate gains; sales were falling in almost every department; the operating figures from several earlier acquisitions did not live up to the promises made to the board when the acquisitions were recommended.

". . . And so, gentlemen, considering the political and economic difficulties we are facing, I hope you will agree that our progress is not unsatisfactory." Cosgrove sat down to total silence. If only they don't ask me about the cash, he thought. Or about that Liechtenstein deal. He could feel the sweat prick at his back, under his shirt. That blasted laundry had starched it again, contrary to his specific instructions.

"Seems to me we're doing damn badly," Leonetti said, breaking the silence. "Other than Interland, practically every division's losing money. I know you're showing a lot of break-evens and even a couple of improvements, but we all know that's more creative accounting than fact."

Several of the directors nodded in agreement. Each knew that there were many ways acceptable to the Accounting Practices Board of making a company seem more profitable than it really was. For example, certain marketing expenses for a new product launch could be spread over three years so that in the first year the company benefited from all the launch sales, but had to pay only one-third of the expenses. The problem, as

Leonetti well knew, was that in the following year the remaining expenses had to be charged, but with no off-setting introductory sales surge.

"I believe we should get down to basics," Leonetti continued. "Start running the company as hard and as lean as one of those rigs I used to push. I say we should get tough new management where we need it. . . ."

My god, thought Blake Richards, does he mean himself instead of me? That was an entirely unexpected attack. He had expected that he would have to fight off Herman Cosgrove's desire to be his successor, but he had figured that would be easy. Leonetti would be a far tougher rival.

"We've got to stop frittering around with this flaky cosmetic company," Leonetti ended, his fist hammering on the table.

"You've made your point," said Blake Richards coolly. "Before we proceed, I'll just remind you of the business and financial situation of the Regina company. A number of you may note that its profits would make a big improvement in our total earnings per share."

"We know what Regina is and what it does," Leonetti interrupted. "It's a huge cosmetics company which had good profits in the past. Word is their profits have been eroding recently, even though they insist they'll show a big increase this year. Goosing their figures, probably, to fatten themselves up before they sell out."

Richards moved toward the second easel, at the head of the table. "Here are the actual figures," he said, ignoring Leonetti's outburst.

The chart he unveiled, unlike Cosgrove's, showed that Regina had a most healthy trend in sales and profits. Only at the very top of the profit chart, where it depicted the last six months' performance, was there any slowdown, and even there some growth continued.

"A merger with the Regina Company would give us an additional profit this year of almost twenty million dollars after taxes on sales of about five hundred and thirty million dollars according to their forecasts. Since our total API profits would otherwise come in at about fifty-seven million dollars, down from sixty million dollars last year, the addition of Regina would be dramatic. Instead of showing a decline, we would show an increase of over thirty-five percent, to seventy-seven million dollars."

"Your increase isn't going to look anywhere near that good," Leonetti said quickly. "The accounting rules will require you to restate last year as if it included Regina in API to make the comparison real."

"That's true," said Richards, "but even so, we'd show an improvement instead of a decline. Combined API and Regina profits last year would have been seventy-four million. This year we'd show seventy-seven million. That's a hell of a lot better than the fifty-seven million we'll show if we don't make this acquisition."

Bronsky nodded. "The point is, Jimmy," he said, looking directly at Leonetti, "that we don't have the time to get back to basics. Hell, you've seen what our stock's doing."

As usual, Bronsky had hit at the heart of the problem. When the news of the impending Regina acquisition had leaked out a week ago, the financial analysts of Wall Street had viewed it as a desperation move. They had already been made suspicious about API because a major newsletter had implied that the company's real-estate investments might not be as solid as generally supposed. Now the intention to acquire Regina, itself rumored to be in some difficulties, was taken as confirmation that there must be something wrong.

Only yesterday Cecil Rand, a corpulent, unappetizing, but wily man who had taken over running Regina from his father, had called up in consternation. "What the hell is going on with your stock?" he had demanded with uncharacteristic aggressiveness, his somewhat effeminate voice almost harsh. "At today's prices the deal's worth a hundred million dollars less to me."

He was right, Cosgrove realized. Whereas the three million API shares to be swapped for Regina had been worth two hundred eighty million dollars when the deal was originally made, now, with the stock price down to sixty dollars a share, they were worth only one hundred eighty million.

"I wouldn't worry about it too much," Cosgrove said. "The stock should come back."

"I'm afraid my colleagues and I would be unable to count on that. We would not let Regina go at less than the two hundred eighty million we agreed."

"I'm not sure we could go along with that." At last, Cosgrove had seen a legitimate way to kill the deal without antagonizing Richards. As always, he could be decisive when he felt it was necessary. "Our stock will, of course, bounce back. If we increased the number of shares we are offering for Regina, we would be overpaying."

"We have no assurance whatsoever that your stock will rebound." Worried about what was happening inside Regina, Rand could not let the deal fall through. On the other hand, API's stock might fall further, and he wasn't about to be played for a sucker by Herman Cosgrove. Cecil Rand might be plump and bad-skinned, but after all those years of surviving under the tyranny of his father, he was not without a toughness of his own. "Of course, if you would guarantee the price of your stock—"

"I shall discuss it with my colleagues," said Cosgrove, "but I do not hold out much hope." He hung up pleased; the deal seemed dead.

But Herman Cosgrove had underestimated Blake Richards' determination to acquire the Regina company. At the time he had not realized what lay behind that determination. He recognized his error the moment Richards returned and burst into Cosgrove's office.

"Listen, we can make a tremendous land deal with the Saudis as soon as we have the Regina thing put to bed," he started.

"I'm afraid we have some problems—"

"Rand called you, I suppose. Wants to renegotiate the deal."

"Well, as a matter of fact, yes."

"How much does he want?"

"He's saying they still want the same value of stock, which means at today's share price we'd have to give them almost four and a half million shares instead of three million. I'm not sure—"

"For Chrissake, Herman, this is the time when we *have* to expand. Stop being so goddamn scared."

"So I'm saying that we don't have time to get back to basics," Bronsky repeated leaning forward across the boardroom table. "Much better to bring in Regina, give ourselves a boost for a year, and use that time to build back API." He leaned back, his point made.

Leonetti listened attentively. "But what makes you think we'll be able to build API back next year?" he demanded. "Hell, there wasn't much wrong with it three or four years ago, was there, Blake?"

Richards merely grunted.

"And now we're in trouble," Leonetti continued, drumming the point home. "You'll be retiring soon, Blake, so it won't be your problem. But who do we have who can pull us out?"

There it was, typically Leonetti, a bold frontal attack forcing Blake Richards either to bow out or counterattack right now.

"Well," Richards started, hesitating in his surprise, "perhaps it would be wiser if I—"

But he was too slow. For Cosgrove had guessed at the same moment as Richards that Leonetti was angling for the top spot at API. In a flash he recognized too that Blake Richards was about to counter that move by offering to stay on. Whichever man emerged victorious from the confrontation that was bound to follow would become the company's next head. After years of waiting, he was not about to let it be anyone but himself.

"I think you're exaggerating, Jimmy," Cosgrove interrupted fast and with surprising vigor. "I have a powerful group of executives working under me who are more than able to run API. If necessary, they could take on Regina as well. After all, although we have some problems, my presentation showed clearly that we are recovering."

"Recovering, my arse. We're falling into a cash problem faster than anyone here even realizes," said Leonetti passionately. "Just because you don't admit the problem, doesn't mean it's not there. We'll have to face a serious profit reduction one way or the other. We can mask it for a while, but—"

"The hell we do," Blake Richards interrupted. "There's no reason why we can't fight our way back up. We've got the products, the sales organizations, the factories. All it takes is some hard-nosed managing."

"Yeah, well, where is this hard-nosed management? How can we wrestle with Regina when we can't even seem to hold API up?"

Christ, Cosgrove realized, he's on another tack. If I don't stop him, he'll offer to run Regina. Then, when Richards retires, he'll take over the whole thing. . . . "The real problem," Cosgrove interrupted again, "is not who is going to run Regina but whether it's even worth acquiring. Admittedly, its profit and sales picture has been sound. But remember, gentlemen, we originally agreed to pay three million of our shares for the business. That was enough. Now it's up to four, which makes it very expensive."

He paused; then, noticing that Richards seemed about to argue, he continued quickly. "The fact is that some sources doubt whether Regina can even hold last year's profit level, let alone show the dramatic increase they are assuring us. Altogether, I would urge this board to look very carefully at this acquisition before we proceed."

"What 'sources'?" Bronsky demanded immediately. "I never heard of such sources."

Immediately Cosgrove backtracked. He had successfuly deflected Leonetti's bid for power; and Blake Richards' impending retirement had been placed squarely on the table without being contradicted. He would see to it that it was mentioned clearly in the minutes of this meeting. Richards would try again, but Cosgrove had clearly won the first round. There was no point now in antagonizing Horace Bronsky. "Perhaps my sources are not completely reliable," he said. "All I am saying is that we should be careful. If we do decide to proceed, we should consider leaving the running of Regina to Cecil Rand. He knows how the cosmetic business works. Alternatively, there is a first-class man running Regina's international company, a fellow called Martin Cohen—"

Leonetti snorted. "If you think they're doing so badly, why keep 'em?"

The president, who had half expected this retort, promptly changed his view. "You have a very good point," he said. "I agree with you. In fact, I had been thinking along the same lines myself. Later, we can reconsider, but for the time being we need a top-rate man from API to run Regina. I have just the man available, competent and ready for the job. A number of you have met him previously, I believe. Alex Petersen." By changing his mind and agreeing with Leonetti, after first seeming to disagree, Cosgrove had made it virtually impossible for Leonetti to advocate his own candidacy. After all, he could hardly state that Petersen, whom he didn't know, was inappropriate. Well, that threat's averted, Cosgrove thought. Now the only question is how to stop the whole damn acquisition and make sure old Blackhead has no excuse for remaining.

There was silence in the board room as each director kept counsel with himself. It was Abrams who spoke next. "Gentlemen, it is not my place to judge whether the acquisition of Regina is sound business. However, I would like to express some concern that I have about the quality of the data we are being fed by the Regina people."

"Why don't you check it?" Blake Richards interrupted.

"We have checked as much as we can, but from the outside even a careful audit cannot give you the full answers."

Bronsky raised his head slowly. "I see no reason to suppose that the Regina Company is misrepresenting anything."

Abrams saw the danger signal and retreated immediately. "Very well," he said. He too had no intention of arguing with the powerful Bronsky.

"I'm not sure we should buy this company. I think Jimmy's right when he says we should stick to our knitting," said Marshall Lyddon suddenly.

"For Chrissake, Marshall," Blake Richards exploded. "We need to expand, not sit still."

"Possibly. But I still say we should concentrate on strengthening API first."

Herman Cosgrove's precise accountant's mind was tallying the probable lineup of votes for and against the acquisition. He himself was against, although he was not yet publicly committed one way or the other. Leonetti was clearly against it. So was Lyddon. Abrams had retreated before Bronsky's attack, but would probably vote against the proposition in the end. Four against, out of ten directors.

Declared for the acquisition were only Bronsky and Richards. But Richards' business friend and Dr. Brittainy and old Cy Baldwin almost always voted with the chairman. That made five probable votes in favor of the acquisition already. Damn it, thought the president, Darwin Kellogg will smell which side is on top. He's bound to go with the five votes to make it a majority.

At that moment Darwin cleared his throat. "As most of you know, I've been friendly with the Rand family for many years. Perhaps it would be a conflict for me to give you my views."

"Not at all," said Richards quickly. Like Cosgrove, he realized that Kellogg would probably be in favor of the acquisition. The chairman was under no illusions; he knew that Regina was having difficulties. But he was determined to push the acquisition through anyway. After it was acquired—and he had protected his own position at API—he'd figure out how to turn Regina around. And if they wouldn't let him stay, well, to hell with them and Regina!

"Very well, then, it's my feeling that we should take over the Regina Company. Even if it's not doing quite as well as it seems, with some expert management planning it can certainly be a valuable asset." No harm, Darwin Kellogg felt, in making a sales pitch for his own management company. "If my firm can be of any assistance, we would be pleased to help."

That's it, thought Cosgrove with resignation. With Blake Richards, Bronsky, and Kellogg already for the acquisition, and Baldwin, Brittainy, and the chairman's golfing buddy almost sure to go along, the majority was already against him.

But surprisingly, Chancellor Brittainy was having trouble deciding how to vote. Normally he would have backed Richards automatically, but in this instance he had a personal conflict: only a few days earlier he had been asked to sit on the board of another huge cosmetics firm. Clearly he could not accept if API acquired Regina. Chancellor Brittainy was a professional director who sat on many boards, accepting the risks in return for a considerable income from directors' fees. Thirteen board memberships at five to fifteen thousand dollars per year each was a nice addition to his chancellor's salary.

"Very difficult decision," the chancellor began, looking at Bronsky.

"We make them all the time, don't we?" said Bronsky calmly.

And Chancellor Brittainy understood clearly that he would have to vote in favor of the acquisition if he wanted to get another penny for his school from the numerous charitable trusts which Bronsky influenced. "Yes, very difficult," he repeated. "But on balance it seems to me that a corporation of our type must move forward into our future aggressively."

"In other words, you want to buy," Leonetti interrupted.

"That would be my recommendation."

I'd better join them quickly, Cosgrove thought. No point in alienating Richards *and* losing the battle. . . .

"I don't favor Regina at all," said Cy Baldwin suddenly, and the entire group looked at the senile old man with amazement.

"I knew a girl once—she was called Regina something. No damn good! The whole family was no damn good. I'd vote against Regina anytime."

"Come on, Cy," Richards said, "that has nothing to do with this acquisition."

"Maybe so and maybe not," said Baldwin, his chin out pugnaciously. "But it's a risk. I wouldn't like any company called Regina mixed up in API. Don't believe in it, myself." He sat back in his chair, breathing heavily. Clearly there would be no changing his mind.

We've won the day, Cosgrove suddenly realized with surprise. With Leonetti, Lyddon, and Baldwin declared, and with his own vote plus that of Abrams likely to go the same way, he had half the votes—enough to have the whole matter delayed for further study. That would certainly let him kill the deal. It remained only for Abrams to declare himself formally against the acquisition—and then screw Bronsky and the chairman. I'll win this one running away, Cosgrove thought, *and* have Leonetti on my side.

"Well, Leonard, where do you stand?" he asked the chief counsel, trying to keep the jubilation out of his voice.

Abrams pondered for a while in silence. True, as Cosgrove assumed, he had intended to vote against the acquisition. Convinced that the majority of the directors would vote for it, he could have afforded to protect his professional reputation by taking the safe legal way. But now, if he voted against the acquisition—and against Bronsky and Richards—he would have to carry much of the responsibility if API's profits declined.

"As Dr. Brittainy has asked, it's a difficult decision."

"Seems clear to me," said Leonetti.

For a moment Abrams almost voted no.

"And to me," said Bronsky. His voice was quieter than that of the ex-trucker, but no less powerful.

"On balance, I think we should proceed," said Abrams.

"Hear, hear," said the chairman's friend.

The president's heart, elated a second before, sank. He feared that his inner groan of disappointment might have been audible. Six votes for the acquisition. Bronsky, Richards, and his friend; Kellogg, Brittainy, and now Abrams. There was no point in continuing to fight.

He said, "I quite agree with those of you who feel that this acquisition would be a sound one. My point was that we should examine their figures carefully before moving ahead. You can rely on me to do so."

"Shall we take a formal vote, then?" Blake Richards asked.

"I think we should vote unanimously to acquire the Regina Company," said Jimmy Leonetti graciously. "May I so move?"

"Second," said Horace Bronsky.

"All in favor?" asked the Chairman.

There was a round of assent.

"Damn glad we decided to go ahead," said Cy Baldwin, rousing for a moment. "Good company, that Regina." He lapsed again into oblivion.

Herman Cosgrove had not relaxed until all the directors had left. Only then did he permit himself to scratch his scalp, dishevelling his carefully arranged hair. Thank God they didn't ask more about the cash, he had thought. Not that they won't find out fast enough if things don't soon improve.

Chapter 4

Blake Richards found his victory hollow. In spite of the acquisition, Leonetti's determination and Cosgrove's guile blocked all his attempts to delay his retirement. Herman Cosgrove, privately exultant and publicly as reticent as ever, moved into the chief executive's office with so little fanfare that even the business journals failed to mention the event. Only one important magazine, *Business World*, where an unusually bright investigative feature writer, Pamela Maarten, sensed serious trouble at API, ran an article of any length on Cosgrove's accession to power. Ms. Maarten, widely known for her biting comments, concluded: "If, as is widely believed, API has growing cash problems, Herman Cosgrove's long experience as an accountant will help him to describe those problems accurately; it remains to be seen whether it will also help him solve them."

API's new chief executive ignored the *Business World* article and behaved as if any problems his company faced were merely typical of any business with API's spectacular five-year growth rate and could easily be resolved. Privately, however, Cosgrove was deeply worried for the company and for himself. After years of sometimes agonizing waiting, he finally had the power to run the show without having to subjugate his own pride to please one boss or another. But no sooner had he achieved power, than events seemed ready to snatch it away. The cash drain from API's real estate operations continued; the company's consumer goods business was not reaching Richard's unrealistic goals; and the more he saw of the Regina Cosmetics Company, the more convinced he became that his original instincts against acquiring it had been right. The place simply reeked with problems. Not that being right was any consolation; it would be his neck no matter what if he couldn't cut back expenses fast enough to stem API's profit decline. He shuddered. If only he could find some escape route. He thought about little else. Or at least some way to cushion the shock if the Board did blame him. Perhaps it was time to have that private talk with Cecil Rand. Certainly Rand had hinted often enough that a meeting would be worthwhile. . . .

Cecil Reginald Rand was the only official child of the legendary Sir Reginald, a larger than life character who had founded his cosmetics empire on a mixture of showmanship and business acumen very like that of his great rivals, Helena Rubinstein and Elizabeth Arden. But neither they nor the latecomer Charles Revson could match Sir Reginald for sheer flamboyance.

In almost every respect, however, Cecil was the antithesis of his father. Where the old man had been elegantly tailored and impeccably handsome, his son was sloppy, his shirt forever bulging over his belly, his face often glistening with sweat. Where Sir Reginald had been determined to the point of blindness, Cecil Rand faced the world with flexible shrewdness. And where Sir Reginald had been loved or hated by his employees, Cecil, always enmeshed in the intrigues and politics of Regina, was distrusted, envied, disliked, and feared; but seldom admired.

Originally an Australian adventurer named Reg Rand, Sir Reginald in his early years had been a buccaneer, a mercenary, a gold prospector, a cowboy, even a French chef—but always a handsome, swashbuckling hero. He made a million dollars in copra in the Pacific Islands and lost every penny speculating in diamonds. Soon he made another fortune, this time in Australian opals, which he helped to popularize. When he lost his opal

mines as a result of an obscure land gamble which did not pay
off, he became one of the first men to dig aquamarines com-
mercially in Brazil. With those profits, Reg Rand acquired a
cattle ranch in the western prairies of Canada and probably
rustled most of the cattle he ran. At thirty-five years old, he was
a tycoon.

He sold his ranch and took his growing fortune to Hollywood. Some said that the movies he made, although brilliant,
were financial calamities. Others maintained that his fortune
grew, but that in one magnificent Byronesque gesture he gave it
all away to the most beautiful movie queen of them all. In any
case, within two years of his arrival in Hollywood, virtually all
his money was gone. What little was left he used as a down pay-
ment on a medieval castle in the "fruit basket" of France, the
Loire River valley. It was from this beautiful but decrepit old
place, which he renamed Chateau Regine, that he and the young
Frances Duke started the Regina cosmetic company as a mail
order business. It became an almost immediate success, and
within less than two years they had transferred its headquarters
into elegant offices on New York's Park Avenue.

By the time Reg Rand was forty-five, Regina had become a
major retail cosmetic house. Somewhere along the way he had
appropriated an English baronetcy. It mattered not at all that
the title was fictitious, for its origin was lost in the hot air of a
thousand public relations officers. From the age of about thirty
to the end of his life at ninety-one, he was *Sir* Reginald—an outrageous star, a satyrical mogul in the fullest tradition of early
Hollywood, a con man, a tyrant. Through it all, he remained an
undaunted romantic who admired and lusted after shop girl and
princess alike and who consummated most of his lusts with cheerful disregard for convention, enraged husbands, or encroaching
age. No one challenged his right to his title. But it was a life
title, as it turned out, for when Cecil tried to appropriate it, not
even his own employees would call him Sir Cecil. He had neither
the charisma nor the gall to pull it off. Sir Reginald was a knight;
Cecil Rand, merely a clever, perhaps devious, middle-aged son.

Throughout Sir Reginald's life—every adventure and scandal
of which was gleefully reported by the press of a hundred countries—he was always surrounded by the most desirable women.
It was said that he entered the cosmetic business in the first place

because he knew more about beautiful women than any other man of his time. Women throughout the world wanted to look like Sir Reginald's women, and he became the great cosmetic authority. Long before Charles Revson invented the idea that "lips should match fingertips," Sir Reginald designated and defined beauty in women. He told them how to be desirable, and they believed his every word. His accent, as he performed on his own radio and later TV commercials, was thickly British but with just a touch of Australian vulgarity which made it earthy and sexual. His bearing was aristocratic and his face so adventure-scarred and leathery that it seemed to say: "I have seen and felt everything." Sometimes he appeared to be all bluff and bluster, but so great was his self-confidence and so steely his spine that the bluster turned to reality and the bluff was rarely called.

"If you can't fix it, fake it," he used to say privately. He was rarely caught in a fake.

In spite of Sir Reginald's many outrageous liaisons, in his own extraordinary way he remained loyal to Frances Duke—Queenie, as he called her. He always told her with glee and gusto of his latest conquest, always laughing about the "scrapes" he got into, like a little boy who is proud of his naughtiness. At first she was shocked and hurt by his behavior, but after a while she learned that women were his lust and his enjoyment, not his love.

"You are my only love," he would repeat to her on many occasions. "Only you are my love."

At first she could not bring herself to believe him, but gradually she became surer. He always returns to me, she finally understood, and he is always so happy to be back. At last she believed him when he assured her, "you are my only love." It was then that she decided that she would like his child. When she shyly broached the idea, he roared his approval and, hugging her, swung her around the room. Then he carried her, laughing and protesting, to the master bedroom and made love to her, first gently and then with such stallion violence that she became excited and then satisfied to a degree she had never imagined possible nor experienced again.

"I *must* be pregnant," she exulted.

But she did not become pregnant, and after about a year both admitted that she probably never would. They hardly talked about it, but gradually she came to realize how very deeply he wanted a child; a son specifically—his own son. No adopted child would do for Reginald, she thought. Nor for me.

She ruminated for many months on the problem and on her solution, considering it from every angle, practical and personal. When she finally decided it was right, she worried for several more weeks about how to tell him. Eventually, late one night, when they had made love and were lying warm and content in each other's arms, she started to explain.

"We can't have the son we both want, it appears—"

"You sound pedantic," he laughed at her. "It must be serious. You're only pedantic about once a year and it's always serious."

"Yes, dear, it's serious. I have a suggestion—" She hesitated.

"Let me guess," he interrupted. "You and I don't seem to be making my son. One alternative would be to get married and adopt a kid. But you don't think that would be the same for me as siring my own. Nor do I. Maybe the kid we'd get would grow up to be some pimply-faced little mite and we'd not want him. Too bad for the kid. And for us. So that means I'd have to beget my own kid with some other woman. Assuming, of course, that the reason we're not having a kid together has to do with your tubes and not my sperm count—"

"Reg!" She was quite shocked. "How could you think that. You are the most virile man any woman—"

"Nothing to do with it, love. You're sexy as any woman I ever screwed, but who knows about tubes. Those things aren't related."

She had loved him more than ever for his good sense. "If anyone heard you wondering about your fertility, Regina's stock would collapse," she teased. "Except that no one would believe you."

"I'm not planning to mention it in public, you know," he laughed.

Tears came to her eyes.

"So you are thinking," he continued, "that I'd better try to have my son with some other gal." He paused. "The problem is, I'd have to marry her to make the kid legitimate." She nodded. "And then divorce her and come live with you."

She looked up from his chest where she had buried her face

and nodded mutely, realizing with surprise that her whole face
—and half his chest—was wet with her tears. "If you'll want to,"
she said in a frightened voice.

"Of course I'll want to come back," he said with every bit
of his habitual certainty. "Why on earth would I want to stay
married to some broad just because she's the receptacle for my
son? Sometimes, my love, your fears are purely daft!"

His mild irritation was more consoling to her than anything
else could have been. She needed his strength at this moment,
not tender reassurances. "I've been worrying for days about how
to tell you," she said. "I feel a little silly that, before I even start,
you tell me."

"You are my love," he said simply. "I understand." Suddenly
he chuckled; she could feel the laughter ripple the length of his
body pressed against her. "Capital idea," he said. Then, his voice
serious again and full of certainty, he repeated, "Capital."

She felt such a zestful lust for him at that moment that she
attacked every part of his body until she aroused him again and
they made love passionately, almost savagely, both reaching cli-
maxes which left them exhausted and caused them to sleep hours
longer than normal.

"Have you chosen the girl?" were the first words he uttered
when they awoke, as if their conversation had never been interrupted.

"No. But I have the specifications."

"So do I!"

"Intelligent, healthy, tall—"

"Beautiful, sexy—"

"Strong, energetic—"

"And available!"

They both roared with laughter.

He was married eight months later, the day his doctor
assured him that Miranda Watkins, the beautiful daughter of
an impoverished Boston family with impeccable social standing,
was indeed pregnant. And divorced one year after their son was
born. The arrrangement cost him one million dollars, which he felt
was a bargain. His only annoyance was that Miranda insisted as
part of the marriage contract that if the child was a boy, his
first name should be Cecil after her father, with Reginald only

his middle name. Nothing that Sir Reginald could do would dissuade her from that condition. It rankled the more because the name Cecil was the one which stuck.

Sir Reginald was inordinately pleased with his newborn son. He announced his birth with a double-page newspaper advertisement in the New York Times and used the occasion to launch an entire line of Regina baby products. For such a loud and often rough man, he was marvelously gentle with the baby, holding his tiny head in his powerful hands and dandling him on his knee by the hour. When the baby cried, Sir Reginald would hug him, but if the baby did not stop at once, his father would quickly become impatient.

"Nanny, take the boy and see to it he stops his weeping," he would say sternly. "He has nothing to cry about."

As Cecil grew, his father's demands increased.

"I made the football team," the little boy would shout as he ran into Sir Reginald's study.

"Fine. Very good. First string?"

"Well, no. Not yet."

"Okay, then it's just a start. Now fight for it." Sir Reginald's voice would show his disappointment. "Only first string really counts."

By the time Cecil was in his early teens it was clear that, although he was a bright and good-looking boy, he would never have the dominant brilliance his father wanted.

"I'm always a disappointment to him," Cecil once told Queenie tearfully. "He's always asking me to do more than I can."

"No, you're not," she tried to reassure him. "It's just his way to get the most out of people. That way he can be proud of them— and they can be proud of themselves."

"He's so much better than I am," the boy wept. "So much better—"

"Oh no, Cecil, you mustn't—"

"But he is! And so are you." Young Cecil rushed out, tears streaming, leaving Queenie to wonder what she could possibly do to help him live with such an evident and painful truth.

As Sir Reginald became more demanding. Cecil's sense of inferiority grew. Eventually, shortly after Cecil turned fifteen, there was a crisis. At first it was just another minor argument; but it led to Cecil's first rebellion against his father—a shrewd and effective rebellion which took the form of giving up all sports, gluing himself to his radio, and eating. For six months the boy ate ceaselessly: three and sometimes four large meals a day, and an endless stream of ice cream, potato chips, candy bars, and hamburgers in between.

Again and again, Sir Reginald berated, cajoled, or bribed him. Once he even beat Cecil. Nothing helped. The boy ate endlessly. Steadily his weight rose. If his father thought he was a no-good lazy kid with no pride or drive, well, he was probably right. His father was usually right. So he might as well live up to his reputation.

The final blow to Sir Reginald's waning parental pride came a few months later when his son developed severe acne. Sir Reginald hated that acne more than anything else on earth. He commanded his chemists to develop a cure. When they could not, his sarcasm and often his fury was boundless. Nothing helped.

Cecil was almost pleased that his acne withstood his father's onslaughts. It gave him a sense of importance. At least here was one part of him Sir Reginald could not overpower.

Eventually, Sir Reginald gave up and left his son alone. Gradually Cecil's overeating eased and he switched from radio to reading. Eventually he graduated from school with sufficiently high marks to earn a grudging compliment from his father.

"You didn't do so badly, son. There's a real spark starting to show now that you've stopped dousing it under manure heaps of food."

Cecil, delighted almost to the point of tears, thought this might be the happiest moment of his life. At last he had pleased the old man. If that's what it took, he would happily lose fifty pounds. "Thank you, father," he said quietly, his voice catching.

"Now," Sir Reginald continued, his enthusiasm and determination for his son evident in every muscle of his body, "now, do even better in college." He was astounded when Cecil burst into tears and rushed out of the room.

"Strange boy," he said to Queenie. "Weak like his mother."

Cecil drifted through college without noticeable successes

or failures, participating in no competitive sports or campus clubs, and graduating near the middle of his class. He went on to Wharton business school because it seemed easier than fighting his father's determination that he take a post-graduate degree. There, too, he graduated with average marks, a totally non-memorable student. Briefly he toyed with taking a job away from Regina but, after a few months' vacation in Europe, he acquiesced to his father's insistence and joined Regina. A while thereafter he married a motherly young woman of unrelenting mediocrity, and moved into a pleasant house in a corner of Sir Reginald's Westchester estate.

But under this placid exterior acceptance, Cecil Rand seethed with subconscious anger. One dream reoccurred frequently from which he always awoke filled with tense, unspecific hatred: his feet were encased in cement, and he carried spears which he thrust at all who came near, mutilating them dreadfully, while he screamed his wrath at the top of his voice. . . .

Sir Reginald vacillated between ignoring his son for days and then giving him some major assignment well beyond his ability. Watching him inevitably fail, he would sigh deeply, shake his head in theatrical parody of tragic acceptance, and return to ignoring Cecil entirely.

The change in Cecil's resigned acquiescence came after he had worked at Regina about two years. He had been summoned into his father's office.

"Yes, sir?"

"How are you, son?" Sir Reginald sat behind his extraordinary swinging desk, a piece of enormous polished marble suspended from the ceiling on polished brass chains and anchored by an even larger chain to the floor. Writing on the desk made it shake, but it didn't matter since Sir Reginald rarely wrote, preferring to dictate short, often vitriolic memoranda or to bark orders into a telephone and have them confirmed in writing by the recipient. The mail he had to sign was wheeled in by his butler, neatly laid out on a desk attached to a silver tea-trolley which was then firmly clamped to the floor by suction cups.

"Well, thank you." Cecil's voice was wary.

"I had assumed you were not well since I have not seen you for several weeks."

"No, thank you. I have been quite well. Eating heartily!"

Sir Reginald frowned slightly, Cecil noted with pleasure. At least that particular weapon had kept its sharpness.

"I have an assignment for you that you should enjoy."

Cecil said nothing. Too many times in the past he had allowed his hopes to build only to have them crushed as the assignment his father gave him turned out to be either demeaningly simple or vastly too difficult.

"Just possibly, you may even be able to handle it."

"Possibly."

"For Christ sake, boy, can't you be a little more optimistic?" Sir Reginald, whose self-control was renowned, could never contain his exasperation with his son for more than a few moments.

Cecil remained silent. It was another weapon with which he could avoid his father's domination.

"Very well," said Sir Reginald with a sigh. "I shall explain it carefully so that the task remains within your scope." He paused. "Just possibly."

Cecil still remained silent, a small, almost supercilious smile on his lips. Was there nothing, Sir Reginald wondered, which could penetrate that smug indifference? At least when he was younger, the boy had tried. Not with much success, to be sure, but he'd made the attempt. Perhaps with enough pushing and guidance he could have made it. But now this utter indifference, this snotty, superior smile. . . .

Cecil, too, was reflecting how much these confrontations with his father had changed. As a boy, desperately trying to please, he would cringe before his father's sarcastic criticism. Most discussions would end with tears; often he would rush away and hide for hours sobbing his heart out. Even when he first started working at Regina he had been deeply humiliated, more disappointed by far than Sir Reginald himself, that none of his assignments seemed to work out right. But now—his smile broadened just perceptibly—he had gained the upper hand at these meetings. Finally he had learned that he could defend himself against his father's attacks simply by waiting until they were over and refusing to show that he was hurt. What could his father do? In a masochistic way, Cecil almost came to enjoy these confrontations.

"Must you stand there with a silly grin?" Sir Reginald would never have stooped to so mundane a complaint with anyone else.

"I am smiling with pleasure that you plan to give me an assignment." Cecil's smile remained unchanged.

"Very well." Sir Reginald controlled his anger with difficulty. "Notwithstanding your facetious tone, I shall take what you say at face value. The assignment I have for you is straightforward; I have pointed the way already. We all know it can be done. I want you to find a way to get us restarted in the mail-order business."

Cecil's smile remained fixed. But, in spite of himself, his heart contracted with disappointment. Clearly the task was beyond him, beyond anyone. It was just one more trick to put him down. A mail-order business, he realized immediately, would have to be started under a new name, not under the name Regina. The huge department stores and drug chains on whom Regina relied would never allow the company to sell its products in competition with them directly to their consumers. But starting a cosmetic company under an unknown name via mail order was virtually impossible; no cosmetic company in the world, except Yves Rocher in France and Sir Reginald himself in Regina's early days, had ever been successful in selling cosmetics through the mail. Far worse, Cecil recognized in a flash, was the fact that his father and Queenie had started Regina as a mail order house, even though they had dropped mail order when they moved to the United States. That meant that whatever Cecil did, short of building another company as successful as Regina, Sir Reginald would never be satisfied. So I'm bound to fail, Cecil thought, becoming angrier by the second. I don't have even a prayer. This time, he'll prove to the whole world just how inferior I really am. As if that needs any more proof. . . .

Suddenly Cecil's anger erupted into his conscious mind like a lava stream from an apparently extinct volcano burning great scars in the land. Why did he have to put up with this shit? Why? Without any thought to the consequences, he spat out the only words strong enough to convey his anger.

"Fuck you," he said, his voice full of hate and scorn. He turned on his heel. "Fuck you, father." He marched out, slamming the door viciously. Sir Reginald sat absolutely still, but his desk vibrated on its glittering chains and the points of light reflecting from their links speckled his granite face with points of gold. It looked for all the world as if he had covered himself with Regina's Gold Dust, one of the season's best sellers.

From that day on, father and son talked only rarely and then with no more than cool politeness. But from that day, too, Cecil gradually began to gather power within the company. Starting first in areas in which Sir Reginald had little interest, he pushed and intrigued his way to authority.

"I would like to see the cost of goods ledger," he would ask the accounting department and they, not daring to refuse the owner's son, would give it to him. He would search through the figures until he found something questionable. "Why are the costs of our 'Kiss Unlimited' lipsticks rising?" he would demand.

"We are facing increased packaging costs and Marketing feels that a cheaper lipstick case would hurt sales."

"Very well, I shall see to it." He dropped a note to the marketing department. "Cost of goods are way out of line on 'Kiss Unlimited.' Please advise me promptly whether you would prefer to raise prices or move to a less expensive lipstick case."

To his delight, Cecil found that usually people did what he wanted. When, occasionally, an executive fought back, Cecil would immediately drop the issue. But he would remember what he considered the personal affront and even the score in some other way. It happened, for example, when he asked about costs on "Lovely Eyes" eye shadows.

"We feel strongly," responded the marketing manager, an unsmiling young man appropriately named Stern, "that moving to a cheaper compact or formula will seriously harm our sales."

Two weeks later, Cecil visited the personnel department. "I'm very worried that entertainment expenses in Marketing are out of line," he explained. An investigation commenced.

A few days later Cecil ran into Hy Weissman, Regina's vice president of sales, apparently quite unexpectedly.

"Hy, how are you? Glad to see you. Listen, I've been meaning to ask you why your guys haven't been given as much money to spend for in-store promotions this year. Is that one of young Stern's ideas to save money?" Cecil laughed. "He'll save money on sales commissions, too, if sales drop off." Before Weissman could respond, Cecil was already walking away. "Listen, good to see you, Hy. Keep in touch."

Weissman, always suspicious of Marketing anyway, was especially touchy about anything that could hurt his sales people. It took him no time to complain about Stern to Sir Reginald.

Within three months, Stern was so investigated and attacked that he resigned. As Cecil won such battles repeatedly, his influence rose. While he never participated in new product development or in sales, which were his father's main interest, he gradually gained power in all other areas. When Sir Reginald was stricken by a heart attack and, a few days later, died of a second one, Cecil Rand was strong enough to become chief executive of Regina. He refurnished his father's grand office, selling the magnificent hanging desk to a second-hand dealer for only a few dollars, and took over. At last, he felt, he could be his own man.

But running the company was far different from surreptitiously acquiring influence in it. Now he was required to be creative and decisive, both areas in which he lacked talent and experience.

Soon, in spite of Queenie's best efforts to carry on the new products department, Regina started losing momentum. Cecil rationalized that his father, in his blind, arrogant way, had just not kept Regina abreast of the modern world. To his keen disappointment, he realized that the company would have to be sold to survive. Finally, after a year of discreet attempts to find a buyer, he had persuaded API to make the acquistion. Now if only he could find a way to get back the job of president, to get it even though his family no longer owned the company, to prove to them all that he *could* do it, to prove to his father. . . .

"Lovely," was Cecil Rand's response when Herman Cosgrove, after reflecting on the matter for several weeks, finally called to accept his long-standing luncheon invitation. "We'll make it Four Seasons. Lovely."

With its spacious dining room, high ceiling, sound-absorbing smoke-gray hangings shimmering in front of the tall windows and central reflecting pool, Four Seasons was an ideal restaurant to choose: the food and service were fine; but, above all, you could not be overheard. Rand made the reservations and, arriving first, was ushered to a poolside table. Only patrons of some importance and loyalty could be assured such placement. Herman Cosgrove, worried and slightly desiccated, in total contrast to the rotund and genial-seeming Rand, arrived a few minutes later, out of breath and harried.

"Apologies for being late," he started. "I'm afraid there's a lot to do—"

"Of course. I quite understand. Taking over a company as large as API—lots of problems, I'm sure, lots of work." Rand smiled charmingly. "Let me order you a quick drink, then we can have lunch. The goujonette of sole—"

"I'll just have a steak, thanks. And a glass of white wine."

"Perhaps a Pouilly Fumé; not too heavy for lunchtime.'

"Just a glass. Anything."

The captain hovered and Rand gave the order with elaborate instructions on how the food was to be prepared.

Lot of nonsense, Cosgrove thought. Secretly, he preferred pizza to all this fancy stuff.

"Well, Cecil, how are your sales this month?" Herman Cosgrove started ponderously as soon as the order was placed. He realized that Rand's objective was to remain Regina's chief executive, but what was he going to bargain with?

"I say, Herman, let's not ruin lunch with business," Rand interrupted. "So bad for the digestion, all those juices churning—"

All through the meal Rand chattered inconsequentially, ordering a wine more to his liking, discussing the food with the owner, demanding more butter—and rarely finishing a sentence.

"His sentences stagger on until they drop dead," Pamela Maarten of *Business World* had said of his speeches.

Only as the espresso was being served—with Cosgrove's patience at breaking point—did Cecil Rand say, "I believe that I could continue to do the job pretty well." He broached the subject without preliminaries, assuming rightly that Cosgrove knew which job he meant. He picked at his chin.

"I'm afraid the board preferred me to put in an API man initially," Cosgrove responded.

"I realize that. Petersen. You told me. But I wonder if he'll have the experience for our rather special business."

"Yes, I doubt that too." Herman Cosgrove paused in order to choose his next words carefully. "In that case, I might persuade the board that you should be recalled." He paused again, for emphasis. "Under the appropriate circumstances, I would certainly choose that option."

"Let us only hope that he has not done too much damage by then," Rand replied. Then, leaning forward over his protruding stomach, he added emphatically, "After all, I shall be one of API's largest shareholders." He paused to make sure his implied threat was clear. "On the other hand," he added, "I shall certainly do anything I can to help—yes, anything I can do.'

"'A certain time will have to elapse—" Cosgrove wished Rand would come to the point. These veiled hints were unimpressive. Even a large minority shareholder would have little influence if the business went well; and if it did not, then Herman Cosgrove would need more than vague assurances of help.

"Of course, of course. I would not want it otherwise. Give the boy his chance." Rand's smile stretched across his jowly cheeks but left the top of his face cold. "In any case, once we do start working together, we shouldn't have much trouble putting things right—provided, of course, they haven't gone too far off the rails. I imagine you and I would work well together, very well."

"I hope we would."

Rand's smile became purely benign. "Then, of course, there is the whole question of our investments—the ones our trust makes. You know my family controls the Rand trust. Sir Reginald set it up years ago. It will receive most of the API shares we get for Regina. The trust has some money now, but when we sell the API stock—lots of funds—if you ever wanted to participate. . . ." He again let his sentence dangle; but this time, Cosgrove knew, he did so on purpose. Here, he realized, was the offer he had been awaiting—a potential reward dropped into the conversation as casually as if it had no value at all. Yet Cosgrove knew that private participation in a large investment fund could be of enormous financial benefit. He could participate in tax shelter investments which he could never afford on his own. And trusts of this size frequently got inside information on investments—even though to do so was strictly against the Security and Exchange

Commission's regulations—which allowed them to make enormous profits.

"I would very much appreciate that opportunity," the president said, trying to sound casual. He paused for added emphasis. "I believe in cooperation."

"Once we are working closely, with me running Regina and you as my, shall we say, general at API, we shall have no difficulty in cooperating."

Herman Cosgrove was not surprised that Rand would not reward him before being reestablished as president of Regina. In such business deals, he knew from experience, the benefit rarely preceded the favor. The luncheon ended with mutual understanding.

Afterwards, as Cosgrove walked down Park Avenue towards his office, he viewed the giant office skyscrapers on either side of the avenue with a mixture of awe and satisfaction. Behind him was the bronze-colored Seagram building from which he had just emerged, with its spacious pools and fountains; opposite, the great Manufacturer's Hanover building; north, the green glass edifice erected by a former president of Lever Bros. who, after that feat, returned to architecture.

When he was younger, these buildings had towered over him and he had wended his way through the sidewalk crowds apologetically. Now he felt a momentary surge of confidence. He could stare back at these buildings, knowing he was a victor in the business battles in which they were the fortresses. He, Herman Cosgrove, accountant from New York University and before that, secretary of his graduating class in Western High, Middletown, New Jersey, against all the odds had become one of the giants of this magnificent avenue. He could command respect, even awe, in every building in sight. He need step aside for no man.

Herman Cosgrove strode forward, head held high. If only it could last, he thought suddenly. Immediately his shoulders slumped again. Head down he hurried back to his office. If only it could last. . . .

Chapter 5

The reception area of the Regina Cosmetic Company was feminine, perfumed; perhaps not beautiful, but opulent. As Alex Petersen got off the elevator he was struck by the contrast to the offices of API. The focal point here was an inlaid Louis XIV desk set on a deep red Persian carpet. The superb bowl of long-stemmed roses on the desk matched the carpet's colors perfectly; above, the Venetian chandelier reflected them gaudily.

Behind the desk sat one of the most beautiful young women Alex had ever seen. She reminded him of an actress he had dated until he discovered how ambitious and self-centered she was. I hope this one's not the same sort of bitch, he thought. She's even more beautiful.

"Can I help you?" Her voice was husky and her smile almost cheeky.

She thinks it's a game sitting in this room, Alex thought. He noted as he approached that the fragrance became sweeter.

"Yes," he said, "yes, I'm—" He hesitated for a second. "Alex Petersen." He stopped, not sure whether to explain further.

The girl knew at once. She arose quickly and walked around

the desk towards him. "Oh," she said, "you're the new president. How nice!"

She grinned at him, while Alex blushed. Then, her hips swiveling, she crossed the reception room.

"Follow me," she called, "I'll take you to Mr. Rand's office." Her smile seemed intimate, as if she were inviting a friend into her apartment.

He opened the door for her rather clumsily, and she preceded him into the lengthy corridor. In the offices on both sides he could see desks covered with papers, secretaries taking dictation, managers with telephones between ear and shoulder, businessmen and women of many ages, some frantic, some relaxed, all apparently busy. The unusual ingredient was that, overtly or surreptitiously, they were carefully inspecting him. Evidently he had been expected. He could sense the men craning and he could hear the women whispering and giggling.

"I seem to be causing some interest," Alex said to the receptionist.

"Excuse me?" The girl stopped so suddenly, Alex had to swerve to avoid bumping into her. As he did, he stumbled and she grabbed his elbow to steady him. The sound of secretaries giggling seemed to rise to a crescendo. What a way to make an entrance, Alex thought. They'll be wagging their silly tongues forever.

Finally they arrived at Cecil Rand's suite of offices. In the anteroom sat his secretary, middle-aged and prunelike, behind another gorgeous desk.

"Hello, Gladys. Glad to see you're looking so happy," said the beautiful receptionist. "This is Mr. Petersen. He's here to see Mr. Rand."

The older woman arose. "Thank you, Georgina," she said gruffly. "That will be all."

Quite unconcerned by the reprimand, Georgina executed a mocking little curtsy. "Most people call me George," she said to Alex. "I'm going to be an actress," she added facetiously. "You'll see my name in lights!" She disappeared with a wink while Gladys seemed to become even more arid and Alex was forced to cough to hide his chuckle.

"Mr. Petersen, may I welcome you to the Regina Company?" said Gladys. "I believe Mr. Rand is ready to receive you. If you

would be so kind as to wait for just one second, I shall check."
She walked stiffly into the inner office. A few moments later she
reappeared. "Kindly follow me, Mr. Petersen."

Alex's first impression was that he had returned to the reception area. The color of the carpet, the chandelier, even the
flowers, seemed identical. But behind another Louis XIV desk
sat Cecil Rand, round and overweight, his shiny face like a pit-
ted apple. He levered himself out of his chair and rose behind
his outsized desk. He scratched his left nostril. "Nice to see you."
He held out a hand in a damp, slightly twisted handshake. "Glad
you're going to be our new, um, uh—" he paused, "president," he
said with very apparent difficulty. Once over this hurdle, however, he talked on more easily. "*Lovely* to have a bright young
man come in. Knew you were bright the very first time I heard
about you from Herman. Seems ages ago! Knew you'd be the
sort of fellow we'd want in this company—" He seemed to run
out of breath.

"Beautiful offices you have," said Alex, feeling the need to
make some comment.

"Oh, marvelous offices; marvelous, yes. My, umm—" Again
the difficulty with a word. "My father might not have liked
them the way they are now. We've had them redecorated,
changed. . . ." Cecil's voice seemed to run down. "Super company the old man founded—" The voice picked up again. "Marvelous what a wonderful line of colors we make, lots of different
colors. Can't sell a woman the lipstick she wants if she thinks
it's the same as all her friends are wearing. Got to have a wide
variety, you know, a wide variety. . . . Takes a lot of learning,"
he added with emphasis.

"Yes, I'm sure it does; and I'm sure you will be able to teach
me—very fast." Alex's emphasis was just as clear.

"Come and meet Miss Duke. You'll want to get to know
her; she's terribly important to this company," said Rand, ignoring the determined note in Alex's voice but raising his eyebrows
just enough to indicate he had heard. "She could give you a
whole beginner's course about cosmetics. Just what you need."

"I'm sure I won't remain a beginner long," said Alex, unwilling to let the needling pass.

"Determined lady, too; brilliant. Knows it all. Queen of

the industry, actually. Do well to listen to her, you know." He paused. "Come on," he said, "I'll introduce you."

They walked, a procession of two, down the corridor and turned right down a tributory corridor. At the end of that, Rand beat out a tattoo on an ornate door and pushed it open.

"May we come in?" he asked.

The voice which answered was clear, firm, and assured. "Yes, come in, Cecil."

Queenie sat behind a modern executive desk in a comfortable but businesslike office. The style was up-to-date and simple, but the focal point was striking: a series of magnificent orchids artfully arranged on glass shelves on either side of the window and emphasized by a single gorgeous flower placed with Japanese care beside the plain black telephone on her desk. On the other side of the desk was a neat row of sample jars.

"Do come in and sit down," she said to Alex after the introductions were complete. "Cecil, there's no point in your staying; you've heard it all before."

"As you wish." Cecil Rand seemed almost peevish as he withdrew.

"I'm delighted to welcome you, Alex. I hope that you are going to be happy at Regina," she said. "My name is Frances Duke, as you know, but most people call me Queenie. I rather like it. What they call me behind by back is, of course, another matter."

The back in question was ramrod straight. Alex observed that the features on her face were strong, her skin smooth and her make-up impeccable. She noticed him studying her face.

"I'm seventy-seven years old and you will agree that I don't look a day over sixty," she said. "That's because the treatment products made by Regina keep the skin young, and the cosmetic products are so tastefully colored that they hide every imperfection." She was apparently wholly serious. "Now," she continued, "I would like to show you some of our key products. Let me start with the treatment products. They are the most important items in any beauty regime."

"We seem to have a long line."

"Of course. There are almost infinite variations in skin, and many different product usages. For example, Regina's Youth Glow

—this product here—is made both in a day cream and a night cream version."

"What's the difference?" Alex asked. This austere old lady made him feel like a schoolboy again and he wanted to interrupt the lecture.

"The day cream is light and vanishes rapidly into the skin," she explained. Her tone was impersonal, her appearance dignified, her neck arched high. "The night cream is much heavier, a somewhat greasy cream to maximize skin moisturization for older ladies. It is slippery, and younger ladies wouldn't like it." She paused for a moment and then, with precisely the same inflection, she added: "Yes, young ladies wouldn't much like it. You see, he would slip right off."

Alex looked up, flabbergasted. He had no idea what his reaction should be. He was not even sure he had heard correctly.

Suddenly Queenie burst into peals of laughter. Her whole frame shook; tears ran down her cheeks.

"I really got you on that one," she hooted. "You looked as if you'd swallowed a whole goldfish." Again she roared with laughter.

Full of relief, Alex laughed too.

"There, now we can be friends," she said.

"I'd love to be friends with you, Queenie," Alex said seriously. He would need as many friends as he could find, he realized, and clearly she held enormous power within the Regina Cosmetics Company. But in spite of Queenie's friendly words and obvious attempt to make him feel at ease, Alex could not quite shake the sense that she did not like him.

Queenie continued to sit at attention until her secretary had escorted Alex Petersen out of her office. Only then did she allow her shoulders to relax. No longer erect and proper, she seemed older; but also softer and more feminine, almost motherly. It was a view of herself which she allowed no one at Regina to see. So this was the young man who was to succeed Reg. There was no way he could do that, she thought. She was not even sure he would turn out to be as good as Marty Cohen. They are all so smooth, she thought, so charming. This young fellow's handsome enough—not as rugged as Reg, of course, but good-looking. But he's just another company man: professional, well-grounded in the business-school lessons, sound. Reg was never sound. But none of them had half his guts; not one had the guts to *feel*. . . .

Marty Cohen's office, into which Alex was ushered next, was garish. The furniture, including a large Victorian desk full of mahogany curlicues, was a brash reproduction. The walls were decorated with olive-green wallpaper covered with felt patterns, and the floor sported a thick carpet of matching color and design. In one corner there was an enormous lighted globe. In his rare and generally unsuccessful attempts at lightheartedness, Cohen described it as his "sphere of influence." He viewed it as the symbol of his position as president of Regina International. Little liked by his colleagues, for he was cold and humorless, he nevertheless enjoyed a considerable reputation as an effective manager and a sound—even brilliant—marketing expert.

"Cohen wanted to become president of Regina," the head of API's personnel department had warned Alex. "And he deserved to. He's done a good job over the past few years in their overseas division; and before that he helped Sir Reginald and Miss Duke administer their U.S. company. No doubt his nose will be out of joint. Be careful."

As Alex entered, Cohen arose from his desk and extended his hand. "I'm delighted to meet you. May I welcome you to Regina. I'll help you in every way I can." The two men shook hands firmly. Cohen's face was still, except for a slight twitch in his jaw muscle.

"I'm sure you know the company very well and can be of a great deal of help to me," said Alex. "After all, we have twenty-five subsidiaries, right? You know them intimately, but they're all new to me."

"I certainly know the company well. I've worked here for almost twenty years. I even married Cecil Rand's daughter."

Alex was surprised by the belligerence of Cohen's tone. It seemed so defensive, almost as if he were challenging Alex to think less of him because he had married into the family.

"Yes, I married Barbara Rand nine years ago," Cohen continued. "She is Sir Reginald's grandaughter, of course, and the old man was still alive then. I was director of sales for the U.S. company and when we decided to get married, I wanted to resign. Sir Reginald wouldn't hear of it. He was a hell of a salesman, so he persuaded me to stay."

"Are you glad you did?"

"I believe I've contributed significantly to the company."

"And I'm sure you will in the future."

"I shall do what I can."

Cohen's words were friendly enough, but his voice was cold. No doubt, Alex realized, Cohen hated his guts. And yet somehow he would have to allay his jealousy and win him over if he were going to make a success of running Regina. The company's international business was almost as important as that of the U.S., so that without control of International he could never control the business as a whole. That meant he either had to gain Cohen's loyalty, or try to push him out. He hoped it would not come to that. If it did, God knew who would win. Alex had the more powerful position. But, as Cohen had explained, he belonged to the Rand family which now owned a large block of API stock. That gave him considerable strength. Moreover, Cohen had worked at Regina for years; presumably many of the key employees would be loyal to him.

Even if he could gain Cohen's support in the end, Alex worried, could he do so fast enough? Before it was too late?

Chapter 6

Marty Cohen walked the short distance up the path to the door of his Manhattan brownstone unsteadily. He fumbled with the key. "Fucking lock!"

"I'm home," he shouted as he entered. "Where the hell are you?"

Barbara came to the door of the bedroom at the top of the stairs. It was after midnight and she had been asleep.

"Where have you been?" she asked.

Even as she said it she realized she was instantly back in the same old argument. It seemed it would go on forever. How old was it? she wondered. Weeks, months, perhaps years?

He looked up the stairs at her. His eyes filled—With what? she thought. With hatred, loathing? There was a violence in them that she dreaded.

"I was with Fifi. Where the hell d'you think I've been?" His voice was thick with alcohol.

"You always say that."

"It's always true."

"It's not true. You just think it's a smart thing to say."

"Most wives accuse their husbands of infidelity," he said, still angry but becoming more petulant than violent. "You accuse me of *not* being a goddamn infidel."

She smiled, thinking the pun was intended.

"What the hell are you laughing at,'" he demanded, new violence overtaking him.

She realized that he was too drunk to have intended the word play.

"It's true, isn't it, what I say? It's true." He was shouting passionately.

"I don't care." Her voice was resigned. "I just want you to tell me as much as you want. But tell me honestly." She knew it was no use. Whenever she tried to explain, he just fought her.

"I *have* told you," he yelled up the stairs, his legs braced apart. "I have bloody well told you. I was out. I was out fucking Fifi." His unkempt hair and dilated nostrils empahized his rage.

Barbara walked back into the bedroom. As she closed her door she heard him curse again, and then stamp up the stairs to the spare room and slam the door.

How different he used to look, she remembered. He's paunchy now, even in his handmade suits. And when he's drunk he seems so vulgar, so *dirty*. She began to weep.

Cohen and Barbara had both changed in the nine years since their marriage. Cohen had been twenty-nine when they met, a young man on his way up. His alert, slightly tough face and his sinewy body made him look arrogant. He showed an assertiveness, almost a cruelty, which Barbara, ten years younger and a softly beautiful girl, fresh, precocious but naive, found most attractive. Yet for all his competence and outward strength, there had also been a neediness in him, almost a hunted quality, which appealed to her even more. All needy creatures attracted her. As a girl, she had filled her parents' house with stray dogs and birds with broken wings. In this respect she took after her mother who, although ordinary in most respects, did have a special quality of sympathy which was exceptional. It was this combination of need and arrogance in Cohen which had really fascinated her.

Barbara continued to cry, more in frustration now. How little she had been able to help him. His neediness seemed to have increased over the years, and she no longer found his cruelty and arrogance exciting.

Over the same years, Barbara had grown into a beautiful and sophisticated woman. At twenty-eight she remained slim by careful dieting, dressed tastefully, and received admiring glances from men and women wherever she went. Even now, with her face puffy with sleep and tears, and her hair untidy, she looked beautiful.

Why do I feel hurt when he comes home like this? she wondered. I know what he's like. Too well. He's cruel and angry, but he's so vulnerable too. I shouldn't hate him for it.

Did we love each other at the start? she asked herself. Or was it only his loneliness and the physical part which attracted her. He had been her first experience with sex, and it had seemed so important.

All through her youth, the boys who trooped to see her had been kept at bay by Sir Reginald, who hovered everywhere like a great bald eagle, slashing at them with his sarcasm, mortifying them, chasing them out of the house with peals of laughter so that they rarely returned.

"They're not good enough for you anyway, little Barbara. You always bring home the waifs and strays. Just like those poor animals you look after," he would say. "One day you'll be beautiful and strong. Then the right man will come along, a young lion who can stand up to me—not some concave-chested weakling with a crack in his voice and a nose that needs wiping."

He was like a tough old eagle, she thought, teaching me how to fly. How does that hymn about eaglets learning to fly go? *Sweeping, swirling*—damn, I've forgotten. I remember singing it as loud as I could in church. Afterwards, Grand would take me for a ride around the estate in the carriage with the two horses cantering and he cracking his whip to make them go faster. He liked the name Grand. I think he felt he deserved it! I hardly had a real father at all, she thought bitterly. Poor dad, he couldn't stand up to Grand any more than my boyfriends could. And now we have no idea how to talk to each other at all. Sometimes I think he'd like to, but it's too late. There's no habit of talking to fall back on, and we're too close to pretend we're strangers who can learn.

Marty was the only one who seemed able to get under Grand's guard. He got the abuse, but he kept coming back. He was strong enough to take it. Grand needed him at the office, too; that counted. He couldn't completely forbid him from coming. So Marty became my passport to being grown-up. . . .

"What a marvelous place to have a honeymoon," everyone had said. "You're so lucky to be going to the French Riviera."

"We would like a double bed," Cohen insisted, tough and stubborn.

"Oui, Monsieur, an excellent bed we have; a beautiful room. Actually, two lovely beds next to one another."

"We want a double bed, not two singles."

"Yes, sir. I'm sure we have such a room."

"Good, we'll take a look at it."

They followed the desk clerk. The two boys carrying their baggage seemed ready to collapse under their load.

"The bed's fine, but the room's too small." Cohen's voice roughened.

The assistant manager joined the procession. "Oui, Monsieur. Au plaisir. But perhaps it may be rather difficult since our larger rooms have two single beds—"

"Then take this bed and put it into a large room." Cohen's voice had risen. "I'm fed up with waiting."

"We shall try to find a room into which this bed can be brought."

"I must see it," Cohen insisted. He seemed so sure of himself, so confident. Only Barbara sensed how he had to fight to stave off the fear that he would not, after all, obtain the room he demanded. How humiliated he would be, she thought. So she smiled at everyone, willing them with all her might to find a suitable room.

The procession, lacking only a drummer boy, it seemed, was led by the now terrorized room clerk, followed by Cohen bristling and Barbara praying silently. Behind them, the pompous assistant manager, the housekeeper, the two small boys still struggling under the luggage and four more staggering under the large double bed. Eventually they obtained precisely the right room: large, romantic, with a beautiful view, and an excellent double bed.

It should be such a happy memory, Barbara reflected; softened and funny in retrospect, a memory to cherish. Not for us, she thought. Even the memory is of arrogance, determination, toughness. No warmth, no gentleness.

Marty Cohen had left his aunt's house without regret as soon as he was old enough, and never returned. He hated his aunt, and with her husband, a bumbling hen-pecked man, he had no relationship at all.

Cohen had chosen New York University to take his undergraduate degree in business because it was the most pragmatic, down-to-earth school he could find. He won a scholarship which covered most of his tuition, and to earn his keep he worked nightly as a busboy—and hated it: the greasy smells, the abusive waiters, the impatient customers—they all added to his anger. But he swallowed his fury and submitted.

Eventually Cohen graduated, but his marks were unimpressive and the only job offered to him was as a salesman for a tobacco company.

At first his career seemed to be an endless round of warehouses run by ugly men and their ugly wives.

"Hurry up and move those boxes," the old bitch at Moscowitz Super Wholesale, who reminded him of Aunt Ruth, would scream at her mate. Then, seeing Cohen arrived on his monthly trip, "Who are you?"

"Marty Cohen. International Tobacco."

"To sell us more of your garbage?" She would regard him with distaste. "Here, move this box before you do anything else. Come on, move it. Your damn suit's not much anyhow. So it should get a little dusty. Who cares?"

When he joined the great, glamorous Regina Company, he could pretend to himself—and boast to his acquaintances—that his career was on its way. But it was only much later that the real power started to come, and it was intermittent. That old bastard Sir Reginald wouldn't stand for any sort of rival. It was always: "Come here, Marty-boy. Do this. Do that. Listen to me carefully and just conceivably you might be able to understand."

No matter how well he did, there was constant derogation; sometimes subtle, sometimes blatant. Even his name became a putdown. Sir Reginald would call him nothing but "Marty-boy."

"Come in, Marty-boy. I want to tell you what to think." Sir

Reginald would be seated in his opulent office, a plate of melba toast, especially baked by his chef, in front of him.

"Why do you need a French chef to bake toast?" Barbara once asked.

The old man had smiled his wicked, happy smile. "It gets us publicity."

Sir Reginald would stare at Marty, sometimes for minutes at a time, without a word.

"Yes, sir, what can I do for you?" Cohen would eventually ask, unable to stand the silence any longer. In spite of his best efforts, his voice always seemed hesitant when he addressed Sir Reginald.

There would be another infinite silence. "What can you do for me? Well, that's a difficult question. Almost unanswerable. It's why I'm sitting here ruminating. I can't imagine. You'd better come back later when I've had time to think about it."

If Cohen managed to remain silent, standing in interminable discomfort, Sir Reginald would occasionally just give him a task and curtly dismiss him. That was what Cohen prayed for. But often Sir Reginald would look at him as if seeing him for the first time, and then start to needle.

"I hear you've been having a little trouble with Kohlmann Brothers."

"Well, I think we're making progress, Sir Reginald."

"Making progress, are we?" Sir Reginald's face would show exaggerated surprise. "What a strange definition of progress. I never heard of progress being used as a word to describe backwards motion." Then, his voice suddenly hard, "Bloody silly to say we're making progress when we're not. Who do you think you're fooling? Just because I can't live on anything but melba toast, don't start thinking I've become totally senile. Sales are going down with Kohlmann's, Marty-boy, not up. We're not making any bloody progress at all."

"No, sir."

Sir Reginald's voice would change again. The kindly professor talking to the backward student. "The trouble is you don't know how to approach Kohlmann Brothers. You've got to have a little flair, a little good manners, Marty-boy. Let me try to explain. Now listen very carefully, otherwise you won't understand. Let me tell you what to think."

"Yes, Sir Reginald," Cohen would cringe. Even now his muscles tensed at the memory.

"The point is you need to invite them to dinner and be charming. Can you be charming, Marty-boy? And dress properly, so they'll be impressed by the quality of the Regina Company. I know we only sell cheap cosmetics—but we sell them at a terribly expensive price." Sir Reginald would chuckle at his own joke. "You've got to pretend that you're elegant, Marty-boy. *Elegant.* Now I'll tell you what to do. . . ." Sir Reginald would proceed with a description suitable for no one older than five. "If you handle it right, you'll be able to triple their sales." The old man would sigh with utter despair. "Think about it, Marty-boy, and if you still don't know what to do, call me." He would sit back contentedly in his chair. "Remember," he would finish with his favorite slogan, "if you can't fix it, fake it!"

The interview would be over, but Cohen could be sure that there would be another and another, ever more full of sarcasm and degradation, if he failed to triple the sales at Kohlmann. Sir Reginald never forgot a task he assigned.

Once Cohen tried to explain that it was expensive to be well-dressed. "Perhaps, if I could have a clothing allowance—" Such allowances were normal for many women in the business. Queenie, he knew, received ten thousand dollars a year for clothes.

"A what?" Sir Reginald thundered. "A clothing allowance? With your taste, Marty-boy? Why with your sense of style, the less you spend the better." He stared at Cohen, critically examining every inch of him. "Money wouldn't help you, Marty-boy," he had said at length. "Moreover, don't I pay you a salary?"

"Well, yes. But—"

"But what? It's not enough? I have to tell you what to think, and then pay you as well, and you say it's not enough."

It was on that occasion, while Sir Reginald continued his lecture, that Cohen decided that, one way or another, he would have to get more money. On previous occasions he had thought of quitting. But already he was well-placed in the company, and gaining power. Except for Sir Reginald, people were starting to respect him. He wouldn't quit! And one day the old bastard must surely die. . . .

Cohen's relationship with Sir Reginald became easier after he and Barbara were engaged. The old man doted on her.

"My only weakness," he called her.

"We had the Kohlmann people out to dinner the other night, Sir Reginald."

"Did they buy more?"

"No, they didn't buy; but they promised us they would."

"We need sales, Marty-boy, not promises. What good are promises? If I paid you in promises, you'd have a lot less belly than you have. Do try to be more charming next time. More elegant. I've explained it to you a hundred times."

But Cohen now had a response. "I think your granddaughter handled the elegance part very nicely, Sir Reginald," he would say smoothly. "I'm sure Kohlmann's will buy more."

Once they were actually married, Sir Reginald rarely even started on his missions of derogation, and he became gentler still when the first girl was born.

"I love our little girl, Barbara," he would say, more gentle and loving than Cohen could have imagined. "I'm daffy about Daphne!" He would grin like a boy. "She's the best thing ever produced by Regina."

"I had something to do with it, Grand," Barbara would laugh. "So did Marty. Daphne wasn't wholly a Regina production."

"You did," the old man would answer her seriously, making sure Cohen was in earshot. "You're part of Regina. Marty was just a coincidence. It could have been anyone."

"Oh, Granddad!" Barbara would try to feel shocked, but she could never quite feel what she should; while Cohen's smile would belie the depth of his wound.

Finally, after Cohen had longed for it during so many hating days and endless vindictive nights, Sir Reginald did die. What an exultant leap Cohen's heart made when he heard the news.

After that he had been promoted, at his own request, to head Regina's overseas business. Cecil Rand, although he became Regina's chief executive, left Cohen virtually unsupervised internationally. And for three perfect years, Cohen had been free, autocratically running his own company as if he owned it.

Suddenly he recalled that his good life, his tyrant's good life, was over; had been unceremoniously stolen by some IBM'd bastard from that greedy, gobbling raider. He slammed his palm onto the edge of the wash basin, suddenly as angry as when

Barbara had asked at dinner earlier this evening what the new man was like.

"Son-of-a-bitch—thinks he knows everything. Just because he works for some damn company that took over. A bunch of accountants."

She had looked at him quizzically. "Frightens you?" It had been partly a question, partly a statement—and so accurate that he had lost his temper entirely. Smashing down his plate, he had stormed out of the house.

Chapter 7

A lex Petersen's living room was small, lived-in, comfortable. Two walls were covered with bookshelves crowded with tennis trophies and well-thumbed volumes. Another was panelled in a mixture of wood and cork. Several lamps cast their warm glow in patches. The window wall, with its curtains undrawn, overlooked a cityscape almost as impressive as that from Herman Cosgrove's office. Now, late at night, a million lights glittered.

Alex sat in his scuffed leather chair as he had almost nightly for several weeks. Before him on his desk were piles of documents and figures which he had collected in his first few weeks at Regina. The papers overflowed into untidy but useful piles on the floor. A snifter of brandy, hardly touched, sat by his hand, and the smoke from a cigarette in the ashtray curled in bluish spirals towards the stucco ceiling. It was a night as dark and soft as velvet.

But the Regina figures, staring at him from the columned papers, were jagged and discordant. One hundred and sixteen million dollars of accounts receivable. He did a quick calculation on his calculator. That's impossible, he thought. Our sales this year are forecast at $530 million. That means we have over eighty days of sales on which we have not collected our money. The company's payment terms require all customers to pay within thirty days. Even assuming that there are many slow payers, the average of accounts receivable shouldn't be more than twice that—sixty-five or seventy days at worst. He looked at another sheet of paper headed "Aging" on which the accounts receivable figure was broken into segments. About one-third of the receivables were less than thirty days old and therefore not overdue. Another third were between thirty and sixty days old. The rest were between sixty and 180 days. These, he knew, would include the habitual slow payers, notorious in the industry for using their suppliers' money to run their own under-capitalized businesses. The bigger suppliers refused to ship if they were not paid reasonably fast. The smaller companies, needing the sales, didn't always have the strength—or the courage—to cut off shipments and tried to make good by giving less promotional support. But we're big, thought Alex. There's no reason why we shouldn't be paid on time. He made a note to tell Sales and the Credit department to get tougher.

Going over the figures yet again, Alex suddenly realized that the accounts on this sheet added up to a total of only $102 million —or about seventy days of average sales. Not good, but what he had expected. Where the hell are the other $14 million of receivables? he wondered.

He shook his head to clear it in the late night, and bent to rifle through a pile of papers on the floor. After a moment he extracted a sheet on which were listed the receivables by name of account. Quickly he looked at the total: $116 million—which meant that somewhere on this sheet were $14 million of accounts receivable which didn't appear on the aging account. Why not? he wondered.

Feeling like a detective, Alex shuffled through yet another pile of papers. The computer printouts, which at first had seemed merely a jumble of figures, were becoming real now as he delved behind their impersonal format and deep into their meaning.

"Ah," he breathed, "Lombard Drug."

His red pencil made a hard slash under one figure. $1.8 million. And good God—more than two years old! No figure like that appeared on the aging tally. Why the devil are we still shipping them if they've owed us money for over two years? And why are their current bills up to date? Normally large chain drug accounts like that pay their oldest bills first.

He searched on, diving from one pile of papers to another, the loneliness of the night forgotten. Suddenly his pencil underlined another name in red. Drew Drug. Eight hundred and twelve thousand dollars, also about two years overdue. Involuntarily he sucked in his breath in surprise. Quite oblivious of the time of night, he grabbed for his telephone.

The sleepy voice of his secretary answered. "Hello?"

"Listen, Sylvie, do you remember whether Lombard Drug and Drew Drug are both owned by the Scarpetti Brothers?"

"Yes, they are," said Sylvie in a tired voice, and then, somewhat more vigorously, "Do you know it's almost one o'clock in the morning?"

"I'm sorry; I didn't realize. Sorry to wake you." He hung up. But he was excited, not sorry. So it's the same outfit, he thought. Over $2.6 million two years overdue from two accounts owned by the same people.

Suddenly the excitement waned and he felt exhausted. If only I knew whom I could trust to ask, he thought. I'll worry about that in the morning. Nothing more I can do now. He yawned. Better go to bed. For the first time in months, he did not stop to ask himself whether all his efforts were worthwhile. . . .

The telephone rang so loudly in the silence that he started, almost as if *he* were guilty of whatever foolishness or dishonesty lay behind the figures.

"Listen," said Sylvie, "I was thinking—they own the Park Discount chain as well. Did you want to know?"

"Oh, yes," he said. "Just a second." He reached for the receivables sheets again and shuffled quickly. "You're right," he said. "Five hundred and seventy thousand dollars, two years old."

"Huh?"

"Both Lombard and Drew owe us money. Two years overdue. Now it appears that Park Discount does as well. All told, the Scarpettis owe us over three million bucks."

"Wow! What are you going to do?"

"It's after one o'clock in the morning," he said.

"I know," said Sylvie, "I told *you* that. But now I can't sleep. Do you think there's something crooked going on?"

The thought had, of course, crossed Alex's mind, but the evidence was inconclusive. There could be a thousand explanations. He hoped fervently that it was not dishonesty. If it were, there would be several people involved. Uncovering a mess like that always undermined morale. What he needed now was a boost to everyone's enthusiasm, not a scandal.

"I hope not, Sylvie. I certainly hope not."

"It wouldn't be good for anyone, would it?"

"No, it wouldn't." He paused. "Now it's time to go to bed."

"I'm in bed!" She pretended indignation.

"Then sleep well."

"Ha!"

"Thanks," he said seriously. "Thank you. It was nice of you to call back."

"Good night," she said, pleased.

"Doesn't that damn boss of yours ever let up," grumbled her friend, roused from his satisfying sleep. "He's impossible."

"Oh no he's not," she said, jumping to Alex's defense immediately.

"Okay, honey, forget it," he said, unwilling to argue. "Let's get some sleep."

"Yes, let's." She switched off her light. If only he were more aggressive, she thought. And slimmer! She smiled ruefully in the darkness, knowing that what she really wanted was for him to be more like Alex. Suddenly she giggled. Wouldn't Alex be astonished if he knew that she had a man in her bed. It would never have occurred to him. Damn, she thought, I wish it would. The idea might turn him on. But the fantasy faded quickly. She went back to sleep.

Alex placed the telephone back into its cradle very gently and then sat quite still, as if any sudden movement would precipitate the collapse of the terribly fragile Regina edifice. For it was not only the receivables which seemed dangerously high, and now suspicious, too. A few days ago he had discovered that there was a massive problem on inventories as well. Seventy-eight million dollars of raw material and packaging inventory showed on the balance sheet at the end of last month. Alex knew that the total cost of goods of Regina—as in most large cosmetic companies—was less than a third of the selling price to the trade. Raw and packaging materials were less than half of that. He had calculated that, with annual sales of $350 million, Regina's usage of such inventory for a whole year should be only about $80 million. That meant the company had a full year's supply of raw and packaging materials on hand. Far too much. At first Alex had assumed that Regina had developed a temporary excess for some reason, but when he checked he found that they were buying as much as they were using. No effort was being made to reduce inventories to a more reasonable level.

"Why can't we use the inventory we have on hand?" he asked the factory manager.

"Not entirely suitable." Ken McAlister was a Scotsman of few words.

"How much of it is not suitable?"

"I could not tell you. My requests for proper inventory computerization have been ignored."

"Can you guess?"

"I'd prefer not to."

"Come on, Ken, you must have some idea how much junk we have in that $78 million."

"Maybe fifteen million. Maybe twenty-five."

Alex was shocked by the enormity of the problem. "Is the inventory merely obsolete, or is it really bad?" he demanded. It was the key question. Obsolete inventory could frequently be sold off at cost or manufactured into low-price unbranded merchandise and sold off, without recording a loss, to discount houses or dumped in distant places like Indonesia. However, if it was contaminated with bacteria, dried out, or otherwise useless, then the problem was irremediable and the full loss would have to be recorded.

"I'm sorry, sir. I don't know what we have and what we don't." McAlister was embarrassed.

The problem, Alex quickly learned, was that a large cosmetic company could have two thousand or more different finished product items. Each such stock-keeping unit, or SKU as the trade called it, was made up of many components. A jar of face cream, for example, required caps, jars, liners for the caps, labels for the jars, an outer carton, and possibly an instruction leaflet, plus the ten or even more ingredients of the cream itself. Many of these components were interchangeable with other products, but Ken McAlister estimated that he still had over twenty thousand different components in inventory. He didn't know how many were temporarily unusable because they didn't fit with other components, how many were "slow-moving" because the company had an excess, and how many were totally useless.

It became evident to Alex as he talked to Ken McAlister, and later to the inventory control people, that there had been little discipline in bringing out new products. Product managers had simply introduced them as they seemed appropriate, without discontinuing old products. So the number of products had increased drastically. As a result, Regina had four different lines of lipsticks, each with over seventy shades; a similar number of nail polishes; almost as many eye shadows; and countless face creams, emulsions, cleansers, make ups, mascaras, eye liners, hand creams, neck creams, body creams, toners, sun products, depilatories, anti-perspirants, shampoos, hair conditioners, blushers, acne products, masks, cuticle creams, nail polish removers, nail implements, and even foot creams. Regina also sold three couturier fragrances and a so-called "lifestyle" fragrance called "Living High" which competed with such products as Revlon's "Charlie" and Rubinstein's "Blazer."

In addition, Alex learned, there were also samples distributed through mail-order houses like *World of Beauty* and *Cosmetique*; gifts to be given away in department stores with the purchase of regular products; miniature sizes to be given away on airlines or in hotels. Then there were reduced-price packages; trial sizes for sale in drugstores; special packs custom-made for major chains like Walgreens—the list seemed endless.

"We have many different components." McAlister's understatement seemed almost comical.

"I might tend to agree!" Alex smiled briefly. "Nevertheless, we've *got* to know how much of our inventory is merely obsolete and how much of it is useless."

"I know. It's a question of computerizing it. That's the only way we can keep control."

Alex turned to his telephone. "Sylvie, get that fellow who runs our computer operation."

"Charlie Legson?"

"Yes. Tell him to move it."

"One problem we have is with warehousing," McAlister explained while they waited. "We are paying a couple of hundred thousand dollars just for space to store the excess inventory."

"How do you take a physical inventory?" Alex asked, concerned about the enormity of that task.

"We haven't taken one in over a year."

"Christ! Then how the hell do you know what you've got?"

"I don't. I just said that."

"I thought you meant you didn't know how much of it was obsolete. I never heard of a plant which doesn't take inventory at least once a year. With a complicated setup like ours, it should happen more frequently."

"We used to take inventory every half."

"Why did you stop?"

"About a year ago, when the question of selling Regina came up, Mr. Rand said we should stop taking all further physical inventories and rely on our book inventories."

"You mean the running total of what you're supposed to have on hand?"

"Yes."

"And that's the only way you know what inventory you have?"

"I'm afraid so."

"But that means that if there is any erosion of inventory, either stealing or, more likely, wastage at the production lines, you wouldn't know—and therefore your assets and profitability would be overstated."

"Right."

"When are you planning to take the next physical inventory?"

"I'm not."

"What do you mean?"

"Mr. Rand hasn't changed his directive: No physical inventories until further notice."

"Now listen, McAlister—you've worked here for almost twenty years. I looked up your record, and it's excellent. So from now on, I would appreciate your running your factory the way you know is right. Is that clear?"

"Yes, sir," McAlister said. "We'll take a physical inventory within two weeks, as soon as we can get ready."

Alex was not sure whether McAlister's sour tone had become more sour still. He hoped not. He needed top-rate people like this manufacturing expert. On the other hand, he could not operate without his executives taking initiative on their own.

"Ken, I just want to reemphasize," he said in a kindlier tone, "that you are in charge of our manufacturing operation. Except for major capital expenditures or policy decisions, I expect you to run it on your own. I know you can. If you need any help, don't hesitate to see me. But don't take orders from anyone else."

McAlister nodded his head. "Yes, sir." His expression seemed less dour.

"Charlie Legson, sir," Sylvie announced, opening the door.

Charlie Legson was short and thin, with a huge smile which rarely left his otherwise foxy face. Unlike most computer men, he rarely used jargon words like "time-frame" and "interface," viewing his task not only as making his computers run but, more importantly, as teaching how they should be used. Consequently, Charlie Legson was almost revered by the various managements for whom he had worked. Alex had borrowed him from API.

"How are things going, Charlie?"

"Terrible," Charlie replied, with his normal big grin, "but probably getting better."

"What should we do about this inventory problem?" Alex assumed that Legson, who was checking through the adequacy of Regina's computer systems, would already have observed the absence of an inventory control program.

"We're working on it," Charlie Legson said promptly. "It's a big gap. The first thing we need, of course, is a physical inventory. We've had a little difficulty—"

"We'll be taking it within two weeks," McAlister said without inflection.

"Great. Then we have to punch each component into the machine—"

"Isn't that done? After all, we must have had an inventory control program at some point," Alex interrupted.

"Yes, but incorrectly. The computer has been told only one use for each component. Actually, many components have several uses. Once we tell the machine all the uses, we can then program it to calculate the best use of our components."

"That way we'll be able to list our inventory not in components, but in theoretical finished products," McAlister said, now looking thoroughly pleased. "I've been recommending that for years."

"How long will that take?"

"The programming will take about three weeks. We can do the key-punching concurrently. But there are many other things for the programmers to work on, so it's a question of priorities."

"What's more important?" Alex asked.

"Receivables, I think."

"I agree. But inventory would be second?"

"I think so," Charlie looked serious for the first time since he'd entered the room.

"So do I," McAlister agreed. And for the first time he smiled.

The memory faded and Alex realized he was totally weary. He undressed quickly, dropping his clothes in an untidy heap, and fell into his bed.

On top of everything else, sales are down, he thought. If we can't rectify that, we haven't got any chance.

I would hardly ask you to run Regina if the job were impossible. Alex could hear Herman Cosgrove's assurance now.

"Like hell," he said, loud and angry. "Like fucking hell!" Even that tough old goat, Sir Reginald, would have had problems the way the company is now, he thought despondently. I wonder what he would have done. Then, just before he fell asleep, he chuckled softly. Faked it, I suppose!

Alex Petersen's alarm rang at 6:30 the next morning. He groaned as he silenced it, rolled out of bed, rejected doing his occasional morning exercises, and staggered to his shower. The stimulation of the previous evening had evaporated and he felt groggy and dispirited.

Across the park, Cohen's alarm sounded almost simultaneously. He too groaned, hung over for the third day in a row, but surprisingly he felt less depressed than Alex. Carefully, so as not to disturb the room's equilibrium, he showered and dressed. A glass of tomato juice with a dash of vodka and some dry toast helped to settle his stomach. The last few days had been quite as difficult for Marty Cohen as for Alex Petersen. All week his anger and frustration had mounted as the name Petersen hovered constantly on people's lips.

"He's awfully handsome," he heard Marcella York, an attractive large-breasted woman recently recruited as a product manager, confide to a script-girl visiting from the television department. "And he's not married. I don't think he ever has been."

"I heard he's divorced."

"Anyway, I think he needs looking after," the product manager giggled.

Cohen walked away, his jealousy corrosive.

The next day had been worse. Cohen visited the accounting department. "How's my computer program for the French factory coming?" he asked Charlie Legson. It had become an urgent matter because Cohen had closed a small plant in Belgium which was running unprofitably, and had consolidated manufacture in France. Also, he had transferred duty-free sales from Switzerland to France. The Swiss franc had strengthened so that the cost of products made in Switzerland calculated in other currencies had risen, while the French franc had weakened so that export prices from France had dropped. Duty-free shops, which controlled captive markets on airplanes and in airports, could push any fragrance they wanted. They used this monopoly to demand rock bottom prices. To compete, Cohen had to take advantage of every currency break he could get.

Charlie smiled broadly. "I'm sorry to say it's been delayed."

"But we need it now," Cohen insisted.

"I realize that. But Mr. Petersen said that the top priority for my programmers, after accounts receivable, is the U.S. inventory control."

There was no point in arguing, Cohen realized. He would have to bring it up with Petersen later. He turned on his heel without another word.

The final straw came yesterday afternoon when he received a memorandum from Alex's office requiring him to attend a management meeting the following week at the offices of a Darwin Kellogg, "who is a director of our parent company and whom I have retained to help us consider how to strengthen our business."

"Christ almighty," Cohen yelled at his garish office walls

when he realized the import of the letter. "Shit!" He had almost ripped it in two. That bastard. *Why couldn't he have asked me first instead of kissing some director's arse? I know more about what's going on, more than Petersen will find out in a year of meetings.* . . .

Beneath Cohen's rage there was a legitimate concern. If word got out that Petersen had not consulted him before appointing an outsider, he would be in trouble; an executive who did not have the ear of the president had little influence. Perhaps word was out already. That would account for Legson giving him the runaround. . . . He smashed his fist uselessly against the patient resiliency of his sofa. Tears of rage pricked his eyes.

For a moment he wondered if his father-in-law, Rand, could help; but quickly he discarded that idea. Then he considered the more useful approach of talking to Queenie. Sir Reginald had always listened to her and had usually done what she suggested. And Queenie had sometimes been an ally to him in the past.

"Seems to me the least Petersen should have done before bringing in Kellogg was to ask us insiders what's going on," he told Queenie insistently as soon as he had confirmed that she had not known of the meeting either. "This guy Kellogg, he's some sort of consultant, isn't he? Probably ready to sell us back what we already know at some outrageous price."

Queenie was not sure how to respond. She harbored no warm feelings towards Alex Petersen. Too smooth and professional, she felt, unconscious that these were characteristics she normally admired. No worthy replacement for Reg. On the other hand, she had known Darwin Kellogg for years as a friend. . . .

"Kellogg's a very good consultant," she finally answered noncommitally.

"Why didn't Petersen ask us first?" Cohen demanded. Then, fearing he sounded petulant, he added, "Well, perhaps he had his reasons." He hesitated. "I wonder if we should offer to brief him in more detail ourselves before the meeting. What do you think?"

"Why don't you suggest it? He might be grateful." She doubted it, however. Her guess was that Alex had decided on an outside consultant precisely so that he could obtain an unbiased view. *It's what Reg would have done,* she had to admit. Even so, Petersen should have handled the matter more tactfully. After all, Cohen was an excellent businessman; he could easily have been the company's president. He still might be, she thought. Admittedly she didn't like him much. . . .

"Cold fish. Malodorous cold fish," Reg used to say about him.

"Contradiction in terms," she would tease. "Refrigerated fish doesn't smell. Anyway, he's good at his job."

"Damned good. Only reason I kept him. Now that he's conned Barbara into marrying him, I couldn't get rid of him if I wanted to. Wish I could have stopped that."

"I know you do," she would sympathize.

I always seem to have been sympathizing with him, she remembered ruefully. Most people would have marvelled how soft he was inside.

"You're the stony one," he used to say to her. "I'm the smart one."

"Then why do I do all the work around here?"

"Because I'm the smart one," he would laugh. Then he would add seriously, "You're perfectly capable of running Regina without me. Yet you put up with the whole thing."

"I do more than put up with it. I love it—and you."

But she had always known that Regina needed Reg more than her or anyone else. He was the spirit of the company, its brilliance and its drive. He had the uncanny intuition for what women wanted. Cecil understood nothing of women. Cohen too, although a fine administrator, had little intuition. She doubted that the new boy had it, Petersen.

"He should have told us," Cohen repeated.

"Yes, I think he should," she answered. "But I wouldn't worry about it. Let's see what happens."

It was too early to worry about anything yet, she thought. Petersen might not turn out as bad as she feared. Obviously, the company had had to be sold. It would not have survived another year on its own. Not under poor Cecil, anyway. She felt so sorry for him, still scheming, still trying to satisfy his father. He'd be happier if he spent more time with his family and a lot less time trying to get back his old job at Regina.

Let's hope Petersen can handle the job, Queenie thought again. If not. . . . There was always a way, Sir Reginald had taught her. And she was not without resources. All that Regina stock Reg had transferred to her. API stock now. No one knew about that, but it might make a difference if things went too wrong with young Petersen. She smiled rather coldly.

"What are you smiling at?" Cohen asked sharply.

"Just a thought," she said. "Nothing important."

Cohen had left Queenie's office not sure whether she was for him or against him. Neither was she.

In spite of his hangover, Cohen arrived at the office only slightly late and went through the routine of his corrrespondence deftly. He had a light luncheon and by mid-afternoon he felt quite well physically. The only symptom which remained was a slight dizziness when he moved his head too fast.

But his anger at Petersen intensified all day until, by mid-afternoon, it had become a writhing dyspepsia, and his manner of calm concentration merely a camouflage.

By five o'clock, Cohen had had enough. The papers he shuffled seemed ready to choke him. The walls gave him claustrophobia. His whole body twitched to break out. . . .

"I'm fed up; I'm leaving," he shouted to his secretary. He had no idea where he was bound. All he knew was that somehow he had to vent his frustration, his disappointment and his rage.

Chapter 8

That morning Barbara had slept late, awakening only when the sun, shifting gradually, had touched her face, warming it awake. It was a beautiful morning. Both girls had gone to school; the younger one, at barely four, still had to be accompanied. Usually Barbara took her, enjoying the clutch of the little girl's hand, loving the sensation of being so wanted. But today, realizing that her employer was still asleep, the maid had taken her, so that now Barbara was alone. She rose, made some coffee, and sat down in front of her typewriter, determined to work on her novel.

"Great potential from a young writer," *Publishers Weekly* had said about her first book. Whatever that means, she thought for the millionth time. Other critics had also been complimentary, although some had complained that it was too easy a book to write, merely autobiographical. The *Times* had concluded: "Barbara Rand has written an entertaining first book, peopled with high society folk of her grandfather's milieu and full of cocktail party banter remembered well and written down succinctly. Now, if she can summon the creativity to feed her knack for facile writing, she will be someone to watch."

She had loved the critics' praise, but hated them for not realizing how hard it was to "remember well and write succinctly." And sometimes she could not help wondering how many reviews there would have been had she not been Sir Reginald's granddaughter.

As it turned out, Barbara now realized, the critics had been right. While it had been hard writing her first book, this new one—which she desperately hoped people would not only read but feel—was simply hell. She had to wrestle with every word. And often the words, appropriating a life of their own, would fight back stubbornly, refusing to bend to her will, seeming stilted when they should be relaxed and contrived when she wanted them to be moving.

The excitement of the first book had been immense. She remembered the opening cocktail party, a giant reception organized by Sir Reginald with as much fervor as he had lavished on the original introduction of Regina into America—and with far greater resources. It had been held in the grand ballroom of the Plaza Hotel in New York. Every beauty editor, fashion personality, gossip columnist, socialite, and magazine publisher was there. A middle-aged film star, her skin still as impeccable as alabaster and her famous red hair as perfect as ever, flowed in chiffon. Next to her, the renowned beauty expert from a competitive cosmetic company entertained all in earshot in her bubbly, English-accented voice with a series of comments on the passing scene as pointed as *Punch* itself. The brilliant associate publisher of the bible of the fashion industry entertained his friends by shocking the very few shockables to be found in this throng of sophisticates. A famous golfer, whose scores had risen with his fortune until both were remarkably high for a man of his profession, talked to a young woman of great beauty and blinding ambition.

But for once this egocentric group's attention was focused not upon itself, but outward upon Sir Reginald and his pretty, talented granddaughter. All small talk started and ended that evening with THE BOOK.

At precisely the high point of the evening—that moment when the last guest had arrived and no one had yet started the inevitable New York departure routine ("I'm afraid I must be leaving. Another affair. *You* know")—Sir Reginald held up a deceptively genteel, manicured hand. The music stopped with a flourish. Carefully, theatrically, his hand now arranged in his jacket pocket, Sir Reginald waited for complete silence before stalking to the podium.

Once there, he waited interminably until the stillness in the room seemed unbearable. Then he spoke only one sentence, but a sentence to launch Barbara's book as few books have ever been launched: "My granddaughter has written a best-seller," he announced, his voice ringing through the microphones, "a sure-fire best-seller!" The audience cheered and cheered. . . .

Overnight, Barbara had become a celebrity, her new status carefully nurtured by Regina's public relations department. Systematically they approached each of the national "talk" shows and also the important single-city shows like Kup's Show in Chicago and Ruth Lyons in Cincinnati, with a pitch explaining why Barbara Rand would be an *ideal* interview candidate. "She knows the *inside* story of life with Sir Reginald, surely the *sexiest* grandfather in American business," they would explain. Then they would add significantly, "And you know how heavily Regina advertises with you. . . ."

Each show's producer received at least one telephone call from a member of Regina's public relations staff. For the particularly important shows, Colonel Brown-Williams, Regina's very British head of PR, called. In almost every case, the caller had some personal relationship with the producer. Sometimes they had worked together; often the public relations caller had done the producer some favor—PR people loved to sow favors, reaping their rewards only when it was really important. A good PR man never wasted valuable indebtedness on minor response.

As a result, Barbara appeared on virtually every important talk show. And the combination of Colonel Brown-Williams' careful coaching on how to make the most of her precocious charm, and her own piquant observations on the social scene, made her quite popular. She was invited back for a second appearance with Johnny Carson and written about in *Time* magazine. For some time, while her husband first smiled indulgently at her success and then started to show increasing irritation at her absences, she basked in her celebrity status. But after a few months, the excitement abated and she disappeared completely from the public eye.

Now, almost five years later, she felt an imposter when she

said she was a writer. It seemed such an exaggeration after only one book, and that out of print for almost three years.

I *must* write something worthwhile, she would tell herself. I will! But it was beginning to be a cry without much hope.

Almost mechanically her fingers started to peck at the typewriter. "Chapter 4," she wrote. She wanted to start thinking about her characters, to start feeling as they would. But she could not. They were happy, whereas her mind was filled with bitterness. Would Marty come home from the office this evening, she wondered, or would he go on another drinking spree? Was he even *at* the office? She told herself she didn't care. . . .

> *Business-man, business-man, out on a spree,*
> *Fuck your whore Fifi, don't father-fuck me*

she typed cynically.

Somehow cleansed, almost purified because she had transferred some of her pain onto paper, she started to write. Soon she lost herself completely in her story. Only once, as she paused to fetch herself a snack, did she brood that she had never enjoyed a love nearly as satisfying as that which made up the central theme of her novel.

I'm writing a wish-fulfillment fantasy, she thought. I wonder how long I can stand living with my own wishes so unfulfilled.

Chapter 9

God, this company has so many problems," Alex complained
to the empty air. A sense of urgency which had been growing for weeks flooded him. "If only I have enough time. . ."

He had come to the office with the rising sun and had felt
invigorated by the cool morning; but after an hour he seemed
to have made no progress at all. Distractedly, he took his water
jug to the window and watered a serenely growing plant. Far
below he could see an office building under construction. Dozens
of men scurried across it seeming to achieve nothing, but the
building grew steadily. He wished Regina were being rebuilt
as surely. On the street further below, tiny cars and speck-like
people played out some child-giant's game. "Did he who made
the lamb make thee?" He smiled. For a moment he wondered
whether he wouldn't have been better off on his grandparents'
farm after all; recalled nostalgically the dog which swung on the
cows' tails to make them hurry to their stalls at milking time,
and the calming drone of the bees. . . .

Those summer visits to the farm in Minnesota were the only
really happy events of his youth. He experienced a sense of freedom on the farm and, strangely, a sense of opportunity. He could

never explain why he felt this, because the farm was small and his grandparents barely eked out an existence. Perhaps, he reflected later, it was because the farm gave him a chance to dream which was missing from the gray New York suburb in which he lived. His parents' house was cramped and always noisy. His mother was perpetually worn, overwhelmed by his loud brothers and browbeaten by his sister demanding better clothes or arguing about how late she could stay out. There was never peace in their house.

Alex looked forward to his annual visits to the farm as a time of quiet, for writing poetry (which he kept more secret than sin) and lying in the sun amidst the drone of the meadow insects. He never felt melancholy when he was on the farm.

"Ever thought of taking over after a while?" his grandfather asked him once. "The farm's hardly big enough, but grandma and me have made a go of it."

They talked about it for a long time, about what his life would be like. Alex had been tempted, and deeply touched by the old man's care and generosity. But in the end he realized that the farm would not satisfy him. "I wouldn't like that, really. Not in the long run. I'd almost feel as if I were wasting my opportunities if I stayed here. I know you and grandma are happy. But I don't think I would be."

His grandfather grunted. "Maybe not. Let me know if you change your mind."

"But thank you, grandpa," he said quickly. He hoped he hadn't offended him.

"Nothing to thank, boy. Just looking for someone to work for me cheap," his grandfather had said gruffly, and patted his shoulder. "You're probably right."

Christ, I'm getting morbid, Alex thought, shaking himself back to the present. But he knew that he was happier than he had been in weeks—happy that the sun was shining and that the business day was about to start. He heard his secretary enter the outer office.

"Good morning, Sylvie," he called, and then as she entered, "Hello, love; what's first on the agenda?"

"Coffee!"

"I'd love some. And then?"

"Then you have a whole stream; you're going to have a busy

day. Your first meeting is the one Miss Duke called on new products."

Alex knew that new products had been the life blood of Regina under Sir Reginald, who himself had enthusiastically generated the ideas. But it was Queenie who supervised the choice of shade and consistency of lipsticks, eye shadows and other make ups; pushed the art department to create superlative packaging; worked with the merchandising department to develop dramatic in-store display material; and saw to it that the agency's advertising combined elegance with hard-sell.

Frequently, the lawyer would object to the advertising. "You can't say, 'Makes your skin young.' That's not true. It's the same age after you use the cream as it was before."

"It looks younger," Queenie would argue.

"Then that's all you can say: 'Makes your skin *look* younger.'"

Queenie would agree, knowing she had again pushed through a strong claim and knowing, too, that if she had asked them to approve ". . . *look* younger" in the first place, they would have asked her to furnish statistical proof which, while perfectly feasible, would have taken months.

About a year before he died, Sir Reginald had particularly liked a commercial with a young woman saying, "I love this cream. I use it myself and it's so *good!*" There was a delay in airing it and Sir Reginald had wanted to know why.

"I'm sorry, Sir Reginald, but we can't use that commercial unless we have a signed statement by the girl that she used the product regularly for at least a week," the lawyer explained. "And we're having trouble finding the girl."

"I'll sign it."

"I'm afraid you can't, sir. How would you know that she used it?"

"I watched her, that's how. She put it on every night before I fucked her!"

The legal department in most large companies, Queenie knew, was the keeper of the corporate conscience. Even Sir Reginald used to tell the lawyers to contradict him—and stop him by force, if necessary—if he wanted to do something which they considered against some law, ordinance, statute, or government rule. For rules varied drastically between countries. In Venezuela, Sir Reginald had learned with cynical amusement, retail prices in some industries were fixed during a negotiation among all manufacturers and by law could not thereafter be changed; whereas in the United States, any collusion between manufacturers to fix prices was a prisonable offense.

After Sir Reginald's death, Queenie continued to manage the new products department with great efficiency. But without Sir Reginald's innovation, she knew that Regina was falling behind. How could she carry on without him? Why even try? It was too hard, just too hard. But she never allowed anyone at Regina to sense the awful loneliness and void she had felt since Reg's death. Only at home in her simple apartment—not the opulent showplace she had shared with him, but her own private place which she had always kept as a symbol of her independence and to which she had returned after he was buried—sometimes her eyes filled with tears, however impatiently she rubbed. . . .

Queenie had called today's meeting some weeks earlier to try to give Regina's new products program renewed vitality. To be polite, she had invited Alex Petersen to attend—for all the good it will do, she thought. When he entered, Queenie was already seated regally at the head of the conference table. The others present were the chief chemist, Dr. Helmut Wagner; the head of new product development, Jean Smith, a loquacious woman given to equal bubbling enthusiasm about every new product; the marketing manager, a flashy young man with blond hair named Garry Gainsborough but nicknamed Garry Glitter; the head of the copy department, a rather languorous lady known only as Cecilia; and two senior product managers, one in charge of new fragrances, the other, Marcella York, of new make up products. Everyone watched Queenie expectantly.

That's the problem, thought Queenie. They're looking to me for the new products, and I'm looking to them. "As background," she started, "I've sent each of you a list of our new products for the last twelve months. Without belaboring the point, I feel it is an undistinguished list. A number of our products have experienced some success, but basically only by cannibalizing other products within our line. Obviously we must do better.

"Now, to open this meeting I am asking Jean Smith to describe to you the products on which she and her people are working."

Jean Smith arose. "I'm delighted, Miss Duke, quite delighted to be able to talk to you today," she said, her words so rapid they seemed to stumble over each other. "We have a great number of very exciting new projects."

"Yes," said Queenie, "please proceed."

"Well, the first product is a new line of lipsticks which will be wonderfully longer-lasting. We'll call the new line 'At Long Last.' Isn't that clever?"

Alex shifted uncomfortably in his seat. The name seemed rather silly to him.

"The second new product is a marvelous line of other make up items which will also carry the 'At Long Last' name. . . ."

The longer Jean Smith talked, the faster her words poured out, and the less impressed Alex became. As far as he could see, her products were unoriginal. Worse, they were hardly different from products already in the line, whereas the whole art of launching new products—as he and Darwin Kellogg had discussed at length—was to find products *not* yet in the line. In that way, sales of the new products would all be extra profit. As Darwin had been explaining to him, most of the competition understood this principle. Max Factor had introduced a luxury Halston fragrance into department stores where they had little business of this type; and Helena Rubinstein had launched a department store fragrance line called "Blazer" by Ann Klein, a line of treatment products for older women called rather appropriately "Madame Rubinstein," and a group of shampoos called "Hair Care"—all new items in mostly new product areas for the company, thus representing additional sales, not merely a substitute of one line for another.

Jean Smith finished, somewhat out of breath with her enthusiasm. Glowing with self-satisfaction, she resumed her seat.

"As you see," said Queenie drily, "practically all the products Jean has described are competitive with something we already have in the line. Few have any real spark of originality."

Jean Smith's face fell. But she knew from experience that it would be unwise to contradict Queenie in this mood. Moreover, she thought to herself, forced to be objective, she's quite right; we haven't had a really *new* product in months. The others held similar thoughts; their faces expressed their frustration.

"The trouble is that we don't have anything that is technically new," said Garry Gainsborough. "If we had that—"

"We have a great deal that is new," Dr. Wagner interrupted, immediately defensive. "The problem is not that we don't have new developments, but that we are not given direction. If marketing tells us what they want, we have every chance of being able to develop it. I cannot think of a single case where we have been asked for a reasonable new product and haven't delivered."

"I've asked you for a dozen new products you couldn't make," said Jean Smith indignantly. "A lipstick which gives a high gloss and lasts a long time—"

"That's definitively impossible!" said Wagner flatly. "Everyone knows that the higher the gloss in a lipstick, the shorter its wear. We can't develop a cancer cure, either—"

"And a wrinkle cream that works—"

"That's another one of those insoluble problems. Our creams help, but they cannot eliminate. I still say that we can develop any new product that is *reasonably* feasible. Sir Reginald was never dissatisfied."

At the mention of Sir Reginald's name, all the people in the room started talking. They live in his shadow, thought Alex; while once again Queenie was thinking, We can't do without you, Reg.

Alex raised his voice just enough to be heard over the hubbub. "In what areas do we most need new products?" he asked.

Immediately there was silence in the room. Everyone looked at him with surprise.

"There must be some parts of our business where our need for new products is greater than others," he urged. "For example, I noticed that our fragrance business is declining. It certainly needs a shot in the arm. Also, we seem to have a very poor shampoo business compared to our competitors—"

"We need something exciting in our colors," said Marcella York immediately.

"We need a new fragrance for sure," said the manager in charge of fragrances at the same moment.

"What are your priorities?" Alex asked.

"We have a great number of priorities—" Jean Smith started.

"I know," Alex interrupted her firmly, "I want to know which are your *top* priorities."

Jean Smith stopped talking and looked hurt. "Well," she said tentatively, "our—"

"Our most important need is for a new fragrance line," said

Queenie firmly. "The trouble is we don't have an idea which pleases us."

"What sort of a fragrance are you looking for?" Alex asked. If he could get an exciting project going in just one area, he felt, he could start the momentum again.

"Our figures clearly indicate that we need a mass-distributed fragrance which will appeal to younger customers," the fragrance product manager started to lecture. "The designer fragrances we now have are well established, but they are declining as our customers get older. Our new item, 'Living High,' has not caught the imagination of young women. However, we have researched what sells and we are now developing a musk line to compete with 'Jovan,' and a life-style line to compete with 'Charlie,' 'Babe,' 'Blazer,' and the others of that type."

"Isn't that simply copying?" Alex asked.

"Well, that's where competitive sales are coming—" the product manager started to justify himself.

"Yes," said Queenie bristling at the criticism. "Yes, we are merely copying." She almost demanded, "Can you do better?" but stopped herself at the last second. Better to give him a fair chance to hang himself, she thought. He'd do it soon enough.

"Then let's bring out something new," said Alex matter-of-factly. "Does anyone have any suggestions?"

There was silence around the table—silence and a certain embarrassment. Even Jean Smith had nothing to say.

"Well, I have a suggestion," said Alex, taking the plunge. He had been preparing for this moment ever since Queenie had called her meeting. "But before I tell you, let me give you some background. As you all know, there has been an accelerating trend towards natural things—health foods, environmental control, cross-country skiing, antipollution devices, organic foods." His audience was fascinated to see their new president in action for the first time. Christ, Alex thought, I hope I don't blow this. "Men have even been allowed to go without ties on occasion," he continued. There were polite smiles around the table. "The guitar has become the national instrument, jeans the national dress, and jogging the national sport." The faces around the table looked at him seriously. They're like school children, he thought. Queenie, observing the same thing, for the first time felt his power. Illogically, she felt a sudden surge of annoyance, almost anger. He's not like Reg, she thought. Not at all. He's too logical and he lacks the glamour. . . .

"In our business," Alex continued, "that trend has shown itself in many categories. In shampoos, for example, 'Herbal Essence' by Clairol has been very successful. And 'Johnson's Baby Shampoo' has become the biggest-selling adult shampoo. Neither of them was a technical advance. Johnson's had been around for years before it took off for adults. But they became successful because they fit into the broad consumer movement to natural and pure products, as does homebaked bread, and natural cereals, and herb teas—I assume you all know Simon and Garfunkel's songs?" Alex asked suddenly.

There were several nods around the table.

"That's the sort of spirit I'm thinking about." Alex paused, looking at the expectant faces. They really depend on me, he thought. Well, here goes. "I suggest we bring out a series of fragrances to capitalize on all this naturalness," he said. "I suggest a line of fragrances based on herbs. It's been done before for shampoos, and for cosmetics of all sorts. But never for fragrances. Individually, they would be a new sort of fragrance—natural, pure, pretty. The first set would be 'Parsley,' 'Sage,' 'Rosemary,' and 'Thyme.' We'd use that Simon and Garfunkel song in our advertising. Packaging would be in modified spice containers, but elegantly done. The line would be far 'purer' than Clairol's 'Herbal Essence.' And it's expandable. Later we can bring out shampoos and soaps and other herbal fragrances."

Alex ceased talking. All around him there were nods of agreement. And smiles.

"Technically simple," said Wagner.

"Brilliant, brilliant, brilliant," said Jean Smith.

"It's just what we need," said the product manager.

Only Queenie showed no emotion. It could work, she thought reluctantly. But it could be a great failure too. Is the trend to naturalness still as strong as it used to be? Does it apply to fragrances? She was not sure. Perhaps. She still felt annoyed, unwilling to trust Petersen. . . .

"How quickly can such a line be put onto the market?" Alex cut through the noise.

"It will take us about six months to develop the products,"

said the product manager, "and a further three to complete the launch details and do the manufacturing."

"I want to be in stores in half that time," said Alex.

"But that's impossible." "Out of the question." "Can't be done." A number of voices were heard around the table.

"In five months," said Alex, his voice strong. "Several of you have told me that the cosmetic industry requires rapid action. Now show me that you can do it."

"Very well," said Queenie. "The products will be on the market in five months." Her voice was cold. If the products fail, she thought, it will not be because we have not moved fast enough.

"Thank you," said Alex. "I'm afraid I must leave for another meeting now." He walked quickly out of the room, hearing the noise rise behind him.

Only Queenie, sitting at the head of the table, remained silent. The products don't sound bad, she admitted to herself. But you never know. Reg had the intuition. Does this young man?

"Colonel Brown-Williams, commander-in-chief of public relations, is here to see you, sir," Sylvie said with mock pomposity.

"Thank you, Sylvie. Do I detect a slight note of sarcasm?"

She giggled. "Colonel Brown-Williams," she announced formally. As the colonel strode in, she winked behind his back.

"Good morning, sir. Glad you could see me. Afraid I have some problems to report." The colonel had a drooping white mustache and greying hair brushed stiffly back. His manner was purely military, his accent as clipped as any colonel in British India.

"Do sit down, George," said Alex.

"Thank you, sir. Sorry to be the harbinger of bad news."

"What is it?"

"Let me show you, sir." He handed over the latest copy of a widely-read marketing newsletter. An article circled in red charged: "New Management at Regina Out of Control, Look for Changes," and continued, "The new management at the Regina Company doesn't seem able to deal with all the problems facing it. Only the International division, under Martin Cohen, an experienced cosmetic executive, remains in good shape. The industry is asking, 'What will happen next?'"

"It's only a scandal sheet and they frequently make vitriolic comments, but I hate to see it happen to us."

"It's not pleasant. But if it's just a scandal sheet, why worry?"

"Because the serious press is starting to pick up similar rumors. *Industry Reports* magazine is going to do an article on cosmetic companies that have been acquired by big conglomerates. The thesis is that many of them have done badly, which is true. But they are planning to single out Regina as the latest example of an acquired company running into trouble."

"Are you sure?"

"Yes, sir." Colonel Brown-Williams seemed ready to snap a salute.

"How did you find out?"

"I was informed, sir."

Alex was aware that public relations executives like the colonel painstakingly built a circle of acquaintances in the media who fed them advance information. In return, the PR people provided their friends with first breaks when a piece of real news —a major acquisition, for example—was announced.

"Can you stop the story? Or make it sound less negative?"

"I don't know, sir. I'll try."

"Are there other bad stories coming out?"

"The worst one by far is likely to be a piece Pamela Maarten is writing about API for *Business World*. I don't know what she'll say. She's very professional; never gives away anything before it's printed. But she's also made her reputation being tough and acerbic. I anticipate it will be negative."

"Will she include Regina?"

"Definitely, sir."

Perhaps it's too late already, Alex thought. As always, he was amazed how rapidly the news media picked up bad news. The newspapers were often accused of exaggerated reporting and sometimes of gross misstatement. But it was his experience that they were often uncannily right. Certainly in this case. . . .

Alex pulled himself away from his thoughts. There was no point in such negative speculation. "What would you suggest?" he asked.

"Three things immediately, sir," said Brown-Williams promptly. "The first is that you should make a series of speeches which we can use as platforms."

Alex was aware that this form of publicity was used frequently when a company wanted to publicize something intangible and therefore not newsworthy—a renewal of its internal vitality, for example. Although few people actually heard these speeches, the company's PR department would arrange to have them reprinted as articles in business magazines or, failing that, would reprint them at company expense—frequently very beautifully—and disseminate them to the desired audience. Effectively used, this technique could make a major impact. However, as Alex knew, it was hard and time-consuming work.

"Very well," he said reluctantly. "I'll do it if you think it's needed."

"I do, sir."

"What else?"

"Well, sir, I propose a presentation to the New York Society of Security Analysts. The most influential stock analysts on Wall Street belong, and what they say about the value of a stock influences its price as much as anything."

"Can you arrange it?" Will they listen to subsidiary companies like us?"

"Regina's so important to API, they'll make an exception."

"Okay. When?"

"With your permission, sir, I would suggest luncheon at the Banker's Club one week from next Thursday. We have to move fast if we are to offset the adverse rumors. And I happen to know they had a cancellation for that day and are looking for someone."

"Another of your informants?"

"Yes, sir." For the first time the colonel smiled.

"I assume you know what's going on inside Regina as well?"

"Yes, sir." There was no inflection in the colonel's voice.

Alex decided to get to know Colonel Brown-Williams better. "You'd better inform API's public relations people so they know what we are planning."

"Very well, sir."

"Apart from that, you may proceed.' Alex was amused to hear himself falling into the Colonel's own military vernacular. "And the third approach? You mentioned there should be three."

"I believe you should have luncheon with *Business World's* Pamela Maarten. It's better than just seeing her in your office, and it's important that she gets to know you—although even if you get on swimmingly together it won't influence what she writes. But it will help if she thinks you're honest. That way she'll check with you before she publishes and she won't print anything you deny."

"Unless she has proof, I imagine."

"Right. And if you deny something and she has proof, she'll never listen to you again."

"She sounds like a tough bitch."

"Very professional, sir."

"Should I have Sylvie call her for lunch?"

"I've taken the liberty of inviting her to lunch today, sir. I'm afraid you were tied up. And Miss Maarten said it was rather urgent. Sylvie said it would be alright. I hope you don't mind."

Alex looked up with surprise. "No, I suppose not," he said doubtfully. "It beats sandwiches in the office. Yes, that will be fine," he said with more certainty. "And, Colonel, may I say that you have done an excellent job. I appreciate it."

"Thank you, sir." Colonel Brown-Williams rose smartly, almost saluted, and marched out of the room.

At the other end of the building the artists and designers chatted, flirted, pouted, bantered, groaned, joked, complained—but always worked. The Regina Company might be doing poorly in the opinion of the newspapers, but it was an active, almost hectic place for all that.

"Most companies, even if they are doing quite badly, do ninety percent of what they do right," one of Alex's professors had explained. "The science of turning an ailing company around is to attack only the other ten percent." His professor had paused. "The *art* is knowing which ten percent!" Alex smiled rather grimly at the memory. The art of turning this company around will be to do it fast enough.

Chapter 10

Alex Petersen arrived at the Four Seasons a few minutes early for his lunch appointment with Pamela Maarten. An efficient young man ushered him to a table beside the reflecting pool and wished him a pleasant meal. The waiter took his order for a glass of white wine and brought it immediately. Alex relaxed and wondered idly what Miss Maarten would be like. In his experience, journalists of her importance were either middle-aged women of great acumen, or tough young feminists who "stood tall" in well-cut suits, flashing their teeth in sarcastic, disbelieving smiles. He expected the latter and prepared for a gruelling lunch.

He watched the room filling gradually with its normal mixture of senior business people and celebrities. Orson Welles arrived with his retinue and was shown to a table immediately across the pool from Alex. The actor started at once to issue orders in a voice which filled the room. The elderly chief executive of a consumer goods company even bigger than API arrived, accompanied by an extraordinarily beautiful young woman who laughed at his every word. A marvelously handsome quarterback from the team presently at the top of the league arrived with two eye-catching girls whom the old chief executive ogled enviously.

Christ, Alex thought cynically, look at me—a cliché of success. But in spite of the exciting novelty of his job at Regina, he felt little satisfaction from his success. Sure, he seemed to have it all: good job, good looks, a talent for tennis, the easy self-confidence of the Princeton man—even appropriately poor but honest parents. But he was also achingly dissatisfied, bored with his achievements, empty in the midst of activity and laughter, guilty about the ambition which had carried him so high up a ladder the meaningfulness of which he now questioned. Alex maintained his normal hard-working habits and hid his growing self-doubts from the world. As much as possible, especially at work, he maintained his customary pleasant, sometimes humorous approach, a manner which had never been mistaken for weakness but which had given him the reputation for being a "nice guy." Nevertheless, those who knew him well sensed that his natural good cheer now seemed forced—and wondered what would happen. . . .

The frustration of Alex Petersen's boyhood had been just as intense, but quite different in quality. In the last few years he had become more and more frustrated because, having achieved success, he was appalled to find that he was still unfulfilled; he was still seeking for something, but without knowing for what. As a boy, his frustration was far simpler—he lived in a rage, fearing that he could not break out of the fixed, solid, immutable society in which he was mired. He was convinced that beyond lay freedom, excitement, opportunity; if he could only fight his way out, everything would be totally different from the all-encompassing ordinariness, the prosaic *decency*, of his family, his friends, his school, his church, his neighborhood.

But the basic difference between then and now was that as a boy he had never doubted—not deep inside him—that he *would* succeed in breaking out; he knew there *must* be a way. Now, having fought his way past the early barriers, he found new ones—less direct, less obvious—which he was not sure he could overcome. He was not even certain whether his undefined goal even existed. His uncertainty sapped the optimism which had carried him through so many boyhood frustrations.

Each day during the school year, rain or shine, winter or summer, he had walked home from his good, sensible school past the same meticulous frame houses with the same postage stamp lawns, each mowed, fertilized, weeded, protected from crab-grass (the only interloper in his entire suburban world) as rhythmically as the passage of the seasons themselves. He longed to hurl rocks right through every clean picture window on the block. Even that, he knew, would not set him free; he would simply be relabelled. That "nice Petersen kid" would become that "kid who went wrong."

Each summer day at 7 A.M and each winter day at 8 A.M. his father—round, red face bovine with contentment—would buss his mother on both cheeks, tell Alex to "watch his step," and depart for work with the admonition, "I should be home by 5:30 this evening," as if in twenty steady years he had ever been home at some other time. Then he would join a group of identical men, all called Lars or Sven or Jon, and together they would hammer roofs, erect walls, or, when the building trade was slow, mow lawns or fix fences. At lunch the men would drink Tuborg.

"Why not try Budweiser once?" Alex had asked.

"No thanks. We always take Tuborg."

The containment of his life would have been more bearable to Alex if he could have found even one friend with whom to share his discontent. But all his mates seemed satisfied to move into their fathers' jobs or, at best, go to the local college because that, too, was the legitimate thing to do. None felt with Alex any limitation of spirit.

At thirteen, Alex's drive for excitement became almost un-containable. Unable to give it rein, he became broody and self-centered, a teenage Hamlet who worried his parents and antagonized his friends. In a fling of defiance, he turned to shop-lifting.

There was a sense of danger when he walked into the Wool-worth store, a sense of aliveness in himself he had never felt before. He prowled the store nonchalantly, looking for the ap-propriate merchandise to lift.

The manager in the office overlooking the store noticed the youth circling. "Look," he said to the woman working there, "see that kid? He's on the hunt, I'd say."

"Yeah," she said, hardly glancing up, "looks like it." They're all the same, she thought; rich kids looking for a thrill.

The manager watched Alex glance around to make sure no one was close and then pocket a handful of pens.

"Christ," he muttered, "why do they do that?" He hurried to the front door and waited for the boy to emerge.

Alex's excitement was intense as he walked slowly towards the door. He pushed through the door into the open air. He was outside. He could do whatever he wanted. He was *free*. . . .

"Give them back," said the manager wearily.

Alex's world collapsed. "What?" he stuttered, his stomach contracting with fear.

"You took a handful of pens from counter four and put them in your left pocket," said the manager, holding out his hand. "Give them back. It was one of the clumsiest pieces of shoplifting I have ever seen."

Slowly, as if giving up his last chance for freedom, Alex returned the pens. "I'm sorry," he muttered. "What will you do?"

The manager, father of three boys himself, paused. The kid before him looked so crestfallen. Obviously he'd been out for some excitement and it had backfired. His first time, judging by his ineptness. Calling the police would make the sordid little escapade seem important, so it was probably better to play the whole thing down. That's what he'd do with his own kids.

He looked at Alex contemptuously. "I'm not going to do anything. You're not worth it. Too stupid." He walked back into the store leaving the boy inundated with shame.

The incident had a lasting effect on Alex. Not only was he thoroughly humiliated, but he was also bitterly angry at himself. How could he have been so foolish? He vowed that never again would he allow himself to be so degraded. From the next day forward, he affected an appearance of good humor, masking his true feelings behind an easy grin.

"What a change in the boy. He's become so happy," his parents' friends commented.

"He's growing up," his father would respond smugly.

Behind his smile Alex would curse at them all silently, fantasizing how amazed they would be if only they knew what he really thought, the tortures he planned for them. . . .

Once he learned how much easier his life was if he appeared

cheerful, he learned, too, how to counter his sadness by a sort of perpetual motion, a driving for success. When he was fourteen he took a paper route in order to earn enough for a car. At fifteen he bargained for an old hulk of a Ford and taught himself enough mechanics to get the car moving, and then, as soon as he had a license, to keep it on the road. He fought to make the football team in high school even though he was too light, and earned a spot on the team and a reputation for ferocity as well. Later he showed the same gritty determination at tennis, which was his passion at college and remained a favorite relaxation.

But even while he was enjoying his teenage success, he still felt hemmed in by the pervasive ordinariness of his surroundings. He counted the days until he was old enough to leave.

Alex graduated from high school with an A average, a football letter, captaincy of the tennis team, enough money to pay for his first year of college—and a soaring sense of relief. His record was so good, he could get a scholarship from any school in the country. He was ecstatic. Success could break him free. That knowledge fired his determination for achievement as nothing else could, and there was born in him an intense ambition that did not wane for fifteen years.

He chose Princeton from the other top schools to which he was accepted because it offered the best scholarship. Once enrolled, however, he became a Princeton man down to his Ivy League bootstraps. Within a year, the Swedish carpenter's son was indistinguishable from the scions of empire builders.

Alex Petersen graduated from Princeton with honors and then spent two uneventful years as a junior lieutenant and ADC to the commanding officer of a small southern army base. His primary function was to play tennis, losing gracefully to his commanding officer in singles and carrying them both to victory in doubles. He missed Vietnam because his C.O. would not allow his transfer.

"All I did while I was in the army was to wait, look sharp, and get married," he told a friend later. "The marriage was the least memorable of the three!"

At the time, of course, Alex thought that getting married was right and honorable. Admittedly, he felt none of those profound stirrings of love he had read about. But after a year of working to suppress his deeper feelings, he found that a relief. He assumed, in any case, that the pleasure he felt in her company was all he could expect.

She was a colonel's daughter, an army brat imbued with military tradition and therefore helpful to him. More important for a bored young man, she had a nice figure and a willingness to adore him. Moreover, she was a virgin the first time they had sex and somehow they both assumed that that fact justified her dependence on him. When he was about to be discharged from the army and therefore leave her, her expression became so tragic that he asked her to marry him instead; and was rewarded with such a look of teary, soulful gratitude that he felt unutterably strong and noble.

Alex's ambition reached its full stride when he left the army and became a trainee in an advertising agency.

At first, sitting at a desk overstrewn with papers, he was nonplussed. Where to start? He read the top piece of paper carefully. It had to do with a motorcycle account. His boss, a peppery little man, sat in a corner office alternately snapping at subordinates and obsequiously answering the phone when the client called. All clients, Alex learned, were godlike and irascible; but this particular client was especially angry because his sales were behind target.

"They won't do enough advertising, and then they blame us," his boss complained.

"Why can't we explain that?"

"Christ, you're naive. You can't ever tell the client it's his fault; half the function of an advertising agent is to take the blame." His boss was particularly sarcastic when he was frightened—and he was in almost perpetual fear. He drank to bolster his courage.

By the fourth week, his boss had taken a liking to him and insisted that Alex join him for a "quick one" most evenings. "I'm almost forty," he confided one night after his third martini. "I've never made it big. If I lose this account, I'm up shit's creek."

"Isn't there something you can do?"

"Nothing." The response was flat and hopeless. "All they care about is their fucking races. If they spent half that much money on advertising . . ."

The next day, presumably embarrassed by his confidences, he ignored Alex entirely. They never went drinking together again and after a while the frightened little man drank himself out of the job and disappeared. Alex, however, had gleaned the information he needed, and the following weekend, briefed on motorcycle racing from several hours of library research, he attended the races. He wangled a pass to the pits and amidst the tearing noise and the panther-like excitement of the participants—masked under their veneer of blasé professionalism—he met the clients, father and son. The three talked together knowledgeably between races.

Alex Petersen visited the races half a dozen times and got to know the clients well before he allowed them to find out, apparently by accident, that he worked for their advertising agency. When they did, they were delighted.

"You're the first guy from that bunch of martini drinkers who's ever been to a race."

Within six months, Alex had the account in his pocket. He was given the title of account supervisor. Coincidentally, sales rose—for which he took full credit even though he had not had time to influence the business. It never occurred to him to question the ethics of his approach.

Alex stayed with the agency five years, learning his trade, picking up other accounts by a mixture of competence and appropriate socializing. He was elected a vice president and shortly thereafter given the prestigious API account. After three more years, he was invited by API management to switch to the company itself. The agency was amenable since it strengthened their contacts with the client. So at thirty-one he became a group product manager for API, in charge of all marketing activities for the snack-food division, his salary a healthy fifty thousand a year plus bonus.

During the next four years Alex Petersen was busy supervising his growing number of brands; worrying about packaging and advertising effectiveness; working with Research and Development to improve product quality or to lower costs; exhorting the sales department to meet selling objectives; fighting with Manufacturing to achieve production quotas; and developing new product ideas. In the evenings, he entertained important chain buyers, socialized with television executives, and kept close contact with important API managers. Gradually he built a power base within the company.

"Why aren't you ever home like other husbands?" his wife would complain.

"Why don't I have a clerk's job you mean?"

"No. You're too good for that. It's just that I'm so lonely without you."

"Yes, dear."

"You make me so happy when you're here."

"Why not go out with your friends? Or get a job?" His voice showed how little he was interested.

"I *hate* other women," she would moan. "I wish we could have a baby."

"Maybe we will. Or the adoption will go through. We've been waiting long enough." In truth, he was relieved that they had no children.

The self-questioning started gradually after Alex turned thirty-five. At first the questions only broke through his busy life occasionally and he ignored them, assuming he was just tired. Once, feeling bored for the first time in years, he had an affair with a rather voluptuous secretary in the St. Louis sales office; but after the girl complained that he did not see her often enough, he never returned.

In the same year, he concluded that his wife was too much of a burden. I'm probably not good for her either, he rationalized.

"You are never home for me," she started one evening. "I'm so lonely—"

"I know," he said, suddenly making the decision he had toyed with for months. "I'm not right for you. I think we should split."

She looked at him as she had when he was leaving the army, her eyes filling with tears. Then, suddenly, her face seemed to fall apart, almost like a mirror shattering. "Oh my God," she moaned. "You can't leave me. I depend on you. You're the only man I've ever known." She flung herself at him rubbing herself against his leg. "Oh my God," she sobbed. "What have I done wrong? Don't leave me. Don't leave. . . ."

He relented. For almost another year they stayed together,

as his work became less and less meaningful to him and his wife became paler and more pathetic. Eventually he could stand it no more. Without a further scene, he left the house and took an apartment. The divorce came fast; the settlement he made was huge, an unsuccessful attempt to buy off his guilty conscience. The divorce didn't end up costing him much since she remarried within a year and his guilt was assuaged as well.

His life at API, on the other hand, became more difficult. Some days the job seemed as exciting as ever, his ambition almost as intense; but often he felt hemmed in, contained, just as he had as a boy. The people are wealthier, he thought, the conventions more elegant—but I still can't move.

He considered quitting, but he hated to give up the career for which he had worked so hard. Moreover, he could think of no preferable alternatives. Instead he slugged on, doing his job competently but with less and less enjoyment. "There must be a better way," he heard a commercial on the radio, and he couldn't shake the phrase from his head for days. "There must be a better way."

Now he had the new challenge of Regina. Certainly no one could ask for more excitement than that, or for more power.

If it can be rescued, he thought again suddenly; if the bitch doesn't unmask me two minutes after she gets here. Where the hell is she anyway, he wondered.

The next person accompanied by an usher down the long corridor leading to the dining room was another attractive young woman—tiny, no more than five-feet two, auburn-haired and very pretty. Alex was impressed by the strong sense of dignity and self-assurance she exuded as she smiled at several of the diners. The chief executive with the beautiful escort rose when he saw her coming and embraced her formally, kissing both cheeks in the continental manner. Alex was delighted when he realized that the usher was bringing the newcomer to his table.

"I'm delighted to meet you, Miss Maarten. I'm Alex Petersen. Won't you sit down. Can I offer you a drink?"

"I'll have the same as you, a glass of white wine." Her voice was incredibly deep coming from such a petite woman. "I'm glad that you can still afford to come here." Her face showed a friendly smile but Alex knew that the interview had begun.

There was a moment's uncomfortable silence. Then the waiter brought menus and they both ordered steaks. He noted with approval that she also liked hers very rare.

"Tell me about Regina's main problems," Pamela Maarten began.

"Well, of course our biggest problem is competition," Alex answered easily, determined to give away nothing which could be misconstrued. "Revlon, Lauder, Helena Rubinstein, Factor— they are all pressing in on us. And the French companies are starting to enter."

"I know all that, but—"

"Our response, though, is vigorous," Alex continued firmly. "We have several new products in the works, including an exciting new fragrance line which will be out in a few months—"

"Look, I realize Regina is still in business—" Pamela Maarten started to interrupt again.

She's very attractive, Alex thought, but she's tough. He'd have to be careful not to make her angry; but he had to hold onto the interview a little longer to make it clear who was in charge.

"We are doing more than 'being in business.' We are enjoying what amounts to a resurgence of energy. Let me give you an example. . . ."

Pamela Maarten hardly listened as Alex recounted his anecdote. How can I get him to answer questions? she was thinking. He's just pontificating now. But contrary to Alex's concern, she was not at all angry. It's what I would do, she thought, if I were in as bad a state as Regina and API.

"What are your profit expectations for the year?" she asked innocently when Alex had finished, knowing his answer would inevitably be standard. "You don't mind if I make notes?"

"Not at all," said Alex, slightly startled. It was not customary for a luncheon interview to include note-taking, but he could hardly object. "Our profits, as announced at the time of acquisition, should reach an all-time high of twenty million. However, given the enthusiasm within our company, there is always the possibility that we can exceed that goal." Christ, he thought, I sound pompous.

The waiter served the meal while Alex continued his recital.

"Excellent steak," Pamela Maarten interrupted. "Try some." She gave every appearance of enjoying herself.

Alex tasted the meat. "It is good," he agreed.

For a few moments they both enjoyed their food in silence. Then she looked up and smiled at him. "Look," she said, "I know quite a bit about the situation at Regina. I remember Cosgrove's twenty million dollar forecast just as well as you do. I also know that you've not had an exciting new product since Sir Reginald died. And that you have a lot of administrative problems. There's a rumor that your receivables and inventories have problems. I've heard rumors, too, particularly from department store people, that your sales are starting to slow down while your returns are up—"

"You seem to know quite a bit," Alex interrupted.

"I do. So you see, I don't need any speeches about 'enthusiasm.' I don't need bullshit of any kind. I can get all the hyperbole I can possibly stand from your PR people."

Alex was about to object, but she wouldn't let him. "What I want to hear from you is the simple truth about just two questions: Can you turn Regina around? And can you do it fast enough to fulfill Cosgrove's irresponsible profit forecast?" She took a large mouthful. "It *is* a good steak," she said somewhat indistinctly. "Take a bite to give yourself time to think!"

Alex laughed, started to say something, flushed, and took a drink of wine. "I do need time to think," he said. "I've never been attacked with such vigor during an interview." He tried to sound reprimanding, but although he should have been annoyed by her words, he actually felt more admiration than anger.

Even more, he felt at a loss. If he responded to her challenge with politician's words—long-winded, meaningless—she would ignore him and write what she had heard about Regina elsewhere. In that case, her article would be, at best, skeptical about Regina's future. He could of course lie and say that everything was fine. But even if he were prepared to do so, which he was not, she would not believe him and would write about the company most critically. On the other hand, if he told her the full truth, describing Regina's problems, but emphasizing that he nevertheless felt that he could pull the company around in time, he would be leaving himself wide open. If she wanted to, she could use all the negative information he gave her without including his optimistic feelings. Such a factual negative article would be extremely interesting to her readers who loved to hear about problems. And it could easily become the company's epitaph. The trade, reading about Regina's troubles in *Business World* under Pamela Maarten's respected byline, could stop supporting the company—which would kill it as surely as anything. . . .

"Well?" Pamela Maarten interrupted his thoughts. "Have you decided whether to trust me?"

"I think I should say 'no comment' and run for cover."

"Of course you should. You hardly know me and if you tell me the truth, you put yourself entirely in my hands. I'm not sure what I would do if I were you." She sounded sympathetic. "But I can promise you that if you level with me I will write the most accurate article I can, neither whitewashing nor—"

"Nor setting down aught in malice?"

"That's right," she said. "I'm more like Othello than Iago."

"As a matter of fact, you're not even remotely like Othello," he said, laughing. "You're very pretty." Immediately, he noticed her face stiffen. "Did I say something impertinent?" he asked innocently.

"Well, no—It's just that it has nothing to do with the subject we were discussing."

"Nor does the steak. It's just that I still need time to think."

They both laughed.

"Cheers," she said, and lifted her glass to him. "Thank you. I like being thought pretty."

Suddenly, he decided to trust her. What the hell, he thought, I've got to trust someone occasionally. "Very well," he said, "I'll tell you all about Regina, its potential, but also its problems."

She was utterly delighted that she had gained his trust so fast. It was more than she had hoped for. Was it because he was very clever, she wondered, or very naive?

For the next half hour she grilled him on the problems Regina faced and he answered her as truthfully as he could. Occasionally, when she trod on confidential ground, he refused to comment; but she was professional enough not to probe where he felt he should not talk. Finally, the interview was over.

"That's all," she said. "Let's enjoy our coffee. And thank you," she added sincerely. "You were most helpful."

"You're welcome," he said wryly.

"You hope," she laughed. "Oh, one more thing. I suppose

you would agree that if API fails, you would go down with it?"

Alex instantly felt his stomach contract. If that was the tack her article was to take, it would be disastrous. He hoped his face did not reflect his consternation. "Yes," he said. "I suppose we would. But I have no reason to expect that API will fail." He wondered whether he had made a terrible mistake by being so frank with her about Regina.

"Don't you be too sure." She sounded ominous. "In any case, I shouldn't be asking you about that. I have a meeting with Cosgrove next week."

Coffee was served and they talked of many things. He found her bright, informed, funny, and, as he forgot his worries about what she would write, increasingly attractive.

As they were leaving, he summoned up the courage to ask her to have dinner with him.

"Business or pleasure?" she asked suspiciously.

He hesitated; should he use business to persuade her to come? Again he decided to be honest. "It would be pure pleasure," he said.

"In that case, I'd be delighted," she replied. "As long as you realize that it won't make me write any more favorably about API—or about Regina."

Chapter 11

I n the days that followed, Alex Petersen barely had time to breathe as he fought to wrest order out of Regina's confusion and struggled to achieve its profit forecast. His chief lieutenant in this fight was John Bryant, the company's controller, a gray man with a worried brow, full of nervous energy, whose idiosyncracy was to talk as if he alone were responsible for the company's performance.

"I've made the profit this month," he would announce, his tone full of satisfaction; or, taking the blame, "I'm afraid I've fallen short this month."

Alex had brought Bryant with him from API and trusted and relied on him completely. Often, as on this morning, they met before the office officially opened; even before Sylvie arrived.

"Good morning, John," Alex called as he heard Bryant enter the outer office. "Come on in."

John Bryant bustled in half-submerged under his papers, looking more worried than usual. "I'm afraid I'm in serious trouble with the accounts receivable, sir."

"Why don't you come and sit down first?" Alex smiled indulgently. "Haven't we known about that?"

"Yes, but it's worse. Seems that the sales people have been making strange deals with some of our customers."

"Huh?"

"Apparently it has to do with our cutting prices."

"They did that to boost sales. Why would that give us a receivables problem?"

"That wouldn't. But in order to hide the fact that they were cutting prices to some customers and not to others—which is illegal under the Robinson-Patman Act—they billed everyone at full price. Then they wrote some customers a separate letter saying only to pay part of the bill. The trouble is they never did put copies of those letters into our files."

"Who signed the letters?"

"Many of the sales people. There was no one person. It was a common procedure."

"Then who authorized it in the first place?"

Bryant shrugged his shoulders. "No one seems to remember. And no one knows how the favored accounts were chosen. To me it.seems fishy as hell."

"Is one of the accounts Scarpetti?"

"How did you know?" Bryant's amazement showed clearly. "You're right. I tried to collect a huge amount from them—over 1.8 million dollars—and they pulled out these damned letters saying they didn't have to pay. It's been going on for several years, apparently. The 1.8 million is the cumulative amount."

"But we show the whole amount as an asset in our books?"

"Precisely. So I have to write it off. And take the loss."

"I assumed you would," said Alex. "What a mess."

"Yes."

"You'll find the Scarpettis are into us for over three million. They own three drug chains: Lombard, Drew, and Park Discount."

"Christ!!"

"Do you know how big the problem is altogether? I assume the Scarpettis aren't the only ones."

"I'm not sure yet. The figures show fourteen million over two years old. But they're not all the same thing. I've already found about nine million which are returns which we received and actually wrote off by setting up a reserve instead of clearing out our receivables."

"I don't understand. Are you saying nine million of the missing fourteen million are no problem—just booked in the wrong place?"

"Right. It's the other five million I don't know about, and there may be more false accounts in our current receivables. We'll have to check every account which owes us money before I can tell exactly. It's not so easy to find out about those letters because the customers feel vaguely guilty. They don't want to talk."

"They are more than *vaguely* guilty," said Alex. "They know damn well we've discriminated in their favor. That's illegal for us to do. But for them it's shady too."

The Robinson-Patman Act, both men knew, meant that every account sold by a manufacturer like Regina had to receive equal treatment. If an advertising allowance was offered to one account, it had to be offered to all. If some accounts were too small to advertise and therefore could not take advantage of the allowance, they had to be offered an equivalent benefit which they could use. Similarly, all accounts within one trading area had to be able to buy at the same price. Certain volume discounts were permissible, but even they had to be kept within strict limits. Both men also knew that Robinson-Patman was frequently violated. In fact, under the law, treating customers differently was justified if it was necessary to meet competitive practices. On those grounds many companies violated the law with their legal department's sanction. But this was different. Scarpetti and the others involved had bought at far lower prices than Regina's other customers and there had apparently been a carefully developed scheme to avoid this becoming known. The discrimination seemed illegal; the cover-up provided circumstantial proof.

"Don't you have any idea what the nonexistent receivables will add up to in the end?" Alex probed.

"I can't be certain, of course," said Bryant hesitantly, "but my guess would be four to four-and-a-half million."

The figure hung in the air as dangerous as a guillotine's blade.

"Son-of-a-bitch."

"Precisely."

There was a long pause. Bryant looked white. Alex sat deep in thought.

"Any ideas?" Alex asked after a while.

"The only good point is that I'll be able to take them as a tax loss, so after taxes the write-off will cost only half as much."

"Are you sure?"

"Yes, I'm sure of that. But there's a far more difficult problem facing you."

"What?" Alex asked, noting that the accountant had said *you*, not *I*.

"What profit should I forecast for the year when I make my official six-month statement next week?" The accountant had reverted to the personal pronoun. "As a major API subsidiary, I have to issue an earnings report publicly every quarter. The second one for the year is almost due."

"Why not issue the earnings report without making a forecast?'"

"Because, if I don't issue a new forecast I'll be tacitly confirming our current one of twenty million dollars."

"I see."

"The trouble is that, with all my other problems, I'm not sure I can bring in the twenty million even without writing off the receivables."

"But you still think you can?" Alex realized that his language, too, was making the assumption that the accountant actually made the profits. "But you think we probably can?" he corrected himself. "And we may even do better?"

"It's not impossible that I could do better," said Bryant in a tone which suggested that it was, "but it's very possible I could do worse. A lot depends on how well the International division does. And that's very hard to tell. Cohen has always come in on target in the past, but this year his figures look pretty tight. It all depends on whether he has any reserves. You asked me to find out exactly where he stands, but his international financial guy, Posen, makes a mute look verbose." Unexpectedly, Bryant cackled with laughter. It was a grating sound, Alex thought, rusty with disuse.

"What happens if we end up below our forecasts?"

"That could be a very major problem. If you announce an earnings forecast and then miss it badly, everyone who bought API stock on the basis of that forecast can sue the company if the price of the stock falls. And sue you personally."

"Me, personally?"

"Absolutely. You issued the forecast. The angry shareholders would claim that you did so falsely, knowing that the earnings projections would not hold up."

"But I don't *know* that. I still have reason to expect that—"

"That's what the lawsuits will be about," Bryant interrupted. "Also, since it's illegal to tout your own stock, the Securities and Exchange Commission might attack you, too."

"But we're not touting the stock."

"The SEC might claim you had if they felt that you had declared a higher earnings projection than you anticipated."

"Then there's the problem of inventory," said Alex.

"I haven't even considered that. I have been assuming that I wouldn't have to write that off this year, that it has some value."

"We simply don't know," said Alex wearily. "We won't know for three weeks."

"That's too late. I can't delay next week's announcement by more than a day or two, if that."

Alex was aware of how quickly rumors start on Wall Street. The analysts and the press were already asking about Regina's health. Pamela Maarten's article was still pending; a delay in the forecast might swing her from neutral to negative—if she weren't there already. In a volatile situation like the one at Regina and API, rumors were the last thing they needed.

"The point is," said Alex, talking partly to himself, "that any reduced profit forecast now—and certainly any drastic reduction—would have a terrible effect on our business. Once people think you're doing badly they stop helping you. That's when you go to hell."

"That's what I'm worried about."

"Of course, if we hold to our forecast, it might become a self-fulfilling prophecy. After all, we have another six months to make up for the receivables problem. And the inventory may not be as bad as it seems."

"It might be worse."

"Yes," said Alex, thinking about the various risks he faced, "yes, it might be worse. I assume you asked Asquith over at API what to do?"

"Of course. He said what you'd expect: 'Do whatever you think is right. But don't fail to meet whatever forecast you make.'"

That was precisely the answer Alex would have expected. API's chief financial officer would certainly not want to share with Alex the responsibility for the Regina profit forecasts.

Somewhat reluctantly, Alex picked up his telephone.

"Sylvie, get me Mr. Cosgrove, please."

He hung up to wait for the call. To his surprise it came through in only a few seconds.

"Yes?" said Cosgrove, his voice gruff. He expected no good news from Alex.

"We have a number of problems, sir, which I thought you should know about."

"Of course you do. Every business has problems," the president interrupted.

"I thought you should know about them because we have to issue our semiannual profit forecast next week."

"I know."

"The two major problems are that we shall probably have to write off about four and a half million dollars of accounts receivable, which would give us an after-tax profit reduction of just over two million dollars. And we have an inventory problem, the dimension of which we do not yet know, but which could be anywhere from nothing to ten million dollars or more after taxes."

"Yes?" The president managed to keep his voice totally unemotional; but had Alex been able to see him distractedly scratching his scalp he would have realized at once how perturbed Herman Cosgrove was.

"I'm not sure what profit forecast to issue next week. We won't know about the inventory problem for at least three weeks."

Cosgrove sat rigidly in his chair, his fist clenched around the telephone. He fully understood the implications of what Petersen was telling him. A reduction in the forecast now would be disastrous, not only for Regina but for the whole company. Worse, if the banks learned that Regina's receivables and inventories were suspect, there would be hell to pay. Asquith had borrowed a sorely needed twenty million dollars against them last week. Petersen didn't even know about that. On the other hand, if he condoned a false profit forecast by Petersen, that could have terrible personal ramifications. . . . .

"You should make whatever forecast you believe is correct," Cosgrove said coldly, realizing that his only option was to force the whole responsibility onto Petersen. Whether that would hold up in court if they were sued by shareholders or the SEC remained to be seen. But it was his only hope at the moment. "Obviously, if you reduce your forecast now you will seriously harm the company. But if you cannot hold to the reasonable profit I forecast at the time of acquisition, then you'd better reduce it." He paused, and then, in the coldest voice he could muster, added, "Really, Alex, the decision is up to you."

What else could I have expected? Alex was thinking. If I was appointed as a scapegoat, I can hardly expect him to share in the responsibility for my forecasts. "Very well, sir," he said. "I shall do as I see fit."

"Of course," said the president, and placed down the phone. His hands were trembling.

The decision, Bryant and Alex both realized, carried far more than financial implications. The future of the whole company was at stake, possibly the future of API as well; and with it the fortunes of hundreds of thousands of employees and shareholders. Alex's future, too, hung in the balance. If he backed down now and watched Regina inevitably sag and then collapse, he would be safe; no one could blame him legally, no one could sue. But could he be satisfied with such a path? What of ambition and achievement and success? Were they worth taking a risk? Were they worth it for *him*? A few months ago, he wouldn't have cared. Now? He wasn't sure what he felt.

"Tell me, John," said Alex, mostly to stall for time, "how is our cash position?"

"I'm very tight," said Bryant. "*Very* tight."

"Will we have enough?"

"I doubt it. Not with Christmas inventory starting to build up."

"And we'll not get any money from API, I suppose?"

"That's for sure."

"Can we borrow for ourselves if we have to?"

"I believe I can; my current assets are still 1.9 times my current liabilities—even with my inventory and receivables problems. I'm pretty sure our banks would lend us at least another fifteen million, maybe twenty. I'd have to get approval from API, of course."

"Would that be a problem?"

"Just a formality. The way they are set up, they do the actual borrowing. But they've always let me run on my own. I just inform Asquith and he tells me to go ahead."

So the decision remained. If Alex declared a lower profit, he took no personal risk. After only a few months as Regina's president, no one would put the blame on him. He could always get another job—that is, if he even wanted one. But the company's fortunes would almost certainly spiral downwards. On the other hand, if he held to the earlier forecast, there remained a reasonable chance that he could save Regina; but if he failed he could be in grave trouble personally.

Suddenly Alex felt angry that there was no one to advise him. Bryant, for all his willingness to talk of profits as if he created them personally, totally abrogated responsibility. The decision was Alex's alone. With this recollection, anger passed and was replaced by a sense of pride. Never before had he been required to decide on a business matter of this importance. It was the reward—or, perhaps, the curse—of being at the top. Suddenly he knew that was precisely where he wanted to be. As a boy, and later at Princeton, he had known that about himself beyond doubt. In recent years he had started to wonder. But now the answer was clear to him again. It *was* worthwhile. Business was a human activity which, in individual cases, could be as great or as debased as any other human activity. There was nothing intrinsically good about businessmen, perhaps, but there was nothing particularly unworthy about them either. And business viewed broadly was clearly a positive force. Economic well-being depended on the health of business—and this supported the quality of life. . . .

His decision was clear; but after all it was a personal decision, he realized, not a philosophical one. He could not explain, nor really justify it; he simply wanted to be at the top. He would take the risk.

"We'll declare that we expect to achieve the profit forecast at the time of the acquisition," he said firmly.

"Very well, sir." John Bryant left the room as busily as he had entered.

Alex, too, had no time to ruminate. Throughout the meeting with Bryant, the phone, tactfully muted, had rung intermittently. Each time Sylvie had taken a message and summarized it on a pink slip to be given to Alex later. Now it rang again, but this time, after listening for a few seconds, Sylvie buzzed the inter- com.

"It's Hy Weissman on the line, sir. He's mad!"

"Again?" Alex asked, amused.

Hy Weissman, the sales manager for Regina, was well over six feet and weighed at least 250 pounds. His voice was naturally loud and he used it fully. In a rage, he was an imposing sight, and his angers were not infrequent—although Alex had noticed that they were carefully timed. A determined man, experienced and realistic, Weissman had worked for Regina for over ten years and before that as assistant sales manager for a large tobacco company. His men, whom he protected as if they were his chil- dren, revered him.

"Alex," he boomed, "listen, I want to talk to you. Can I come up?"

"I'm a little busy—why not just tell me on the phone?" Alex had had experience with the loquacious Weissman.

"Damned West Coast deliveries. We can't get anything out there in less than four weeks."

"I know, you've told me already."

"But not a damn thing's happening."

"Who's working on it?"

"Nobody's working on it." Weissman seemed more annoyed than the problem warranted.

"Now, listen," Alex said. "What's so special about the prob- lem today?"

Weissman instantly caught the edge in Alex's voice and muted his anger. "They say the problem is that it takes too long for my salesmen to send in their orders. That's crap. Just an excuse—"

"Why don't you put in a WATS line?" Alex interrupted. "Huh?"

"You know, one of those telephone lines on which you can place as many long distance calls as you want for one fixed monthly fee. Then have the salesmen telephone in their orders the day they take them. The orders will get in fast, and it will force our people here to give the West Coast priority."

"I'll inquire about it," said Weissman uncertainly.

"Goddammit, Hy, don't inquire about it—do it." It was Petersen's turn to be overbearing. "You're the one who's complaining. Now I've got a solution for you. So handle it. By the way," he added aggressively while Weissman was still off balance, "what's with those overdue receivables at Scarpetti's?"

If Alex had hoped that Weissman, surprised by the sudden attack, might reveal something, he was disappointed.

"I don't know," Weissman said promptly but without any concern in his voice. "I'll handle the whats-its line today. There's something strange about those receivables. Bryant just told me about the problem. I'll get back to you."

Alex's first thought was that he had learned nothing at all. Then, as he continued to reflect, a small question started to creep into his mind. Was it believable, he wondered, that Weissman had never heard of the special discounts? He must investigate Weissman a little further, he decided.

Sylvie entered and started to clear away the coffee cups. "Young John Samuels is here with a new promotion package," she said.

"You'd better send him in."

"Yes, I'd better. He's terribly important!"

Alex was still chuckling as a pompous young man hurried in.

"I'm here to present our fragrance 'Summer Special,' upon which we would appreciate your formal concurrence. We judge it to be excellent, Mr. Petersen."

"Yes, I'm sure it is. May I see it, please?"

"I believe it is very commensurate with the efforts conducted in previous years, but there are some meaningful improvements—"

"Just show me."

The young man looked hurt. "Yes, sir." He placed a bottle on the table. It was a cooling body splash which the company marketed throughout the year, but sold mostly in the summer. Each year a price reduction marked on the bottle further boosted sales from May through September. The label of the bottle now in front of Alex was inscribed with the words "Summer Special" in orange, and the S of "Summer" had been made to look like a sunburst.

"You know, if you call it 'Summer Special' the trade will send back every piece that hasn't been sold as soon as the summer is over." Alex hoped he was not sounding too much like a school teacher. "Why not call it something nonseasonal? How about 'Splash Special'?"

"Well, we believe there is considerable merit in calling it 'Summer Special.' We considered many alternatives—"

"Look," Alex interrupted, his voice only barely patient, "there's good reason not to call it 'Summer Special' and there must be other good names. So you can avoid the risk and still get the job done. Maximum action with minimum risk is the objective of all business decisions." With a smile he added, "That's one of 'Petersen's Platitudes'."

"Thank you, sir." The young man left rather sheepishly.

"You must have cut him off at the knees," said Sylvie when she came in a moment later. "He was taking very small steps."

The telephone rang again while Alex was still laughing. She picked it up.

"Mr. Petersen's office. No, I'm sorry, he's in conference. Yes, I'll try to have him call you back; but he'll be leaving shortly. For some time, I'm afraid. Perhaps you could drop us a note. Thank you, good-bye."

"Who was that?"

"Somebody trying to sell you insurance."

"You are a consummate liar."

"Aren't I?" she said pleased. "I'll get your mail now." She whisked out. A second later she was back with an enormous pile of paper.

"Oh, my God!"

"I've put the important stuff into a separate pile." She pointed to a thick folder at the top.

"All that? It can't all be important."

"It shouldn't be, but it is," she said with finality and left, closing the door firmly.

Immediately the office became as calm as a professor's study. Alex reached for the "important" folder and quickly became absorbed in the so-called "vital statistics report" from Regina's international companies. The full year forecast in most countries seemed to stand up well compared to the sales levels which had been promised to API at the time of the acquisition. But as Alex scanned the actual performance of the last three months, the figures looked much poorer. Sales in several European countries were below budget. Japan, too, looked terrible. Suddenly he was acutely worried. In some ways this was the worst news yet. If he could not rely on the profits from International, then time would certainly run out before he had any chance of turning Regina's U.S. business around. In that case his directive to Bryant had been quite wrong. Then. . . .

Instead of finishing the thought, he punched his intercom. "Get Cohen up here right away," he told Sylvia.

Quickly he took the next piece of paper from the "important" file. It was a note requesting approval for a price increase on lipstick from $2.00 retail to $2.15, on the grounds that the cost of goods had risen to over 35 percent—compared to the corporate objective of 30 percent. A fifteen-cent increase at retail meant that dealers, who made 40 percent profit margin on cosmetic sales, would get an additional six cents, while the company would take in an additional nine cents, resulting in a cost of goods of 30.7 percent. The memo explained that there was a danger that moving over the magic two-dollar mark for a lipstick might make the Regina products seem too expensive, but recommended that the risk was justified.

Alex thought for a moment, then scrawled across the top of the paper: "Why not $2.25? If consumer has to pay over $2.00 anyway, won't she pay $2.25 as easily?" He did a quick operation on the calculator. "Gives cost of goods 29.3 percent—below 30 percent objective." He put the initials of the marketing manager on top of the note and signed it *Alex* with the date. As his hand dropped it into his "Out" basket, he was already devouring the next sheet of paper.

It was a form headed "Obsolete Inventory Destruction Request" filled in by young Samuels and requesting permission to destroy $8,200 worth of obsolete packaging material. Under "Reasons for Necessity," Samuels had written "Obsolete." Alex picked up his dictating machine.

"To all product managers," he dictated rapidly. "Some of your Obsolete Inventory Destruction Requests do not adequately justify the proposed destruction. Since destroying inventory wastes money, we must try every alternative before we resort to destruction. Please make sure that all inventory disposal requests carry with them a complete explanation of why nothing can be done to salvage the material. Thank you for your help." He thought for a moment then added, "P.S. to John Bryant: Please prepare a summary of the inventory we destroy each month so that we can keep overall track. Thanks."

The buzzer from Sylvie's desk sounded. "It's Weissman again," she said.

Alex punched a button on his telephone. "Yes?"

"Listen, I've asked about those receivables. I told you wrong. I've known about those special discounts for years. I just didn't realize that's what all the fuss was about—thought you meant something new. Sir Reginald actually started those. He told us which accounts to work with. I had no idea Bryant and you did not know about it."

"Sir Reginald authorized the discounts?"

"His letter is quite clear: 'Cut the price as far as necessary to get the order.' It's in my files. I'll send you a copy." Weissman hung up, leaving Alex totally nonplussed.

Almost immediately Sylvie announced that Cohen had arrived. He entered, accompanied by the head of international accounting, a somewhat sinister man of indeterminate accent, age, and background. His first name was Mynar, but he was addressed by his staff and peers alike as Mr. Posen.

There was something vital, almost dangerous, about Cohen, Alex thought—like an animal not fully tamed. And Cohen's choice of Posen as his chief financial advisor did nothing to reassure Alex; for Posen had about him something of the baleful air of Peter Lorre, the sinister little actor Alex occasionally caught on the Late Late Show.

"I've been looking at the international vital statistics reports," Alex decided to attack. "It seems to me that in several countries you are way below your budget year-to-date, and aren't going to make your annual forecast."

"Oh, I think we will," said Cohen smoothly, far too experienced to be bowled over by such an attack. "The figures in some countries, France for instance, seem a little optimistic. But France is an interesting country; they've always achieved their estimates in the past—even when they seemed impossible. No doubt they will in the future. We have to give them a certain amount of leeway—"

"Leave them alone, you mean?"

"No, not entirely alone," said Cohen judiciously. "I keep

close control. But we should not pressure them too much." He continued talking reassuringly for a few moments. "The important thing is that I keep firm but gentle control," he concluded. He placed just the slightest hint of emphasis on the word *I*. "I have done it for several years."

"What about the other countries, Marty? What about Italy?"

"Ah, we have problems there, too."

"Their figures look better."

"They *look* better, but in Italy things are never as they seem." Alex found Cohen's knowing smile extraordinarily irritating.

"How are they, then?"

"Well, the best I can say is that, while our business seems to be in sound shape, it's very important that I keep a tight hand on the tiller." Again the slight stress on the *I*.

"The same thing applies in Germany, I suppose?"

"They require more determined supervision. They are a much harder people."

"Their figures look weak."

"I shall see to it that they make their budget," said Cohen sternly. There was an uncomfortable pause at the reprimand.

Alex realized that Mr. Posen had said not a word. Turning to him now, he asked, "Is our spending in France on budget?" Since sales were behind budget, advertising and sales-promotion spending should also have been kept below budget. However, Alex knew that subsidiary managers hated to cut spending when sales were already soft, fearing that such cuts would soften sales further and lead to a downward spiral.

Cohen smiled easily as Posen unfolded a chart fully two feet across, covered with an apparently infinite pattern of tiny numerals in *trompe l'oeil* patterns. "Let me show you first this," Posen said in his indefinable accent. "Here we have each country's sales performance and spending last year, this year to date, and the balance required for the next three months—"

"What the devil does all this show? Please get to the point," said Alex. "Is our spending on budget or not?"

"Fully commensurate with our present and anticipated sales," Cohen interrupted smoothly.

"Many papers are needed to tell the complete story," said Posen, sounding apologetic and folding up his chart.

Alex realized that, as he had feared, he would obtain no

real understanding from Cohen. "Well, well," he said, sitting back in his chair, "things seem to be in pretty good shape after all. I assume that I can count on your budget figures when I issue my semiannual forecast."

"You can," said Cohen. But Alex was not much reassured. If the figures were wrong, he realized, Cohen would simply apologize. But I'll bear the brunt, he thought angrily.

Cohen relaxed in his chair. The change in his bearing was barely perceptible, but Alex knew that he felt he had won. A small victory, perhaps, but a victory nevertheless.

Time to attack, Alex thought. Aloud he said, "Today is Monday; tomorrow we have the meeting with Darwin Kellogg, and on Wednesday evening we leave for Paris. I would like to see for myself what's going on. Sylvie has made the reservations."

He buzzed Sylvie, who quickly ushered Cohen and Posen out of the room.

"I'd better make those reservations, hadn't I?" she said when she returned.

"You were listening," he accused.

"I wouldn't have missed it for the world!"

Marty Cohen returned to his office feeling more surprised than angry. But by the time his secretary entered twenty minutes later, his surprise had turned to rage.

"Get me Paris," he roared. "Hurry!"

When the phone rang he snatched it.

"Just a moment, M. LeVecque is coming," said the French operator, "*ne quittez pas.*"

Cohen's knuckles rapped on his desk.

Then the suave, French voice of Claude LeVecque, directeur general of Regina France, came onto the line.

"Marty, how are you?" LeVecque had spent a year studying in Cambridge University in England before graduating from the Sorbonne in Paris, so that his French accent was superimposed with a British one. He would have died before dropping an *h.* "How happy I am to hear from you."

"Here's how it goes—" said Cohen. He had no time for the normal amentities. And he knew he could count on LeVecque. For all of his suavity, the Frenchman was frightened of losing his job. Top positions in the cosmetic world in France were not plentiful, and "Directeur General, Claude LeVecque" looked good on his business card. He could hardly expect any place on the rungs of the Legion d'Honneur ladder—an honor he craved mightily—without a card which said at least that.

"Our new boss Alex Petersen is coming over to Paris—leaving on Wednesday night and arriving the next morning at eight. I intend to leave tomorrow evening so that you and I can spend Wednesday together before he gets there."

"It's an honor," said LeVecque automatically.

"Bullshit. It's merely unavoidable."

There was no response from LeVecque. He knew this mood in Cohen well and had decided long ago not to respond to such outbursts.

"But since it's inevitable, let's make the most of it."

"I'm listening." The accent seemed to become less elegant.

"I've told Petersen that the figures from France, as submitted in your latest estimate, are our best forecast. He felt that we might not be able to achieve the figures and wanted me to explain how we were in a position to continue to make such an estimate."

"How indeed?"

"What did you say? I didn't hear." Cohen's voice sounded menacing.

"Nothing, Martin. I was just making an interlocutory exclamation."

"Right," said Cohen. "Now to continue—I told Petersen that it was only because of the strength of our French management, assisted to some degree by myself, that we could be so comfortable with our figures."

"Thank you." There was only a hint of sarcasm in the Frenchman's response.

"Don't thank me," said Cohen roughly. "I believe that it's important at this time to support each other."

There was only a momentary pause before LeVecque said clearly and emphatically, "I understand. What you were saying to Mr. Petersen was that although the evidence of the past months' sales and profit figures gives cause for reconsideration of the future, it was nevertheless the opinion of the French management, ably supported by yourself, that the annual budget figures were capable of being achieved by the continuation of the policies and practices which experience has taught us have been so successful in the past."

Cohen smiled for the first time that day. When it came to the use of sophisticated words adding up to nothing, the French were unsurpassed.

"Precisely," said Cohen.

"Precisely," echoed LeVecque, his voice fruity with smugness.

"I would like you to make a detailed presentation to Mr. Petersen, starting with a complete rundown of the French economy. However, since it will be his first day, we should not continue too long into the afternoon. He will doubtless be tired."

"Precisely," said LeVecque again.

"Good. I would also suggest that we have a decent luncheon for once—not our normal sandwiches in the office."

"Yes, I do see your point."

"Other than that, I will leave the decisions of what to include—and what to omit—in your able hands. I realize the time you have is short—"

"Indeed, it will be difficult to prepare a full set of business data," said LeVecque. "But we shall certainly be ready with a broad overview."

"Right. A broad overview."

"It would certainly help us if the basic economic presentation could be made in French. Our people are not all as fluent as am I."

Cohen smiled broadly this time. "What a good idea. Queenie tells me Mr. Petersen spent some time in France."

The conversation with the Italian general manager, whom Cohen ordered to Paris, was similar.

Only with the head of the German company was Cohen more direct: "I want you to stonewall—to give no information. Just say your experience is the substantiation for your forecast. I've told Petersen that we are not in difficulties in Germany in spite of your poor first five months' figures, and I want you to back me up on that; is that clear?"

"It is."

You always have to order those goddamn Nazis, thought Cohen; and Dr. Krause, the general manager of Regina Germany, thought his normal uncharitable thoughts about Jews. Practically everyone in the American cosmetic business was Jewish. Sometimes he wondered how he had entered the business so many years ago without anyone even mentioning that. . . .

It was mid-afternoon before Marty Cohen's preparations were complete. His ear ached and his voice was scratchy from the shouted telephone conversations. Petersen would have no easy time in Europe.

Cohen buzzed his secretary. "Get me Rand," he said.

"Hello," said Rand's voice a few seconds later. "How are you?"

"Cecil, I need your advice. Let's stroll over to the Plaza and have a drink."

"Great idea."

It was a warm and breezy day. The girls' skirts hugged their bottoms. The two men crossed the street and walked up Fifth Avenue past F.A.O. Schwartz, probably the most expensive toy store in the world, with its windows charmingly decorated with moving trains, tiny figures of animals, dolls that moved and smiled and cried.

Suddenly in Cohen's brain there flashed an image of his closed room, locked on the outside by his Aunt Ruth, and the toys he was supposed to play with. One was a doll. He hated dolls. He pulled at the doll's arms and legs until they broke. He smashed her head. . . .

A pretty girl, her blond hair blowing in the breeze, turned away from the store window just in front of them. Rand looked at her appreciatively. "Lovely day," he said inconsequentially. "Beautiful people."

Cohen's inner vision switched to a scene of a thousand girls, all as young as this one, deformed and broken, piled at Auschwitz. He had seen the picture somewhere. Somehow this horror became the fault of his Aunt Ruth and of the young girls walking in the sunny street. Bitches, he thought; jabbering, screwing bitches. "Yes, it is a lovely day," he said in an ordinary voice.

Afternoon tea at the Plaza had hardly changed in twenty years. Elegant, unhurried men, well-dressed dowagers, young women from Barnard or Smith, all still entered through the same ornate gate and were superciliously shown to a table of the maître d's choice where they watched their neighbors and listened to the string quartet's afternoon music.

"Well, what can I do for you?" asked Rand. "I have a feeling you're a little tense, a little—"

"I'm worried about the progress of the company. I certainly don't want to say anything against Petersen—I'm sure he's a competent executive—but I am concerned."

"I'm sure you are." Was there irony in Rand's response?

"We're in severe difficulties in the U.S. company already," Cohen insisted.

"We needn't be."

"You think not?"

"Well, of course, I'm not running it—"

"That's my point."

"Oh," said Rand, suddenly realizing he was being flattered, not attacked. "Oh, I see—"

"Now that API has brought in one of their own," the phrase dripped with sarcasm, "the industry is saying we're about to become just another inexpensive cosmetic line.

"And you could rescue it." The irony became unmistakable.

"No, damn it. That's not the point I'm making. All I want is to avoid a similar calamity in International."

Cecil Rand looked more serious. "Is there a problem there, too?"

"Petersen doesn't know what to do about America, so now he's decided to move in overseas. I'm not going to stand for it." Cohen's voice was rising. "I've built the business internationally these last three years. I'm not going to have him destroy it."

"Do you have a choice?"

"With your help, I have a choice."

There it was. The two men eyed each other. They were natural allies: both shared the objective of eliminating Petersen; they were related by marriage; they had worked together for years. Yet the pause lengthened as Cecil struggled to decide. He had never been confident of Cohen. There was something indefinable about him which made him uncomfortable. Queenie felt it, too. She had told him. . . . Then, quite unexpectedly, Cecil's doubts were swamped by a sudden surge of sympathy for Cohen. He was his son-in-law, after all, part of the family. And certainly Sir Reginald had given him little enough reward for his efforts. Just like me, Cecil thought bitterly. Of course he would help Cohen if he could.

"You can't stop him going, you know. If he wants to visit Paris—"

"You knew?"

"He informed me in advance."

Cohen was stopped in his tracks. Petersen was no mean rival.

"Of course, Cecil. I understand that. We'll welcome him overseas, and I'll keep him fully informed. It's just that I hope we can stop him from screwing things up. And please forgive me for being so straightforward. I get emotional when someone attacks Regina. I feel so deeply about the company."

"I'll see what I can do," Cecil assured him. "Actually, I do own half a million shares of API, don't I? Perhaps I could have a little talk with Herman Cosgrove."

Cohen was delighted.

The moment Sylvie interrupted, Alex knew there was a crisis.

"Mr. Bryant is here to see you again," she said. "It's urgent."

Bryant hurried in looking even more worried than usual. For once he carried no papers.

"I just talked to Asquith. He absolutely forbade me to borrow any money against my inventories or receivables."

Alex was shocked. "Why?"

"He wouldn't discuss it. Simply gave me the order and hung up. When I called back, his secretary said he was busy."

"What do we do now?"

"I don't know. We have enough cash for another six weeks. Maybe I can stretch it a little by slowing down payments to our suppliers. But we'll never last till the money comes in from the Christmas merchandise. Most of our customers don't pay until January."

"Why the hell won't API let us borrow?"

"I'm not sure, sir. I can only assume that they have already used our assets as collateral to borrow for themselves."

Chapter 12

B arbara Cohen and Queenie met for lunch at least once a month. They faced each other in almost total contrast. Barbara was softly beautiful, gentle, caring. On the surface she showed a diffidence which sometimes seemed like weakness—although underneath lay much of the strength of her grandfather. In her writing, there was also some of his ebullience and creativity. Frances Duke, on the other hand, looked strong, almost austere. She was always erect, impeccable, dignified. Sometimes, when she was tired, she seemed almost craggy. Even in private, when she allowed her rigid control to slip and her body to relax, she always retained her extraordinary dignity.

For all the contrast between them, however, Queenie and Barbara had been good friends since Barbara was a little girl. In those days Queenie, in her early fifties, icily beautiful and totally dedicated both to Regina and its founder, had often welcomed the little girl into her office while they both waited for the notoriously unpunctual Sir Reginald. They had talked together, sometimes for an hour at a time, like equals. Barbara had been such a precocious, self-confident eight-year-old. . . .

"Queenie, I don't know what to do anymore," Barbara was

saying. "Marty is so angry, so violent." She toyed at the salad before her, reminding Queenie of an unhappy child.

"He has some reason for being angry, you know. He deserved to be Regina's next president. Then API put in Petersen, and—"

"What's he like?" Barbara interrupted, veering away from such a simple explanation. She knew there was more to her husband's anger than the lost presidency. If only he would tell me so that I could help him, she thought.

"I'm not sure about Petersen yet." Queenie's voice interrupted her thoughts. "At first I thought he was just a gray flannel shell. So excessively proper. Now I'm not sure. Once or twice I've started to think he just might turn out to be brilliant." Queenie's voice became perplexed. "But I don't like him." She stopped, suddenly annoyed at her candor.

"I don't suppose you do," said Barbara, "not after Grand."

Queenie's face became totally still. Yes, she thought, that's true. I *have* been comparing them all along. No wonder poor Alex doesn't stack up. She looked across the table at her companion wondering whether her remark had been as innocent as it sounded. "At least he's handsome enough," she continued with a laugh. "A little too slight for my liking, but wiry. Probably good in bed."

"Oh, you're outrageous." Barbara was more amused than shocked.

Queenie smiled. "When he was first introduced to me I thought he was so pompous that I decided to loosen him up a bit—"

"I know," Barbara interrupted. "I heard that story. Apparently Petersen has told it all over town. I saw George Brown-Williams the other night at a party, and he told me." She giggled.

Queenie looked pleased. "It turns out he's not as pompous as I feared. He's not Hotchkiss and Harvard either, although he looks it. Princeton on a scholarship, actually."

"You've been doing your homework."

"Darwin Kellogg told me. He's—"

"Oh, I know, Darwin always knows about everything. And he's so sweet—" She paused. "Marty mentioned that Darwin's going to do some work for Regina. Marty seemed very annoyed."

"Yes, it's another sign of his power eroding. And Petersen

handled it tactlessly. I can sympathize, really. After all these years, what does Marty have? He's not the president, he didn't get any stock—"

"But I have two hundred thousand shares. And the children have six hundred thousand between them—"

"In some ways that makes it worse."

"You're right. That's why I didn't agree when Grand wouldn't make Marty an executor of the children's trust."

"Reg was adamant on that."

"I know. It really hurt Marty. That's why I changed it after Grand died. He wouldn't have approved, but it made Marty so happy. And it's not as if he gets any benefit from the trust himself. Anyway, he doesn't need it now that he finally has some money of his own."

"Does he?" Queenie was surprised. "There was nothing in Reg's will for him. I tried to suggest it several times, but—"

"No, he's had to earn it himself. Investments and things. Grand could be so adamant—"

"Yes, he could be—occasionally." The two women laughed together at the understatement. "Yes, Reginald was stubborn," Queenie said seriously, "but he was usually right."

The two women looked at each other tenderly, the bond strong between them. In different ways they had both loved Sir Reginald very much.

"I'm frightened of Marty's angers," said Barbara suddenly, reverting to her troubles. "He's more violent now, different. I wish I could help him."

"You wish you could help everyone," said Queenie with a smile. Then, almost severely, she added, "He's under great stress, you know. I wouldn't worry about him too much."

Barbara would not be so easily consoled. "He drinks more than he used to," she said, close to tears.

Queenie reached over silently and touched her hand. "Is the marriage over?" she asked softly. "Are you going to divorce?"

"I don't know, Queenie. I'm afraid what that would do to the children. And to Marty too. Oh, and I feel so lethargic."

Queenie nodded sympathetically.

"Do you remember how precocious I was when I used to come to your office all those years ago?"

Queenie nodded. "Not *that* many years."

Barbara would not be diverted. "Well, I was still precocious when my book came out five years ago."

"Reg was so proud of you."

"But I'm adult now; I'm past being an ingenue. I've got to make it on my own now, without Regina or Grand, or even you. That's part of what makes Marty so angry at me. Sometimes I think he needs me more than anyone, including him, realizes. He hates it when I'm engrossed in writing and not concentrating on him."

"Yes, I suppose he would."

"I'm writing another book. I want it to be really good this time. It's terribly important to me. I keep plugging away at it, but I've lost objectivity. I can't tell anymore whether it's good or not."

"What does your writer friend think?"

"Solly? He hasn't seen it recently. I gave him the first draft and he wrote me a detailed critique. He said it had great promise—all except the plot, the characters, and the writing!!" Barbara laughed somewhat bitterly. "Oh, Queenie," she said suddenly. "Help me. What shall I do?"

"Why not go and stay at the Chateau Regine for a while? Watch the Loire flowing and the fruit ripening. It's what I always do when life gets a little heavy. I love it more than anywhere else on earth. When I think of Reg it's usually in the setting of the Chateau. . . ." She shook her head, impatient at herself for being nostalgic. In her normal businesslike voice, she continued, "Go there. Stay as long as you like. The children will be fine with your housekeeper, and Marty really can do without you. Go, write your book."

"I think I will, Queenie. I need to get away. Thank you."

"Don't thank me, dear. You can use the Chateau anytime. You loved him too."

The two women left the restaurant together and hugged each other goodby. Barbara walked towards Park Avenue, feeling calmer than she had in days.

Queenie entered her waiting limousine to be rushed back to the Regina offices. She reflected on Barbara's comment about Alex Petersen. Everything moves forward, she thought suddenly. Am I just holding on to the past, trying to slow down the future?

Perhaps it would be better to hand over to the younger ones. Maybe, after all, young Alex isn't such a bad alternative. She smiled wryly. With a little help, of course, she thought.

Chapter 13

Darwin Kellogg was the senior partner and the major force of Kellogg Associates, a business consulting firm which, for huge fees—at least five thousand and up to twenty thousand dollars per month—advised corporate clients on running their businesses more profitably. For weeks or months they would study the client company to pinpoint its shortcomings. Then, as Darwin deemed necessary, they would invent new products, reorganize accounting departments, strengthen sales organizations, improve marketing plans, or even, at the secret request of a dissatisfied board of directors, find a more appropriate chief executive officer.

Most of Darwin's clients were in some sort of trouble before they retained him. And all were highly sensitive. When he exposed the unpleasant truths they had paid him to unearth, they usually hated it, and accepted his proposals only because he combined great tact with extraordinary business acumen and creativity—and because they'd paid a lot for his advice.

Above all, Darwin gave the impression of being a kind, gentle, and trustworthy man. His prematurely white hair, almost jolly face creased around the eyes and mouth with laugh lines, and his beautifully full, smooth voice, set people at their ease. Yet, like his voice which was powerful enough to fill a hall with a mellifluous carpet of sound, so was his personality strong and determined as well as kind.

At the moment, Darwin and two of his junior executives were completing the preparations for a presentation to be made jointly to the Regina Company, headed by Alex Petersen, and its advertising agency, Blom Bentsen Beame, headed by Charlie Bentsen. As always, this presentation would have to be handled with great care; no doubt many feathers would be ruffled by their findings.

Susanna Brightwood, in charge of research, finished putting the charts in place.

"What sort of man is this Alex Petersen?" she asked.

"Good businessman," said Darwin. "Very hard working."

"He'll have to work harder than ever if he wants to fix Regina."

"He sure will," Darwin agreed. Susanna loved to hear his voice; *creamy* was how she described it to herself. She thought him one of the most desirable men she had ever met, incredibly warm, and sexy too.

"I feel so safe with Darwin," she explained to her girlfriend, Marcella York, "as if I could risk the forbidden things with all their excitement but without their danger."

"Do you?" Marcella asked.

"Risk them, you mean? No, it's all businesslike," Susanna said rather sadly. "So far!" Suddenly she remembered that Marcella had recently joined Regina. That should give me a good contact inside our client, she thought. I just hope I didn't say too much about Darwin. . . .

"Yes, Petersen has an excellent reputation," said James Moran, noisily. Since his recent elevation to the rank of vice president of Kellogg Associates, he felt constrained to contribute heartily to every conversation in earshot.

"All set, Sue?" Darwin asked.

"How wrong can you go with five charts?"

"Very wrong!" Darwin said and they all laughed.

Over the next few minutes the other "guests" arrived. Two English maids, supervised by a butler who looked as if he moonlighted as a church deacon, served tea and coffee. Sweet rolls were offered but mostly declined. Darwin hovered everywhere, introducing himself and bringing together those people who didn't know each other.

Cohen entered, immaculately dressed in white shirt and dark blue suit, both inexpensively tailored in Hong Kong. The number of times he visited Regina's Hong Kong subsidiary seemed more dependent on his need for clothing than on the subsidiary's need for supervision.

Charlie Bentsen, red-faced, gregarious, the born salesman, arrived moments later. He boomed greetings. In contrast, Alex Petersen arrived quietly; nevertheless he was promptly greeted by Darwin Kellogg. My God, Susanna thought the moment Darwin brought him over, I'm surrounded by sexy men. Marvelous!

Queenie arrived next—swept in, really—head high. She nodded to Alex, acknowledged Cohen, shook hands with Charlie Bentsen, hugged Darwin, and ensconced herself in one corner of the room where she received in turn each of the other guests.

Last came Cecil Rand, his suit even baggier than usual. He made his way fussily across the room, acknowledging greetings with a barely perceptible nod of his head or flutter of his fingertips. He was the emperor, he implied, and they his subjects. But the greetings of the subjects were perfunctory and each immediately turned back to whatever conversation had been so briefly interrupted. Eventually he reached Queenie.

"Hello, Cecil," she said. "About time we got started. We are all glad you could come." There was a half-smile on her face, difficult to decipher.

Under Darwin Kellogg's careful direction everyone was quickly seated. He himself stood at the end of the room next to an easel. On the other side of it, like good children in school, sat his two associates. On opposite sides of the long table facing each other, as if sitting in judgment, sat the clans. On the left, the clan of Regina; opposite, the ad agency's personnel, anxious, subservient—yet itching to take offense at whatever Darwin would say.

Kellogg cleared his throat. "May I welcome you to our offices." His voice, stronger to address the group, remained as smooth as ever. "In particular, we would like to welcome Alex

Petersen who, as you all know, has had extraordinary success at API. Alex, we hope we shall see you many times in the future. And, of course, we hope that this first meeting will help to put the problems and the opportunities we see for the Regina Company into perspective."

Alex nodded his head. "Thank you," he mumbled, embarrassed.

"The first thing we would like to show you," Darwin was continuing, "is a profile of cosmetic users. Who are our customers? Since Susanna Brightwood here has done a great deal of this research work, I shall ask her to tell you about it."

The young woman rose abruptly, took a collapsible pointer from the inside pocket of her blazer, and extended it with a sharp click.

"In order to determine precisely into which category of consumers the Regina customer falls, we interviewed 2,125 women," she started, her nervousness making her speak a little too fast. "Each interview provided both numerical and subjective data. Thus we now know which products our respondents use, and what sort of people they are, psychologically and psychographically." She paused, slightly winded. Darwin Kellogg gave her an encouraging smile and nodded his head. Her muscles relaxed.

"Our research showed that cosmetic users fall into five reasonably well-differentiated categories." She uncovered a bar chart on the easel. "As you will see from this chart, the first category of women represents about ten percent of the population. These are women who have such a poor self-image that they just don't care how they look. We have nicknamed this type—" She paused, and then with a flourish unveiled a large picture on the wall. " 'The Slob'!" The photograph was thoroughly appropriate: a picture of a famous television actress in the role of a sloppy cleaning woman. There was an appreciative rustle of laughter.

"In any case," Garry Gainborough interrupted, adjusting his gold tie-clip, "the Slob wouldn't have enough money to buy our products."

"Perhaps not, but these are actually psychological, not economic groups."

"Oh?" He didn't seem convinced.

"The early Caroline Kennedy might be an example of someone who did not care about her appearance," said Susanna. "When you compare her with Caroline of Monaco, you can see how types vary even among the rich."

"I see," Garry Glitter repeated, but this time with conviction. He smoothed his already perfectly groomed hair.

"The second group is characterized by a better self-image, but an equal lack of caring," Susanna continued. "She is so busy with outside interests that she has no time to look after herself. We call this category, which represents eight percent of the population, 'The Worker Bee!'" Susanna unveiled a large photograph of Betty Friedan, chin and nose jutting, and without make up.

"Actually," said James Moran, "Betty is carefully made-up most of the time, but the picture was appropriate." He was delighted to drop her first name into the conversation.

Susanna continued as if there had been no interruption. "The third category, some twenty-two percent of consumers, is made up of women who follow the mass, who are sheeplike. They tend to be competent but subjugated." Susanna paused and wondered whether she might be in this category. Could she marry Kenny and become a subjugated wife the way he wanted? Last night when he had been so dominant and she had felt so turned on. . . . "I don't think—" she started to say and then, realizing the phrase was appropriate only to her thoughts, coughed to cover up. "I don't think," she repeated determinedly, "that this group, which we call 'The Girl-Next-Door,' is a particularly good customer for Regina." She unveiled a photograph of freckled innocence. "She uses cosmetics tentatively—and mostly on Saturday nights!"

I'm not in that group after all, Susanna concluded. I'm certainly not tentative! She smiled to herself remembering how aggressive she had become back at Kenny's apartment.

"Category four is a good customer for cosmetics, but more for Estée Lauder and Helena Rubinstein than for Regina. Although she uses makeup and treatment products regularly, and constitutes twenty-eight percent of the population, she's not quite exotic enough for our company. She has great dignity, though, and she's very feminine, competent, and poised. Understated in her loveliness. We call her 'The Queen.' She is typified by one of our own." With a warm smile, Susanna unveiled a remarkably beautiful portrait of Queenie.

There was general applause. Queenie bowed slightly in her chair and endeared herself to everyone by blushing. "That you should use me to illustrate people who don't use Regina!" she said in mock horror. "I can't imagine why I feel so flattered."

"It is in the fifth consumer category that Regina's main audience lies," Susanna continued when the audience quieted. "This consumer represents the balance of the population—that is, thirty-two percent of all women. She is a generally self-assured woman, a little brasher than 'The Queen.' She definitely wants to make the most of her looks and is therefore particularly interested in color. Sometimes she may also be compensating a little for feelings of doubt. She is probably somewhat more sexually aggressive than the other categories—and even a little obvious about it. So she wants to use makeup to, let us say, get across her story." There was chuckle from the audience. "On other occasions, it helps her cope."

Quite a few of us could use makeup, then, Alex though wryly.

"We call her 'The Fashion Model' and she is our prime target," Susanna continued. "Unfortunately, she is also the prime target of Revlon and Max Factor."

"Thank you," said Darwin, as Susanna, relieved and elated, took her seat. "Very cogent." He waited for the audience to resettle itself, then he continued.

"So there we have the ideal customer for Regina. She feels attractive and free, and she wants to be glamorous. Yes, that's the key word—*glamour.* If we lose that, we lose the foundation of our business."

Although Darwin's voice had hardly changed timbre, it had taken on an impressive solidity. He paused and then continued in a more ordinary voice. "Now let us see to what extent our glamour remains intact. To find that answer, we did a second piece of research. Mr. James Moran, a vice president of our company, will now outline the results of that research. James—"

"Thank you, Darwin. Our task, ladies and gentlemen, was to determine precisely what is the reputation of each cosmetic company with consumers. It was quite a task!" He gave an exaggerated sigh intended to be humorous.

No one smiled and Moran hurried on. "To do this we first asked women which companies came to mind when they thought of cosmetics. The responses were generally what we would expect: The bigger the company, the more 'top-of-mind' awareness it enjoyed. Unfortunately, Regina was an anomaly; we are the second largest company in America, but our 'top-of-mind' was only fifth."

"Did the research company know what they were doing?" Cecil Rand interrupted.

"They did," said Darwin Kellogg, brooking no argument. "There are many firms in the research field. Some of them are indeed unethical and arrange research so that their results are what they think their client wants. But the bigger, better-known companies—Gallup, Roper, Yankelovitch, and many others—do objective research and report the results they find. We chose one of those."

Cecil Rand was silent.

"Next," Moran continued, "we asked half our respondents to rank the eight leading cosmetic companies on a scale from one to ten for the following characteristics: 'fashionable,' 'modern,' 'good product,' 'good for skin,' 'expensive,' 'glamorous,' 'meant for young women,' and 'exciting.'

"Finally, we took the other half of our respondents and asked them to describe in their own words each cosmetic company they knew about.

"We took all this data and tabulated it, cross-tabulated it, analyzed it, charted it—and here it is!" Moran again paused for the laugh which never came.

"We're looking forward to your results," Alex said to overcome the uncomfortable pause. Moran looked at him gratefully and continued.

"First let us consider which companies consumers think are 'fashionable.' This chart is based on a statistical correlation between the respondents. . . ."

Alex's mind wandered as Moran described the technical basis for the chart. Why did experts need to feed their listeners boring, technical data? He only half-listened for the next fifteen minutes, understanding that Regina still had a sound reputation for color, but had lost the excitement it used to enjoy. There was little news in that. Nor was he surprised that Revlon was very closely associated with color in consumers' minds, that Estée Lauder was considered to be the 'Jet Set' company or that

Rubinstein showed consumer strength in 'good product' and 'good for skin.' It was not until Moran was closing his presentation that Alex started to listen closely again.

"Finally, the most important chart of all; for this one deals with glamour—the whole foundation of the house Sir Reginald built." With an exaggerated flourish, Moran unveiled his final chart. "You will see, ladies and gentlemen, that Regina is still near the top of this chart together with Estée Lauder, Revlon, and Helena Rubinstein."

Cecil Rand smiled in spite of his determination to remain aloof. Moran beamed as if the good results reflected favorably upon him. He was just about to expand on his success when he caught Darwin's forbidding eye. "Thank you," Moran said hurriedly and sat down.

Cohen started to interrupt, but Kellogg was too quick for him. "Let's complete our presentations," he said blandly. "I shall summarize." He unveiled a chart on the easel. It was empty except for four strips of colored paper.

"I think we all agree that Regina still has quite a reputation for glamour." He peeled back the top strip of paper. Underneath was the word *Glamour* in beautifully illuminated gold letters. "And our reputation for color and fashion is still good." Off came a second strip of paper, revealing those two words delicately photographed in shades of lipstick and makeup.

"When it comes to product quality we are merely satisfactory." He removed the third strip to reveal the words *Product Quality* written in large typewriter letters.

"But, oh dear, when it comes to excitement—" He removed the bottom strip to show the picture of a woman with an enormous yawn. Everybody laughed as if there were a good joke in the recognition that the company was dull. "I think we must do something about that."

A pall settled on the room. There was an uncomfortable shifting of chairs. Alex Petersen suddenly realized that Kellogg had accused the management of Regina of rank incompetence, of almost killing a company that was the very symbol of sexy fun, of dreams that could come true—and had made them smile at the accusation. What a clever man, he thought.

He's right, Queenie reflected ruefully. Regina has lacked excitement since Reg died. So have I, for that matter. But perhaps I could do it. . . .

Bentsen, too, acknowledged to himself the correctness of the findings. At least it's not the agency's fault, he thought. We recommended exciting advertising and plenty of it.

But in Cohen's head there burned the conviction that somehow he had been tricked—and with it came another flash of anger so strong it felt almost as if he had been punched. He blinked and shook his head to clear it.

It was Queenie who spoke first. "You are right, Darwin. We need a new image. We need someone to set that image, to recapture the excitement of Sir Reginald." For one brief moment she meant herself, but it was a weak try. Her lips mocked herself even as she talked. Her eyes doubted.

It's the tiny parts of the face which tell their story, Alex reflected. How awful she must feel knowing that she cannot rebuild the company's modernity and verve. Quickly he scribbled a note, folded it, and passed it down the table to her. Queenie opened it carefully.

"I wish it were ten years ago so that you could have your just deserts," Alex had written.

For a moment she was delighted, amazed. My God, he understands, he really understands. But as fast as her elation, there came, too, the cynical thought that Alex was simply trying to ingratiate himself. He needs my support, she thought, so he's making himself likeable. Reginald was never like that, never tried to please, never manipulated me. Suddenly a wave of longing overtook her, of hunger for Reg when he was still young, lean, beautiful—a wave so powerful that she feared her eyes might spill her tears of longing; and then a wave of bitterness and resentment that, instead, only Petersen sat there, writing her silly notes. As if I'm a school girl, she thought. How dare he! She tore and crumpled the note and placed it firmly in the ashtray.

Alex watched her tear up his note, observing the glint in her eye which he assumed was scorn. Seeing her stony face, he realized that his effort had misfired. Christ, how stupid, he thought, angry at himself and embarrassed that she evidently thought him either childish or a fool. Now what can I do? I'll need her, no doubt. . . . He could have kicked himself.

Charlie Bentsen cleared his throat. "I quite agree," he said. Bentsen's statements always started with those words, but it was an affectation; for he was neither weak nor particularly agreeable. Frequently the sentences that followed contained strong disagreements. But they always started in the same ingratiating way. "I quite agree, I quite agree. . . ."

"Indeed, I have said for a long time that we need a return to the excitement of yesteryear. I agree with Queenie that we need a new image of excitement." The phrases of affirmation rolled off Bentsen's tongue. "The agency stands determined to join with its client, as it has offered to do so many times in the past, and to take whatever steps are decided upon in mutual session among men and women of good will." He paused, not sure what to say next. "I quite agree," he reiterated. "I quite agree."

"Well, I don't," said Cecil Rand. "We have the excitement of Sir Reginald. That's what we're all about. As far as I'm concerned, Sir Reginald *is* our excitement. Of course he is! What I really mean is that it's completely possible to create the excitement, but since we *have* the excitement there's no reason. . . ." He rambled on. The others, apparently attentive, ignored him. When he finished there was a silence so long it became painful. Finally, as if by general acclaim, it was time for Martin Cohen to make his inevitable statement. Slowly he rose to his feet.

"I recognize that you have conducted some valuable research in the United States, and I am aware that you claim to have conducted some similar research in other countries." He spoke in a flat, emotionless tone which, rather than camouflaging his anger, served to emphasize it. "But there are some key differences between our United States and our international divisions. Let me enumerate—"

"'Please go ahead," said Alex Petersen.

Cohen was instantly livid that Alex should thus presume to give him permission. A sarcastic rejoinder hovered on his tongue, but he managed to control himself. Coldly, almost rudely, he listed the differences between the international company and its American parent:

"We have had more new products in International in the last twelve months than the domestic company has had in three years. That is because we have recognized a need for the excitement of new products. As a result, and of course also because of tight business controls, our profits have risen by 11.3 percent per year in the past three years while our sales have grown an average of 9.2 percent per year. Over the same period, sales in the U.S. have also risen, but far less, and the U.S. company's profit as a percentage of sales has declined."

Alex recognized the figures as being technically accurate, but nevertheless misleading. Actually, International had done far less well than it seemed. The reason was that companies like Regina, which reported their sales and profits in U.S. dollars, had to convert local currencies into dollars. If the dollar weakened—as it had in the last three years relative to the German mark, for example—then it took less foreign currency to buy one dollar. Thus, all assets in such countries became worth more when expressed in dollars, even if they did not rise in value expressed in local currency. Such dollar increases showed as a profit, even though they had nothing to do with an improvement in the real profitability of overseas operations. Not all Regina foreign subsidiaries had improved their dollar earnings this way. Some, like Mexico, where the peso had fallen against the dollar, had lost money. But in total, Regina International had come out well ahead; last year International's profits would have fallen, not improved, had the dollar risen even slightly.

However, Alex decided against interrupting to dispute the profit figures. Instead he made a note to ask Posen to break out operating profits separately from currency gains or losses in the future. Also, he offered up a silent prayer that the dollar, which had been strengthening lately, did not continue to do so. With all the other problems he had, that would be disastrous.

"Even more important," Cohen was saying, "the international company has spent an average of ten percent of sales on advertising, while the U.S. company has cut back its advertising—and thus its means of creating excitement—to a mere four percent of sales.

"For all these reasons, it is wrong to consider the international company's image as being similar to that of the U.S. company. I grant that more could be done—all things human can be improved—but I think we should reject any research which suggest that we are no longer exciting." His face knotted as his anger grew. "We are a growing, profitable company internationally," he almost shouted. "It's unfair and incorrect to say that we have lost our excitement—"

Alex realized that Cohen was on the edge of his self-control. "I completely agree that the international company has done a remarkable job," he interrupted quietly but emphatically. "You have done well, Marty. But, as you have emphasized, you have not been given the tools by the head office. You have been forced to operate with many so-called new products which were not really new—"

"We must do them all ourselves in the future," Cohen interrupted. "We've never been given the opportunity. Before Sir Reginald died he kept the reins himself, and then after his death, the difficulties started. We have done more than our best—"

Alex cut him off in mid-sentence. "I'm sure you have," he said. "We shall discuss it later. The day after tomorrow I shall be in Paris. That will be a good opportunity."

Cohen was stopped short both by the determination in Alex's voice and by the sudden reminder of his forthcoming visit to France. Reluctantly he resumed his seat while Alex, anxious to avoid disruption, started to address the whole group.

"I think that we are all in agreement that at least in America, where our heart is, the company today lacks the excitement upon which glamour is built; that it lacks modernity, and a sense of immediacy and action. On the other hand, we have many assets— and the greatest of these is the dedication of our management." He looked slowly around the table. "I know I can count on each one of you to help recreate the excitement we had in the days of Sir Reginald."

"Here, here," said Bentsen, "I quite agree."

"I shall do what I can," said Queenie formally, not sure how much she really wanted to.

Even Cohen, still wracked with his silent storm, managed to indicate assent.

"Sir Reginald will show us the way," said Cecil Rand. "Definitely."

"Our real problem," Alex Petersen continued, "is that we must recreate the excitement without spending much money. For the fact is," he said slowly, "that although we have continued to report rising profits, this has been an accounting illusion. The truth is that both our U.S. company and our international subsidiaries are in dire circumstances. If we cannot turn our business around, and do it fast, we are in grave danger of spiraling downwards. Down, and eventually out."

There was a sigh from around the table, almost of relief. At last the admission had been made. The secret calamity with which they had all lived—almost as with a sin—had finally been voiced.

"Oh, I say," said Rand. But his protest was so weak as to seem like acquiscence.

Without waiting for further comment, Alex continued. "One reason we have to turn Regina fast is that otherwise the department stores, our most important customers, will lose faith in us. You all know how quickly they stop supporting a company they think has no future."

His listeners nodded. They all knew how vital the great merchandising department stores, like Bloomingdale's in New York, Rich's in Atlanta, Marshall Fields in Chicago, Bullock's in California, were to the status of a prestige cosmetic company. It was in the luxurious surroundings of such stores, at least one of which existed in every important city in America, that consumers evaluated and compared cosmetic companies. They might later buy specific products from a drugstore in the generally mistaken belief that they were cheaper there, but they would have made their decision about which companies were glamorous and exciting in the department stores. It was for this reason, Alex had learned from Hy Weissman, that the competition among cosmetic companies for the most space and the best location in department stores was so fierce. For this reason too, the major cosmetic houses paid for their own beauty consultants to serve behind department store counters, and for their own promotional advertising, counter decorations, makeup artists, and much more. Estée Lauder and Charles Revson had fought legendary battles over the best space in the most prestigious stores.

"Few cosmetic companies make profits in department stores," Weissman had explained.

"Do *we?*" Alex wanted to know.

"We do not. And I don't believe we should," Weissman sounded belligerent. "As it is, our competition is saying that our business is weakening. If we cut spending, we'll lose space and location for sure. Department stores have no loyalty when you're going down."

"The point is," Alex said, not realizing that he was mimicking Weissman's very words, "that department stores have no loyalty when you're going down. You all know that better than I do. Nor, for that matter, do drug chains. They buy what their computer tells them they sold. If sales go down, they buy less and display less—which usually means they sell less. It's a vicious circle." Alex paused, and then in a voice so emphatic as to seem harsh, he said, "Our only hope is to turn Regina around, and do it fast."

Each man and woman considered the truth of what Alex Petersen had said. In the lengthening silence, each realized that had the acquisition not occurred, the company Sir Reginald founded and built could not have survived. Even Cohen, faced with this overriding fact of his business career, could not argue the point. The question was, could the company survive even now? The room was full of doubts.

Alex allowed the silence to continue for an interminable minute before he felt it was right to start moving forward again. He turned to Darwin Kellogg. "Well, Darwin," he said, his voice no longer somber, "that was a remarkably lucid and accurate presentation. I want to thank you most sincerely. The problems are quite clear. Now what do you think we should do about them?"

Darwin Kellogg rose to his feet. "I appreciate very much your compliments," he said.

Suddenly Alex realized he had made a mistake. Bentsen's face had hardened, Queenie looked angry, Cecil Rand's mouth had fallen into a pout. Oh Lord, thought Alex, if he answers, everyone will think I'm going to let him run the company. If that's what they think they'll ignore me and try to screw him for sure.

"But," Kellogg continued smoothly, "I think that the solutions to our problem will only be found by careful discussions and considerations involving all of us."

"A wise statement," said Alex immediately and with relief.

Darwin looked at him with a half-smile. He realizes he almost muffed it, he thought. Good man!

"I very much appreciate your all coming," said Darwin.

"And I thank you very much," said Alex, rising.

The meeting was over.

There are certain restaurants in Manhattan where a five dollar bill to the head waiter is the key to obtaining the "right" table. In others it is fame which counts: You cannot be seated in the front half of New York's expensive Club 21 unless you are at least a minor celebrity; nor without a long wait at P. J. Clark's, a sawdust-floored beer and hamburger joint, unless you are a political candidate. But Orsini's is different; to get the best seat in the house, all you have to be is a regular customer or a very beautiful woman. You may, of course, be both.

Charlie Bentsen, a very regular diner at Orsini's, was already seated at one of the prime tables when Alex Petersen arrived.

Alex had never eaten at Orsini's before, hardly had time to observe the surroundings as he was swept in by the captain. Even so, he could not overlook the unusually beautiful women, with or without escorts, placed as if decoratively on either side of the narrow part of the restaurant. He wondered whether Pamela ever ate here. She was just as beautiful, but what a difference, he thought; he would never dream of describing Ms. Maarten as merely decorative. Beyond, where the room widened, Alex got the impression of airiness, ease, and more infinitely beautiful people.

Nothing like my apartment, Alex thought; nor for that matter like home. The words of the song "If my friends could see me now" came to his mind. Even after years of eating at lush restaurants, he still felt like an outsider.

"Hello, Alex, how nice to see you," said Charlie Bentsen, rising.

At the far side of the room a slight man with frizzy hair and a well-cut, conservative suit was holding court. He reminded Alex of a Shakespearean sprite—Ariel in *The Tempest* perhaps—animated, mischievous, physically active even when seated—and, without trying, very much the center of attention. On his table was a half-empty bottle of Dom Perignon champagne and sitting with him were two beautfiul women. The women laughed, the man waved and smiled at people seated throughout the room.

Suddenly he jumped up and, still waving to his friends, walked over to an imposing elderly woman being hovered over by waiters on the far side of the room.

"I see the editor of *Women's Wear Daily* is paying court to the cosmetic industry," said Bentsen. Alex realized that the woman in the midst of the waiters was Estée Lauder, the most powerful beauty monarch of them all. "I'll introduce you to *Women's Wear* as soon as he's through with the competition. He's very smart and totally informed about everything that's happening in the industry."

Before Bentsen could do anything further, the editor turned and approached their table. He was even more striking at close hand. His slight double chin and vaguely disheveled look clashed with the excellence of his clothes, and the contrast made him seem both vibrant and very human. He shook hands with Bentsen and sat down at the table. Immediately the waiter brought over his Dom Perignon.

"Let me introduce Alex Petersen," said Bentsen.

"I'm delighted to meet you," said Alex.

"Bullshit." The editor looked prankish, wickedly waiting for something to happen. Just like Ariel, Alex thought again. "But welcome to the industry anyway. We need some new blood." His hand swept around the room. "See how inbred we are," he said in a loud voice. Then, turning back to Alex, he added, "Let's have drinks one night."

"Just you and me alone?" Alex asked in mock horror.

The editor laughed. "I'll probably bring some friends."

"Good," said Alex. "I'll call you," he said.

The editor returned to his table to be greeted with enthusiasm by the two young women. The waiter brought him a new bottle of champagne. Bentsen and Alex shared the old one.

"It's good champagne," said Alex.

"He's a good guy to know. And honest—which doesn't apply to everyone in this industry."

A serene, beautifully dressed young woman with alabaster skin and an air of shyness came down the aisle in their direction.

"Who is that?" Alex asked enchanted.

"She's the beauty editor of *Fashion*," said Bentsen, referring to the only fashion magazine as prestigious as *Vogue*.

"She looks shy."

"She is reticent, not really shy."

"Very beautiful, very beautiful."

The young woman walked over to the editor who jumped up, suddenly seeming like a gangling boy. They embraced formally and murmured something to each other. Smiling, she turned away, waved to the beauty monarch, and then joined a group of middle-aged people at a large table in the corner.

"Department store buyers," Bentsen explained.

"So tell me," Alex started, feeling it was time to talk business, "what are we going to do to get Regina moving again?"

"I thought you'd never ask!" They both laughed. Then Bentsen launched into his carefully prepared speech. "I am committed to the idea that we need excitement. That's what Regina is all about. And I agree, too, that our excitement must be in context with our all-important glamour image. Yesterday, Darwin confirmed what we at the agency have long been saying." Bentsen warmed to his theme. "But to achieve new excitement, we need a *new* sort of glamour, not based exclusively on Sir Reginald but on a totally modern idea." He was just about to continue when the waiter arrived bearing food. Immediately Bentsen leaned back. "Ah," he said smoothly, "let's see what good things we have to eat."

They waited until they had both sampled the food before Bentsen continued.

"What we must do—as we shall recommend to you at a huge and unnecessary meeting when you get back from France—is to make consumers believe that all the beautiful people use Regina: Sir Reginald's old friends, Hollywood, the people in *Woman's Wear*—all the beautiful people."

"Wonderful," said Alex, verging between the sarcastic and the impressed. "Wonderful. But how do we even start to get that idea across?"

"The most important part is public relations. I realize that coming from me, your advertising agency, that's nothing short of heresy. But I believe it."

Alex nodded, interested that Bentsen would start by recommending an approach on which his agency would make no profit, but confident that an advertising proposal on which the agency would make its standard 15 percent commission would follow.

"We must have Regina and its people appear in all the social columns in New York, in L.A., even in Dubuque, Iowa. Don't ever think the columns have lost their influence. Eugenia Sheppard, Earl Wilson—they're devoured!

"Beyond that, we must appear all over the world: in the society pages in London and the visiting dignitaries columns in Japan; in *Modern Romances* and the movie magazines; in *Playboy's* 'people in the news,' and in *Fortune's*, for that matter; in *Time* and *Penthouse*; in *TV Guide*; on the TV talk shows, too." His voice crackled with excitement. "Just imagine the impact! Just imagine how, first in limited degree, and then ever more widely, the name Regina will be reassociated with exciting glamorous people—"

"But how?" Alex stopped him in the midst of his fantasy.

"Well, of course Queenie can help."

"Yes, and I hope she will." Alex hesitated. "But you know," he said carefully, "she's not quite as young as she used to be."

"I quite agree. We need more, much more." Bentsen took a deep breath, summoning his resources like a skier preparing himself before a jump. "Our first major step in obtaining the public relations we need is, paradoxically, advertising—"

"I would have expected nothing less," Alex interrupted.

Bentsen laughed, but hollowly. "It's necessary," he said almost coldly. "Advertising is at the heart of what we want to do."

"I know," said Alex seriously. "I agree that we need a great deal of advertising to get Regina moving."

"What we are aiming for is an advertising campaign using many different 'beautiful people,' known and unknown," Charlie Bentsen continued, unaccountably flattered by Alex's words. "It's the variety which is important. We mustn't use only celebrities; we must use *everybody*. All *sorts* of people; all ages and nationalities and colors. They will *all* be part of the infinitely glamorous 'Wide World of Regina.' That's what we'll call it: The Wide World of Regina."

"Like Marlboro Country?" said Alex, not quite facetiously.

"Exactly, exactly. Vistas of glamour. Rivers of fashion. Acres of Veblen. Conspicuous consumption taken to its exaggerated extreme. A world-encompassing vision of glamour. An infinite vision of Orsini's." He waved his hands grandly around the room. "That's why I suggested we come here."

"Will advertising help to get us that sort of public relations?"

"It will do much more than help. Magazines and newspapers like to support major advertisers with public relations if they can. But for most of them it's tricky because endorsement of advertisers' products is against their editorial policy. In our case it will be different. All we want is mention of our celebrities. If they're in the news while also associated with Regina because they're in our ads, we'll have our PR impact."

"Was Sir Reginald really like that, Charlie?" Alex interrupted as a thought struck him. "Was he really part of the glamorous world of the sophisticates?"

"Of course not," said Bentsen. "He was a tough old Australian bastard with a hard-on for shop girls. He had no sophistication in that sense at all. Smart as hell, and tough—but not *civilized.*" Then, reading Alex's mind, he added, "But Cecil doesn't realize that. That's why his publicity always touts him as being an elegant man-about-town. Surely you've noticed how pleased he is when he appears in the columns."

"Of course. That's why I'm wondering whether he'll go along. After all, your approach spreads the glamour emphasis away from his father. And if Cecil disagrees, we'll never attract the right celebrities. They wouldn't want to get involved in any sort of fight."

"He will definitely cooperate, and most enthusiastically."

"How can you be so sure?"

For all his professional control, Charlie Bentsen could not quite contain his smirk of satisfaction. "I'm certain," he said, "because Cecil Rand has already agreed to be one of the beautiful people we illustrate in our advertising."

Alex Petersen was surprised. He would not have guessed that the agency would be able to develop such a complete, far-reaching campaign so fast. But would it work? There was no way Alex could be sure—and the risks were great. If the company spent heavily against the campaign and it failed to catch consumers' imagination, there would not be enough money to try again. And yet, if they were conservative and spent lightly against the idea, it would have no chance. Only a massive effort would make the Wide World of Regina effective. . . .

Alex Petersen leaned back in his chair, the beautiful women, the editor of *Women's Wear,* the food, even the restaurant itself forgotten. In spite of his doubts, logical and coherent, he had felt an intuitive conviction as Bentsen talked that here was an advertising idea which would work. He tried to focus his full concentration on it. And the more he considered it, the more his doubts faded and his rational judgment supported his original intuition. The 'Wide World of Regina' had all the hallmarks of a great advertising campaign. It was memorable because the people in it represented a lifestyle to which every cosmetic user aspired. It was believable because glamour was the birthright of Regina, and this was an expansion of that idea. It appealed to all customers since it would include all sorts of celebrities. And its public relations impact would be enormous. Moreover, Alex knew that other great advertising campaigns had been used to build the image of a product. The "Marlboro Man" campaign, for example, had made that cigarette brand into the biggest seller of them all.

"I would like to see some executions of the campaign," Alex said.

"I agree. I quite agree," said Bentsen promptly. "That's what we'll show you at our giant meeting. We already have some impressive roughs at our offices."

"Oh, do you?" Alex was excited now. "Could I see them this afternoon? Maybe I can show them in Paris. I'll need something to help me build some enthusiasm over there. The whole campaign is a hell of an idea—"

"Darwin thought so too," Bentsen interrupted. "We talked about it a while ago." He was naively pleased with himself.

So that's it, thought Alex; that's where the idea originated. No wonder it was ready so fast. And Bentsen doesn't even know.

"Excellent," Alex repeated, "simply excellent. I'm sure Cecil was genuinely pleased. Please move as fast as you can with getting the advertising into the magazines and onto television. And let's hope it works."

Chapter 14

J immy Leonetti's office did not hum with action; it screamed!
He needed two secretaries to answer his phones and bring
coffee, and two others to handle the mail and the typing.
In addition, a beautiful and sophisticated woman acted as his
full-time private secretary, traveling with him, arranging his
calendar, handling his private mail, breaking dates for him, occasionally even organizing his laundry—but rarely, any more,
sleeping with him. When she had first joined him five years before, they had enjoyed sex together. But he was interested in
variety, and his energies were ever more consumed by his growing network of business dealings while, for her part, she found
that her ego was better fed by having him permanently interested
in her professionally than fleetingly titillated by sex. So they had
remained friends and she had become invaluable to his business.

"I only screw him once in a while, just to prove I'm not hard
to get," she explained to one of her better-liked boyfriends. "If he
thought I was some sort of prize, I'd never get a moment's sleep."

Leonetti's office was large and dramatically untidy. Stacks of
files half covered the floor. Books, magazines, and real estate

brochures crowded the bookshelves. The three telephones on the huge desk were camouflaged by the jumble of papers, folders, briefs, new product samples, blueprints, and prospectuses for stock offerings, known as "red herrings." The ashtrays, which interspersed the other flotsam deposited there by some careless business tide, overflowed with ashes and cigar stumps.

The most noticeable phenomenon about Jimmy Leonetti's office, however, was that it was permanently noisy. In the background was the clatter of typewriters and telephones. The main body of the noise was the cacophony of human activity: men and women shouting over poor international telephone connections; doors slamming; back-slapping greetings of football almuni turned businessmen; laughter; and the infinite babble of salesmen's persuasive, sincere, urgent pitching. Dominating the rest of the noise arose the powerful, confident voice of Jimmy Leonetti himself, as he grabbed at telephones, shouted exuberantly into the intercom—or directly to the secretaries in the adjacent room when he forgot to punch the intercom—laughed uproariously, and enjoyed himself enormously.

By character and by vocation Jimmy Leonetti was a promoter. He loved making deals. He enjoyed people, the more exciting and entertaining the better. If they were controversial —or worse—he cared little. Only if they were dull did he refuse to do business with them. He knew everyone: Mafia chieftains, union bosses, politicians, Wall Street financiers; but also priests, athletes, businessmen, inventors, writers, actors. He knew countless women: models, singers, starlets; all young, it seemed, all voluptuous. His taste in women was elementary. He wanted them gorgeous, nubile, full of laughter, and highly orgasmic.

He sat now with one leg resting on the desk, the other slung casually over the arm of his chair, waving an enormous cigar like a fat black baton in one hand and cradling a telephone receiver near his ear in the other. He exuded a sense of pent-up energy and rarely sat still for more than a few minutes. Even when he did, his fists were forever pounding at something: the air, his desk, an imaginary opponent. . . .

Even as he continued to listen to the phone he stabbed at his intercom and, covering the mouthpiece, instructed his secretary, "Get me Bandini back, sweetheart. Pronto." The word rolled off his tongue in pure Italian. "Yeah, and make it fast," he added in Brooklynese.

The girl laughed, but she moved fast to track down Harry Bandini, chief investment officer of one of the richest and toughest unions in America. He had called Leonetti an hour earlier, sounding upset.

"For Christ sake, tell him to shove it," Leonetti yelled into the telephone suddenly. "If he doesn't want the deal our way we'll go over to the other side. He'll take it if you get a little rough. He has no choice." He hung up abruptly.

"Harry Bandini on line two, sir." The girl's voice was sublime.

"Hello, Harry. What do you want?" Leonetti started his greeting before the telephone had reached his mouth, so that to the listener the booming voice seemed to rise to a crescendo.

"I'm concerned about that investment in Techno-Service you recommended. The return's good at seventeen percent guaranteed, but I've been asking around, and it's risky—"

"For Christ sake, of course it's risky. Where the hell have you been? You want a risk-free investment? Go get ten percent from your friendly bank, maybe nine. You want seventeen percent, you gotta take a risk."

"I know that, but—"

"But nothing. Shit, man, just think of the risk some of your guys took getting the money."

"Yeah, that's just—"

"Listen, I got an even better one. For a hundred, you can get a share of a new property deal I've got going in Florida. Market's depressed as hell, so we can get it cheap. Real sweet. A lot of local money's in it with me, so we can be sure of good rulings. The kicker is that on top of fifteen-and-a-half percent with a possible bonus, you'll get free hotel space. Use it for your conventions and you don't pay; or if you do pay, the money's got a rubber string attached—"

"A what?"

"Rubber string. Bounces right back!" Jimmy laughed uproariously.

Before he hung up Bandini had taken three shares for his fund.

"Another three hundred grand for the Florida deal," Leonetti shouted to his secretary above the din. "Easiest deal I ever sold."

She made a careful note into a folder.

"That's great," she said, hurrying into the room. "But you sold out on that one already. You only had two shares left."

"Yeah, I know; but I've decided to add ten more shares."

"Won't that dilute the deal for the buyers you've got?"

"Of course, sweetheart, by ten percent." He grinned at her. "But they'll agree because I'll keep it in reserve and use it to boost their bonus, if necessary. If the bonus is enough without it, we'll use it for the start of the next deal. Get Roger to draw up the notice."

"Your broker on line one," said another dulcet voice over the intercom. Leonetti grabbed for the phone.

"Listen, Leo, keep buying Associated Vending, you hear?"

"Very well."

"We've got about twelve percent of it now, right? For about ten million?"

"Twelve point three percent, ten million, two hundred and thirty thousand."

"We'll need twenty percent to be sure we have no trouble taking them over."

"Word's out that you're after the stock. If we push, the price will keep rising. Another 7.7 percent, which we need to reach twenty, could cost you another twenty million."

Leonetti hardly hesitated. "Get it," he said.

"What about API? You control a million shares. That's partly what you got for Interland and partly the purchases you made before you joined their Board. Shall we hold or sell?"

For the first time Leonetti seemed unsure. "I'll let you know," he said after a moment. "Hold it for now. I can't sell anyway without a public announcement, because I'm an insider." He hung up.

"Was that your broker asking whether to sell API?" asked the girl with the dulcet voice, walking into the room. "He called to ask whether to sell just before you came back, but you haven't been free for a second. I'm new here, and I wasn't sure what to do." She did not add that she had purposely waited until she could use the message as an excuse to meet Leonetti alone.

"It's okay. We can't sell anyway." Leonetti was paying little attention to the girl. "But next time, get any message to me real quick, okay?"

"Yes, I will. I'm sorry." She stood there, searching for something else to say. "Why can't you sell?" she asked abruptly. "And what's an insider?"

Jimmy Leonetti glanced at her closely. Pretty girl, he observed. And clearly interested. Good tits. Could be worth training. He grinned at her. "An insider is anyone who's got confidential information about a company, stuff the general public can't get. The Securities and Exchange Commission insists you can't make money by having that sort of inside information." Leonetti was speaking fervently from personal experience. On two occasions he had been accused of violating S.E.C. rules. The second time he was almost disbarred from working in the securities industry.

"But why?"

"Well, in the old days, before the Federal government established the S.E.C., speculators on the inside of companies used to make killings at the expense of other shareholders." Fair enough, he thought. Fools deserved to lose out.

"So what?" she asked, echoing his thoughts. "Nobody forces them to invest."

"Yeah, honey. But the do-gooders didn't like it." He looked at her with more interest. She smiled back at him. "And there were some real abuses. Sometimes if a company was going broke, its managers—who should have been screwed not rewarded—could get rich by selling short and then announcing the company's situation—and watching their profits mount as the stock fell." Leonetti was enjoying his didactic role. "Under the insider rules," he continued, "it's also illegal to feed some stockholders confidential information without giving it to all." That was his problem with API, he realized. Being an insider, the only way he could sell his stock would be after announcing his reasons for doing so publicly. But that would knock the bottom right out of the stock prices. . . .

Suddenly he realized the girl was still standing there. Good tits, but a little slow, he thought. He liked them with more spirit. Georgie would have flung an ashtray at him if he'd ignored her for that long. Or shoved her cunt right in his face the way she had once at a party when he'd sat down to discuss a deal instead of paying attention to her. He grinned at the memory. "Get Roger Knight in here," he said to the girl. He had lost all interest in her even before she left the room.

Roger Knight III, Leonetti's key assistant, was the scion of a wealthy, enormously conservative Boston banking family which dated back, with the Lowells and the Cabots, to the beginnings of the American colony. His father was tyrannical, reactionary and sarcastic.

"Roger, it's something of a disappointment to me," he would announce to the seven-year-old boy at the dinner table, "that when you eat, you apparently seek to emulate the manners of a horse."

"I'm sorry, Father."

"Your sorrow is noted and justified. But your manners remain appalling.

"Yes, sir."

"What did you learn in school today?"

Like most little boys, Roger could never quite recall what had happened several hours previously. When he first left kindergarten and went to his elementary school, he was always in trouble with his father over such a situation.

"I don't know," he would mumble.

Whereupon his father would lecture him severely on the penalities of not paying attention. By the time he was seven, Roger had learned to have an answer ready.

"We learned about the history of how America was founded, sir."

"Very well." His father's interest never lasted long enough to probe.

In all, Roger's childhood had been repressed and unhappy. His father was always stern; his mother Roger remembered only as a flitting, gorgeous creature, usually full of distant laughter, but on several unaccountable and terribly frightening occasions racked by sobs. He rarely saw her. Instead he was dressed, washed, and talked at by a series of nannies who seemed for the most part thoroughly displeased to be forced to look after him.

The only joy he experienced in his early years was when he was taken skiing. The moment his first skis were strapped on

at the age of four, he started sliding around in delight, an un-
accustomed grin on his face.

"He seems to enjoy it," he heard his father say.

"Good," his mother replied. "Then we won't have to stay
with him all day. Thank God!"

By the time he was six, Roger was skiing with wonderful
abandon. Head encased in a ski helmet, legs bent into the perfect sitting position, he would tear down the slopes, his skis
chattering and bouncing every time he hit a bump. After a series
of miraculous recoveries, he would arrive at the bottom and skid
to a triumphant halt at the lift line, throwing out a shower of
scraped snow.

Later he started racing, and by the time he was fifteen he
was touted as having Olympic potential. He was interviewed by
the head ski coach of the American Olympic committee. Roger
recalled him as being encased from head to toe in leather: leather
jacket and trousers, leather boots, even leather skin.

"You have a chance to make the Olympics," the leather man
had promised. "You must work hard and let nothing distract you."

Roger's elation lasted for weeks. He could hardly believe his
good fortune and he practiced harder than ever before, falling
into bed each evening at the end of his endurance.

It was then that he was hit by the first of his depressions.
By no means the worst he was to experience, it was so unexpected that he would remember it for the rest of his life. Earlier
he had suffered from time to time from moodiness. Inevitably his
father had ascribed this to naughtiness and had threatened appropriate punishment.

"If you don't know what you're unhappy about, I'll give you
something. . . ."

But those moods had been minor compared to the sense of
despair he experienced when this depression hit. Awakening
after an ordinary night's sleep, he encountered such a feeling of
bleakness that it seemed like a physical weight pressing down
on his chest and in at his temples. Alternately he found himself
utterly unable—and unwilling—to summon the energy to move,
and conscience-stricken that he cared so little. He could concentrate on nothing but the weight on his chest, the dreadful
sense of claustrophobia, and the despair which overwhelmed him
and seemed to spread through his memory of things past and

hopes for things to come. He failed to struggle out of bed that day.

The next day the abject despair had abated and he was left with a deep sense of sadness—and also with bewilderment and fear about what was happening to him. He got out of bed, but he couldn't face the ski slopes. After a few days the sadness dissipated and he returned to the ski slopes with almost all his previous enthusiasm.

As he grew older, however, his depressions became more frequent and severe until, by the time he was seventeen, his life seemed to move through a series of gray plateaus and black valleys.

"For God's sake, stop being so damned depressed," his father would say. "You have an excellent life. Why do you make such a problem out of it?" Roger, at a loss to know the cause of his depressions, worried that he was going crazy. "I'll try," he would mumble. There was no one to help him.

In the winters it was a little easier. Then he reached for his skis as for a life raft and, pointing them at some almost suicidal drop, raced crazily downwards. . . .

The risks of skiing really fast seemed to shake him out of his depressions. He switched from slalom to downhill racing and ski-jumping because they were faster and more dangerous. As he grew older he became wilder and wilder.

As the depressions became worse, coming with the power and frequency of waves crashing onto the shore, the fantasies started—of death, of suicide in a fast car. But there was never anyone to turn to; no one to understand.

On his twentieth birthday, he had a skiing accident which almost killed him and forced him to give up competition. After months in a cast, with the depressions more painful than the damaged bones, Roger recovered sufficiently to take up car racing. Driving a brilliant red Maserati, he started to make a name for himself on the Grand Prix circuit. Eventually, in a dramatic crash on a wet night at the twenty-four-hour race at Le Mans, he smashed up his car and only barely survived. He still fantasized about that crash sometimes, half with fear, half with desire. . . .

It was in the hospital, as he lay severely injured and wishing fervently that he could die, that he finally found help. A young psychiatrist diagnosed his condition and prescribed lithium carbonate. The drug helped. The worst depressions ended, and his condition so improved that sometimes he became almost happy. Even at his worst moments he no longer experienced the total despair he had known earlier, but only a feeling of listlessness he described as "gray walls pressing in."

Roger was well enough by the time he was twenty-five to enter Harvard. Eventually he took his law degree, graduating near the top of his class, and drifted into banking. He was having difficulty with his depressions again when he met Leonetti and, almost at once, started working for him slavishly. "Tough Jimmy" provided the excitement Roger had lacked since he was forced to give up racing.

"What do we know about API?" Leonetti asked as Roger Knight hurried through the door. "Everything. Fast."

Roger had anticipated the question. "We know a lot. To start with, you are into Interland Trucks in depth. They'll make good profits—"

"But less than they used to. The teamsters are raising their demands."

"Right. And the new contract's due next month."

"That new son-of-a-bitch at the local, Cassidy, would love a strike. It would strengthen his hand more than anything else."

"So he'll be tough to bargain against."

"Yeah. He wins either way. If they raise wages enough, he's a hero; otherwise, he's a martyr—"

"Which is even better than being a hero," Roger interrupted drily. Leonetti chuckled. "API's biggest division is its food division," Roger continued. "A major revenue source is a network of regional potato chip companies which also distribute Mexican tortilla chips, cheese snacks, that sort of thing. That division is running headlong into new national competitors.

"Will it make money?"

"A little, but down from last year."

"Shit," said Leonetti, but without rancor. He was expecting bad news.

"The one bright spot is API's pudding and pie-mix business which had been on the decline. About eighteen months ago, this fellow Alex Petersen started some new promotions and some rather exciting advertising. The business started to go up—"

"Let's hope he does the same at Regina."

"Right. The problem is it's nowhere near enough to offset the money they seem to be losing on their real estate."

"Cosgrove keeps saying the real estate's profitable."

"It's not," said Roger Knight flatly. "They may be making it look good on the books, but it's a disaster."

"Shit," said Leonetti again, this time with more feeling.

Actually, it's not the profits that are the main problem. It's the lack of cash. The real estate is a huge drain."

For a second Leonetti was quite still, looking at Roger. "How bad overall?" he asked succinctly.

"I'm not sure, but it seems pretty bad. I picked up a rumor that they're borrowed to the hilt. And it seems that every day less cash is coming in than is flowing out."

"But if they're still making profits—" Leonetti said angrily.

"That's not always—" Roger Knight started judiciously.

"Yeah, I know, forget it. I figured it out already." Then, moving to another thought, he added, "What about Regina? Can they get money there? Profits? Cash?"

"That's where things get more difficult. We don't have as much information. They've been getting bad publicity. But the company claims that's all it is; no real problem. Personally, I think there may be more to it. It's possible that they can do as well as Cosgrove claimed, but I suspect they've got internal troubles, personnel troubles."

"So I hear from George. She tells me everyone's at everyone's throat."

"Who's George?"

"Beautiful receptionist screws virile banker," said Leonetti. He drew an exaggerated version of Georgina's figure in mid-air. "I met poor Herman at a cocktail party the other night," he continued, his mind jumping quickly forward. . . .

"Scintillating man."

"Yeah, isn't he. Most of what he said put me to sleep. But I did pick up the same thing you're saying about the cash."

"What did he say?"

"I don't remember exactly. I said something about the 'wide boys' in England—the ones who run the gambling—always having lots of cash, while our guys put all theirs into laundries and never have a spare cent. Cash-paupers. He said something like 'aren't we all?' Then he quickly explained that he meant his wife and him, not API. I would have missed it without the explanation."

"Did he say anything else?"

"Not on that subject. But he had a point he wanted to unload. Cosgrove never goes anywhere unless it's on business. He's an ass, but a stubborn ass."

"What did he want?"

"Wanted to tell me Alex Petersen was messing up. Says he has no feel for the cosmetic business. 'Bit of a wing-tip-shoe man,' he told me. 'Even Cecil feels he doesn't have enough taste.' "

"Fat Cecil? He's a hell of a one to be talking about taste."

"Yeah, I agree. But he's been around a long time, and he's bright. Nasty, but bright. The problem is, Cosgrove and Rand could be giving out that story for some chicken-shit reason of their own. Also, I can't tell whether Cosgrove is down on Petersen because he's really screwing up Regina, or because Cosgrove's afraid he's doing too well."

"We ought to be able to find out."

"George says that Petersen is 'super.' Of course, she has a special bias. I also called Darwin Kellogg. I've known him for years. He says the company's image is improving and that Petersen has been helpful. Then again, Darwin praises everyone. Professional failing."

"Seems to me we ought to find out what's really going on," Knight said.

"Yeah," Leonetti responded immediately. "Get started by—" The intercom buzzed insistently. "What is it?" he demanded, grabbing the phone. "Oh, put him on." He winked at Roger Knight. "It's Wolfschmidt getting timid."

There was a click on the phone as the connection was made. "Now what?" Leonetti said in a weary voice quite out of keeping with the mischievous grin he directed at Roger. "Now what's wrong?" He listened for a moment. Then, all of a sudden, he took a deep breath and yelled into the phone, "That's pure crap. I don't give a damn what your bank told you. I'm telling you that they *will* take our price. Listen, Wolfschmidt, just do it, that's all." Leonnetti's voice calmed slightly. "Now listen. Just write out the check and give me the power of attorney like we agreed. Then I'll do the bargaining. Do it today, you hear me?"

His voice rose to a bellow. "Today!" He hung up looking pleased with himself. "Fucking Krauts. You always have to shout at 'em if you want action," he said to Roger in his normal voice.

Before Roger could respond, Leonetti picked up their conversation at the point it had been interrupted. "Get started by putting O'Hagin into Regina so we can get a real feeling for the figures."

O'Hagin was a rather gaunt and pessimistic accountant who was retained by the Leonetti organization for special accounting assignments—meaning he would get himself hired as a bookkeeper in some company in which Leonetti was interested and from that junior post scrutinize all the figures and pass them back to his boss. Years ago, Roger had remonstrated that this was both illegal and unethical.

"Right," Leonetti had agreed readily. "It's not 'specially legal. Nor is speeding, but it's done all the time. As for ethical, if the guy finds nothing, he's not stolen anything confidential. So what's unethical? And if he finds they're fixing the books—same question."

"Okay," said Roger, "I'll tell O'Hagin to quit checking out Patelli's. He's found everything he's going to over there anyway. He can apply at Regina tomorrow. He's good at interviews. Just the right mixture of self-confidence and servility for a permanent junior. And the resumé he made for himself is perfect for him. He should have no trouble getting in."

"The other thing is, Roger, you should go over to France and find out what's happening with Regina there. It's part of this fellow Cohen's territory, and since he's the obvious alternative if Petersen screws up, I'd like to know how he operates."

Roger's heart sank. He hated the thought of the overnight trip to Paris. The five or six hour time difference meant that he missed a night's sleep, which always aggravated his depression. "I'm very busy—" he started tentatively.

"Yeah, I know. You'd better only stay two or three days. Fly over tomorrow night and let me know where they stand before the weekend—" Again the buzzer interrupted Leonetti.

"Mr. Wolfschmidt says he's sent over the papers," said his private secretary. "I've got Bandini on the phone. Says he wants ten more shares of the Florida deal for the union and 'whad'ya mean they's sold out?' Also you're late for lunch with that deputy mayor you like so much."

"So what's new?" Leonetti demanded. The girl laughed. "Put Bandini on. He'll only take a second."

Leonetti cupped his giant hand over the phone once more. "Listen," he said to Roger. "One more thing. Find out the names of all the big shareholders in API. 'Specially the ones in street-names we're not supposed to know about."

"I'll try."

"We might need them in a hurry some day if the shit really hits the fan. Which it probably will."

Chapter 15

Queenie sat in her favorite chair in the center of her austere living room listening to the music from *Giselle*. Usually she could relax almost instantly when she heard it and, closing her eyes, recreate the vision of the incomparable Ulanova floating ethereal, tender, utterly weightless on the stage of the great Moscow theater. But this evening no image came, and her impatience made her feel jumpy and brittle. Thank God, Darwin is coming to talk to me, she thought. He has such good sense. She walked over to the record player and took off the playing head. The music stopped with a jarring cough.

Queenie paced around the room like an old lioness who hears the hunt but cannot join. She checked the plants for water and found they needed none; rearranged a book which was misplaced on the book shelf—poems were supposed to be on the lower shelf—and rejected the idea of finding herself something to eat. She would be going out for dinner with Darwin; there was no need to snack. She never had while Reg was alive, afraid that she would become fat and unappealing to him, and there was certainly no need to now just because he had left her. Might show some sign of human weakness, she thought, cynical about herself.

No point in giving in, she answered her thought. There are enough people who would gladly point out how I can't exist without him.

Can I? she asked herself. Damn, she thought, I'm having one of my conversations again. I must be getting senile. Next thing I'll be muttering out loud. On the other hand, she thought, cynical again, who is there better to talk to? Darwin, maybe. But he's twenty years younger. Almost all the people my age I really cared about are dead. . . .

She walked back to the plants determinedly and watered one anyway, just for something to do. Christ, she thought, I'm getting maudlin.

The doorbell rang as if in answer to her need. She almost ran to open it.

"Hello, Darwin. Am I glad to see you!"

"You sound like it." He looked her over carefully, surprised by her greeting—outburst, almost—since she was normally so very contained.

"Come in. Take your coat off." She helped him hang it in the closet by the door. "Don't just stand there. Come and sit down." She was chattering almost meaninglessly, her brittle gaiety in contrast to her carefully prepared, almost regal appearance. "I am so fed up," she continued, "fuming about nothing in particular." She laughed to take some of what she viewed as the childishness out of the statement. "I could stamp my foot," she said, "like a little girl. But I don't suppose it would help."

"Don't you be too sure. There is a whole school of psychotherapy that believes in pummeling pillows to get out your aggressions. Why not foot-stamping?"

"Bio-energetics?"

"That's it."

"Rubbish. Any excuse is good enough for a basic lack of self-discipline these days. Anyway, that's my view."

"Mine too. But then, we're just old fogeys."

"Are you making a point, Darwin Kellogg?" She looked at him appraisingly. "I assume you have an ulterior motive in that statement. Anyway, you're twenty years less of a fogey than I am. Don't you try to put yourself in my generation. Even with two face lifts and a positively masochistic schedule of exercises, I'm still at least ten years older than you."

Darwin just smiled at her. "If I asked nicely and promised not to encroach on your generation, do you think I could have a drink?" he asked.

"Oh, I am sorry, of course. Scotch, as usual?"

"Please. One lump of ice and soda. But I can get it—"

"No," she said, "let me." She smiled at him, noting again his remarkable capacity for making her feel relaxed. "I need to assuage my guilt for not offering." She moved briskly to the bar in the corner of the room. The ice rattled in the bucket and then clinked into the glass. "What do you think of Alex Petersen?" she asked casually.

"Nice chap." Darwin decided not to understand that this was to be the central topic of the evening.

Queenie brought Darwin's drink over to him and placed it on the small, pearl-inlaid table next to his chair. Reg had bargained for it, she remembered, in an Egyptian bazaar almost thirty years ago. She would never forget how *hot* it had been in Cairo that year. . . . She sat herself into the chair opposite Darwin and sipped the sherry she had poured for herself.

"Now," she said, "answer my question. We're not leaving here until you discuss him with me. And you'll find nothing worth dining on in my refrigerator."

Darwin laughed. "You never miss a trick," he said.

"I lived with Reg all those years. He was the past master. Always knew what the other side was thinking—"

"Was *going* to think—"

"Right. Do you remember when he—" She interrupted herself. "There, now you've got me off my question again. It's not fair." She paused. "It makes me feel so old when I catch myself reminiscing," she said seriously, "old and senile."

"You're not that, Queenie. Quite the contrary, you're remarkably sharp and tougher than ever."

"A mature old chicken—scrawny, wily and suspicious. Right?" She was pleased to think of herself so. "No one's going to wring this old fowl's neck."

Darwin smiled at her again and decided the time had come to answer her question. "Not even young Alex Petersen?" he asked, watching intently for her reaction.

"Ah yes," she said ruminating, "Alex Petersen. Everyone seems to like him. That bright young woman at your office, Susanna Brightwell, told me he's marvelous."

"Perhaps he is."

"Perhaps her criteria are different from mine," Queenie said cynically. "You're right, of course," she added. "I am suspicious of him. He's so smooth, so goodlooking and professional."

"Those are hardly indictments."

"No," she said, "that's exactly what Barbara pointed out to me."

"In her own way, Barbara has uncanny intuition."

"All except when it comes to Marty," Queenie said sternly, veering away from the uncertainty of her own feelings. "She doesn't understand the pressures he's under, and she doesn't recognize that he's strong and can take care of himself."

"Is he?"

Queenie looked at him sharply. "Of course he is."

"Hm."

"Do you doubt it?"

"Yes. I think he's a great deal more vulnerable than we think."

"He's angry, of course. I don't blame him. But vulnerable?"

"Why have you never had the feelings about Cohen you have about Petersen?" Darwin asked abruptly.

"Because he's not—oh," she said, suddenly doubtful.

"Because he's not man enough to usurp Reg's place? Is that what you were about to say?"

"Certainly not." Suddenly she grinned. "But it may have been what I was about to think!"

"I think Alex is quite a find for Regina."

"Not an accountant?" She used the term purely derogatorily.

"No, and not a weakling or a kid."

She sat silent then for a very long time, sipping her sherry and remembering the years with Reginald. The crises when they almost went broke because he overspent on some product he had fallen in love with, or because sales softened unaccountably and even his natural optimism began to flag; or because he decided movie-making—and usually some exotic star in whom he lost himself—was his life's real purpose. . . . The good times, when everything they touched sparked and the money rolled in and they could travel together for months on end, happy in each other's company, opening new subsidiaries in lands she had barely dreamed of as a girl. . . . And the hard, work-a-day times when they arose every morning at six and slaved cheerfully throughout the day to keep the multitudinous details of the business in working order . . . the constant striving for excellence. . . . What would it have been like if it had been Alex Petersen, not Reginald?

"He's not like Reg Rand, you know," Darwin interrupted her reverie. "He could never have done the things he did. Wouldn't have wanted to. But then, would Reginald have wanted to run a big institution like Regina is now?"

Queenie listened intently as Darwin spoke. "No," she answered, utterly certain. "Of course he wouldn't." She finished her sherry in one swallow. "The question is not whether Alex Petersen is a replacement for Sir Reginald, but whether he's good enough to succeed him."

"Yes," said Darwin, "that's the *right* question."

"The point is," she said with sudden emphasis, "if Petersen's not good enough we're in real trouble."

Barbara Cohen threw open the tall, leaded glass doors which connected Chateau Regine's master bedroom with the parapet overlooking the Loire. She shivered slightly as the cool morning air touched her bare skin and scuttled back into the big four poster. Near her window a robin warbled his matins, his clear, full throated song emerging like an aria through the jingle of sparrows chirping. Beyond, the warning croaks of several blackbirds, disturbed while pulling at their wormy breakfasts, provided the depth of a percussion section; and in the far distance the wail of the peewit added woodwind strains of sadness. . . .

Barbara felt beautifully relaxed in the splendor of the room, with its chintz curtains, rough pine furniture, and handmade rug; and, for once, at peace with herself. Queenie had been right in suggesting she come here to think. After only a few days, she felt resuscitated, able to cope. Yesterday she had written a whole chapter with hardly any effort. She could lose herself here, lose her worries, her fears. Later she would stroll outside into the gardens and smell the wetness of the leaves. . . .

She turned over in the bed and felt the warmth of her own body, the smoothness of her skin, against the perfect linen sheets. She stroked her breasts and felt them harden under her touch. Her hands were so gentle on herself, so different from Marty's demanding caress. One of the men in her book was gentle like this, soft and loving, like a child. He would understand the fresh loveliness of the morning, she thought. She would write about him later today, write a love scene between him and Belinda.

Barbara's hands smoothed over her breasts and hips and stomach until they felt the contrasting soft roughness between her legs. How she loved to touch herself there. If she could only write about how Belinda—who was herself, of course, as she wanted to be—also craved the gentle warmth of this exploration, adored the feel of his hands, not hard and purposeful like Marty's, but infinitely safe and gentle like hers now. She let her hands glide over her gauzy mound and insinuate themselves, so circumspectly, so very very slowly, between the smooth lips, tugging so carefully, over and over again, until she couldn't help shivering with the delight of the feeling and speeding up the motion of her fingers inside her warm wetness. Gradually the birdsong seemed to shift from the outside into her body and become fuller and sweet until at last she was filled with an incredible warmth and love and her whole body felt like the river and the song and she climaxed with a poignant, awe-inspiring tenderness. . . .

Afterwards, she lay enveloped in her happiness. That was the way it should be, she thought. Then with disappointment, with resignation, but not with real sadness, she realized that Belinda was a wonderful fantasy; it could never be like that with Marty, perhaps not with any man. Men were hard and strong, like Grand had been; or clever and devious like her father; or harsh like Marty. . . . After a while, she rose and started to write.

Chapter 16

The taxi raced down the autoroute, exited adroitly at the Porte de Clignancourt onto the Boulevard Périphérique which encircles Paris, and rushed on. Alex was amused to note on the seat in front of him a fluorescent yellow sign which said, "Please try to not smoking."

Paris had long been Alex's favorite city. He had known it first when he lived there, practically without money, during one of his college vacations. All he had been able to afford was a tiny "bed-sitter" with a communal bathroom where you washed with the water from the large china jug and emptied the dregs into a foul-smelling slops bucket. Disgusted, he had solved the problem of keeping clean with the same mixture of initiative and originality he was later to show in his business career. Each morning he would don his one good suit, pack his toilet articles into his only other possession, a satisfactory briefcase, and invade an opulent hotel. With outward assurance but a fluttering heart, he would take the elevator to one of the top floors and walk through the corridors until he found a newly vacated room being made up by the maid.

"Towels," he would demand, as if he were the tenant returned.

"Oui, Monsieur." The girl would fetch the towels and discreetly leave.

He had bathed in the most luxurious bathrooms in Paris without being caught. A year later, equally impecunious, he had tried the same trick in Rome. But at the first hotel he entered, the porter had demanded rudely what he wanted and Alex fled in confusion.

The Hotel Lancaster, near the Champs Elysée at the Etoile end, one of the hotels in which Alex had bathed, remained one of the most luxurious small hotels in the world.

"Monsieur Petersen, I am delighted to welcome you back." The old gentleman who kept the door recognized him.

"I'm delighted too, Maurice."

"Do not worry, I shall take care of your bags."

Maurice opened the large glass door, and Alex moved through with a sense of infinite importance. As he reached the free-standing elevator, all gilt and mirrors encased in a lattice-work of wrought iron, he was greeted by the head porter and by the assistant manager, resplendent in his morning-coat. The three men bowed their heads slightly towards one another, equals in their recognition of the quality of the hotel.

The elevator moved smoothly upwards and they exited into the beautifully carpeted corridor with its warm, slightly perfumed air and then entered the delightful room with its plump bed and glistening chandelier. A few moments later the bellboy arrived with the bags, arranged them neatly, and graciously accepted the tip. Then the room was empty.

Alex yawned loudly, stretched his arms above his head and wished he could stay relaxed and alone for the rest of the day. Instead, he started quickly to undress, trying to shuck off his weariness with his clothes, and hurried into the bathroom.

The entrance to Regina France was darker, mustier, but kin in style to that of the Lancaster Hotel. It might have been the residence of an older but poorer branch of the same aristocratic family. The address, just down the road from *Dior*, was excellent.

As Alex entered the elevator, it lurched desperately but managed to carry him up the three floors to the main reception area. He noticed as he alighted that the rug was worn and the floor creaked.

"What can I do for you, sir?" The receptionist matched the building.

"I am Mr. Petersen. I imagine Monsieur LeVecque is expecting me."

"Yes indeed, sir. One moment." She picked up the phone and in rapid French, with frequent sideways glances at Alex, announced his arrival.

A few moments later Monsieur LeVecque, the general manager of Regina France, emerged majestically. He was a tall man, gray himself and dressed in a perfectly tailored gray suit, and he gave the impression that no crisis that this inferior world could impose could shake his smooth politeness. The greeting between him and Alex was a parody of business etiquette; but after they entered the inner sanctum the cordiality ended abruptly. LeVecque remained in the background and Alex found himself standing isolated in a noisy, smoke-filled conference room in which the hostility was thicker than the smoke.

At the head of the table sat Sam Cohen, cigar clamped firmly in his mouth, tie loosened, forehead glistening with sweat. He looked for all the world like a caricature of an early railroad baron. The chair on his right obviously belonged to LeVecque. In front of it, the pencils were sharp and parallel, the papers neatly arranged in piles. Over the rest of the table there was a mass confusion of scattered papers, filled ashtrays, and rubbish.

Flanking Cohen and LeVecque—huddled together like chicks looking for warmth—sat the remaining European executives. Opposite Cohen, the table was devoid of papers. Pulled back from its shiny expanse was an ornate arm chair, evidently awaiting Alex.

For an interminable second Alex stood under the hostile scrutiny of the people in the room. The noise continued. He started to clear his throat to say something, but at the last moment, just before he had to assert himself, LeVecque glided up.

"Won't you take a seat here, Mr. Petersen." He pointed to the isolated chair. "I shall make the introductions.

"Ladies and gentlemen," he continued as the room quieted, "allow me to introduce Mr. Alex Petersen, the new president and chief executive officer of the Regina Company."

For a man as obviously versed in protocol as LeVecque, the fact that Alex was presented to the Europeans rather than the other way around could not have been an oversight. It was, Alex realized, a small but carefully calculated insult.

"Now, Mr. Petersen, may I present the staff of Regina Europe: Dr. Krause, the general manager of our German company; Dottore Vittorio Borelli, director general of our Italian company; Madame Housen, the managing director of our Swiss subsidiary. . . ."

Alex realized that the noise level had risen again and that each person introduced merely nodded and then returned to conversation with his neighbor. It was evidently their carefully rehearsed objective was to put him firmly in his place.

"I realize it must be very difficult for you to remember the names of all these people," LeVecque sympathized. "After all, we and Martin Cohen have been working together for quite a long time. For us, it seems easy, doesn't it? For you, it will be a process of considerable learning. Of course, we will help— But let me proceed: Monsieur Guerland-Ladoucq, the marketing director of the French company; Madame de Vourevinne, the head of European training and education. . . ."

Alex sat, hardly listening, trying to control his mounting anger. Unconsciously his jaw muscles clenched, which Cohen noticed with pleasure.

"Signore Castel Romano, who is now operating as the controller of France, on loan from our Italian company. . . ."

Finally LeVecque completed the introductions and walked slowly back to his place. The room quieted. All eyes turned toward Marty Cohen, who moved his chair back an inch and took a breath preparatory to speaking. . . .

"I'm delighted to be here," said Alex in a strong voice. Reluctantly the eyes turned back toward him. Got you, he thought, pleased to have at least slightly altered their prearranged choreography. "And to meet each of you. I look forward to getting to know you better as we move forward together into the future. The Regina Company has a strong past—but a stronger future." He knew he was overdoing it, but the very pomposity of his words gave him back some of his self-confidence.

There were several eyebrows raised in appreciation. He is not as weak as Cohen said, LeVecque was thinking.

"And now over to you. It's your meeting, Marty."

Cohen was furious to lose his carefully established advantage. It cost him an intense effort to appear relaxed. "Thank you, Alex. It is a privilege to present to you our plans and progress, and give you the information you will need to—" he hesitated, "to, let us say, evaluate our excellence!" There was a polite laugh around the table. "First, let us discuss the agenda.

"We'll interrupt our meeting to prepare for lunch. We are eating at Maxim's, where I have taken the liberty of having Monsieur LeVecque order us a light lunch. I'm sure you will not wish to eat too heavily on your first day in Paris. Do you know the city, by the way?" The condescension of the remark was superbly rude. "Never mind, we'll discuss that later. Now back to business. After lunch I suggest that we hold some preliminary discussions on the French economic situation. Then, in deference to the inevitable fatigue which comes from traveling across the Atlantic overnight, I think we should probably finish early; I've arranged for the car to bring you to your hotel at about four o'clock.

"Tomorrow, I think, the trade. We have set up a meeting for you in the morning to talk to the head of the Retail Merchants Association of Paris. Luncheon, I suggest, will be at La Fourchette, which is very pleasant. You may not have had the opportunity to eat there before." Again the biting condescension. "Then in the afternoon, a more detailed review of the French economic and political situation—depending, of course, on how deeply you wish to explore our business. The following day I have asked Dottore Vittorio Borelli to give you an update on our very challenging situation in Italy. Dottore has, as you know, run that company most efficiently—ignoring all the help he's been getting from New York!" Again there was polite laughter in which Borelli joined, perhaps a shade too noisily.

"The following day, if you care to stay so long, we are suggesting that you look closely at our German company. Our general manager, Dr. Krause, is ready to fill you in."

Nothing, thought Alex bitterly. They have done absolutely nothing. I should have made my telex more specific and demanded the information I wanted. Now they're just going to waste my time. "Is there a specific business agenda?" he asked.

"We can certainly make one up as soon as we have decided on what part of the business you would like to review."

There were jeering smiles from the helpful executives around the table. Cohen had clearly reestablished the upper hand.

"Very well, ladies and gentlemen," said Cohen. "We shall now break and reconvene in twenty minutes, in time to leave together for lunch." Clearly and meaningfully, he added, "I very much appreciate your all being here so early this morning. I believe we were able to complete a great deal of useful work."

"Good meeting!" said someone else in the room.

"Yes, fine."

"Fine and useful."

The compliments echoed around the room as the executives quickly departed. Alex Petersen was ignored. Should I stop them, he wondered. He realized he had missed his chance.

"A fine bunch of people," said Cohen, walking towards Alex. "They're very experienced, and very loyal."

"Yes," said Alex dryly, "that is clear."

"Excuse me, I have a few tasks to do," said Cohen. "I'll be back shortly."

Alex, looking and feeling forlorn, was left alone. He opened his briefcase and shuffled his papers to seem busy. The pretense was thin. A few moments later, LeVecque's secretary poked her head around the corner of the door. "Mr. LeVecque asked me to get you a copy of today's Paris *Herald Tribune*," she said in a friendly voice. "He said it would help pass the time."

It was three-thirty before the meeting reconvened. Cohen rose. "We have had an excellent luncheon," he commenced, as if addressing a gourmet club. "Now I believe that the time has come to start thinking more seriously about our situation in France. For that, it is important to understand the economic and political situation, and I have therefore asked Monsieur LeVecque to make a report on these matters."

"Thank you, sir. I shall be delighted," said Monsieur LeVecque in his perfect English. "However, since I understand that Mr. Petersen speaks French, and since my own knowledge of English is limited, I am sure you will forgive me if I make my presentation in the French language."

"Naturally," said Cohen quickly, "we quite understand."

Alex was so stunned by the pure insolence of the approach that he said nothing. Then, when it was far too late to protest, he had no alternative but to agree. "Of course. That's quite all right. I hope my French will be sufficient." He was livid at his own confusion. Of course he was tired, but that was no excuse; he had the power, and yet Cohen and his gang were breaking his neck. Then, suddenly, his anger was over, replaced by cold determination. "I shall take very careful notes," he said to Cohen. "If I miss something, you will be able to clarify later."

Alex extracted a pad of paper from his briefcase and laid upon it a golden pencil. The moment LeVecque started to speak, rolling sonorous sentences full of Gallic complications off his tongue, Alex studiously started to write. From time to time, like a schoolboy taking notes, he looked up at the speaker. Once he smiled, causing LeVecque to trip on a word. His ingenuousness was startling. Slowly the group's attention shifted away from the speaker. Alex's chair became the room's focal point. Cohen realized what was happening but could do nothing.

Suddenly, Alex rose. Without even a look at the speaker, he walked out with his sheaf of papers, closing the door firmly behind him. LeVecque's flowing sentences ebbed to a stop. Two minutes later Alex returned, sat down and stared fixedly at the speaker.

"May I continue?" LeVecque tried to reprimand Alex.

"I know of no reason why not," said Alex in surprise. "Were you not at the middle of your presentation? I trust my momentary absence did not interrupt you."

The response was so polite that LeVecque's reprimand seemed out of place. He inclined his head and continued somewhat falteringly while Alex opened his briefcase ostentatiously and put away his papers. Thereafter, Alex remained quite motionless staring at LeVecque who, becoming increasingly flustered, accelerated his remarks, almost stuttering in his desire to be done.

"And so our future lies in the hands of the unions and of the Government—mitigated by the everlasting strength of the middle class and the church, and modified by the growing power of the industrialized community and the intelligentsia of both the far Left and the far Right. I hope you can agree with these conclusions." LeVecque, slightly out of breath, ended abruptly.

"I think it's time for our coffee break," said Alex. He rose and the rest followed his lead. Only Cohen remained seated, hopeful that not all his people would leave the room. When it became clear that he would soon be left alone, he quickly rose and hurried out to where the coffee was being served.

"Come, Krause," he said in a loud voice. "we have some important matters to discuss." Ostentatiously he pulled Krause to one side.

Apart from Cohen and Krause, there was little talk as the coffee was sipped; each executive contemplated where now to place his loyalty.

Vittorio Borelli, the most impulsive of the group, sidled up to Alex. "Our company in Italy is doing remarkably well—in spite of some difficulties of direction," he hinted in confidential tones. "You heard Mr. Cohen joke that we indulge in what you Americans call 'doing our own thing.' Sometimes it is necessary. Sometimes, if we didn't do that, we wouldn't do the right thing."

"I'm looking forward to hearing about it." Alex nodded politely and went to pour himself more coffee.

Everyone in the room, most of all Cohen, noticed Borelli's approach and Alex's reaction. And everyone, too, noticed the secretary who walked in a few seconds later and handed Alex a sheaf of papers. He thanked her and returned to his seat. "I believe the coffee break is ended," he said in a clear voice.

The executives moved back to their seats rapidly. Only Cohen, although he returned to the meeting room, remained standing. "I believe the next thing we must do is to decide—"

"I have already decided," Alex interrupted. "While you're up, Marty, would you please distribute these agendas?" He held them so that Cohen had no alternative but to take them and hand each manager a copy of the detailed agenda, complete with probing questions.

"I believe the agendas are self-explanatory," said Alex. "Basically what I want to know for each country is the history of sales and profitability broken down by the industry's usual split of 'Treatment,' 'Makeup,' 'Fragrance,' and 'Others.' Then further subdivide 'makeup' into 'lips,' 'eyes,' 'nails,' and 'face.' I'm sure the data is available.

"Now," Alex continued, "it is about four-thirty so that you have several hours to collect all the figures before tomorrow's meeting. We shall convene here at eight-thirty in the morning. My car is waiting, I assume, so I shall have no trouble getting myself back to my hotel. Marty, you'd better stay here to help. Good afternoon."

Alex Petersen rose and walked rapidly towards the door. He left without a backward glance, closing the door behind him firmly. Even LeVecque, normally of imperturbable politeness, failed to stand.

At eight-fifteen the next morning when Monsieur LeVecque's secretary entered the conference room, Alex Johann Petersen, the president and chief executive officer of the world-wide Regina Cosmetics corporation, was sitting at the head of the conference table, waiting. Before him was a pot of steaming black coffee, which he had evidently purchased on his way in, and a copy of his agenda. He was talking into a small dictating machine. The secretary was astonished. For the second time in less than twenty-four hours, a member of the French Regina Company forgot the traditional forms of Gallic politeness. Failing to say good morning, she rushed out of the room to report to LeVecque, who came hurrying in a few moments later.

"Ah, you are here so early, Mr. Petersen. I am, of course, delighted."

"How nice of you to say so," said Alex as they shook hands. Then without a trace of detectable irony, he added: "I was so much looking forward to today's meeting." The sarcasm was the more effective for being apparently absent.

Cohen and Vittorio Borelli came in at the same moment.

"No chicory," said Alex, pointing to his coffee. "It made my morning."

Cohen smiled weakly. "I could do with some coffee myself," he said. "We were up half the night."

"Well, let's get started then. I hope you won't have to go on too long today."

The other general managers entered as, with an effort, Cohen composed himself. "Yes, I'd like to get going. You remember Dottore Vittorio Borelli, Madam Housen, and Dr. Krause?"

"Indeed, I do."

"We spent a great deal of time working together last night." Cohen added just a touch of emphasis to the word *together*. "We found that we were not entirely clear on what you wanted. So we felt that—"

The door opened and Castel Romano, the young man on loan to the French company from Italy, hurried in. In rapid Italian, he informed Borelli that the figures he had asked for the previous evening were largely complete.

"I suggest we could present what we have with no problem," he said.

Borelli, looking thoroughly annoyed, shook his head vigorously. "Definitely not until everything is finished," he said in Italian. "And not today in any case." Then, turning to Alex, he continued in English, "I fear we do not have the information to answer your questions. We did our best—" He shrugged his shoulders.

"Quite the contrary," said Alex clearly. "I will be delighted to follow Mr. Romano's suggestion and see largely completed the figures he now has."

Borelli's face bleached white. "Oh," he started, "I didn't realize that you—I mean I'm afraid that some of the answers are not quite right—I mean—"

"You speak Italian?" Cohen asked in irritation.

LeVecque said simply, "Mon Dieu!" under his breath.

"I just thought that it would be useful to review the answers as far as they are ready," said Alex blandly. "But if you feel they are not yet reliable, I certainly agree that they should be withheld." He felt that there was no advantage in pushing Borelli; he alone had even hinted at allegiance.

"I very much appreciate your understanding," said Borelli. "Most generous." Alex hoped he had gained at least an occasional ally.

Cohen, although shaken by the encounter, continued with his set speech. "We felt that we should hear from you more precisely what you had in mind. Your agenda was clear but we felt that we should understand more completely your underlying reason for wanting this information—especially as much of it is hard to obtain."

"My purpose in preparing the agenda was simply to obtain the data I need to understand our business," said Alex coldly. "I would like to know what lies behind your financial projections which I receive in New York."

Under his calm exterior, Alex was very worried. What sanctions could he impose if they refused to give him the data? I can hardly fire them all, he thought. In fact he knew that in most European countries—and certainly in France—firing any executive involved paying him a large indemnity and possibly making the company liable to substantial damages for "abusive rupture of employment."

Realizing that he dare not risk open rebellion, Alex continued: "You are all quite clear on what I want." His tone was neither accusatory nor angry, simply factual. "But I feel that you deserve more explanation of how the American company has started and will continue to move forward."

They all listened intently, watching to see from which direction his counterattack, if any, would come. At the moment, Cohen had the upper hand. Would Alex fight back? Perhaps there was nothing he could do. . . .

"This is the first time we have met, and therefore it is important that we understand one another. It is important for me, as your president, to recognize your strengths, and indeed your weaknesses, individually." Alex stressed the last word so that each executive understood that, although he was part of a group at the moment, sooner or later he would come up against Alex Petersen alone.

"It is also important that you understand as much as possible about the American company. After all, there can be no doubt—" he repeated emphatically, "there can be no doubt whatsoever that it is from the American company that Regina's world-wide direction emanates." He paused for so long that the words which followed were full of meaning and threat. "That is where the power lies.

"As long as things go well for Regina, we shall remain independent of daily control by API. But if things ever go sour—" He left the end of the threat unstated.

How would it look if I were asked to resign from Regina? thought LeVecque. He'd have to pay an indemnity, of course. But would he care?

Alex continued in a businesslike voice. "The major problem we face in Regina is the problem of our identity. While he lived, Sir Reginald was our sole identity. He made the company glamorous and exciting. Now he is dead. If we are not careful, Regina will lose its glamour and excitement. It will die too." There was silence and apprehension in the room. "There is, of course, a more optimistic way of regarding the situation. After all, most of our millions of customers didn't know Sir Reginald personally. To them he was only a series of publicity stories, a glamorous concept. His inconvenient death does not necessarily destroy that concept. Our products are still those that Sir Reginald created and his women used. The only problem is that his death prevents the concept of Sir Reginald Rand from being kept up to date. If we continue to equate our entire corporate identity with him, we will inevitably become old-fashioned."

Several heads nodded.

"On the other hand, we obviously cannot disavow the heritage of Sir Reginald."

"Then what is the logical answer?" Dr. Krause asked. "You are saying that we must stay glamorous," he pronounced it with the emphasis on the second syllable—glam*or*ous, "but you also say that we cannot rely on the glam*or* attached to Sir Reginald." Krause's gutteral voice made it clear that he hated conundrums.

"The answer is that we must create a new concept of glamour, a concept of which Sir Reginald is a part but not the whole. A concept which encompasses *all* the beautiful, glamorous people of today: Film stars, socialites, career women— Here, let me show you."

With a flourish, Alex pulled from his briefcase the mock-ups Bentsen had given him after their lunch at Orsini's. "This is a rough of the first step."

There was a stir of excitement. "Excellent," someone said. The advertisements the agency had prepared were fully as exciting as Charlie Bentsen had promised.

"Beyond that, we have to create a whole new sense of excitement for Regina through public relations. Regina must be part of the elegant scene. People like you must be seen in the right social circles. Monsieur LeVecque, you and your friends must help us create social prestige."

LeVecque swelled his chest. His hand stroked the lapel of his jacket where he seemed already able to feel the rosette.

"And of course we need new products, new fashionable ideas. We must once again become the leader in fashion."

"You are right, Alex," said Cohen, seeking to reenter a meeting which had largely forgotten him. "Our research and development people need a push."

"Yes. And in addition our marketing people, our general managers—we ourselves—must come up with new ideas, new and better products."

"Sales are not always commensurate with the level of excitement," said Krause dryly.

"Completely true, Dr. Krause," Alex hoped he could convince Krause without having to contradict him. He sensed that contradiction would only make the German stubborn. "We all know that in most countries half a dozen of our older, less exciting lipstick shades represent three quarters of our lipstick sales. We also know that sales of those shades would drop drastically if we didn't have exciting, but slower-selling new shades. Women want the feeling of excitement in a shade range, even if they end up buying the same old colors. They want to *be* safe and *feel* sexy."

"You are right." Krause was utterly certain.

"Similarly, we must all come up with exciting new products —even if our old products remain our best-sellers."

"I have suggested a silvering stick," Borelli joined in the conversation.

"You mean a high-frost eyeshadow or lipstick?"

"No, I really mean a stick which lays down a layer of silver wherever the woman wants it—or a layer of gold."

"Like in *Goldfinger*," said Krause. "I like that."

"Yes, I suggested it to New York. I told them sales would be terrific—but they wouldn't buy it."

"I think maybe 'they' have changed their minds," said Alex. Both men looked at him with the beginnings of admiration.

Suddenly Alex again changed the mood of the meeting. "Ladies and gentlemen," he said, "I must ask you whether there is any point in our continuing. You have not, have you, prepared the agendas I asked for?" The executives around the table hung their heads like naughty children.

But Cohen had had enough. "It was impossible to complete your agenda in the time available," he said. "While we can run our businesses profitably, sometimes we cannot find the time to prepare such thorough briefings."

Cohen had stopped only barely short of open defiance—and there seemed nothing Alex Petersen could do about it. The sentiment in the room started to waver back towards Cohen. For just a moment, Alex almost gave up. Then quickly he pulled himself together.

"Then we shall break now and I shall return to New York on this afternoon's plane," he said. "I would ask all general managers to be in the United States next week to brief me fully, in line with my agenda."

"We shall do it the week after next," said Cohen. "That will give us the time we need."

Cohen and Alex Petersen stared at each other, measuring, daring, bluffing. In Alex's case, however, the confidence was illusory. What could he possibly do if Cohen refused? For Cohen, the opposite applied: His confidence was exaggerated and arrogant. He had the power; Petersen could do nothing. He *knew* Petersen would have to back down, knew with such certainty that he almost laughed aloud. . . .

But Alex would not give in. "Next week," he said simply.

Cohen's surprise was total. He experienced also a sense of keen deprivation. Gone was his fantasy of total superiority. All that remained was—unbelievably, incomprehensibly—a business meeting with Alex Petersen and a lot of strange people staring at him and wondering whether he would fight—people who would mock him, just as Sir Reginald and Aunt Ruth had always mocked him, if he lost. They would love to see me lose, he thought. But he would be too sly for them, smart enough to submit when necessary. He would not lose, not against some upstart prick.

"Very well," he said, "we shall try for the end of next week."

Alex's relief was so great that he could say nothing for a moment. At last, feeling that his voice was under control, he said simply, "That will be fine. We can run into the weekend if necessary."

He pushed back his chair, placed his advertisements back into his briefcase, took his coat, and left the room. This time Monsieur LeVecque held open the door, and Cohen accompanied him to the sidewalk. A taxi pulled up almost immediately and Alex entered. As it drove away to the airport, he could see Cohen walking back into the building, his right fist slamming into his left hand.

Alex leaned back against the cushions, his face drawn, filled with a mixture of self-doubt and elation. I wonder who really won that round, he thought. And I wonder who will win the next one in New York.

Chapter 17

R oger Knight III had a difficult time in Paris. It was hard to
know where to start on his investigation of the Regina Company. Worse, his tiredness aggravated his tendency to depression
and, despite the lithium carbonate, the gray walls pressed at him.
There was nothing in Paris exciting enough to dispel them, no one
like "Tough Jimmy" to add zest.

Nevertheless, Roger worked doggedly and learned a great
deal about the Regina Company. The first morning he checked
parfumerie stores in the city. Then he rented a car and drove to
the old city of Rouen, where he visited several more perfume
stores nestled incongruously among Renaissance churches. "I am
here from the United States to learn how cosmetics are sold in
France," Roger explained to each storekeeper. "I wonder if you
could give me some information."

The storekeepers, flattered, talked volubly. From one he discovered that there had been no very successful new Regina
products in the last two or three years; from another, that, although Regina products were always delivered on time and sold
reasonably well, frequently there were formulation problems.

"What do you mean?" he asked, not quite understanding the French word.

"The emulsions, the creams the ladies put on their skins to moisturize them. They liquify, they separate."

"Do these sort of problems occur frequently?"

"Oh, yes," said the dealer, with a casual wave of his hand.

That day, too, Roger visited the giant Paris department store, Printemps. The main floor was largely taken up by the cosmetic counters of competing manufacturers. Each manufacturer, Roger learned, provided the decoration of the counters and the beauty consultants who served behind them—in some cases as many as half a dozen girls to a counter. Each competed in providing the most exciting makeup artists, gift-with-purchase promotions, and other "events." There was considerable prestige in having a good share of Printemps' business, so that most companies gave the store their best promotions. While Roger was there, Revlon had a magician doing card tricks to attract customers, and Estée Lauder was giving away a hundred franc gift with each purchase of twenty-five francs of their products. As a result, Printemps was bustling with customers, and enjoyed enormous sales.

Almost all the retailers shared the same attitude towards Regina: it was sound, prestigious—and dull.

On the second day, posing as a security analyst, Roger met the editor-in-chief of French *Vogue* for lunch at Maxim's and heard from him that Regina still sold good products but was losing its status as a fashion house. During the rest of his time he met with bankers, lawyers, accountants, newspapermen, fashion experts, stylists, employment agents, advertising agents, consultants. For each he developed a special story.

"I'm interested in making an acquisition," he said to a consultant. "What do you know about the Regina Cosmetic Company?"

To a fashion stylist who specialized in obtaining accessories for couturiers who did not design their own, he said, "I'm interested in opening several boutiques in France to sell fine quality accessories. Which cosmetic company would be the best one to tie up with?" The woman did not recommend Regina and when Roger mentioned it, she merely pouted.

It had been a long two days. Roger sat in his small hotel

room, condensing his findings into a streamlined report. His head was pressured and his eyebrows seemed to push into the front of his brain. It was eight in the evening. The sound of the traffic was a dirty noise beyond the smog-filmed window. Under Malraux, the whole of Paris had been steam-cleaned until the buildings gleamed in their original white stone. A law had been passed which said that all buildings must be recleaned every twenty-five years. Not often enough, Roger thought, looking through his dirty window. He wished Jimmy Leonetti had come with him to Paris. Things would be lively then. As it was, everything was dull. He wondered why he bothered to live at all.

Roger shook his head like a fighter rising on a long count. "Leave me alone," he said loudly. The grayness of his depression curled back like the devil shrinking before the cross. I'll go out, he thought; I've got to do something. He undressed and entered the shower.

As long as the water ran and the shampoo bubbled in his hair, he could hold the illusion that a friendly evening lay before him. Prolonging his preparations, he toweled himself dry to the tiniest part of his body, clipped his nails, manicured his cuticles, shaved meticulously. Finally, he dressed as slowly as his self-delusion would allow, his depression dangerously close. It was barely nine o'clock. It was Paris. He was ready—and he was alone.

He successfully used up two hours by going to a movie on the Champs Elysée. The film was macabre and worsened his mood. Emerging from the theater, he pretended to himself that he was on his way to see some friends, to whisper with a beautiful girl, to have someone ruffle his hair. He walked down the Champs Elysée, envying the couples he saw just for being together, jealous of their laughter. When he reached the park, he turned left, past Le Drug Store with its sexy, self-aware girls and slim men, towards the most expensive shopping street in the world, the Faubourg St. Honoré. He admired here a window with silk scarves at a hundred dollars apiece, there some miniature painting priced at ten thousand dollars. On the gracious Rue Royale he turned left. Then past the Church of the Madeleine and right into the Boulevard des Capucines, with graceful trees lining both its sides.

He stopped for a few moments to buy a sandwich in a stand-up store. Excellent! Momentarily the evening brightened.

But with no one to share it, it faded again. All alone in the city of pleasure, he thought miserably.

A sports car the color of his old Maserati hurtled into a side street where several prostitutes paraded. It screeched to a halt in front of one of them. After a brief conversation she entered the car. It raced off, tires cursing.

Roger took a sidewalk table at the Cafe de la Paix on the Place de l'Opéra and ordered a coffee. When it came, its saucer was dirty with spilled grounds. The car he had seen pick up the whore only twenty minutes earlier skidded to a stop at a traffic light almost in front of him. The driver was alone again.

Into Roger's mind flashed the memory of his Maserati screaming down the track so fast that the trees blurred. Then, as fantasy replaced memory, he could almost feel himself wrestling with the wheel as the road turned in front of a huge stone dike. He felt himself give up his fight to turn—and the car leapt upwards, almost flying, and spun in slow motion towards the utter finality of the solid wall. . . .

"Hello. You seem to be all by yourself," said a voice with a charming accent full of melody. A still attractive woman sat at the table next to him.

"I am alone," he said, pulling himself together with an effort. "I don't much like it!"

"May I join you then?"

"I'd be delighted."

She picked up her coffee and sat down next to him. For a fleeting moment he thought he had found a friend.

"We can go to my place," she said. "It's very close."

"Oh shit," he said, "I thought you were a friend." He got up to leave.

"Where are you going?" the girl asked.

"To my hotel."

"I can go with you?"

"No," he said. "I'm depressed—and dog-tired."

Next morning Roger's depression had receded and he worked hard all day, learning more details about Regina, but nothing that altered his overall view. He persevered only because he knew that new data turns up when one least expects it. As it happened, he was right. During his very last meeting a new piece of information which was to make a very important difference came to light.

Roger had arranged to interview a man looking for a job, a ruse which he knew worked well if he could find an applicant who knew the company being investigated and felt free to talk. Roger had found this man by posing as a member of an accounting firm looking for someone to work on their cosmetic client's business. The employment agency, which probably suspected that Roger was not a genuine employer, but was too interested in their fee to care, had submitted several resumés. Roger had picked one from a young man who had been dismissed from the French Regina Company, guessing he would therefore have no loyalty towards it and would talk openly to make a good impression.

"Did Regina make good profits while you were there?" Roger asked.

"Much better than we pretended," the young man responded.

"What do you mean?"

"Well, I was in charge of setting up a system of reserves so that when we made more money than we forecast we didn't have to tell the parent company."

"Why did you need such a system?"

"So that we could keep track. We called them 'hidden reserves.' "

"No one in New York knew about them?" Roger feigned amazement.

The young man defended himself. "Mr. Cohen, who was the head of International, knew. He asked us to set up the system."

"They couldn't have been big," said Roger.

"Oh yes they were. Why, last year we had over half a million dollars in hidden reserves."

Roger Knight arrived at Charles DeGaulle Airport in a rush, barely in time to catch his plane back to New York. Almost before he realized it, he found himself at the entrance of the 747.

"Welcome aboard. Your seat is this way." The stewardess lead him to the first-class section. Roger sank gratefully into the armchair seat. Pushing one button he reclined the seat slightly; pushing another he inflated the back support cushion.

"If the cabin loses pressure, an oxygen mask will fall automatically from the rack above your head," the chief stewardess intoned as she had a thousand times before. "Place it over your nose and mouth and breathe normally."

"Excuse me," said the man sitting next to Roger to a pert stewardess checking the seat belts. "How can I breathe normally if I'm screaming?" The girl laughed.

"Will the cabin crew please be seated in preparation for take-off," came the captain's voice.

Then the plane was accelerating and, a few seconds later, in obvious contravention of the laws of nature, it was flying high above Paris.

"The last outpost of total luxury, isn't it?" said the man sitting next to him.

"It really is."

"Like a completely isolated Grand Hotel."

"Yes." Roger put on his stereo headset. The sound of some great orchestra, piped through a flexible plastic tube, filled his head.

After a while Roger noticed that two seats ahead of him across the aisle a rather beautiful woman was rising from her seat. Restively she went to the pile of magazines and leafed through them briefly. Then she walked to the spiral staircase in the back of the first class section and climbed smoothly out of Roger's view. He felt deprived by her departure. Quickly, as though she were an old friend he was in danger of losing, he rose from his seat and climbed the staircase after her. She was standing by the bar, helping herself to some cashew nuts.

"Hello," said Roger, and then hesitated, not having prepared anything appropriate to say. "You seeemed sort of restless down there." He said precisely what was on his mind, and only realized afterwards how easily she could have taken offense.

"You're very observant." How anxious he seems to talk, she thought.

"You shouldn't be restless, not as a guest in such a luxury hotel-in-the-sky."

"I don't feel like a guest at the moment, more like a prisoner in a beautifully padded cell."

"What a pity. You ought to feel serene, you know, relaxed. So should I," he added ruefully.

Immediately she felt the loneliness emanating from him.

How silly of me, she thought. I must stop making up characters for everyone I meet. She sipped her drink. "I would like to feel serene," she said. "And I am beginning to feel more relaxed." She tossed a nut into her mouth and devoured it with gusto.

"Shall we sit down and talk together?" he heard himself asking.

"Lovely idea," she smiled.

Roger thought it was a perfectly enchanting smile. He was just about to say so when he stopped—She would probably think it forward.

"What were you about to say?" she asked, sensing his hesitation.

"Well," he started, embarrassed, "I was going to say you had an enchanting smile.'

"Oh, how very nice," she said seriously. "Why didn't you say it?"

"I was afraid you might think it forward."

She considered a moment. "Yes, I suppose I would have—a pick-up line."

"It's a pity we can't always say what we mean without being understood to say what we don't mean—if you see what I mean," he said, amused at his own confusion.

"If one of my characters attempted a sentence like that my copy editor would have a field day," she said.

"Oh, you write! Do tell me what."

"Not really. I wrote a book once, years ago—and now I'm trying to write another one, but it isn't coming very well."

" 'Lots of promise' the critics said, I suppose. Now you're worried."

"You read minds, don't you?" She was impressed.

"One of my most endearing characteristics," he said, being flippant to cover his pleasure at the compliment.

"Don't be embarrassed by compliments," she said very seriously.

"Now who's reading minds?"

"Most people don't know how to take a compliment. I had to be taught. All you have to say is 'thank you.' It's difficult. Have you ever seen how women react when someone says, 'I like your dress'? They say something like 'Oh, I've had it for years.' So the person who made the compliment feels like an ass for thinking that such an old dress could be attractive. I think one reason it's so difficult to make compliments is that we're scared of what the recipient will do with them."

"I never thought of that."

"I like your tie," she said, grinning.

"Thank you," he said, "It's very old."

They chuckled together like old friends..

"Would you like to have dinner up here, or go back to your seats?" the stewardess asked.

"Oh, would you join me for dinner?" Roger turned to her.

"I'd love to."

"We'll have our dinner here," he said to the stewardess, and turning back to his companion, he said, "You know, I'm really delighted to meet you. I think this is going to be a wonderful flight."

He is lonely, she thought. "Yes," she said. "I think so too."

They were quiet for a few seconds, and Roger thought how strange it was that they could already accept silence together. Usually that came only after a long friendship.

"The nice thing about luxury hotels-in-the-sky is that it's possible to indulge in friendship without the risk of everlasting-ness," she said suddenly. "I suppose that's why people fall in love so easily on cruisers."

Roger hesitated. "Perhaps we can pretend this is a mini-cruise?" he asked tentatively.

"Perhaps," she said pensively. Then, seeing the hope in his face, "Yes, I like the idea. I really like the idea. Let's be on a mini-cruise." This time she knew that his relief was not just her fan-tasy. In a more ordinary voice she continued, "We haven't intro-duced ourselves yet. My name is Barbara, but I'm not going to tell you my second name because this is a temporary cruise, and that will make it seem too permanent."

"I'm Roger," he said simply.

They smiled at each other.

"Tell you what," said Barbara. "I'll describe a little about myself, so that you know who I am. Then you can tell me about yourself."

Roger nodded in agreement.

"Well then, I'm twenty-nine and a somewhat fraudulent writer, as I said. I'm married with two children, girls—one is four and one is eight—and they're very pretty. One day they will be beautiful, particularly the eight-year-old."

"You are very beautiful too," said Roger.

"Oh, not—" She stopped herself. "Thank you," she said. "Now don't interrupt anymore. I'll lose my train of thought. I'm married, but it's not a very happy arrangement and I don't think I want to talk about it too much."

He looked at her inquiringly.

"This has become such a soft evening, and we seem so warm. To bring in the anger and the pain and the shouting, and all the plain nastiness, the exploitation—that's not—it doesn't feel—" She paused, not sure how to continue.

"Why don't you just walk away?"

"I don't know why. I worry about the effect on the girls, of course. But that's not the only reason. Perhaps it's that I think he needs me too much. Not that it seems that way. But sometimes his rages are so violent. And if he were alone—" She paused. "I suppose I will one day," she said sadly. Then she brightened again. "But let me tell you the other things about myself. I'm delighted with this game! I was born in New York, and I love the city; it's exciting. I don't think I could even pretend to write if I didn't live in New York—"

"I don't like your putting yourself down about your writing," he interrupted. "I've never read your book, but my sense is that you don't lack talent or discipline. To me you just sound as if you're scared."

"Yes," she said, looking at him with growing admiration. "Yes, I suppose I am scared. You're right—it's because I don't really think that I lack talent. If I *knew* I had none it wouldn't be so frightening."

"Perhaps you have a very great deal."

"I should say, *oh no*. But yes, perhaps I do. That's why I continue to write. I so hope that I have—and the discipline to go with it."

"I know it sounds presumptuous, but I really think it will be good. I feel a muse sitting on your shoulder!"

"Do you?" she asked seriously. "I half believe it's possible to sense musicality or writing talent."

Roger, who was not expecting her to take him so seriously, looked surprised.

"You see, the creative process has to do with an ability to express yourself through media other than surface coherence. That's more obviously true in composing or abstract painting than in writing; but even in writing, the flow of the words, the hidden meanings and the feel of them, is communication which goes deeper than surface comprehension. It seems to me that if the artist has such communication potential, then it could be noticeable in him."

"An aura?"

"Not exactly an aura, although that's probably a useful analogy. I really mean some sort of extrasensory communication."

The stewardess arrived with their dinner, served with tasteful silver, bone china, and white linen. Their talk was intimate and soft. At one point, speaking of her children, she talked more about the effect divorce might have on them, and her eyes filled with tears. Quite naturally he reached across the table to hold her hand.

"I'm afraid I forgot to tell you when the movie started about an hour ago," the stewardess said as she cleared away. "I hope you don't mind missing it."

"Oh, we don't mind at all," said Barbara.

"Not at all," he echoed.

Roger's description of himself started gradually, first with the business facts. He talked at length about Jimmy Leonetti, describing with gentle humor some of his idiosyncrasies. His devotion was obvious.

"What happens if you don't agree with him?"

"We fight."

"And—"

"Sometimes I convince him. Sometimes he lets me win. Sometimes he convinces me." He smiled at her. "And sometimes none of those things happen and he tells me to do it his way."

"How does that make you feel?"

"It depends. Not too bad, usually. Except when my depression is close—" He hesitated, somewhat embarrassed.

"Does that happen often?" she asked.

He hesitated again. "Yes. Often," he said with rare openness.

"Gray walls?" she asked.

He was amazed. "How on earth—"

"I had a friend who described depression to me once. Gray walls pressing on him. He had to keep moving."

Barbara put her hand over Roger's. "Tell me," she said simply.

Talking softly, out of place and time, he confided in her; told her about his blackest moods, his teenage and student years when the depressions had threatened to swamp him altogether, his fantasy of smashing himself to pieces in the Maserati, his bouts with the psychiatrist, his fear that he was mad, his eventual recognition that depression was a disease, probably chemically induced, and now his frequent periods of grayness. He talked to her as he had never talked before. She, for her part, felt a gratitude from him which she had never received from anyone. . . .

The captain, requesting on the intercom that all passengers return to their seats for landing, interrupted their out-of-time sojourn long before they were ready to give it up.

They were silent and helpful to each other as they cleared immigration and then customs. When they had collected their bags, he got her a taxi. As her bags were stowed and she entered the cab, his sense of loss became too great.

"I want to see you again, Barbara," he said.

"I know; so do I."

"Is it alright?"

"Oh, yes.'

"But we'll lose our anonymity then."

"It was only a game. Nothing is lost if we decide to stop playing."

He smiled at her. "We'll have a formal dinner together and decide whether our everyday selves have as much in common as Barbara and Roger."

"I'd like that," she said. "I'd like that very much. Tell me your name. I'm Barbara Cohen. Here's my number. I'll call you."

He gave her his business card. As the taxi departed she smiled and waved at him.

For the first time in as long as he could recall, Roger Knight was really happy.

Chapter 18

Pamela Maarten and Alex Petersen were both mildly apprehensive as they prepared for their first evening together. She, in her apartment, fussed over which jewelry to wear with the simple black dress she had chosen. Eventually she settled on a delicate pearl brooch she had bought wholesale in Tokyo. He, in his apartment a few blocks away, tried two different ties before finally settling for a third which seemed to achieve just the right amount of dash without seeming flashy. He felt slightly ridiculous changing ties.

As his cab pulled up to the apartment building, Alex was surprised to see Pamela chatting to the doorman, a dignified black man with white hair who towered over her protectively. She waved gaily to Alex and was at the cab's door before Alex could even get it open. " 'Bye Joe," she called to the doorman.

"See you later," the doorman called back. "Be good!"

"Be good?" Alex asked as she jumped into the cab.

"He thinks he's my father," she laughed. Alex raised his eyebrows. "Lots of people do," she said simply. "When you're barely over five feet you get a lot of protection whether you need it or not." She smiled at him. "I'm glad to see you," she added.

"I hope I didn't keep you waiting."

"Oh no. I always get downstairs a few minutes early so I can talk to Joe. He's such a nice man and so lonely since his wife died."

Her compassion pleased Alex. She was much warmer and more natural than he remembered. Almost girlish, but without being silly. Suddenly he realized that they were sitting in the cab going nowhere. "One If By Land, Two If By Sea," he said to the cab driver. "That's—"

"What?" both the cabbie and Pamela interrupted. "Whaddayou want?" the driver repeated, while Pamela laughingly said, "I'm not dressed for warfare."

"It's a restaurant."

"Never heard of it," said the driver, giving every indication that he did not intend to learn.

"It's in the Village," said Alex, a slight edge coming to his voice. He gave the address. "Let's go," he ordered. The cabbie remained stubbornly silent, but he pulled the car away from the curb, bounced into a pothole, and took off in the proper downtown direction. Pamela and Alex, jostled backwards in their seats, grinned at each other.

Alex had given some thought to the restaurant and it turned out to be ideal. Its beamed ceiling, early New England artifacts, and giant old fireplace gave it a warm and friendly atmosphere. The pianist, who usually played background music alone, was accompanied this evening by two of his friends. They played happy old tunes together and interspersed them with a lot of friendly banter.

The head waiter greeted Alex warmly. "I've given you a table upstairs," he said as he lead them up the slightly creaky staircase to the wooden balcony. "Up here you can still hear the music, but you can talk too."

"It's a lovely place," said Pamela when they were seated. "A good choice."

"Thank you."

The waiter came to take an order for drinks.

"I'd like some red wine, please." She spoke directly to the waiter.

Alex ordered the same and the waiter left. "You know what you want," he said, pleased by her decisiveness.

"For the small things it's easy."

"And for the larger ones?"

"Some of them. For example, I've always known I wanted to work."

"At journalism?"

"No, I didn't know what I wanted to work at. Just that I didn't want to be a housewife. And that I did want to travel. Both were considered out of the question when I was a girl."

"Cooking, sewing, marriage, babies, and church work?"

"Well yes, except that where I lived there wasn't too much church. That's not a lower-middle class ideal. Westchester County and Harlem—the extremes—are strong on church work. My Dad was grass-roots union and Mom was with the union wives and into complaining that Dad drank too much beer."

"Did he?"

"Only if you think a couple of six packs a day is too much."

Alex laughed. "Did you have brothers and sisters?"

"Two sisters. Noisy!"

"So was my family. I was browbeaten by the noise."

"I just knew I had to get out," she agreed enthusiastically. "When I saw the dishes some evenings, and Dad belching, and the TV set, I could have screamed. I did once, screamed my fool head off. Dad just told me to shut up. It was the inevitability of the whole thing that got me. They just couldn't imagine that there could be anything else to life. This was how it was, and would be for ever and ever. My sisters both just naturally assumed they would get married like Mom did, and Grandma before her, and have kids of their own. They were right. They did get married and have kids. And they are living out the same lives as we did when I was growing up. The same women's complaints. The same beery Saturday night bash. The same endless piles of dishes. Hair in curlers during the day. Not a book in the house." She smiled ruefully. "I'm aberrant," she added.

"It must have been difficult to break out."

"It was," she said with a sigh. "Almost impossible. Not the practical problems so much. It was the assumptions which were so difficult to fight. Everyone—my parents, my sisters, the school, the whole community—just assumed that girls would get married, pregnant, and fat—not necessarily in that order. All my girlfriends were boy crazy. By the time I was in high school, boys were all anyone talked about. And whether they had missed their period. And if they had, would he marry them. He always did."

"The gradual day, leaking the brightness away," he said.

"Stephen Spender," she said, slightly triumphant at recognizing the quotation. "Yes, that catches the problem exactly. Sometimes I almost gave in. Except the boys were so dull and so one-tracked. Talk about groping! Also, I didn't grow to my present towering height until I was seventeen, so I was absurdly small. In a way, that saved me. I seemed too young to go steady, and by the time I looked old enough I'd got away."

"It was easier for me, I think. A boy has more freedom."

"Not that easy, I imagine."

"Well, I did get itchy." He smiled, amused at his own understatement. "I had to do something to use up my energy, and there was an old wall where the richer kids practiced their tennis strokes. I got hold of an old racket and some balls and went there most days and pounded the hell out of that wall. It helped, but I was still jumpy."

"My God," she agreed, "I used to get as jumpy as if I was on a caffeine jag!"

"How did you get away?"

"I met a friend—" she started, but then hesitated. Their conversation had started too rapidly, she thought. She was not ready to talk about Martha yet. . . .

The waiter arrived with the menus, giving her the opportunity to change the subject. "I'll tell you about that later," she said. "Let's concentrate on what to eat."

As she investigated the menu and made small talk with Alex about the food, Pamela remembered Martha. I haven't talked to her in so long, she thought guiltily. It was Martha, the big-city newspaper woman passing through town on an assignment, who gave Pamela her chance to break out. Martha was visiting the school where her country cousin taught when Pamela bumped into her.

"Sorry. I was going too fast."

"No harm," Martha said. "Where the hell can I smoke a cigarette without all these no smoking signs staring at me?"

"In the lounge. I'm going there. I'll show you."

"Like one?" Martha asked. Pamela, then just seventeen, was

captivated to be treated as an adult by this older woman. Martha, it turned out, was fifteen years her senior.

By the end of the afternoon, they had become friends and Martha decided to stay over for the weekend. Pamela was ecstatic. Martha was proof that there was more to living than kitchens and babies, and as she talked of New York, of her newspaper assignments, of traveling and of the celebrities she had met, Pamela's ambitions all crystalized into the determination to become a journalist too. Later, on that rainy Sunday afternoon in Martha's motel room, when the older woman initiated Pamela into a form of sex she had only heard whispered about, Pamela felt that she now had the ultimate weapon to break away from her small-town life.

"Men are fun," Martha explained, "but women together can be fun too. And with women you don't have to lose your identity."

Pamela hardly understood. But when Martha left, she found in herself a new strength and self-confidence which made the last months at school bearable and gave her the determination to leave home right after graduation.

"I can recommend the stroganoff," Alex interrupted her thoughts. "Or you can be safe with a steak."

"I'll have the lobster," she said to the waiter, "and a bibb lettuce salad." She grinned at Alex "No offense," she said. "It's just that I don't like stroganoff. And I hate being safe!"

Extraordinary how competitive she is, Alex thought, as he ordered his own food. Yet she doesn't seem hard. He smiled at her.

"It's nice here," she said, returning his smile. "I'm afraid I'm talking too much—"

"No you're not," he assured her. "You were going to tell me how you got away."

"Ah," she said, "I ran away to the evil big city and broke my poor mother's heart." She was being flippant but there was a great deal of truth in what she said. Her parents both felt so insulted, Pamela remembered. As if I were slighting them personally by choosing to leave.

"And when you got to the big city?" Alex asked.

"I stayed for a while with my friend. And I got a job at the copy desk of the *New York Times*. At night I went to New York

University and studied journalism. When I graduated I joined *Business World.*"

"Small town girl makes good?"

"Not exactly. Not that fast. At first it was drudgery, checking out facts and figures at the company library. It was a big treat when I was allowed to check facts at some other library!"

The waiter served their food and they both tasted it.

"Excellent," she said, her enjoyment very evident. "Going out like this will always be a treat for me."

"I know. I feel the same way. Is this really me, Alex Petersen, the carpenter's son?"

She laughed at him sympathetically. "I know exactly how you feel. Exactly."

"Go on, tell me about what you did at the magazine."

"Oh, well, I got to answer phones, proofread unusable manuscripts, attempt opening paragraphs which were always altered and rarely printed, and listen to seasoned journalists air their cynicism over yesterday's soup at the company cafeteria—"

"The cynicism entirely missed you," Alex chuckled.

She grinned back at him. "You're quite right. I developed a serviceable protective layer."

"How did you move forward?"

"Partly seniority, and having learned the basics."

"Of course; but there were surely others who achieved as much and never became *the* Pamela Maarten—"

"Oh, come on." She was almost flustered.

"I'm perfectly serious. You know you didn't get the powerful reputation you have just by seniority and knowing your trade."

"Well, I did get a big break which got me started. It was when I was asked to research the Singer Sewing Machine Company in 1974. They were expanding vigorously in the computer business—"

"I remember."

"I looked up all the facts, read all I could, and the company's strategy made no sense to me. So I decided on my own to do some inside investigation. What I learned convinced me they really were headed for disaster."

"You must have been excited."

"I was. Wildly. I rushed back to the office and wrote up a

whole article on Singer which predicted that they would have to close down their computer operation within less than a year and that doing so would damage the company terribly, if it didn't destroy it altogether. I slaved over that piece for a whole day and the following night, polishing the words, checking all the facts—"

"And the article made you? It all turned out as you predicted."

"Yes. It turned out just as I predicted. And I made quite a name for myself at *Business World*."

"And outside, I imagine."

"Well, not exactly," she laughed. "You see, it was never published. Too controversial. Not enough proof. I tried to persuade them for nine months without success. Then in 1975, Singer lost an astonishing $452 million and almost went under. I became *Business World's* pet prophet. Now they let me publish almost anything I want." She became very serious. "It's a responsibility," she said quietly.

"Do you ever make mistakes, wrong predictions?"

"Of course I do. I try to be accurate and fair, but sometimes I blow one."

"What does that do to the company you're writing about?"

"Sometimes nothing. Sometimes it hurts them."

"I hope you don't hurt us."

"No business, you said. Remember?" She was angered beyond the degree justified by his remark. Was it because she knew that her article on API was going to hurt? He wondered.

"Sounds as if you have a bad conscience."

"Oh really, Alex," she said even more crossly, "that's an absurd thing to say. Why would I have a bad conscience if I write the truth?"

It was Alex's turn to be annoyed. She sounded so superior. "If you are so sure of what truth is, you have solved a problem which has eluded our savants."

"I'm talking about business facts, not philosophies of truth. A balance sheet isn't that complicated—"

"I don't agree with you. There can be large variances in the meaning of the figures on a balance sheet. You should know that. Surely the Singer balance sheet looked good when you first looked at it. The truth only emerged gradually. And even then there must have been some doubt, otherwise your editor would have printed the story."

"Nevertheless, there *are* facts to be unearthed and reported." Her voice sounded stubborn. "Facts I can be sure about, whatever my editor thinks. I'm paid to find those facts and interpret them correctly—even though half the time companies in trouble hire gangs of accountants to mislead," she said, realizing he was right but hating his lecturing tone.

"That's rash nonsense," said Alex, incensed.

"The hell it is. When things are going wrong, corporate accountants always splash whitewash around."

"That is a completely scurrilous statement," Alex said coldly. "Exaggerated beyond all justification. Of course there are cases of whitewash. There is dishonesty in every field. There is also the question of optimism. A manager may honestly feel he will do better than he ends up doing—and, in the meantime, the figures he publishes may reflect some of that optimism. But that is wholly different than whitewash." Alex wondered how much of his anger at her was due to his own vulnerability, and how much of his lecture was a rationalization. Were Bryant and he whitewashing Regina's performance?

"Is that what you're doing at Regina?" she asked, sensing the direction of his thoughts.

"For Chrissake," he said bitterly. "I thought this was to be a social evening."

"Now who sounds as if he has a bad conscience?" Her question, childishly phrased though it was, punctured to the very center of his thought.

"Goddamn it—"

They sat glaring at one another. For a moment Alex considered simply leaving this opinionated, angry, beautiful woman. That would teach her a lesson, he thought peevishly. But he wanted to stay.

Pamela, too, considered walking out. He is so arrogant, so pompous with his lectures, she thought. She was angry enough to shake him, angrier than she had been for a long time with anyone, she realized. She wondered how he had gotten so far under her skin.

The music grew louder, drowning the conversation from the other tables. They had finished their food. They were angry and arguing. Each wondered what to do next.

"Let's call a truce and dance," Alex suggested suddenly.

She looked reluctant.

"You can lead," he said smiling.

"You bastard!" She laughed in spite of herself.

For several hours they danced and joked and talked. She told him of her near marriage to a brilliant writer who, in the end, had turned out to be too possessive for her independent nature. And in response to her questioning, he hesitatingly told her about his marriage and divorce, and how guilty he had felt.

"You still do?"

"No. She remarried and now she's happy."

"And you?"

"I don't know. I'm enjoying myself this evening. But happy? I used to think I was. Now I don't know." It was the first time he had voiced that thought to anyone.

They left the restaurant only when the waiters started rattling chairs. In the taxi on the way back to her apartment, they held hands. When they arrived, he accompanied her through the lobby and up the elevator. At the door of her apartment they hesitated. Each realized they wanted the other; they had felt their bodies pressing at each other when they danced. But each perceived too that it was still too soon. Somehow, they sensed, they would become better friends if they waited. There should be more commitment. . . .

She opened the apartment door, still not sure what to do, half wanting to prolong the evening by inviting him in for a drink, half realizing that if he entered they would more or less have agreed that he would stay.

He drew her to him, intending to kiss her good night and leave. She held up her lips and they kissed gently. She seemed incredibly soft to him, so soft that suddenly he wanted her so strongly that he trembled. He pulled her towards him and her desire rose to match his.

At precisely the instant that he was deciding to scoop her up and carry her into her bedroom, kicking shut the door behind him—and she was deciding that if he did, she would welcome it—the elevator opened and a large, rather, drunk man stumbled out. Alex and Pamela drew apart.

"Don't mind me, kids," he said thickly, leering. "Carry right on." He fumbled with the key to his apartment and disappeared inside.

"It was a lovely evening," Pamela said, reaching on tiptoe to kiss Alex briefly.

"Yes," he said, also realizing that the spell of their excitement was broken. "Yes, it was. Can we repeat soon?"

"Anytime you like," she said.

"Next time, can we make the evening a little longer?"

"Longer?" she asked. "Isn't it late enough?" She glanced at her watch. "I've got to work tomorrow." Then she saw him smiling down at her. "Oh," she said, suddenly blushing. "Oh, I see what you mean." She paused for a second considering. "Yes," she said. "Yes, I'd like you to stay longer next time."

"I'll call you tomorrow," he said, feeling elated.

"No need to call," she reminded him. "We'll see each other at the analysts' meeting."

"Oh, yes. I'd forgotten."

"Good luck," she called after him as he walked towards the elevator.

"Thanks," he said.

"You're welcome," he heard her say as the elevator closed. "You'll need it."

Chapter 19

Herman Cosgrove was nervous about the presentation he was about to make to the security analysts. Such meetings became necessary whenever the investment community started having doubts about a company. Like skittish horses, they needed the reassurance of a calm voice, Cosgrove thought. But he knew they could be like jackals too, tearing at any weakened body.

On previous occasions when he had talked to the analysts, he had nothing to hide. Now the situation was different: API was desperate for cash and only if he could obtain some good publicity, Cosgrove felt, could he expect more money from the banks. But it was a hell of a risk. If someone trapped him into saying the wrong thing, API would be finished.

Perhaps, he thought, he should have let young Petersen handle it after all, instead of taking over himself. At least that way the analysts would have had to limit their questions to Regina rather than being able to probe into API. Or he could have left the group as a small luncheon gathering, the way that colonel fellow from Regina had set it up, rather than tripling its size and making it into a formal afternoon conference. That way less harm would result if he did make a mistake. But no, neither way would have generated the publicity he needed. He *had* to persuade the analysts, and through them the investing community, that API was still strong. Otherwise another stock price decline would start, the banks would not even consider new loans, it would be over. . . .

Nothing should go wrong, Cosgrove told himself for the tenth time. I've just *got* to make it work. He had schemed so long for his position at the top of API that he could not stand to lose it now. His preparations had certainly been thorough enough. As regards Regina, he had been fully briefed by Petersen, in writing and in person; and as for the rest of API, he and his speech writer had refined his speech until neither could improve another word. Nothing should go wrong. Nothing. He would see to it. But the nervousness continued.

The analysts were diverse in age, sex, experience, corporate affiliation, and appearance; but they were all cynical. Each represented a major bank, insurance company, pension fund, or investment banker; and each was constantly exposed to carefully muted hyperbole from one company or another seeking to boost the price of its stock. The Security and Exchange Commission forbade any form of false statement. But there was no law which said that the legitimate activities of a company could not be described in an impressive way. This was done all the time. It was the job of the security analysts to advise their investors which companies were really sound and which were merely telling their story well. Thus, they listened with deep skepticism to the presidents and chairmen who addressed them and often they asked questions as much to trip as to learn. Still they were frequently convinced by the virtuoso performance of some persuasive chief executive. Again and again, business tycoons presented their case to the security analysts of Wall Street—and pushed up the price of their stock.

"Ladies and gentlemen," Herman Cosgrove commenced, "I am delighted by this opportunity to speak to you and I would like to thank the organizers of this event, and of course all of you for attending."

The audience settled.

"The performance of Associated Products Incorporated has been good." He was careful not to sound as if he were exaggerating. "We believe that this has been partly because we have been very successful in some of our acquisitions."

There was a restless movement from the audience at the words *very successful.*

"Now, when we acquired the Regina Company, *Business World* suggested it was 'perhaps the worst blunder that API has ever made.' I believe they have been proven entirely wrong."

There was a skeptical mutter from the audience. Cosgrove waited for the silence to resume.

"I suggest to you, Ladies and Gentlemen, that on this occasion, *Business World* did not adequately conduct its research." He paused. "They completely failed to realize the size of some of our other blunders!"

There was a momentary interval and then, like the thunder following the lightning with a few seconds' delay, a giant laugh rose. The rest of the presentation went smoothly.

"Another salesman makes another sale," Alex whispered to the colonel sitting next to him when the president finished to a solid round of applause.

"Yes, sir," said the colonel. But his response was not as confident as usual. Questions were a tradition of security analysts meetings and they could be barbed.

The first question, however, was simply a request for information. It came from a respected analyst representing a conservative—and very large—pension fund.

"Is API's liquidity adequate? Do you have enough cash?"

The president had, of course, expected the question. He and Asquith had discussed for over an hour how best to answer it. A flat denial of any shortage of cash would be unbelievable—and so inaccurate as to leave the president vulnerable to a charge of misleading his audience. On the other hand, he certainly did not want the audience to realize how desperate a problem API's cash shortage had become.

With a broad smile at the questioner he said, "In all my experience in big business, I have never found liquidity to be adequate. Neither at work—nor at home—do I have enough cash!" There was a murmur of laughter. "We do have what it takes to run the company at the moment."

"Thank you," said the questioner. He and the rest of the audience evidently accepted the response. The president was tremendously relieved. He was over the biggest hurdle of all. Dammit, he *would* persuade them that API was strong. If he could just stop the adverse rumors, perhaps the banks would lend them some more.

A young woman in the front row jumped to her feet. "How much profit are you planning to make this year from the vanity of women?"

"None whatsoever," Cosgrove shot back. The audience laughed appreciatively.

"Seriously, though, you've indicated that Regina profits will be about twenty million this year. Are you still on that target?"

"We are on target for this year. As for the future, we anticipate that Regina's profits will continue to grow."

"Isn't all this business of cosmetics rather a passing fancy?" A long-haired young man, a newcomer to the analysts' group, started to launch into a diatribe. "This business of painting and perfuming yourself. It's all a waste of money anyway. And with consumerism—"

"What brand of aftershave did you use this morning?" Cosgrove interrupted. The young man blushed as the laughter rose.

The moment the next questioner arose, Cosgrove sensed trouble. He seemed thin and sinister, dressed in a tight black suit, his hair unfashionably oiled close to his head, his face as emaciated as a skull.

"It is rumored," he said, his voice as dry as he looked, "that Regina's accounts receivable have approximately four million dollars of uncollectibles. Would you comment on this widely heard rumor?"

Immediately the audience was silent. The skullman stood very still. Even though Alex had mentioned the existence of the problem, the president's heart sank. He had hoped nothing as specific as this would come up. At least not with such an accurate figure.

"Regina does have certain accounts receivable which may not be fully collectible." He spoke urbanely, knowing that his only chance lay in putting on a good front. "However, I would be disappointed if the amount turned out to be nearly as large as you imply. In any case, we were fully aware of the problem, such as it is, before the acquisition. It is nothing much to worry about."

"I am worried," said the skullman with finality.

"Since your worry is hardly justified, sir, perhaps there is an organic reason for your feeling." Cosgrove smiled to imply that he was joking, but there was no laugh from the audience.

The dark man remained standing, completely unaffected. "Does this receivables problem aggravate API's overall cash shortage, which I think is more serious than you have implied?" he asked.

"It does not," said the president promptly and definitely.

"Does Regina have a cash shortage?"

"No." In spite of his emphatic denials, he noted that some of the more experienced analysts were looking interested or making notations. No doubt there would be closer investigations of API's cash situation in the coming days.

"Are there any other questions?" Cosgrove asked quickly, looking at the rest of the group.

"I have another question." The skullman remained imperturbable.

"Perhaps we should give someone else a chance."

The audience, aware that the skullman was discomfiting the president, kept silent.

"Since there are no other questions, I shall continue," said the skullman. "My next question deals with Regina's inventories. I understand that you have a substantial amount of obsolete inventory. Would you comment?"

"Well, of course Regina has some inventory obsolescence. All cosmetic companies do. However, we should be able to keep it under control."

"I understand the obsolete inventory figure is between fifteen and twenty-five million dollars."

Someone must have told him, the president realized, and with that recognition came the parallel one that he dare not deny the allegation entirely. Petersen had warned him that there might be a substantial problem of obsolete inventory. In fact he had confirmed it in writing. I should never have let him do that, Cosgrove thought, and glowered at Alex. Now I cannot say I didn't know. "I shall have to investigate those figures more closely," he said, aware of how weak a response it was, "but I—"

"It would seem to be worthy of your time," the skullman interrupted sarcastically.

"Of course it is. But I suspect it is grossly exaggerated. I am sure that our president of Regina, Mr. Alex Petersen, has the matter well under control. You are welcome to discuss the matter with him after this meeting. It is nothing serious to worry about." He realized he was repeating himself. "Are there any other questions?"

A gray-haired, fatherly man rose slowly. One of the deans of the securities business, for many years he had advised a large insurance company upon its investment portfolio.

"Yes, John, what is your question?" said the president, recognizing him deferentially.

"You've sure been asked a couple of beauties today," the gray-haired man drawled in his country style, a style which had fooled no one in twenty years. "My question is much straighter. You see, I always feel that the mangement of a company is really the most important thing it has going for it. It occurs to me that a company like Regina must have some real personnel difficulties. Its founder died a few years ago and now it's been acquired by a new company; that always causes some restiveness. It may have an inventory problem, an accounts receivable problem, possibly a cash problem; no doubt it has other problems floating around. Now all these problems can really only be taken care of by smart, tough, and *experienced* management."

The room was totally still.

"What I'm wondering is whether you have that sort of *experienced* management. I know that API has lots of good people, but the question is, do you have lots of good cosmetic people? Sir Reginald, now there was a cosmetics man! Who do you have who can take his place and deal with all those problems?"

He had of course hit at the heart of the matter. Briefly Cosgrove wondered whether he, too, had been briefed—by Cecil Rand perhaps. Had he asked his question earlier, without the jagged accuracy of the skullman's interrogation still clear in the minds of the audience, Cosgrove could have responded merely with syrupy assurances. As it was, however, the answer would have to be specific and persuasive if he were to rescue the meeting from disaster. And rescue it he must.

"Ladies and gentlemen," he said decisively, "I can assure you that we have the very finest executives running Regina. Mr.

Alex Petersen is not himself an experienced cosmetic man, but he is extremely well supported by an experienced staff including Sir Reginald's son, Cecil Rand who, as you know, ran Regina after Sir Reginald's death, and Martin Cohen, who has run Regina International very successfully for several years. I am fully confident that Mr. Petersen and his team will be able to build the company's profits in line with my earlier forecast. I understand from Mr. Petersen that we are on target. I have every confidence in him." The president nodded towards Alex, but his smile was cold. Then, pulling his shoulders back and for once standing to his full height, he added in a deeper and stronger voice, "Obviously my confidence in Mr. Petersen will last as long as Regina's profits continue to meet their target."

There was a small turmoil of surprise in the audience. Rarely did it hear a threat so public or so blatant.

"It wasn't an easy meeting, was it?" Pamela Maarten greeted Alex as they were leaving.

"Difficult questions," he answered carefully. "Obviously our president handled them very effectively. I think the outcome was fine."

"He's covering up," she said flatly. "I'm uncovering him in my article."

"Jesus," Alex said, "don't look so bloody exultant."

"It's a good article. I'm pleased with it," she explained. "Come join me for a cup of coffee?"

"Thanks. And you can pay for it." He looked at her with admiration. "Why do I like you so much when you're all set to ruin me?"

"Do you?" she asked seriously.

"Yes." It was a simple statement but they both realized that it carried with it the answer to much more than she had asked.

She leaned against him on tiptoe then and gently kissed his cheek. "I'm glad," she said. "I like you too. I'll pay for breakfast as well, if you like."

Roger Knight hurried back to Jimmy Leonetti's office. "I just got back from Cosgrove's security analysts meeting—"

"Yes?" Leonetti was impatient.

"I have the impression that API's in worse shape than we realized."

"What happened?"

"One thing was that Regina appears to have a major receivables problem and possibly a very large inventory problem. We'll hear more about that from O'Hagin, the fellow we put in there—"

"Yeah. Anyway, they've got those reserves you found in Paris," Leonetti interrupted. "Anyone bring them up?"

"No. And I'm not certain any more they've still got them. I asked O'Hagin, and he couldn't find any trace. Perhaps they've been used up since my informant left."

"Yeah. One thing's for sure, if Cosgrove knew about them, he'd have grabbed them long ago."

"Actually, Regina was not the main problem. It was the questions about API's cash situation that worried me. Cosgrove implied they had no serious shortage, but he didn't outright deny it. He handled it rather well. But I was looking at him carefully and my guess is that they have a worse crisis on their hands than even we realized."

"Was anything specific said?"

"No. But I noticed one or two of the better analysts making notes. I'd guess there'll be some more selling."

"Shit," said Leonetti.

"Can we sell?"

"My broker asked me already. I'm sure we can't. I'm an insider. But I'll double-check." Leonetti picked up the telephone. "Get me Berkowitz," he said. To Roger he added: "He's the best lawyer on Wall Street. If there's any way, he'll find it—Hello, George? Listen, I've got a tough problem. I control about seven hundred thousand shares of API, out of a total of just under fifteen million."

"Congratulations," said George Berkowitz drily.

"Yeah. Well, my assistant, Roger Knight, tells me that several people just left an analysts' meeting with the feeling that API has a cash shortage. We're afraid there's going to be a run against the stock. I'd like to sell right away. Not on the basis of anything I know, but because of the analysts meting."

"You're a director of API, aren't you?"

"Yes."

"So obviously you're an insider. And you want me to let you sell the stock just before a major decline."

"Right."

"And you're trying to tell me you're selling on the basis of public not inside information?"

"Other investors will be selling. Why can't I? Is there any way?"

"No." Berkowitz's voice was annoyed. "You know damn well no one would believe you didn't have inside information if you sell a large amount without advance notice and then the stock crashes. You'd be sued by every investor who lost money. And then you'd be sued by their cousins—"

"You answered the question."

"Yeah," said Berkowitz. "Dumb question." He hung up.

Jimmy Leonetti looked at Roger Knight with a somewhat shamefaced grin. " 'Dumb question' is what Berkowitz said."

"Okay," said Roger Knight. "Then the first thing to do is check out my suspicion—"

"I already know you're right. Got the information two days ago. I was just hoping the analysts wouldn't pick it up so that we'd have a bit more time."

"Do you have any plans for raising more cash?"

"Not yet. But we've got to do something. And fucking fast."

Chapter 20

At least twice a year, the major cosmetic companies announced a new makeup look. The "Not-So-Innocent Pinks," the "Nude Look," the "Iced Teas," the "New New Glamour"— these and hundreds of others had been used in recent years. Each look consisted of new lipstick shades, matching nail polishes, coordinated eye colors, and, frequently, new foundation and blusher shades. Often the look involved a whole new line of products. One year Revlon introduced "Formula 2" lipsticks; Max Factor had countered with a new line of makeup products called "Maxi"; and Helena Rubinstein had announced "Shadows Français" eyeshadows, a line of eighteen blushers called "The Blusher," and a new form of lipstick in a pan called "Brush-on Lips." Each look was accompanied by advertising, frequently very heavy, and merchandising material, sometimes brilliantly eye-catching.

A most important aspect of any look, as Colonel Brown-Williams had explained to Alex, was to create enough excitement around it to cause the fashion and beauty magazines to write about it. Queenie had asked Regina's marketing people to present next January's look and to discuss how it was to be given news value.

When Alex entered the studio where the presentation was to be made the first thing he saw—could not fail to see—was a wall-sized poster of a giant blue sky filled with swirls of blue cigarette smoke rising from giant surreal ashtrays just visible in its bottom corner. On the near wall, cloth swatches were pinned in a variety of smoky shades—smoky blue, umber, gray-silver, charcoal—while on the far wall there was a gallery of photographs of languorous dresses and sweaters picking up colors of the cloth swatches.

"Beautiful," Alex murmured as he entered.

"Welcome to our smoke-filled room," said Queenie. "The colors of winter—"

"Aren't they marvelous?" said Jean Smith, the permanently enthusiastic head of new product development. "I think this is the *most* fabulous—"

"Let's give Mr. Petersen the full background," Queenie interrupted. She motioned for everyone to sit down. "As you know, Alex, we keep a very close eye on fashion trends. As much as two years in advance we talk to the big fiber manufacturers to find out which new colors and materials they will be pushing. Then we attend the couturier showings about six months in advance of each season to see how the French, and increasingly the American, designers are interpreting them into fashion. In addition, of course, we keep close contact with the beauty and fashion editors of virtually all women's and general interest magazines; but especially *Vogue* and *Glamour* for high fashion and *Cosmopolitan* and *Millie* for younger trends. And always *Women's Wear Daily*—I understand you know the editor quite well now," she interrupted herself.

"Quite well," said Alex, remembering an entertaining evening, full of Dom Perignon and beautiful girls, that he and the editor had spent together the week before. He wondered how Queenie knew. Gossip, he concluded again, was rampant throughout the cosmetics industry.

"These investigations give us a good idea, six to eight months in advance, of color and fashion trends. That's about the time we need to launch a new look. Next January, which is the season we're working on, the fashions will be loose and flowing, and colors will be smoky like the ones you see on the board. So 'Smoky' is our theme." She looked across at Cecilia, the sad-looking woman who headed Regina's copy department. "Please describe the theme in more detail," she requested.

"I'd love to," said Cecilia, her voice deep, drawling and Bostonian. "I'm very excited about it." She sounded totally bored. "As you can see from our display, we believe that smoke should be our theme—blue curling smoke rising in beautiful lazy patterns to the sky. You may recall that Victor Hugo said, 'Smoke rising through the trees may signify the most charming thing in the world.' "

Alex, looking around the room, concluded that he was not alone in failing to recall that particular quotation.

"So picture, if you will, a hearthside, complete with a smoky-colored cat and a beautiful young woman with her man in the background. It is a cold January night. Outside there is an indigo sky through which the chimney smoke gently curls, while inside the house the smoke from her cigarette . . ."

As Cecilia talked, Alex stifled a yawn. Christ, he thought, am I tired, or is this as boring as I think it is? He forced himself to concentrate.

"So what we need," Cecilia was saying, "is a newsworthy, compelling name to dramatize our smoky look." She moved to the center of the blue poster and pulled at a tab. To Alex's surprise, one of its panels fell off revealing underneath, drawn in large letters of curling smoke, the words *The Fireside Smokes*.

There was no stir in the room at the revelation. Most of the participants had seen the name before. Those who had not remained silent. Alex felt almost embarrassed. The name seemed such an anticlimax to the build-up of the presentation.

Cecilia returned to her seat and Marcella York, the product manager on color products, took over. "With that background in mind," she said in a businesslike tone, "we have developed six smoky lipsticks and matching nail polishes, and ten eyeshadows." She showed the colors as she talked. "In addition, we have developed a smoky mascara which we don't think will be a big seller, but which completes the line. Finally, we have developed a series of chiffon scarves, berets, a couple of handbags—all done in smoky colors—which we plan to use as gifts and in our publicity shots."

Her presentation finished, she was replaced by the head of merchandising, a rather emaciated man with a thin bald head who had been with Regina for many years. He seemed to regard the "Fireside Smokes" as dull but necessary.

"To present this new look in its most appropriate setting," he commenced in a monotone, "we have created a pre-pack display and tester unit." He pulled a model from a box at his feet. It consisted of a plastic tray molded to hold several of each of the products included in the look, plus testers for consumers to try out the colors. The back of the display was a card illustrating a fireside scene. The name *The Fireside Smokes* was rendered in the same curled-smoke script Cecilia had unveiled. "The pre-pack will sell for two hundred dollars."

The whole approach, Alex knew, was in line with normal practice. For their looks, cosmetic companies typically created pre-pack displays ready for drug store counters without extra store handling. He had seen dozens of them during his numerous store visits. Most stores bought the pre-pack plus "open stock" merchandise to put onto their shelves or peg racks, while a few chains refused pre-packs and bought only open stock. Then, if they could negotiate a favorable display allowance with the manufacturer, they ran their own displays.

"We plan six thousand pre-packs." The merchandising man concluded bluntly and sat down.

Alex knew it was an unambitious quantity. The whole program, it struck him, was unambitious, lacking in flair. It seemed professional but mundane. Somehow, these people had learned to accept mediocrity as inevitable.

The presentations complete, there was silence in the room and everyone looked at Alex expectantly. But he found himself in a quandary immediately. If he accepted "The Fireside Smokes," he would be going against his own instincts; but if he rejected the look, the people here, and especially Queenie, would doubtless resent the criticism of an inexperienced outsider. Temporizing, he turned to Jean Smith. "What do you think?" he asked kindly, giving the impression that he had his own views but wanted to hear hers first. "You're always very enthusiastic. Do you like this look as much as some of the other things you've seen?"

"Oh, I think it's absolutely marvelous. I think that—"

"Do you really?" Alex asked more sternly. "Are you really excited?" He thought he had noticed some doubt in her voice.

"Well, I think it's very exciting." He was sure now that her voice hesitated.

"*Very* exciting? Compared to our competitors, compared to what we used to do?"

"Well, it's right on strategy."

"I didn't ask that, I asked is it really exciting? Will we get the sort of publicity we all want?"

"Well," said Jean Smith, "I think—" She lapsed into silence.

"And you, Cecilia, what do you think?" Alex asked. "Are you really excited by the approach?"

Cecilia was silent for several seconds. By temperament she was less given to bubbling enthusiasm, and her judgment was experienced and sound. Moreover, she had seen an unexpected sternness in this new president and she was not about to lie to him. "I'm not sure," she said finally. "But I do sort of like it—"

"And its PR value?"

"Not very great, I'm afraid. The whole look is good, but—"

"But boring," Queenie interrupted. Obviously Petersen felt the stuff was no good; and he was right. Why the hell didn't he just say so the way Reg would have done? She remembered so clearly how he would have reacted—sarcastic, humorous, cutting, but daring in his opinions, and always clear and instructive. Well, if Petersen wouldn't say it clearly, she would. "Dull as hell," she repeated. To her surprise, she felt a rush of relief. At last there was someone to share the burden of maintaining excitement. . . .

"Dull as hell is right," said Alex, but now he smiled and the tension in the room evaporated. There were several nods around the table.

"Well, it could be more interesting," said Jean Smith.

"We could give a discount on the deal when we launch it," interrupted the merchandising man. "That way stores would put the displays up more willingly."

"I'm not sure—" Alex started tactfully.

But Queenie exploded in annoyance. "No!" she snapped. "Definitely not. If that's the only way we can get in-store display we should all be ashamed. Sir Reginald would never have allowed price cuts."

Oh, wouldn't he, Alex thought bitterly. Only three million dollars to the Scarpetti's. . . . He shook himself free of the

thought. At least this meeting seemed to be going his way. Without arousing too much antagonism he had made them see how
boring their promotion really was. Now, how to build up their
enthusiasm again, how to spark their creativity? It was what he
had to do at the agency when the copywriters ran down and at
API when the new products department went dry. The theory
was simple: start an informal brain-storming session, throw out
some ideas, get people talking, thinking, excited. But it wasn't
so easy to do. . . .

"Why not use cats' eyes?" he asked tentatively. "Aren't cats'
eyes smoky? Couldn't we have a feline look—something with
tigers and fire? How about calling it 'Fire and Smoke, the Moods
of a Cat'—Could we give away tiger's eye rings as premiums?"
Christ, he thought, they're all just sitting there. He had a moment
of panic. Would they stay stolidly silent while he rambled on
making a fool of himself. "Or cat's eye mood rings? All flame
one minute, and sexy dusk the next," he plunged on, slightly
desperate. "Why not—" he paused, searching for new idea.

"'Sultry Smokes' could be sexy," said Cecilia, her voice
doubtful.

"Yes," said Alex, grateful beyond belief that someone had
broken the silence. "You're right. Let's get some sex appeal in.
How about the girl, the cat, both sets of beautiful eyes, a man
hinted at in the background, just a wisp of a sheet over the girl
—and call it 'Just Smoke'?"

"Or 'Smoking Hot' for the brighter reds, said Marcella York,
suddenly joining the conversation.

"Think of the display material," the merchandising manager
added ruminatively. "We might have some fun with it." He
sounded as if the idea of having fun at his job was a novel thought
to him. "We could light fires—"

Gradually the others joined in. When the conversation
lagged, Alex was ready with some new line of exploration. It
was not real creativity, he knew, just a knack. But it often sparked
genuine creative thought in others. Within a few minutes, everyone was engrossed in an idea session, with people silent before
talking animatedly. There was noise and laughter. The merchandising manager was sketching furiously. Cecilia had jumped
up and was leaning over his shoulder almost shouting instructions. Alex sat back relieved. He looked over to where Queenie

was also watching the proceedings. At first she was passively attentive. Then, very gradually, her eyes started to brighten and a smile lit up her previously drawn face. She felt a rising enthusiasm she had not experienced since Reg's death. She felt alive.

After another few minutes, Alex rose. The noise in the room gradually subsided. "When can I see a re-presentation? Something exciting. Fascinating. Three weeks' time?"

"You'll have it a lot faster than that," said Queenie.

Bryant always seemed to be waiting when Alex returned to his office. This time he had the data on the inventory.

"As of three weeks ago when we took a physical count, I had nineteen million dollars excess or obsolete," he said.

"At least we know," Alex said, trying to appear calm.

"It's not as bad as we thought. Some of the approaches you suggested are beginning to work. The computer program has been completed so that we know know what our theoretical finished inventory would be if we used up all our excess packaging. That means we know what we have available to sell. Also, we're able to cut down on our purchasing and use up components we own instead."

"How is our special sales group doing?" Alex asked.

"They're selling the stuff for every conceivable purpose— fund-raising for women's clubs, gifts for test-driving new automobiles, VIP gifts at hotels. They've already sold almost two million dollars of the nineteen—and made a profit on it."

"How much will we be able to get rid of?"

"I don't know. Maybe a third, maybe half this year. But that's enough. It means I won't have to write off nearly as much as I'd feared; I'll be able to demonstrate to the auditors that the inventory has value."

That, Alex knew, was the key point. If the auditors felt that the inventory was valueless, they would insist that it be written down to zero and the loss taken immediately. But if they felt it was worth what it showed on the books, then no loss would have to be incurred.

"What's your best guess how much we'll have to write off this year?" Alex requested. "If we have to write off more next year, we'll be stronger and it won't hurt so much."

"I'm still not sure. Maybe three to five million dollars. That's the stuff which is really hopeless. Fortunately, we're reserved up to three million."

"You mean you planned to dispose of that much inventory this year?"

"Yes, that's what I assumed in my forecast."

"Are you telling me the problem is resolved?"

"I'm not sure that it's resolved," said Bryant judiciously, "But it looks as if it won't be too serious."

"How's that deal I made with that fellow who wants to sell our old inventory to Poland?"

"That was a major part of the solution. He agreed to take almost three million dollars of our stuff at only a bit under cost—all of it old. If he hadn't, I'd certainly have had to write it off."

Alex had been very concerned about the deal he'd made with the exporter to Poland. There were grave risks involved, he knew. Wally Korsakoff was a known handler of old cosmetic inventory, buying at a few cents on the dollar and disposing of it through discount market areas in many large cities. He was considered reliable and could dispose of fifty or a hundred thousand dollars of inventory with little danger of the merchandise finding its way into cut-rate drugstores to be discounted and harm the image of the company.

This time, however, Korsakoff had approached Regina to buy three million dollars' worth of merchandise. Alex had agreed to talk to him.

"It's very simple. I buy the merchandise, I pay you cash, I sell it to Poland. I give you all the papers and the bill of lading to make sure it gets on the boat. You make the money." Korsakoff talked in a loud staccato voice, his hands flying, his shoulders shrugging. He had the lined, mobile face of an old comedian.

"How do we know that the merchandise won't bounce back into the United States?"

"Because I give you orders from the Polish government; also bills of lading to prove it's on the boat. So what else could you want?"

"An order from the Polish government doesn't mean a thing. And the bill of lading is simply a paper which claims that the merchandise was put on the boat. We don't know that it really was; and if it was, we don't know that it wasn't unloaded again."

"So send your inspector. Send somebody to the dock. He can watch. We put everything on board. He watches the boat leave."

Alex continued to look doubtful.

"Look," Korsakoff said, "I do business in cosmetics for years. If I let schlock merchandise bounce back into regular channels, how much merchandise you think I'll get to buy next year? I'll put myself out of business. So now I buy three million dollars worth of goods. I pay cash. You got my personal guarantee. The stuff gets onto the boat. It goes to Poland. You don't never see it again."

He had a sound argument, Alex realized. On the other hand, Korsakoff normally dealt with much smaller quantities of merchandise, usually under a hundred thousand dollars. To divert that into regular trade channels would have given him only a small extra profit and would indeed have destroyed his business. But if he diverted a three million dollar order, even after expenses, he could make a million dollar profit. Enough, Alex considered, to maybe not care about his reputation. More assurances were needed, Alex decided. "That's not good enough," he said. "Even if we see the merchandise loaded onto the boat, we don't know that it won't be unloaded when we're not looking. Neither the bill of lading nor the Polish order mean a damn thing."

Korsakoff looked hurt. "You telling me you don't trust me?" he demanded, his voice almost a whine.

"I'm telling you that the only way we'll do this deal is if you will guarantee in writing to pick up from the trade any merchandise which is diverted from the Polish order. You'll probably have to pay full retail for the stuff because, if there is a diversion, the retailer won't give it up for less."

"That's outrageous!" Korsakoff argued. "I would have to pay five times as much as the merchandise is worth."

"At least five times. However, since you're not planning to divert, what harm is there in guaranteeing?"

Korsakoff knew he was trapped. If he refused to go along with the guarantee, the implication that he was preparing to divert the merchandise would be overwhelming. Nevertheless he hesitated.

"Listen," Alex said, "this is a big deal. We need you because we can't sell three million dollars worth of excess inventory that quickly. But you need us too; there aren't many companies willing to make a deal like this."

"Yeah," Korsakoff said, "you mean there ain't many companies with that much obsolete. You still got sixteen million after I buy the three."

Alex hid his surprise at how well informed the man was.

"Do you want the deal, Mr. Korsakoff, or not?"

"Sure, I take it. And I give you a guarantee. Hey," his face crinkled into his comedian smile. "Hey, and call me Wally."

"How is that deal with the mail order company going?" Bryant asked now.

Alex's face lit up. "I think we'll get a huge order out of them," he said quietly. "At least a million dollars to start, and much more to come."

"For what?" Bryant's voice reflected some of Alex's excitement.

"They send free gifts, which they advertise will be worth at least three dollars, to every customer who buys from them," Alex explained. "However, since they can only afford to spend forty cents per gift, they have a hell of a time finding enough items. One of the best is cosmetics. For forty cents we can give them a retail value of almost four dollars—even more sometimes when we're using up obsolete components."

"They must use millions of pieces."

"They have a fantastic operation. I went up there to see it. I was awed. The mail comes in at one end of the building in trucks like an industrial product. It's moved by fork-lifts and automatically opened by huge rotary letter openers able to handle any size envelope without touching the letter inside. Most of the opened mail is sorted by machines because the order blanks are coded with dots visible to computers. Only a trickle of orders come in handwritten and have to be handled by people."

"Filling the orders must take a huge staff. Every order must be different." Bryant shuddered at the thought.

"No, they have surprisingly few people—just hundreds of computer terminals. Virtually every clerical employee has one."

"It sounds incredible."

"It is. If you write to them saying that you didn't get the

item you ordered, they'll immediately send you another one. If it happens again, even five years later, they'll send you a letter saying this has happened before and advising you to check with your post office!"

Bryant and Alex laughed together.

"Things seem to be going a little better," said Bryant returning to the business at hand. "Fortunately; because my next quarterly estimate is due within the week—"

"I know," said Alex, "and we're still damned tight. We've been lucky up to now, but a thousand things could go wrong. And I'm still worrying whether Cohen will bring in International's profits. He's got obvious problems in several countries. And I don't know whether he has enough reserves to cover them."

"Neither do I, but I do know that the closer we get to year-end, the less excuse you have if your forecast comes in wrong."

"I know." Alex rather bitterly noted again in his controller's habit of switching from "I" to "you" when the risks loomed. "But after the analysts' meeting, do I have a choice?"

"You're right; if you were going to miss your forecast, you should have said so there. I'll issue your forecast accordingly."

After Bryant left, Alex stood up, stretched his arms above his head feeling the tension in his shoulder muscles as a tautness very close to pain. Briefly he wondered, as he used to so often, whether all the effort and struggle was worth it. But it seemed a less important question now than before. He was so busy. I don't have any time left to be dissatisfied, he thought wryly. Then he thought of Pamela whom he would see again this evening and felt a warmth. . . . He turned back to his mail hoping he could get through most of it before his next meeting.

As it turned out, however, the very first letter on the pile stopped him. It came from the assistant personnel manager and was addressed to the Latin American Division manager:

> In answer to your question, personal insurance for manufacturing executives normally continues for three months beyond termination. However, in this instance, the special circumstances in Uruguay would warrant stopping such insurance immediately.

"Get me Personnel on the phone," Alex called to Sylvie. When the personnel manager answered, he said, "I've got a letter here from your assistant dealing with termination of insurance for a manufacturing executive in Uruguay. What's it all about?"

"Oh, don't worry about that," said the personnel manager promptly. "That should never have been copied to you."

"I'm not worried, I just want to know what it is."

"Just a matter dealing with the factory manager."

"What matter?" said Alex, annoyance edging into his voice. "Kindly explain."

"Well, as you know, the factory manager was fired for stealing, and this deals with—"

"Thank you, I understand now." He hung up.

"Get Cohen in here right away," he said to Sylvie.

When Cohen arrived, Alex's voice continued to sound peremptory. "What the hell is this about the factory manager in Uruguay being fired for stealing?"

"We had a little problem," said Cohen. "I didn't think you'd want to be worried."

"What do you mean, a little problem?"

"Apparently the man was taking some of our supplies to a small plant of his own. He was making products very similar to ours and selling them at a much lower price."

"This had been going on for some time?"

"I believe it had. But it was not a very important operation."

"Why wasn't I informed? We have a clear policy that any legal violations are to be reported to me immediately."

"Well, you weren't available," said Cohen defensively. "You must have been out of town somewhere. How the hell could I?"

"I have been here since my return from Paris last week. You could easily have told me." Alex was not willing to be conciliatory. He felt sure that if he were, he would rapidly lose all control. As it was, Cohen had too great a tendency to run his operation as a personal fiefdom. "In the future," Alex said coldly, "please see to it that I'm informed immediately. Even if I am out of town, there's always a telex machine or a telephone close. Thank you, that will be all."

Cohen left, both angry and surprised at Alex's tough stand. His fear grew. Perhaps he would lose after all. . . .

For his part, Alex felt thoroughly uneasy. Not reporting a

case of systematic stealing was obviously against all the company policies. Yet he could see little reason for Cohen to violate the procedure in this case. . . .

The intercom buzzer interrupted his thoughts.

"Yes?"

"Dr. Wagner on the phone," Sylvie said. "There seems to be a crisis."

Alex picked up the phone. "Yes, what can I do for you?"

Dr. Wagner's German-accented voice quavered with indignation. "I am in charge of quality control," he said. "Is that not right?" He spoke English perfectly, but the r was formed in the back of his throat, giving it a guttural sound.

"Of course."

"Then why are my orders overridden?"

"I don't know what you mean, Dr. Wagner. Perhaps you would explain."

"I issued orders that the soap was to be destroyed and not shipped. It is contaminated with metal—"

"Dr. Wagner, I'm sorry, I still don't know what this is all about. Please explain from the beginning."

"And my orders were countermanded."

"Now listen, I understand you have a problem. But I don't know what it is. Kindly explain it coherently." Alex allowed his voice to rise.

Immediately the German became obsequious. "I beg your pardon, sir. I am a little upset. The problem is this. A week ago one of my quality control people reported that certain batches of 'Gentle Soap' had metal particles embedded in them. I immediately ordered all shipment of the product to be stopped."

"Where do we sell that?" Alex interrupted, not recognizing the name.

"Export only. The Caribbean, mostly. Also Central America."

"Very well. Continue."

"In the meantime, I had investigations made of all recent 'Gentle Soap' batches. I found that all batches have at least some metal contamination. The product is made on very old machinery, and evidently the mixers are rusty or corroded so that tiny particles are being scraped off the blades. It is probably not very dangerous. In my judgment, however, it is unacceptable merchandise."

"Have any contaminated batches been shipped?"

"They hadn't when I stopped shipment. Now I have just discovered that my orders were countermanded and that most of the merchandise was shipped. It's continuing to be shipped. I want it stopped." His voice rose and became harsher.

"Thank you very much, Dr. Wagner," said Alex, not commenting. "I will get back to you within a few minutes. Let me just check. By the way, who countermanded your orders?"

"Mr. Cohen."

As he hung up Alex felt a wave of anger. "Get me Cohen again," he shouted to Sylvie.

She connected him immediately.

"Listen," Alex snapped as soon as he heard Cohen's voice, "is it true that we are continuing to ship 'Gentle Soap'?"

"Well, yes," said Cohen.

"Wagner tells me that he placed a stop ship order on it because it's metal-contaminated."

"Wagner always makes a fuss," said Cohen, still angry from his earlier conversation with Alex. "Goddamn it, I said to ship it. It's my territory and my responsibility. I checked the soap myself. There's not a goddamn thing wrong with it."

"Metal particles—"

"There aren't any fucking metal particles in the soap," said Cohen. "You need an electronic molecule detector to find the damn particles in the first place. Wagner's been crying wolf for years. I won't—"

"Marty, I'm ordering stop shipment on all 'Gentle Soap.' Any shipments already made must be returned."

"Goddamn it," Cohen exploded. "I—"

"Did you hear what I said?"

The light flashed in Cohen's brain for just an instant and with it, another flash of fear. "Yes," he said finally, his voice sounding strangled. "Yes, I understand."

To his own amazement, Cohen became icily calm. He felt unreal, pervaded by a cool glow just beyond his perception, like the glow of a city you cannot see, lighting up a dark night. He called his secretary into his office and, in an unnaturally flat voice, dictated the necessary memorandum to the export department. He followed with a temperate note to Wagner informing him of what he had done. His secretary, more used to his sudden rages, observed him with something akin to terror. She would hand in her notice to Personnel in the morning, she decided. His tantrums were bad, but this rigid control was awful.

In Alex's office, Sylvie buzzed to say that Ms. Duke was on the phone. He took the call immediately.

"I hear a rumor that we have metal in 'Gentle Soap,'" Queenie said without preliminaries. "I understand that the product is still being shipped. I called Wagner and he tells me his orders were countermanded."

"Yes, I'm afraid they were," said Alex. "However, I have put things right; all shipments have been stopped. Those which have already been made are being returned."

"I'm relieved."

"Also, you're very quick."

"I've been around for a while." Queenie was pleased with the compliment. "By the way, have you told Cohen?"

"Yes." Alex paused for a second. "He was not happy."

Queenie, appreciating the degree of the understatement, laughed. For a moment she felt almost warm towards Alex Petersen.

Cohen's icy control carried him through the business day and stayed with him while he took some drinks at the Regency bar and arrived home at seven that evening.

"Would you like your normal martini, sir?" the maid asked him as he stepped into his door.

He nodded.

"Hello, honey. How are you?" said Barbara, determined to allow no argument this evening. "Is the girl bringing your drink?"

He barely grunted a response and sat down. For a few moments they were silent. Then, just as Barbara was about to say something about their daughters in school, the glow in Cohen's head exploded into flashes like a sudden electrical storm—the most brilliant flashes he had ever seen, he thought, beautiful and full of power.

"I don't give a shit what obstacles he invents," he said in a low, cold voice. "I'll get that bastard Petersen."

Barbara looked at him with surprise, unsure if she had heard correctly.

"What did you say, honey?"

"I'll get that shit Petersen!" His voice still carried its unnatural rasp. "He can't make it without me. If I don't bring in the profits, he'll never find them. He'll be run out—out of Regina, out of API. Fuck him. That's when I bring in my reserves." He laughed, but without humor, almost wildly. "They'll have to make me president then. They'll have to. You'll be proud, kitten. Grandaughter of one, daughter of the second, wife of the third—"

"I want a divorce," she said coldly, unaware before she mouthed the words that she would have the courage to say them.

"What?" he said. "*What?*" Her voice seemed to be coming to him through a gale in his head; he could hardly understand her words. "What?" he repeated.

"I want a divorce."

Instantly he could hear quite normally again. The flashes, even the haze which had stayed with him all day, were gone.

"No," he blurted. "No, you don't want a divorce. Why? Why now?" He couldn't understand her. "But why?" he asked again. Then, suddenly realizing that he would have to use a totally different approach to avert this new catastrophe, he made his voice change totally and started to cajole. "Barbara, love, I know it's not easy. But why do you want a divorce?"

"There's nothing left of our marriage."

"Oh, but there is—there is for me. I need you." He paused, searching for something else to say. "There are the children. What will it do to them?"

"I don't know. It worries me sick."

Cohen felt a violent rush of anger shake his body. How could the bitch be doing this to him? First Petersen and now his own wife. It crossed his mind that they might be out to double-cross him together.

"Now look—" he started, ready to vent his anger at her. But at the last second his craftiness won. "Now look," he repeated, but in a softer, wheedling voice. "You can't divorce me, honey, I love you. I need you. I need you." He repeated the words softly, insistently until they became a litany she hardly heard, but which affected her deeply. "I need you," he kept repeating, not sure himself how much what he said was true but knowing how those words always moved her.

Perhaps he does need me, she thought. I know he did when we were first married. . . .

"Barbara, I can't stand it if you leave me," he said. He moved over to the sofa beside her and put his arms around her. "Please, honey, don't say you want a divorce. Not like that. Let's at least try."

He sounds so sincere, she thought, becoming convinced for the moment, wanting to believe, even now, after all these years of disappointment. . . .

"It's been ten years," he was saying, echoing her thoughts. "You can't give them up just like this." He saw from her face that he was making progress. "Please, honey," he begged again. "You've put too much into our marriage."

"Yes," she said. "Yes, that's true."

"Don't say anything to anybody yet. Please, honey. Let's try to work it out. Then, if it doesn't work, there's always time to make the move. But right now it's so inconvenient—"

"What do you mean?" she asked coldly.

"Nothing, I didn't mean—"

"You meant it's inconvenient for your job." She was certain. "That's all you care about, isn't it? No, I'm not going to wait," she said with renewed determination. "Not one more day. I want a divorce now."

Cohen, realizing that he had lost, let go. Like a wild thing, he howled his anger at his wife. The maid, hearing her employer scream, cowered in the kitchen. After a few minutes she heard Cohen storm out of the living room. Then the front door slammed so hard that she jumped. The martini she was holding spilled. When she tried to steady it, the glass slipped right off the tray and smashed on the floor.

Chapter 21

C ohen stormed into the streets of New York. Frowning men and women scurried past, caring no more for him than he cared for them. Within a few minutes he found himself before a small, nameless bar. Inside was a row of bar stools at a dingy counter of partly ripped black vinyl. One of the three lights above the bar was out.

The barman looked up briefly. "How are you?" he inquired, but it was clear that he was not interested.

"Scotch," Cohen said taking a stool at one end of the bar. "Double."

The barman shoved the drink towards him. Cohen gulped it.

"Gimme another double."

The bartender pushed the second drink over the counter. "That's four bucks."

Cohen drank again at a gulp and paid. He stared at the three hookers leaning against the far end of the bar. The whiskies began to numb his fingertips. Suddenly he felt his erection start and his anger seemed to rise with it. The most blatant of the three women caught his attention. She wore a thin blouse through which her sagging breasts were clearly visible, their nipples standing up as if they alone had been siliconed. Her face was so flat and cold it seemed dead. Her lower figure, accentuated by a tight miniskirt and plastic boots, was as available as the merchandise on a Woolworth counter.

Cohen walked rapidly over to her and gripped her elbow roughly.

"How much?" he demanded.

She looked at him, coldly appraising. As his grip tightened on her elbow, she looked down the bar towards the bartender who was washing glasses, apparently oblivious to Cohen or the girl. Barely perceptibly he shook his head.

"Nothing," said the girl.

"What?" Cohen asked, not fully understanding.

"I said nothing. No dice. I'm not going with you at any price. You're one of the bad ones."

Cohen looked at her with pure hatred. The barman started to move towards them. Suddenly Cohen turned on his heel and walked out.

The girl turned to the bartender. "Thanks," she said. "I was pretty sure but I'm glad you agreed."

"Yeah," said the bartender. "He had the look."

His head bowed as if against a storm, his face livid, his hands deep in his pockets, Cohen made his way westwards on 57th Street, with its elegant shops that never seemed to sell anything. He turned south on Broadway and, crossing the street diagonally, paused outside a "Ham and Eggs" joint. Through the greasy windows he could see the black hookers with their brazen red wigs, playing up to their pimps or cursing and laughing together. Wild and vulgar as hyenas, he thought. Between them, sullen at their tables and as sad as outcasts from the herd, a number of cleaning women and janitors were taking their evening snack.

As he stared at the women in the snack bar and parading on the street, he became aware that two hookers, silhouettes in a store entrance across the street, were starting to scream at one another. Suddenly the taller, a muscled black woman with hair bleached so blond it was visible even in the darkness, grabbed for the thinner and younger girl who, lithe as a cat, started to squirm and scratch.

Faster than any cop could appear, a stunningly tall black pimp moved towards them.

"Cut!" he ordered. When they did not obey instantly, a small whip apeared as if by magic in his hands. "Cut, Ah said," and the whip slashed twice—crack, crack—so that each of the women screamed once more and then, threatened with the whip again, only whimpered.

The whole action took no more than a minute but that was enough for an excitement to rise in Cohen of an intensity he had rarely experienced. Without another glance, the pimp sauntered across the street past the place where Cohen stood in the shadows, so transported in his excitement that he could no longer sense the ground upon which he stood.

"Give me the whip," Cohen said as the pimp passed him. "Give me the whip." He held out a fifty-dollar bill.

As if in slow motion, the tall man came to a fluid pause in front of Cohen. Insolently, his glance raked Cohen's body from polished shoes to untidy hair.

"A hundred dollars," said Cohen, fumbling in his wallet.

The black man took the money and handed over the tiny whip. "Yeah, man."

As if struggling through air turned liquid, Cohen crossed the street. A car traveling south on Broadway swerved at the last instant to avoid him.

The women, wise in their profession, knew he was coming and understood why.

"What do you want, honey?" The bigger one, older and more experienced, took the initiative.

"You."

"All right, honey, my place or a hotel?"

"Both of you."

"Oh, that's extra. What do you want with two women?" She tried to flirt.

"Both!" He shouted the word.

"Twenty-five bucks apiece."

Cohen's hand went to his wallet. He took out another hundred dollar bill.

"Here," he said, holding it out.

The big whore grabbed for it, but he snatched it back. Deliberately he tore it in half giving one piece to each girl.

"Both, I said, and for as long as I want."

They nodded in agreement, looking at each other for support. He stopped a passing taxi.

"Get going," he ordered the girls. "The Ace Hotel," he said to the driver, "Broadway and 110th Street."

The sour-looking desk clerk gave them a room where they would not be heard and they climbed the stairs together. He had little conscious sense of what he was doing, knowing only that he was there and the women were there. . . .

Later that night, when he had paid much more money and they had let him revile them, whipping them first with words and then with the tiny whip, his head burst open and he was in a vast black cavern full of visions of his Aunt Ruth and the mangled bodies at Auschwitz and a thousand trillion dying things. Then he started to beat mercilessly at the women until their blood and the rushing river of blood behind his eyes seemed to merge. He wanted to kill. They held him down while the younger girl screamed for help and he slashed and hit. He seemed like a snarling mad thing to them, but he knew what he was doing. He was exhilarated at feeling his body struggling on the bed; he rejoiced as he kicked the younger girl in the groin and she doubled over in pain. Then when the older whore, suddenly crazily incensed herself, attacked him, scratching with all her strength, his excitement became so intense that he was drained in an overwhelming orgasm. With a final violent effort he threw both girls off the bed and relaxed, at last knowing that he was satisfied, and laughed in their terrified faces, exulting at what he understood to be his victory.

Barbara was still asleep when Cohen returned. He showered, shaved, ate a pleasant breakfast, and reached the office in time to prepare for a busy day. He felt relaxed and ready to fight. He even relished the prospect.

Alex Petersen and Pamela Maarten felt that their first night together was a great success. From the moment they met, touching their lips together, until they walked back to her apartment holding hands, they could feel their friendship ripening. Occasionally they would stop to glance into a store window or watch some street vignette—two drunks squaring off to fight and then bursting into laughter and together staggering back into the bar; a teenage couple writhing against one another under the canopy of an X-rated movie called *Young Love*.

"You are so comfortable to be with," she said once.

"Comfortable?"

"Yes. Easy. Not boring. Exciting, but without being pushy."

"What a nice thing to say."

"Perhaps it's the evening that makes me feel comfortable. It's warm and we're not competing. Usually men try to dominate me. They want me to be their toy. Perhaps it's because I'm small. Whatever—it turns a date into a power struggle. I don't want to be subdued by my lover."

"You don't seem subdued."

"I'm not with my lover," she said and grinned at him. "Yet."

At another point in the evening, she talked about how much she enjoyed traveling. She had been everywhere, it seemed to Alex.

"What places do you like the most?"

"New York," she said unhesitatingly. "I love to travel, but I like New York best of all. There's a dynamism here which no other town can match. But although New Yorkers are often hard, striving, competitive, they share with the rest of the country a moral sense."

"Moral? What do you mean? All I hear about is rapes and muggings."

"There is a caring throughout America which other countries don't have. We have lots of problems: dying cities, discrimination, venal politicians, vicious cops, pampered crooks—you name it. But people care about the problems, and try to cure them. We all do. We write and read about them. We join concerned citizen's groups. We elect people who seem likely to resolve them—and get incensed when they don't! We castigate ourselves when we can't find a cure fast enough."

"And in other countries?"

"In Europe, they sweep their problems under the nearest elegant rug. 'Let's have another cuppa tea,' they say in England. In Italy they strike—but for themselves, for more wages, not to resolve problems. In France they merely sneer."

Alex laughed, touched by her zeal. "For a cynic, you really hold tight onto your ideals!"

"Sure. In case someone steals them!"

They laughed together happily.

When they finally reached her apartment door, she opened it and they both went in, their excitement mounting. He picked her up and kicked the door shut with his heel just as he had been tempted to do the last time.

"You're so light I can't resist the he-man approach."

"If you don't resist, I won't," she said. "Some ways of being subdued are better than others."

"Okay, doll."

She pretended to beat on his shoulders with her fists and then kissed him all over his face as he carried her across her living room. "The second door on your left will be more convenient," she said. "The one you're heading towards happens to be the closet."

"I love intimate places."

"I imagine you'll find several in a while," she teased. "But I'd prefer your searching for them in bed!"

"I want you very much," he said, as he carried her into her bedroom and placed her gently onto her bed. "You look very beautiful. Very vulnerable." He stood above her looking down.

"I want you too." She spoke softly, raising her arms to him. "Come here."

After that they spoke only in whispers as they undressed each other.

"Oh," she said touching him when their clothes were finally gone, "is it alright if I have just a little sense of awe?"

"It's not alright if you don't."

"I do!"

They made love expertly, but also innocently, playing with each other until their tension mounted to a peak and then experiencing their own and each other's orgasms with storms of elation, relief, and satisfaction.

In the morning they awoke in each other's arms.

"I think we are lovers now," were her first words. She cuddled closer to him. "And I feel wonderfully unsubdued."

Chapter 22

The omens were bad for this day on which Regina's European general managers were finally to meet in New York, two weeks later than the deadline Alex Petersen had set. Alex's cleaning woman had forgotten to buy coffee; at the pancake house where he went for breakfast there was a grease fire which left his clothes smelling of smoke; and after breakfast every taxi had disappeared so that he had to walk several hundred yards, craning his neck, until he was able to flag down a rickety gypsy cab. Then he found he had forgotten his office key and had to wait, pacing impatiently, until Sylvie arrived a few minutes later and showed him where she hid the spare.

Part of the delay in the meeting was legitimate: LeVecque had been faced with a series of mini-strikes in the French factory which required his attention; and a national economic crisis in Italy—another in a long series—had made it undesirable for Borelli to leave. But the main reason for the delay was that Cohen had found a series of excuses for procrastinating.

"You smell well done," said Sylvie wrinkling her nose.

He explained about the fire. "I'll air out, I suppose."

"I suppose." She sounded doubtful. "Would you like another cup of coffee?"

"Later, when they're all here."

"They're beginning to arrive now," Sylvie said, as Monsieur Claude LeVecque, gray and elegant as ever, rounded the corner of the corridor.

"*Bonjour*, Monsieur Petersen," he said. "I am delighted to be here." There was no delight visible in his eyes. "I anticipate we shall have an interesting meeting."

A moment later Borelli arrived, closely followed by Madame Housen of the Swiss company and Dr. Krause of Regina Germany. Within a few minutes coffee had been served and the conference room was already filling with smoke.

Marty Cohen's entrance, carefully timed for effect, took place a few moments later. "Good morning, everyone," he said heartily, taking a seat at the head of the table opposite Alex. "I think we are all gathered and the meeting can now start." There was no doubt that he meant to maintain control.

"Good morning, Marty," Alex replied with equal vigor. "Glad you could be here."

Cohen glanced at him to see whether the remark had been sarcastic, but could not tell.

"May I welcome you all to New York," Alex continued. "I—"

"Thank you," Cohen interrupted noisily. "We shall start now since we don't have much time." He arose to show the meeting was underway. "We are here, as you all know, to answer a series of questions which Alex Petersen wrote out for us in his agenda. I think we have the answers, Alex, to satisfy your—" He paused for a moment. "Curiosity," he added.

"My need to know," Alex corrected.

"Your need to know, perhaps—and your curiosity." Cohen laughed slightly to avoid seeming too rude, but he gave not an inch. "Claude, would you start?"

"I shall be delighted," said Monsieur LeVecque.

I wish he would stop saying that, Alex thought.

Each manager rapidly and efficiently presented his data. Not one volunteered any information not specifically requested and, where there was a choice of how much data to give, each presented the minimum.

They are defiant, Alex kept worrying; united, strong, and defiant. It was quite evident that, since the Paris meeting, Cohen had fully reestablished his weakened influence and welded his managers into a cohesive, antagonistic force. The smoke from LeVecque's expensive Turkish cigarettes and Borelli's Cuban cigars hung in the room in spite of the air conditioning and smelled sour, almost as if the room's psychological atmosphere had turned it rancid. Although Cohen continued blandly to state that Regina's European profits would reach their forecast, it was clear that was most unlikely.

Sandwiches were brought in at lunchtime while the meeting continued. It was almost three o'clock as the final speaker ended. Cohen sat back with just a hint of a smirk. The general managers watched closely to see what Petersen would do. What could he do?

Alex realized how desperate his situation was. Without the profits in Europe, he could not possibly achieve Regina's worldwide profit forecast. He also knew that Cohen could choose from several ways to make the profits if he really wanted to: Probably there were hidden reserves; additional sales could certainly be generated from major customers who had been helped by Regina in the past and who most likely would, therefore, be willing to help Regina now; and no doubt savings could be made too. But only the Europeans, under Cohen's tight rule, knew where these profit opportunities lay—and Alex realized that Cohen would have to be given some major incentive to uncover them.

With an involuntary sigh—which, as he realized a moment too late, signaled his weakness—Alex started the probe. "Very well," he said, trying to cover his mistake with hearty good humor, "apparently we have a few profit problems. So let's spend a while in finding solutions. It shouldn't be too hard to turn up some reserves. First France—"

It was a hollow try, lacking authentic optimism. No one in the room was impressed. Moreover, Cohen had obviously been expecting the request.

"There are no reserves anywhere, hidden or otherwise," he said with flat finality. "None."

Immediately Alex was faced with a dilemma: if he insisted that there were reserves hidden, he would force Cohen to make ever more vehement denials, and thus place him in a position where his "discovering" them later, even if he changed his mind and wanted to, would be very difficult; but he needed those re-

serves desperately. Alex decided to try another attack and return
to the reserves later. "Then we must discuss other ways of guaranteeing the profits you forecast," he started, emphasizing the
you to point out that the responsibility lay with Cohen.

Cohen merely smiled. He knew as well as Alex that if Regina
failed to make its profits it would be Alex, having made the forecasts publicly, who would be in trouble, not himself. Later, when
Alex was out, he could always find additional profits—particularly
if he were Alex's successor. . . .

"Please give me your thoughts on how to improve the situation," said Alex sternly. "The position you have presented is not
good enough."

Cohen knew such a question had to come and his answer
was well rehearsed. "The most important part of the solution is
that we regain the confidence of the trade by assuring them that
Regina is more than merely a subsidiary of API; that we are an
entirely autonomous company."

The French general manager, evidently acting on cue, produced a copy of a French newspaper—something of a scandal
sheet—which gave a profile of Alex Petersen and described him
as a "tool of Associated Products Incorporated."

"Look," LeVecque said severely, "look what the press writes
about us. How can we expect the trade to help us resolve our
problems if we are viewed as a tool of an American conglomerate?
The French are too proud to be manipulated like this."

"It is ridiculous to say that we are manipulating the French,"
Alex retorted angrily. "We are merely trying to sell cosmetics at
a reasonable profit, a profit in line with the one that you projected." Again he stressed the word *you*. And again Cohen merely
smiled, but no one in the room continued to pretend that the forecast profits would be achieved. All seemed to have tacitly agreed
that Cohen's European division would fall short—and so would
Regina overall—unless some as yet unforeseen bargain was struck.
"There is no reason why your profit projection should suddenly
be unattainable," Alex continued, his frustration mounting. "A
few months ago you thought it was—"

"A few months ago I had no idea we would be acquired by
API," said LeVecque, his tone matching Alex's in vigor. "A few
months ago I did not know that we would be thought of as anyone's tool."

"I have precisely the same problem," said Borelli.

"So do I," said Krause of Germany firmly. "I cannot run the Regina Company effectively if I am viewed as a powerless messenger of Associated Products." His already short hair seemed to stand on end, giving his bullet head a look of infinite stubbornness.

Madame Housen of Switzerland nodded primly in precise agreement.

"The fact is," said Cohen, his voice redolent with dignity and wisdom, "as long as the trade feels that we are a tool of API, I cannot guarantee that Regina International will contribute the profits it originally predicted. We may fall far short. We are losing our credibility. Some changes are essential if we are to hold the profits we projected."

A wave of consternation overtook Alex Peterson. How often had Bryant and the lawyers warned him against making public predictions about profitability and then not achieving them? And they were *his* predictions. Neither Cosgrove nor Asquith would stand with him if they were wrong. Certainly, if the Securities and Exchange Commission and irate investors attacked him for disseminating misleading profit forecasts, it would be he, not the officers of API who would have to resign. Even if he won the cases, the legal costs would be astronomical. . . .

"Some fundamental changes in the structure of the company," Cohen was saying, "so that the trade does not view us as a tool of anyone."

My God, Alex suddenly realized, he intends to push me out altogether. That's the price he's asking in return for his profits!

"Seems to me the only viable approach is to make Regina Europe an autonomous company and not part of Regina worldwide," Cohen continued, echoing Alex's thoughts.

And have it report through Cohen directly to Cosgrove, Alex thought, his heart sinking as he saw the whole strategy clearly.

"And have that autonomous company report directly to API," Cohen said. "That way it would be a strong and impressive company in its own right—"

"Then you would be *willing* to bring in the profits?" Alex asked.

"Then I would be *able* to."

In the silence that followed, Alex could hear the hammering of the workers on the new building which had now risen to just a few floors below Regina's windows. It was ironic, he thought, that the vigorous sound of those builders, which he had come to view as a symbol of his own determination to rebuild Regina, should be the only sound he could hear at precisely the moment he was losing control. For he saw no hope. If he gave up Europe, he would be unable to run the rest of the company effectively. And if he did not give in to Cohen, the profits would not be achieved. . . .

The silence in the room was interrupted by the blast of an air hammer. Alex waited for it to stop.

He already had his mouth open to concede when the idea came to him. He closed his mouth again, pretending to cough, and pondered his new thought for a moment, turning it quickly around in his mind to look for flaws. It might work, he thought. I might be able to beat him back after all. It was a risk, of course, because if Cohen called his bluff, Alex would still be giving up his power, but at least not to Cohen. Anyway, what have I to lose? he thought. He took a deep breath. "I believe we should ask Cecil Rand to hear this whole problem," he said smiling to Cohen. "He is the strongest figurehead the Regina Company has. I am sure he can help us solve our difficulties."

There was a rustle around the table as the general managers in the room looked at one another. Slowly their heads turned towards Cohen. It was clear to everyone that Alex was threatening. If Cecil Rand took over as the head of Regina Europe, the company would have all the autonomy it needed. It would be even more completely separate from API than under Cohen's plan.

"After all," Alex added, following up his advantage, "Cecil is a major stockholder of API—certainly no tool of theirs; it might even be the other way around." He laughed. No one in the room reacted at all. Then, very hesitantly, Borelli smiled.

Cohen saw Borelli's tentative smile and realized its import. His stomach contracted sharply. Christ, he thought, Cecil will end up on Petersen's side, particularly once he learns that bitch Barbara has decided to walk out on me.

Alex buzzed for Sylvie. "Please ask Mr. Rand whether he would be kind enough to join us," he said as soon as she entered. "Then come in yourself so that you can take down the full proceedings. I am most anxious that our decisions be completely recorded."

"I'm not sure that it's necessary—" Cohen started in a strangled voice.

"It is essential," Alex contradicted. "Sylvie, please get Mr. Rand."

A few moments later Cecil Rand, untidy, rotund, entered the room, appraising the participants shrewdly.

"Cecil, I appreciate your joining this meeting," Alex said quickly before Cohen, in any case too angry to speak, could interrupt. "We have some problem with the profits of several of our European companies. I thought it would be helpful to bring you in so that you can see for yourself how grave the problems may or may not be. Then we can all decide together what steps must be taken." Everyone in the room except Cecil Rand understood the threat behind the innocuous words.

"Okay," said Cecil Rand, sensing the tension in the room, but unaware of its cause. He worked himself into a chair slightly too small for him. "Let's see what I can do," he said pompously.

"I think you may be exaggerating the degree of the problem," Cohen interrupted, his voice flat with anger and the acuteness of his disappointment. "I believe that our profit problems are not as grave as you fear."

"I had understood that you had no reserves with which to support your profits if necessary," said Alex, watching Sylvie to make sure she was taking down every word. "Without such reserves, I think we all agree, your profit forecast cannot be guaranteed."

"It will be very tight."

"Is it your judgment that you can or that you cannot guarantee the profits you projected?" Alex asked. Then, with emphasis, he added, "Under the present circumstances?"

"I believe that a change in our organization might be helpful," said Cohen hesitantly, "but—"

"What sort of a change?" Petersen demanded. "I believe you said you were concerned that Regina seemed to be becoming a tool of an American conglomerate."

Cohen's anger almost overwhelmed him. His face went completely white; he seemed to be struggling for air.

Cecil Rand picked at a pimple on his cheek as he watched

Alex Petersen and Marty Cohen closely. Obviously there was some sort of fight going on between them, but what? He was about to demand an explanation when the pimple he was playing with broke and his attention was distracted for a moment as he found a handkerchief and dabbed at it.

It was Claude LeVecque instead of Cohen who answered Alex. "Certainly there is some danger of that problem," he said. There was a look of distaste on his face as he watched Cecil Rand dab at his spot. "However, I believe that our continued strong management will obviate this danger."

"Do you feel that my presence as both an appointee of API and your chief executive is harmful in this respect?" Alex demanded, determined to leave no ambiguity.

"Well, certainly there is always a danger," said Monsieur LeVecque, "that such a—"

"Life is full of dangers," Alex interrupted, purposely rude. He had to hurry LeVecque to a conclusion; if the conversation did not end quickly, Rand would be bound to want to know what was going on. Alex was surprised he had not interrupted already. And once he understood, he would certainly start a power bid of his own.

"Of course," said LeVecque, "but I don't think that the problem in this case is too severe."

"And you, Marty?"

Cohen's answer came with tremendous difficulty. Twice he began to speak and stopped without uttering a sound. Once Cecil Rand started to interrupt, but Alex would not let him. "Well, Marty?" he demanded leaning forward as if he were interrogating a suspect, "what do you say?"

"I suppose so," Cohen said finally, almost inaudibly. "I suppose we should stay as we are."

"Then will you find the reserves to guarantee your profits?" Alex pushed his advantage with full determination.

There was another long pause as they all waited tensely for Cohen's response. Even Rand, who still did not understand what lay behind this struggle, realized that Cohen's answer would be its climax.

"Will you?"

Cohen finally admitted defeat. "Yes," he said, his voice strangled.

The tension in the room collapsed with a sigh.

"What the hell is going on?" Cecil Rand demanded at last. His voice sounded petulant. He realized that he had been used in some way but he had no idea how.

"Well, Cecil, the key to our problem in Europe," said Alex Petersen carefully, "is that we are very tight on profits. We shall give you the figures in writing. No point in taking your time now. But we wanted you to join us to see if you have any suggestions as to how things could be improved."

"I don't," said Cecil Rand with complete certainty. He left the room still mystified and now thoroughly annoyed.

The others started to pack together their papers. Hardly a word was spoken.

Alex Petersen sat absolutely still at the head of the table. The tension which had built in him all day drained so suddenly that he felt totally weak, almost ready to faint. He looked down at his fingers and saw they were twitching as they relaxed.

Gradually, Alex recovered enough to be able to move. As he picked up his papers and walked the short distance back to his office, the shakiness in his stomach and limbs persisted. At one point he almost vomited.

He reached his office and closed the door, saying not a word to Sylvie as he passed her. She looked at him in surprise but kept silent also. Even more slowly, he walked over to his desk and, with infinite relief, sank into his chair.

It took several more minutes before his relief turned to elation. I managed to hold on, he thought. By God, I held on. I made it! I really made it. A smile lit up his face and unconsciously he straightened his shoulders. "I won," he said in a whisper, and then more loudly, he repeated, "I won!"

But his manic mood could not last for long; there was still so much left to do. I did win, he thought again, this time without exultation; but I wonder for how long. . . .

Chapter 23

F ollowing conferences of Regina International's management,
it was customary for the senior man present to host a dinner
for the conferees. The restaurant chosen was invariably filled
with self-confident men in five-hundred-dollar suits and even
more expensive sun tans.

Jack and Charlie's "21" Club, or just "21" as it was known
to its habitués, was typical. It carried an extreme air of clubbi-
ness, the men's room so inconspicuous that first-timers had to
make themselves known by asking.

The front part of the downstairs restaurant—noisy but highly
visible—was available only to celebrities. Upstairs, the front of
"21" was acceptable, but the rear was considered a social Siberia.
Alex had circumvented this hierarchical structure, however, by
reserving a private room. It was severely masculine, full of leather
chairs and pictures of long-forgotten racehorses waiting, sleek
and bored, while their owners proudly accepted accolades on
their behalf.

In keeping with the atmosphere, LeVecque had unearthed
a pipe and was drawing on it elegantly; Madame Housen had
dressed in a long tweed skirt which accentuated her shapeless-

ness and gave her a vaguely ecclesiastical look; and Borelli had chosen to sport an all leather suit.

He looks like a successful racetrack tout, Dr. Krause thought, typically Italian.

As each person made conversation with professional competence, the room hummed with small talk. Snatches of discussion about golf or skiing, the rate of growth of the money supply and the latest fashions intermingled with comment about families, the weather, traveling, and, of course, cosmetics. Occasionally, one or two of the managers would group themselves privately and start to talk seriously, but in a moment either Cohen or Alex, each for different reasons, worried about small groups gathering, would wander over and interrupt whatever underhanded plot or harmless conversation was in progress. But underneath these social conventions, there lay the ocean of their private worries.

"What effect do you think a change in your government would have?" Alex asked of Krause politely. He was not, in fact, interested in Krause's reply, so that while the German answered, his mind raced over the events of the day. Obviously Cohen would not accept his defeat gracefully; he would fight back and he had the weapons. In spite of his public promise, he could still renege and fail to bring in the profits; all he had to do was claim he was mistaken. Or he could form an alliance with Rand to share the power. Or—the list is endless, Alex thought. As long as I can't bring in the profits without him, I'm on the hook.

"So I tell you, the economic policy will remain very much the same," Krause concluded, as certain of his views as always. But the German's inner directions were less clear. This fight between Cohen and Petersen is going to destroy us, he worried. How can we concentrate on cosmetics? Already, his wife was noticing that something was wrong.

"What is going on with you?" she had demanded the other day. "You are muttering in your sleep and working late at the office again. Is there still that girl?"

"I have told you a hundred times there is no girl. Don't you understand that there is a major power struggle going on between two dangerous men, the Jew Cohen against the API man, Petersen."

"How can that do us harm?" She had sounded as belligerent

as if the fight were his fault. "They are all Jews, the Americans in cosmetics," she had exaggerated, adding that to the list of things she held against him.

Across the room Cohen, downing his third martini, had been cornered by Borelli.

"Interesting meeting," Borelli said to him. "How did you feel about it?" Perhaps, he thought, he could get a sense of who was going to win. His own guess was Petersen. He had been very nimble this afternoon. Then again, Cohen was very strong, and very well connected. If only I could be sure. . . .

"Yeah," said Cohen noncommitally, "I suppose it was interesting." His voice was so controlled it had almost a robot quality. That son-of-a-bitch Petersen, he kept thinking, that son-of-a-bitch Petersen, that son-of-a-bitch. . . .

When Alex Petersen returned to his apartment after dinner, he was exhausted but sufficiently elated over the day's outcome that he did not feel ready for sleep. He wished Pamela were in town so he could share his victory, but she was in Washington again, interviewing some senator who was in the news, or wanted to be. Instead he slumped into his comfortable leather chair and poured himself a brandy—only his second drink for the evening.

I won that one, he thought. Just. Now if we can start showing some real success. If all the probes would turn up something on those Scarpetti receivables. If I could be sure Cohen will really bring in those reserves. If only we had more money to build the business. He'd had a conversation with Regina's marketing manager, Garry Gainsborough, and Charlie Bentsen the day before.

"Our spice fragrances have all the hallmarks of success," Gainsborough had said pompously as they rode up the elevator to the advertising agency's offices. "But we need more money. We can't launch three new products with less than a million for advertising. Revlon spent ten million to launch 'Charlie.'"

The elevator reached its floor and opened smoothly onto the agency's reception area full of chrome and teak.

"I know your problem." Alex sounded sympathetic. "But we can't afford to spend more. Unless the products are so successful that you exceed forecast—"

"I am of the considered opinion that they will not attain such success levels if we don't spend enough—"

"May I help you?" the receptionist interrupted.

"Yes," Alex said, relieved. "I'm Alex Petersen. Mr. Gainsborough and I are here to see Mr. Bentsen."

"Ah yes, he's expecting you."

"We need more advertising," Bentsen demanded as soon as the formalities were completed. "You had a magnificent idea, Alex, when you suggested 'Parsley,' 'Sage,' 'Rosemary,' and 'Thyme'; but even the best idea will fail if we can't tell people."

"How much?"

"At least two million dollars for the rest of this year. A million more than we've got. That would give us an annual rate of four to five million. With that, we'd almost guarantee giving you a tremendous success.

"We just can't find another million dollars."

"I quite agree." Bentsen started the way he always did. "But I fear that if we spend only what we now have budgeted, we'll snatch mediocrity from the jaws of victory." He seemed rather proud of the phrase.

"Damn it, Charlie, I know it's going to be rough. But a million dollars should give us some impact. With really persuasive copy—"

Neither Charlie Bentsen nor Garry Gainsborough, both experienced men, was convinced.

Neither am I, Alex thought now, brooding in his apartment. Even though the commercials the agency had created had caught precisely the right spirit of purity and charm innate in the products, he knew that without more money for television the new fragrances would be a limited success at best.

Alex's phone rang so loudly in the silent night that he jumped, almost spilling his drink. "Shit," he said as he reached for the receiver. "Hello." His voice carried his annoyance.

"Hello, darling," Pamela's voice was full of fun. "The bear's hibernating?"

Alex felt a sudden surge of pleasure to hear her voice. "How nice of you to call!"

"I called earlier but you weren't back yet. How did your Europeans behave?"

"I survived!" He tried to sound facetious.

There was a pause at Pamela's end of the phone. "You sound as if you almost didn't," she said. "Did something go wrong?"

"It all went right in the end," he said, impressed again by her intuition. "In fact, I had a bit of a victory on my hands by the time we finished."

"Feeling good about yourself?"

"Yes, I suppose so—yes, I am. Wish you were here to share it."

"So do I."

Alex could feel his desire for her mounting. "Damn," he said, "I want you."

"Don't damn it. So do I. I'm still an awe, you know."

"Hurry back, love," he said urgently.

"I will."

He knew she would hang up now if he let her. She always ended conversations abruptly the moment she had heard or expressed what she wished to. "What sort of a day did you have?" he asked quickly.

"Mundane. On the phone with about sixteen press aides to arrange where and what for the interview. Then research so I know what to ask the old fart. Oh, and I went shopping. Found a gorgeous Oscar de la Renta scarf—"

"That's it," Alex said suddenly, as the solution struck him. He would license the name Regina to companies making accessories! You could buy Dior bed sheets and Cardin bathroom fixturies, why not Regina? No cosmetic company had ever done it, but why not? That's how they could finance the fragrances. . . .

"What?"

"Nothing, love. Just an idea. You're too much a reporter to understand." He wished he could tell her all about Regina, the problems, the money they needed, but. . . .

"Too much of a reporter not to understand, you mean," she said, slightly offended that he should be thinking of his business in the middle of their conversation.

"It just came to me," he said, understanding. "I wish I could share everything."

"I know," she said, forgiving him. "But I *am* a reporter."

"First and foremost," he said, teasing gently.

"Yes," she said, very seriously. "Yes, first and foremost." He must never forget that, she thought, whatever happens to us.

"I wish you were here anyway," he said, laughing at her concern. "But I do understand."

"See you tomorrow or the next day," she said and hung up.

Gently he replaced the telephone receiver, smiling. It *had* been a good day after all. Now, he thought, arising to get ready for bed, if I can only make it last. Or at least last through tomorrow.

Chapter 24

S tupid cunt was the first thought that came to Marty Cohen's mind as he awoke in the spare room. What a stupid cunt his wife was. His head pounded from the martinis at "21" the night before. But he knew he had to get her to change her mind about the divorce. He needed Cecil's support if he was going to beat out that shit Petersen. His father-in-law was devious at best, and what he would do if he heard that his daughter was asking for a divorce God only knew.

Cohen left his bed carefully so as not to make himself dizzy, then he showered and shaved. Barbara was still in her room. He put on the silk dressing gown she had given him on their last wedding anniversary and went downstairs to prepare a breakfast tray for her. Toast, coffee, a glass of the fresh orange juice the maid left in the refrigerator each evening. He added his usual morning shot of vodka to another orange juice and drank it quickly. It made him feel strong and confident.

When Cohen entered her bedroom, Barbara had been awake a long time.

"I brought you some breakfast, darling," Cohen said in a contrite voice. "Am I disturbing?"

"No, I was just waking," she lied. "Thank you."

He placed the tray on the bedside table and poured them each a cup of coffee, while she pulled herself half-upright in the bed, tugging the sheet up to her neck. Then he sat down beside her.

"I'm sorry about what happened," he said after a moment. "Deeply sorry."

"It's all right," she said, "about the anger and all that. But I'm firm in what I said."

"I know." He let his face show sorrow.

"It's really over between us," she said, realizing she would do better to say nothing, but needing to explain. "You don't need me—"

"I do!" he interrupted vehemently. "Don't say that. I do need you."

"But only for business—" That was the only need he ever allowed himself to show. At first she had been sure she could do so much more than that for him. And sometimes, in the early days, after they had made love or when the first of the girls was just a baby and Barbara would let her lie, gurgling contentedly, on the bed between them, he had softened, giving her heart hope. Once, when he had told her of his Aunt Ruth, there had even been tears in his eyes. But quickly he had covered his vulnerability by becoming angry. And as the years of their marriage progressed, he had held her ever more distant, refusing all but purely physical contact. "Only for business," she repeated sadly.

"No!" He was adamant. "You can think that, but it's not true." He knew he had to convince her. "It's not true," he repeated passionately. "I need *you*." For a moment he half realized it was true; he didn't need her just for business, but for himself. But no, he would not allow that sort of weakness to intrude. It was only because she was fat Rand's daughter that he needed her, so that he could be president. If it were otherwise, he would be dependent, as weak as a bitch himself.

"But you don't," she said sadly. "You never talk to me about yourself. You never let me hold you—"

In spite of his resolve, he felt his anger grow. The cunt. She would ruin his whole chance. "I do," he repeated. His voice started to take on the strange, almost robot quality she had heard the other night. "Why do you refuse to believe what I say? Why do you always argue with me? Why?"

It was the tone not the words that made an impact on her. "Marty, I would help you if I could—"

"You can," he said. "You must! I need your help."

Perhaps he does after all, she thought. More than he knows. She shook her head in doubt.

Cohen saw the movement but misunderstood. She's refusing me, he thought, the bitch is refusing me. For a second he felt for her the same hate he had felt for the whores before he had subdued them. He wanted to lash at her, subdue her too, make her cry in pain as they had cried.

She saw the constriction in his face, saw the muscles in his neck cord harden. She could not tell what he felt, but there was no mistaking his passion. "I don't know," she said, "perhaps—" He seemed so vulnerable in his violence.

He sensed her doubt through his rage and managed to hold onto his control. "I need you, Barbara," he said in a gentler voice. "Please think about it. Please reconsider."

"Yes," she said in a small, almost girlish voice, "I will. I'll think about it."

"Thank you," he said. Quietly he left the room. He was not sure where he stood, but at least he had won a reprieve. If he could only keep her quiet long enough for Cecil to talk to Herman Cosgrove. . . .

The licensing idea filled Alex's mind from the moment he awoke. Would other companies buy the name? He thought so. Regina carried enough prestige, especially with the "Wide World of Regina" campaign starting to attract attention. Could he get money quickly? He believed he could by demanding an advance of royalties. Hot dog! he thought, smiling at the anachronism. He could hardly wait for the business day to start.

Hurrying more than usual, Alex arrived at the office earlier than his normal 7:30 and waded impatiently through mounds of paper until Sylvie arrived just before nine.

"My God, you've been busy," she said in mock horror.

"Yeah, and I've got a magnificent idea."

"Your ideas always are," she teased him.

"Listen," he said, amused but busy, "get me Bob Stills over at Continental Jewelry." Regina often purchased fragrance pendants, Christmas premiums, and other jewelry items from Continental, one of the largest companies in the fashion jewelry field. In addition, Bob Stills, its president, was a longtime friend.

"He won't be in till 9:30. He's a senior executive." Sylvie grinned at him cheekily. He pretended to lunge at her. "I'll get him, I'll get him," she said, scampering out of the room.

"Bob, I've got an idea," Alex said without preliminaries when Sylvie finally contacted him half an hour later. "How would you like to license the name Regina and give some of that crappy jewelry of yours some prestige?"

There was a pause on the other end of the line. "Are you serious?"

"Of course I am. You don't think the name's got value?"

"Hell, yes, it has value. I'd be delighted to use it."

"So why don't you? Got to pay me a royalty, of course."

"Of course we will. We suggested a licensing deal to Regina two or three years ago—and to Revlon, Rubinstein, and Lauder. You all turned us down. How come you're interested now?"

"I know how rich you've become." Alex decided to keep it light. No point in exposing Regina's problems in detail, even to a friend. "You can afford a nice fat minimum."

"How much do you want?"

"About four times as much as you're willing to pay." Alex had no idea what to ask.

"I'm willing to pay whatever it takes, provided it's reasonable," said Stills, his voice very serious.

"How much? What order of magnitude?"

"Well, I don't want to commit myself. But I believe the offer we made last time was something like two hundred thousand dollars minimum guarantee against a seven percent royalty on the first five million dollars of sales, declining to a two or three percent royalty thereafter. That's the deal we normally make on this type of royalty. We have quite a few of them."

Alex barely managed to keep the elation out of his voice. That was more than he anticipated. "Well, perhaps not four times as much as that," he said lightly, "but certainly more than you offered then. After all, we're even more successful now— and the dollar's half its size."

"I think it's worth talking about," said Stills. It was clear to both men that a deal could be made. "When?"

"Anytime."

They made a date and hung up.

"By Christ, it's going to work, Sylvie," Alex hollered excitedly. "Ask Rand whether we've ever been approached by other potential licensees. He remembers everything. And get me our damn lawyers on the phone so they can tell me it can't be done." Alex's voice sounded jubilant. "Then get Glitter up here."

"Who?"

"Garry Glitter. You know, Gainsborough."

"Oh," she laughed. "I forgot he's nicknamed Glitter."

Alex's elation was not long-lived, however, for a few seconds later Sylvie hurried back in. "The man from the mail order house, John Simpson, is waiting in the lobby. Wants to talk to you."

"Damn."

"He wasn't expected," Sylvie said disapprovingly. "You've got several other appointments and—"

"I'll have to see him anyway, I'm afraid. He's potentially one of our largest purchasers. Reschedule Gainsborough for this afternoon, and bring in Simpson. I hope nothing is wrong with that order."

Alex realized there was indeed something wrong the second the nervous, hurried Simpson entered the room. He feared that the order was about to be canceled. Probably the competition got to them, he thought. Lower prices.

"Can I offer you coffee?" Alex was anxious to slow the meeting down so as not to be stampeded.

"No, I'm afraid I'm somewhat rushed." Simpson would not be put off. "You recall that we gave you a preliminary order when you visited our offices—"

The word preliminary was a terrible sign. "Yes indeed," Alex interrupted, thinking quickly. "Actually it was more than preliminary. We have already started manufacturing the product. My factory manager reported to me only today that he has bought all the components and has already completed a large portion of the order. As I told you, we are determined to provide even faster service than we committed."

"Oh," said John Simpson, suddenly doubtful. "Oh, I see."

"Now, what can I do for you?"

"When will the order be ready?" Simpson asked.

"I'm not sure, but it should be completed quite soon," said Alex, hoping that he could back up his bluff. He doubted that any manufacturing had commenced.

"The point is we're having some second thoughts."

"Oh really?" said Alex, his heart sinking but his voice steady. They could cancel if they wanted; he had no firm order. "Are you looking for a change in quantities or what? We shall certainly do what we can. Frequently orders like this one can be modified up to the last moment. We have a great deal of experience, you know."

"Well, we did have an opportunity to buy the same merchandise at a rather better price—" Simpson was becoming increasingly hesitant. "And since we anticipate larger quantities—"

"Certainly we can give you a price break if you are anticipating larger quantities," said Alex quickly. "Part of the price quoted is the amortization of the bottle molds and set-up times. The longer the runs, the less is the amortization per unit. If you would give us the new quantities, we'll recalculate our prices."

"Well, we are not sure that you would be able to—"

"Let's leave the decision of what we can do until we know precisely what you want," said Alex firmly.

"Just how long will your delivery time be?"

"We committed to six weeks," said Alex. "I believe we should have no difficulty in hitting that schedule." He knew that Simpson would push for quicker delivery and, while the tactic of claiming that the merchandise was already manufactured had reduced the danger of outright cancellation, it would be difficult to claim now that delivery could not be completed very quickly. The trouble was that he had no idea how fast the products actually could be made.

"We'd like to have the merchandise within a week. If you have already produced large quantities of it, I suppose you would have no difficulty with that?" John Simpson was an experienced purchasing agent. Already he was starting to sense that Alex was bluffing.

"Let me check," said Alex, buzzing the intercom for Sylvie. "Get me McAlister on the line," he said to her, referring to his factory manager.

"Yes, sir."

"I'll let you know in just a second precisely how fast we can move," Alex said, turning back to John Simpson.

McAlister was as taciturn as usual. "Yes?"

"You know that order you are manufacturing right now for the mail order house? Well, I have John Simpson, their V.P. of Purchasing, in my office and he's wondering just how rapidly we can complete the order."

"We're not onto that yet. You said six weeks two weeks ago. We'll have it done in three to four weeks' time."

"I know. Can you speed it up?"

"No."

"That's wonderful. You say two weeks you'll have the whole thing completed?"

There was a pause as McAlister digested what Alex was saying. "I could do that," he said hesitantly, "but it means delaying some regular business."

"Fine," said Alex.

"Also, we'll have to modify the small fragrance bottle they want and take a stock item. It's very similar except the neck is not quite identical."

"Less than two weeks then?"

"Probably complete by the end of next week. Nine working days."

"Fine, go right ahead."

"Right," said McAlister and hung up.

"We'll be done in two weeks," said Alex smoothly to Simpson. "The only holdup has been delivery on the fragrance bottle, and we've been able to develop one which is almost identical, although the neck shape differs by about a millimeter. I assume you have no objections."

"If it's indistinguishable to consumers, we wouldn't mind. Please send me a sample."

"Very well, then, let's talk about the increased quantities."

"We want to double our initial order," said Simpson, "but we have an offer for a price about thirty percent less than yours."

Alex knew that the profit margin Regina was making on this order was about thirty percent above cost. He knew too that Regina's manufacturing costs were comparable to those of other major cosmetic companies. Even with the higher quantities, the competitive bid was barely above cost. Probably the competitor assumed that future orders could be sold at higher prices once a business connection had been established. "Low-balling" was an old trick in contract manufacturing: make the initial bid very low and raise prices later.

"I'll match that if you insist," said Alex. "A 'low ball' is always possible. Of course, like your other supplier, I'll then raise prices to a significantly higher level over the next two or three purchases. We, like they, have to make a profit in the end."

"They said they wouldn't have to raise prices unless costs went up."

"If you have that in writing, believe it," said Alex coldly. "Otherwise I know they're losing money on their initial order and intend to raise their prices later. It's an old trick in our business."

"What would be your bid for double the order quantity?"

"I'd have to calculate it in detail, but I imagine we could reduce by about ten percent—and we'd give you a contract not to alter those prices for the first twelve months, and then only to raise them for known increases in components or union labor."

"That's fair."

"You will not find any competitor willing to beat that offer," Alex said with determination, "not at our quality."

The discussion became increasingly amicable; an hour later the men shook hands and Simpson left.

"Did you hold the order?" Sylvie asked anxiously.

Alex's voice was alive and boastful. "I doubled it!"

"You're meeting Bill Cerutti for lunch, sir," Colonel Brown-Williams telephoned to say a few minutes later.

"The Donohue Report?"

"Yes, sir. He wants to have a general discussion."

"He wants to crucify me."

"Well, they have to please their readers."

Alex laughed. "I suppose so."

"They have fifty thousand subscriptions at three hundred dollars a year," Brown-Williams explained, "all executives anxious for the latest piece of scandal: who fired whom, who's joining whom—"

"Half the time they're wrong."

"True. Actually, they're not as accurate as the Gallagher Report, which they try to copy."

"Nevertheless, everyone hangs onto their every scurrilous word," said Alex with irritation. "Do I really have to meet them?"

"I'm afraid you should, sir. I've put them off three times already. If I do it too often they'll print bad rumors about us. Even if they are false, they can do us harm."

"I'd better hurry then. No point in keeping Cerutti waiting." God knows, he thought, there are enough true rumors; Donohue wouldn't have to resort to false ones.

Alex hated the luncheon meeting, hated the false sense of camaraderie among the sharks, and the knowledge that if he said one wrong word it could be quoted out of context and damage not only Regina but himself. How different this was, he reflected, from that first luncheon with Pamela.

"How is Regina doing? Are sales going ahead?" Cerutti asked.

"We're doing fine."

"I know that. That's the universal answer of every businessman I talk to. What I want to know is *specifically* how are you doing? For example, what about sales of your new fragrances?"

"Our profits are improving fast," said Alex, ignoring the question entirely. He had no intention of giving away confidential information on the new fragrances. "I have every confidence they will reach twenty million dollars this year."

"I know all that," Cerutti repeated. "That's your official forecast. What I want to know is your own personal inside guess."

"My inside guess is that we will do precisely what we said we would," said Alex, realizing again how damned he would be if Cohen failed to bring in the profits needed; or if the Polish exporter diverted any of his inventory to discounters; or if more false receivables like those from the Scarpetti brothers turned up; or if . . . . "We're doing fine," he said, but he feared his voice sounded so somber that Cerutti would see through his bluff.

By the time Alex Petersen returned to the office, relieved that his luncheon ordeal was over but worried about what Cerutti had gleaned, even Sylvie had started to look harassed. Throughout the afternoon the problems accelerated.

First there was a round of budget meetings because the marketing department's forecasts for the balance of the year simply would not reach the overall profit level Alex needed. Again and again Alex went over the figures, first with Bryant, then with Garry Gainsborough, and finally with the individual product managers: digging into specific product or packaging costs; cross-examining on the need for promotional programs; vetoing an unessential piece of display material here; raising a price there. Following his example, the managers started to look at their own business in a new light and suggest ways in which money could be saved without hurting sales. Gradually the profit gap was closing.

"Okay, I'm going to stop now," Alex said. "But I'd like you to continue, and get back to me by Monday with a revised budget that hits our objective—and works!"

While the budget review was in full swing, McAlister arrived with the detailed briefing Alex had requested on the money needed for new equipment. Sylvie placed him in the adjacent conference room, and Alex and Bryant shuttled between the two meetings trying to keep the figures separated in their heads, trying to reduce expenses, trying to make ends meet.

No sooner had Alex dismissed the budget group than Sylvie announced that Mr. Posen, the international controller, was urgently requesting a meeting to describe the adverse effect of recent changes in the international exchange rate.

It hadn't taken Cohen long to counterattack, Alex thought.

"I have him waiting in my office," said Sylvie, "and I can't get a damn thing done while he's there."

"Put him in here. I'll finish off with McAlister."

Then there were more assaults. "A fire has been reported in our Colombian plant," Sylvie said. "Mr. Cohen's office just called. There's no one hurt though."

"Thank God for that," said Alex. Then, as his second thought, "Are we insured?"

"I called the insurance department," Sylvie said, pleased with her own efficiency. "They say they will reimburse the loss, but only in Colombian pesos."

"Hell," said Alex. "We'll have to negotiate on that. Lots of replacement parts have to be paid for in dollars. And it's damned difficult to obtain permission to convert pesos to dollars."

"There's also a telex that the Uruguayan situation is worse than anticipated. Apparently several people in the Uruguayan company knew about the stealing but kept quiet about it."

What the hell do I do? Alex thought as he read the telex. I can't fire everyone down there. And yet they all seem to be implicated. He brooded about the matter. It's really Cohen's responsibility, he thought. But he knew that he would be comfortable only if he handled it himself.

In the middle of this problem, a message arrived from the union's shop steward and grievance committee saying they wanted a meeting with Alex because planned working-condition improvements were not progressing fast enough.

"As if that isn't enough," said McAlister when Alex told him, "we have just heard that the FDA inspectors have found—"

"Why wasn't I informed that they were here?"

"We have inspectors from the government here almost every week, sir. These days, all cosmetic companies do. There seemed little point in alerting you."

"What did they find wrong?"

"They're paid to find things. So every now and then they have to earn their money—"

"They found something this time?" Alex asked, noting cynically how long-winded McAlister had become now that he was on the defensive.

"Yes, I'm afraid they found a code violation. It will be expensive to fix. It was not in the capital review you just agreed—"

Alex's head spun. "Why the hell not?" he demanded. The expenditures he had approved were already in excess of what Bryant and he had previously estimated. "How much more?"

"Almost half a million. We weren't sure that should be part of our normal review.

"For Christ sake," said Alex, his exasperation mounting. But there was no point in antagonizing Ken McAlister. "Never mind. Just send me the details."

"Yes, sir. I will."

"Can I approve a capital expenditure budget overrun of that much on my own?" Alex asked Bryant after McAlister had left.

"No, I have blanket board approval for the original capital budget. But I'd have to go back to API for any supplements."

"Would they approve?"

"I doubt it. Not with the shortage of funds throughout the organization."

"Well, they'll just have to agree if the Feds insist. The question is do you have the money available?"

"Hell, no. But we can probably borrow most of it."

"I thought we were borrowed up to the hilt."

"We are. But machinery is different. We can buy that on time, just like buying a car on time."

"Costs more, I suppose."

"Yes, it would cost more. Still, if it's the only way—"

"Seems to be. Unless our new licensing scheme brings in some unexpected money."

"Oh, good Lord, I forgot to tell you," said Bryant. "I got a call from Len Abrams at API. He got a note from you. Says he's fighting a trademark case and he's concerned that if we license the Regina name to unrelated companies it may suggest to the court that we see no harm in disseminating our trademarks broadly. Says it 'could have a deleterious effect' on the damages he might collect."

"For God's sake!" Alex exploded. "We can't worry about a far-fetched possibility like that. If there's nothing illegal about licensing, we'll damn well do it."

"I told him essentially the same thing. He said if you want to see him you should meet him in the courthouse. He simply cannot break away because he doesn't know when the judge will call his case. He'll be there until five."

"How do I know that he's not going to be in court?"

"Abrams says the chances are his case won't be called. In any case, there's no way of calling him, so you'll have to trust your luck."

"Shit," said Alex succinctly.

Bryant left, and for almost the first time that day, Alex was alone in his office. But all around problems continued to mount, and the frenetic pace gathered further speed. He wondered if he would ever be able to catch up.

"There's a Mr. Somerset Wentworth on the phone," Sylvie interrupted through the intercom. "He says it's personal."

"Somerset Wentworth? What sort of a name is that?"

"An old, established, New England name," said Sylvie, her voice without inflection.

"Okay," said Alex laughing. "I'll take it."

"Well, yes," said a voice with a strong Bostonian accent in a bored drawl. "My name is Somerset Wentworth. I represent a firm of the same name; we are executive recruiters."

"Oh," said Alex, guessing what was coming next. "I suppose you are calling to seek my advice."

"Well, as a matter of fact, that's precisely why I am calling."

"How can I help?"

"We have been retained to hire the chief executive for a major division of a Fortune 500 company. It is in the consumer goods area, dealing partly with fashion goods. I was wondering whether you would be able to suggest anyone for the job."

It was the standard approach, Alex knew. "Headhunters" looking for executives to fill major positions would call a likely candidate and ask whether he "knew anyone." If the executive gave any indication that he might be interested himself, a direct pitch would be made. Otherwise, the executive would usually recommend someone else. In either case, the headhunter benefited.

For a moment Alex was tempted. The problems at Regina seemed overwhelming. Would he ever be able to fight his way through? But the temptation was only momentary. A few months ago, Alex had not even been sure he wanted to remain in the business world. Now, sometimes to his own surprise, he cared deeply to make Regina a success. He couldn't just walk away. Nevertheless, he realized, it would be sensible to leave the door open. The risks he took by staying at Regina were colossal. But he had regained his zest, his sense of freedom. To hell with Wentworth and the safe way, he thought.

"No thanks, Mr. Wentworth," he said, his voice casual. "I'm not interested. Sorry."

"I was really asking about whether you knew someone else," said Wentworth, taken aback. Rarely did executives refuse to play the game.

"Were you?"

"Well, of course, if you yourself—"

"I'm really not interested, Mr. Wentworth. I don't mean to be rude, but Regina needs my services, and I enjoy the position. Thank you very much. Good afternoon." Alex hung up the phone, leaving a most impressed Somerset Wentworth on the other end of the line. Every executive started by saying no, but this man had done an unusually good job of sounding convincing. A tough bargainer, Wentworth concluded. It never occurred to him that Alex had merely been saying what he meant.

"You'll have to hurry if you want to get to the courthouse on time," said Sylvie.

"Right." Alex left the office almost at a run. As he rushed through the perfumed elegance of the reception room, he waved at Georgie, the receptionist. God, she's beautiful, he thought as he did every time he saw her.

"Why don't you ever stop to talk to me?" she called as he paused to wait for the elevator.

"I don't trust my self-control," he said just as the elevator door opened.

She giggled. At least he's not pompous, she thought. I wonder if Jimmy knows what a good man he is. She resolved to mention it to Jimmy Leonetti the next time she saw him, which would probably be this evening. Jimmy had not seen her for a day or two. Knowing him, he wouldn't be able to wait much longer. She fantasized about the dynamic ex-trucker and shifted slightly at her desk.

It was four-thirty when Alex entered the municipal courthouse building. The interior of the building, one of the busiest legal centers in the world, was also one of the sleaziest.

After searching through the crowds for a few minutes, Alex found the API general counsel ensconced in one of the few reasonably well-furnished offices. Leonard Abrams had been an assistant district attorney for the City of New York; his experience, his friends, and his present position gave him considerable status in the building.

"Hello, Lenny, how are you?" said Alex. "Glad I could catch you."

"Good to see you," said Abrams, putting down his newspaper.

"I gather you have some problems with our licensing idea?"

"Yes, I don't think you should do it."

"Why not?" Alex's hackles started to rise.

"Well, there is a certain risk—"

"Of course there's a risk," said Alex, his annoyance mounting, "but we need the money. The risk of not moving ahead is considerably greater."

"I'm not sure I agree."

"On what basis?" said Alex, trying to control himself. "Bryant told me you were concerned because our actions might harm the case you're working on. Seems to me that's a little far-fetched."

"It's worth considering," said Abrams defensively.

"Of course. But is it the real reason for your objections?"

"Well, no."

"Then what is your point?"

"Well, from a business point of view, I don't think—"

"From a business point of view, I shall make the decisions for Regina," said Alex, thoroughly angry now. "Please tell me whether there is anything illegal about the matter."

"No, nothing illegal."

"Then I see no reason not to proceed."

"Well, I cannot take the responsibility," said Abrams, becoming pompous. "There are considerable risks."

"How can Cardin, Dior, and a thousand other companies afford to license their names if the risks are so great?"

"Many people break the law; that doesn't mean we should."

"We're not breaking the law—"

"I was merely making an analogy."

"Damn it, I need the money from the license fees," Alex shouted. "If I don't get it, I'm not sure I can bring Regina's profits in on target."

Abrams, recalling that he had voted for the acquisition, reconsidered his position. "Very well," he said at length, "go ahead. I'll support you. You realize, however, that if something goes wrong it will be entirely your responsibility."

"Yes, I realize that," said Alex, still angry. "Of course I realize that if something goes wrong with Regina, it will be entirely my responsibility."

Chapter 25

The executive committee of the board of API met in rather stern session two days in advance of every board meeting to decide which items should be included on the agenda and to make sure that everything that was included would be approved automatically by the rest of the directors.

"Any group as large as a board is essentially mindless, quite incapable of making good decisions," Horace Bronsky had once told an interviewer from *Fortune* magazine. "That's why I never agree to sit on corporate boards unless I'm also a member of a much smaller steering committee which tells the board what to do."

"Fucking right," was Leonetti's comment when Roger Knight showed him the quote. "Fact is," he added, "most groups of more than one are pretty much mindless—although old Horace and me make a pretty strong team."

Bronksy and Leonetti were indeed the dominant members of API's executive committee. Normally, decisions with which they disagreed, although not vetoed outright, were delayed indefinitely in the committee.

Since both men were extraordinarily busy, executive committee meetings were usually short to the point of abruptness. Herman Cosgrove, the *ex officio* head of the committee, always felt himself harried. He would preplan for hours with Asquith how to complete the agenda in the time available and with the minimum questions. If he succeeded, he and Asquith, who was not a member of the committee but usually attended its meetings to provide technical assistance, would offer up a silent prayer of thanks. Sometimes, however, either Bronsky or Leonetti found something with which they disagreed and then all Cosgrove's preplanning was useless and the questions came with machine-gun rapidity, disconcerting him and sometimes leaving him thoroughly annoyed. When that happened, Darwin Kellogg, recently named a member of the committee, intervened to smooth over the argument. Fortunately, disagreements were infrequent, for even the powerful Bronsky and Leonetti rarely knew enough of API's operations to argue intelligently. Today, however, was different.

"Your presentation to the security analysts went badly," Bronsky said before the committee had even found their seats.

"Well," said Cosgrove trying to slow down the attack, "well, not so badly really. We certainly had a few tricky questions, but I think I handled them alright."

"Are we as bad off as it looks?" Leonetti demanded bluntly.

"I don't think that we have fundamental problems," said Cosgrove carefully. His stomach always gave him trouble when he was nervous, and his face was gray; but his training and self-control were such that his voice seemed normal as he continued. "We are having some difficulties with Regina. Also it is true that our cash situation is tight, but it can be rectified. And I don't believe it is becoming worse."

Is he just saying that, or does he believe it? Asquith wondered. For a moment he was tempted to contradict his boss publicly. "My God, we're in terrible shape," he wanted to cry. "We're goddamn broke!" But he saw Cosgrove's determined eye, and his rebellion withered.

"Then what was the damn problem at the analysts' meeting?" Leonetti demanded angrily. "I heard that some emaciated son-of-a-bitch in a black suit seemed to know more about the company than we do!"

"Well, I'd like to discuss that in more detail," said Cosgrove. "I suggest we get this meeting convened somewhat more formally."

Reluctantly Leonetti pulled up his chair and waited for Cosgrove to complete the formalities—the minutes of the previous meeting and the approval of a number of technical items such as the selection of auditors.

The formalities completed, Cosgrove rose to address the other men with full emphasis and pomposity. He was pleased he had slowed down the attack. Now if he could just keep control of the meeting.

Christ, what a windbag, thought Leonetti. But he could hardly interrupt the president's speech.

"Now, let me tell you this," Cosgrove started. "Our problem is not primarily that API is in cash-flow difficulties but rather that we are having major difficulties at Regina Cosmetics. Mr. Petersen, who is supposed to be running that operation for us, is either unable or unwilling to keep us informed of his progress. We are constantly in the dark. We don't know how much profit the company is presently making or is anticipating in the coming months. Worse, they suddenly developed an unexpected need for cash and were forced to ask us for about eight million dollars in order to be able to continue to run their business." Cosgrove's face set itself into a mask of total outrage. "Naturally, that has put us into a tight situation at API itself."

This time Asquith felt he had no option but to intervene. In his view, the president was grossly misrepresenting the facts and, as chief financial officer, he would be guilty of fiduciary malfeasance if he did not correct the record. As he and Cosgrove both knew perfectly well, API had borrowed over $20 million on the assets of Regina without mentioning that fact to Alex Petersen or his financial staff. Then, when Regina needed part of this money for its Christmas inventory build-up—as it did each year— there was no borrowing base left for the company to use as collateral with its banks. Petersen had been forced to demand that API return $8 million of the borrowed amount for its use. "I feel that—" he started to say, when Leonetti interrupted.

"For Chrissake, that's not what caused API's cash problem," he said. "You know goddamn well—"

"Seems to me that if eight million hurts you that much you're in worse shape than you're admitting," Bronsky said at almost the same moment.

"Well, now, gentlemen, I wonder whether I might—" Kellogg started to say. He was drowned out, however, by the others.

"I insist that one of our major problems is Regina," Cosgrove almost had to shout to make himself heard. "The man's gotta go." Cosgrove's stomach remained as taut as the core of a golf ball, but his fear gave him strength. The color in his face had heightened, and for a moment he looked almost powerful. "I cannot continue to operate with a man who removes cash from our company and places us into difficulties," he said, his voice stern.

"Perhaps I could say a few words," Horace Bronsky's voice was calm, but it was clear he would brook no interruption. "There seem to be two questions: Is Petersen a good man? And, separately, is it desirable for us to keep him or to fire him? Obviously those two questions are interrelated. But you will concur that they are not entirely dependent upon each other. Letting Petersen go might buy us some time. It would give us a story explaining why we're doing so badly. API's problems can certainly be obfuscated by suggesting that all we are facing is a little trouble with our cosmetics subsidiary."

"So you want to get rid of a good man so you have an excuse, is that what you're saying?" Leonetti demanded.

"That, I think, is what Herman would have us do," said Darwin Kellogg. He looked disgusted.

"The thought has some merit," said Bronsky, "particularly as there are questions about how good Petersen really is."

"Not much merit," said Leonetti rudely. "Anyway, who would run Regina?"

"We'd gain the greatest degree of credibility if we reinstated Cecil Rand," Cosgrove replied fast, thinking that if he could pull that off he could write his own ticket with Rand's investment funds.

"No," said Leonetti, instantly shattering Cosgrove's fantasy.

"Definitely not," said Bronsky at the same moment. "I would be quite unwilling to accept Rand. He has demonstrated a total inability to run the Regina Company in the past."

"Then we have an obvious alternative," said Cosgrove smoothly. "Martin Cohen. He has run Regina International very successfully for three years. He knows how the company works. He would be an entirely appropriate chief executive."

Cosgrove had agreed earlier with Cecil Rand that if he could not sell the board on reinstating Rand himself, he would do his best to have his son-in-law appointed instead.

"It really is time you became part of our investment group, you know," Rand had emphasized. "Once Cohen is working so closely with you, I think my colleagues would agree that . . ." As usual, he let this most meaningful sentence dangle significantly. Strange, Cosgrove now reflected, how anxious Rand had become to help Cohen.

"I'm not sure Cohen has the necessary stability," Darwin said quickly. "He has not—"

"He seems the best alternative," Bronsky interrupted firmly. "Unless you know something definite against him, Darwin, I would consider appointing him in place of Petersen the best thing to do."

"I suppose," said Leonetti reluctantly.

"Fine," said Bronsky. "That's decided. I understand your distaste, Darwin, but if we don't buy some time for API, all of us, including Petersen, will be in trouble. I'm afraid we have no alternative."

All this time Asquith remained silent, worrying whether he should clarify to the committee that the cash problem at API had little to do with Regina. They seemed to understand, but yet if they really knew how serious. . . . I'm not a member of the committee, he rationalized. I don't actually have the right to say anything.

"You got anything else for today, Jimmy?" Bronsky asked.

"That's it," said Leonetti, rising.

"The meeting of the executive committee of the board of directors of API is closed," said Cosgrove, barely managing to complete the sentence before Bronsky and Leonetti left the room.

"Sylvie, I've got to talk to Alex right away." Darwin Kellogg's soft voice was agitated. "Where is he?"

"He's taking a stroll through Central Park," said Sylvie. "He wanted to think."

"Damn," said Kellogg with feeling. "How long will he be?"

"I don't know. He usually walks from here to the zoo, then once around the little lake and back."

"When did he leave?"

"A few minutes ago."

"I'll catch him at the zoo."

"If you hurry." Sylvie giggled. "But it sounds ridiculous to me."

"And me," said Kellogg, also chuckling in spite of his agitation.

The moment Alex saw Darwin striding towards him he realized there must be a crisis. "What's the matter?" were his first words.

"I have some bad news for you, Alex. The executive committee of API has decided to fire you."

Alex's initial reaction was violent anger, so violent it amazed him. He had known he was a potential scapegoat from the day he was appointed. What he had not reailzed was how much of himself he had invested in Regina. "Is it definite?" he asked, barely keeping his voice under control.

"I'm afraid so. It will be ratified the day after tomorrow by the board."

"Shit!" said Alex suddenly and violently. He realized his fists were clenched and made an effort to relax his fingers.

"You really care."

"More than I thought."

"I tried to stop it, but it was three to one—"

"I know. Thanks anyway. I was put in as a scapegoat. What's so unfair is that Regina's turning around. There's no reason—"

"API's the reason. They're on the brink of disaster."

"I realized that when they borrowed money against Regina's assets without even telling us."

"They're trying to divert attention. Cosgrove says they need time. I don't know. I just don't know."

The two men stood in front of the cage where a lion paced backwards and forwards. Without a word they turned their backs on the animal and started walking into the park. Gradually their pace quickened until they were striding across the meadow, their steps as uniform as soldiers marching.

"Shit," said Alex again. Suddenly he stopped. "What do you think I should do?"

"I don't know. Do you want to fight?"

"Damn right."

"Probably the best thing for you to do is to see Leonetti. I don't think it'll help, but it might. They're not really after you, you see. It's only to take people's mind off the real problem."

"They might have told me," said Alex bitterly.

"They can't yet, not until the board meeting makes it official. No doubt Cosgrove will call you then."

"Yeah. No doubt."

"Is there anything really wrong with Regina now?"

"There's a hell of a lot wrong, but much less than there used to be. We've got it turned. The company can grow; I know it can. You can feel that it's just on the verge of gathering its full power. We're still coughing and spluttering, like a racing car that's a little cold, but any moment you'll hear the roar and our car will be off—"

"I'll call Leonetti as soon as I get back," said Darwin, "and tell him to see you."

"The trouble is that if API goes down, it will drag Regina with it. If the trade loses faith in our parent it will lose faith in us. If that happens, we'll die," said Alex, expressing his own thoughts rather than responding to Darwin. He suddenly remembered the trouble to which his friend had gone. "Darwin, I really appreciate it," he said. "I don't know how—"

"Okay," said Darwin. "Okay, I understand."

"Did Darwin Kellogg find you?" Sylvie asked the moment she saw Alex.

"Yes," he said tersely, "he did." His voice was harsh, almost rude.

She knew better than to pursue her questions. "I think you've got another problem," she said, sad to see him looking so drawn and beleaguered. "Hy Weissman is waiting for you. He's with Bryant. They are very anxious to see you."

"Send them in." Alex's voice was flat, emotionless, almost hopeless. He wondered what more could go wrong.

"Sorry to disturb you, but you've got a serious problem," Bryant started without preliminaries. Alex observed that Bryant had said *you*, and knew it was serious indeed.

"Fucking right," said Weissman.

"What's the problem?"

"The problem is that all the stuff you sold to that schlock artist who was going to export it to Poland is bouncing back," said Weissman. "We've found it in a dozen stores already. A discount chain up in Boston has it and we're getting complaints from our regular customers. Another in Washington has it; it's turning up all over the place."

"Christ," said Alex.

"It's already affecting our receivables," said Bryant. "People we've been pushing to pay on time say they need longer terms because of the diverted merchandise."

"We have Korsakoff tied up," Alex interrupted. "I don't see why we can't stop him and force him to pick up the merchandise. I'll call."

"Good luck," growled Weissman skeptically. "You'll never stop him."

It took Sylvie only a few moments to get Korsakoff on the line.

"Listen," said Alex the moment the exporter answered, "that stuff we sold you for Poland is being diverted into the U.S. How come?"

"I dunno, Alex, I couldn't help it," said Korsakoff. Alex could imagine him screwing up his wrinkled vaudeville face and shaking his head. "I dunno what happened, but don't worry about it. There couldn't be much."

"You owe us an indemnity in any case. You've got to pick the stuff up."

"Listen, Alex," said Korsakoff, his voice becoming a whine, "it's not so important. Like I tell you, the problem isn't so big."

"It's big to us."

"So, I'll do what I can. I'll look into it. Just don't push me too hard. Otherwise, if you push me too hard, I can't pay—"

"For Christ sake, you can pay perfectly well. It was you who pointed out that you do business all around the industry. You buy two, three hundred thousand dollars worth of stuff at a time—"

"And I don't divert."

"Right. Now this one's got diverted for whatever reason. You see to it that it gets picked up and you pay for it. That's our deal and I'm going to make you stick to it."

"I couldn't help it."

"That's not the point. The point is you owe us an indemnity. Or do I have to take you to court and get an injunction?"

"You take me to court, I go broke." Korsakoff emphasized each word as he spoke.

"The hell you will."

"I will. I don't have no choice."

"Your choice is to play by the rules."

Suddenly Korsakoff became angry. "How come you expect me to play by the rules when your own top people don't? How about the kickbacks? How about all that stuff that's going on in Latin America?"

Suddenly Alex felt the Regina house of cards start to crumble. If Korsakoff knew, then the problems must be widely known. "I don't know what you're talking about," he said coldly. "All I know is that I demand that you pick up the merchandise or reimburse us for our costs if we pick it up. If you have any accusations to make, give me the names of the people—"

"For Chrissake, I'm not gonna give you no names. You figure it out. You're the one with the kickbacks and all that shit going on and you know it."

"I know nothing of the sort. There is none of that at Regina."

"Oh, isn't there?"

"If you know something, tell me the names. Otherwise get off it and stick to the contract you made with us."

Out of the corner of his eye Alex was watching Weissman for any sign of concern. The big sales manager's face remained entirely impassive.

"Listen," said Alex, "somebody has to pick up that merchandise from the discounters, otherwise it will ruin our reputation. Our contract says you're responsible. So you pick it up." Before Korsakoff could say another word he slammed down the phone.

"Oh, shit," he said. "Korsakoff's going to go broke if we push him to pay. I don't give a damn, but it won't get the merchandise picked up."

"It can't stay out there," said Weissman aggressively.

"You think I don't know that?"

"I don't think anything," said Weissman. "I just know it can't stay out there if we're to make even close to our sales target."

"I know. If we can't get Korsakoff to pay, which I doubt, we'll have to pick it up ourselves."

"You'll have to pay triple what you sold it for," said Bryant shocked. "More."

"Yes, it won't be very good business," Alex admitted in classic understatement. He sounded tired. How much would he have to repurchase? he wondered. If all the stock for Poland had been diverted, Reginna could not possibly pick it up and still make its profit forecast. Maybe he should just let them fire him. Would he really care? He shook himself. Yes, dammit, he *did* care. Maybe there was still a way—even though he couldn't see it now. At least he'd try. "Hy, to start with I'll need a complete report on where this product is and how much is out there," he said in a determined voice. "We'll decide what to do once we know how bad things really are."

"Okay." The word was a growl of thunder in the sales manager's stomach. He was still growling as he left the room.

"You don't have a chance if you can't find a way around this," Bryant said as soon as the door closed. "If you have to pick it all up it's going to cost six, seven million dollars, maybe more. I'd have to advise you to take down your profit forecast immediately."

"I know," Alex said impatiently. "I know the implications. But before we do anything, let's get the facts. They may not be as black as they seem."

"Very well," said Bryant stiffly. "I suppose it won't hurt to wait a day or two." He hurried out.

Wonderful, thought Alex, his bitterness and disappointment finally overwhelming him. I'm forced to announce a decline in Regina's profits, the board fires me—which they were going to do anyway—and no one on Wall Street even thinks to ask about how API is doing. They've got all their explanations pat so no one ever has to dig for the truth. Just wonderful. . . .

Chapter 26

When Roger called her, Barbara Cohen intended to refuse to see him. It would be wrong. She still had a duty to Marty, a commitment; and he seemed to need her more all the time. "I don't think I should," she started hesitantly. "You see, I—"

"Please don't explain," he stopped her at once. "I understand."

But his voice was so disappointed—and her own desire to see him again so strong—that, in spite of herself, she found herself changing her mind. "Well, perhaps for a drink, or lunch—"

"Oh, anything." He sounded quite joyous.

"You shouldn't be so accomodating," she told him severely. "I'm selfish enough as it is without being spoiled even more."

"Very well, I'll be masterful," he said pretending to be stern. "Kindly see to it that you meet me for dinner tomorrow night. I'll pick you up at—"

"Oh, I can't. We're giving a dinner party. And I don't know whether my husband—" A new wave of guilt swept over her. She wasn't even sure whether Marty would come. What should she say to their friends? She shouldn't be starting something new.

"Never mind," Roger said quickly, sensing that she was about to back out. "How about the next day? Thursday?"

"Yes, I could do that." She was still doubtful. "You know, I really meant to refuse."

"You can't. It's because I'm so masterful."

"Only when I tell you to be. You're really meek," she teased.

"I'm not. I'm really a wolf in meek's clothing."

"Oh, that's awful. How dare you!" They both laughed, feeling their intimacy returning.

They arranged for him to pick her up at the entrance to the Waldorf Hotel on Park Avenue.

Roger Knight thought deeply about where to take Barbara on that first meeting. He was intensely concerned that they would be unable to keep the surprising sense of closeness and trust they had experienced on the airplane. He was determined to do all he could to hold and build that intimacy. Eventually he chose a charming old country inn overlooking the Hudson River, about an hour's drive north of New York. It was near Sleepy Hollow where Rip Van Winkle had been lulled into his entranced slumber.

As they drove out of the city together, Roger and Barbara talked only superficially; they felt reticent with one another, almost shy, confused that in some ways they were already intimate friends while in others they remained strangers. Barbara also felt guilty.

But once they were settled at a quiet window table their sense of peace returned. They blew out the candles on their table so that they could see more clearly the stars and the reflections in the quietly flowing river. The homes silhouetted between themselves and the water seemed quaint and as full of enchantment as when old Rip slept.

"It's lovely here," Barbara said.

"Yes, it's—"

"Let's eat!"

Roger laughed. "You're full of romance, I see."

She grinned at him. "True. But empty of stomach."

He signaled the headwaiter for the menus. They were hand-lettered, simple, pretty.

"I hope the food's as nice as these," she said. "I'm starved." Then looking at the menu, "What's spanikopita?" Here, under first courses."

"It's a Greek spinach pie," the headwaiter explained in a

strong Italian accent. "My wife, she's Greek. It's very good."

"Oh, does your wife do the cooking?" Barbara asked. "Do you own the inn?"

The waiter nodded.

"Then I'd love the spanikopita. It sounds marvelous. And the breast of duck as the main course. With corn."

"I'll have the same." Roger was too intent on her to care to choose for himself.

"The corn is on the cob," the owner explained.

"Perfect. I love it." As the waiter left, Barbara leaned towards Roger. "I love biting it," she said, baring her teeth, and then blushed at how suggestive she sounded. Quickly she dropped the subject. "How funny that such an Italian man should own such a very early American inn."

The wine waiter arrived and Roger ordered a Pontet Canet. A few moments later their food came. She tasted it at once.

"Oh, it's superb!" she cried. "And I'm so hungry." How long it had been, she reflected, since she had felt so eager for food.

Roger smiled at her. "Eat. It's good for you."

"Is that what your mother used to say? Mine always did."

Roger became suddenly distant. "No, I'm afraid not," he said politely. "As a matter of fact, I didn't see much of her as a child. She was very social. And she died a while ago."

"I'm sorry."

"Oh, no. It's been some years."

"No, I meant I'm sorry she never made you eat your food," she said softly, feeling a sudden rush of sadness. "Oh, I'm silly," she said quickly. "I tend to make everything into a soap opera. I love the wine," she added, hurrying onto safer ground.

"It's what they serve on the French railroad," he told her. "Stands up well to shaking. Funny to find it here."

"Tell me what you are thinking," she said suddenly. "I want to know about you. All I know so far is a bit about your job and Tough Jimmy and a little about 'the gray walls.' I don't know anything about the other people you work with, or your friends, or—"

"There's not much there, I'm afraid," he said. "I was thinking only obvious thoughts." He was not ready to make a commitment to her yet—too frightened of the feelings she unleashed in him, too aware of his own limitations to dare to share himself with her.

After all, this was only the second time they had met.

Going too fast for you?" she asked, smiling gently. "After all, it's only the second time we've met."

He looked at her with awe. "You know exactly what I am thinking!"

Suddenly she was terrified that he would discover that it was not real, this business of knowing what he thought. It just seemed to come to her once in a while with someone to whom she was close, Queenie for instance, and sometimes her kids, and now Roger. . . . "Oh, I can't," she protested. "You mustn't make more of me than I am. You'll be so disappointed."

"No," he said with utmost certainty. "No, I won't be disappointed to find out about you. I only hope you'll give me the time." The ordinary tone of his voice magnified his sincerity and emphasized his need.

Barbara felt a wave of emotion, like nothing she had ever experienced, sweep through her. She reached across the table to touch his hand.

"The only way you could disappoint me," he continued, still in the same mundane tone she found so moving, "is to stay hidden from me—or to go away altogether." He stared at the table. "How's the food?" he asked, shying away from his feelings.

She watched him across the table, her hand resting on his, but ignored his question. He looks like a sad little boy, she thought. "I don't really know what's going to happen," she said with the utmost gravity, "but I have a strong feeling that we won't be forced apart so that we can never see each other again; and I'm certain that as long as I'm here I won't ever go away in the sense you mean—"

"You may when you see me depressed and miserable," he interrupted sadly. "You've only seen me happy." He paused. "I'm rarely happy," he added factually.

Their absorption in each other was suddenly interrupted by a commotion at the next table where four businessmen were negotiating roughly over some real estate venture. One of them, evidently slightly drunk, started to pound the table. "Goddamn it," he shouted, "and I'm telling you the price'll triple in two years. Quadruple—"

Roger drew in a deep breath. He felt as if the interruption had let him come up for air. Barbara released his hand and poured herself a glass of water from the pitcher on the table.

"Tell me some more about your depressions. Is there a reason?"

"Oh, yes, but not in the sense you mean. Not what my father would call a *good* reason, like the loss of a friend, or financial calamity. The doctors aren't sure, but they postulate it's almost entirely chemical. That's why lithium helps. Apparently, part of the chemical imbalance is its absence."

"But not all?"

"No. Taking lithium helps, but it's not nearly a complete cure."

"Can just being happy help?"

"Of course. Happiness always helps. But only in the sense that it helps a broken leg. The leg is just as broken whether you're sad or happy, but you obviously feel better if you're happy."

"What are they really like, those depressions? I would like to understand more. How did they start?" Barbara touched his hand again. "Tell me."

Immediately he forgot his surroundings again. "I've never really been able to explain, not even to the psychiatrist." He hesitated, searching for the words to explain. "You see, just going to a doctor like that meant I was admitting to myself I must be crazy."

"But you weren't."

"I thought maybe I was but I didn't want to admit it."

"How awful for you."

"It was awful," he said, and Barbara realized it was an admission he had probably never made aloud before.

Then for a long time, Roger talked about his depressions, describing less about the facts and more about the feelings than he had before. He told her of the relief he felt skiing and later car racing, dwelled, at her insistence, on how the pain from his accidents had been almost welcome as a counter-irritant to the depressions, shared with her the despair he had so often felt. He talked hesitantly, terribly afraid that what he said would destroy Barbara's respect for him and kill her nascent love. Instead, he actually succoured her love until she was so overwhelmed by it she could hardly refrain from rushing around the table to cradle his head against her breast.

"You poor love," was all she could say when he finally stopped talking. "My poor darling. My poor love—"

They were silent then for a long time, gazing at each other and at the rippling streams of light on the river.

"The stars look closer than the lights across the river," said Roger, becoming nervous again at this intimacy, frightened of the vulnerability he had shown.

"Yes, they're very close tonight," she said pensively. "I believe this evening and these special stars will be with me for a very long time. But what will become of us and other evenings I don't know." She paused. "I'm married, you know," she said angrily. "With children and—" Her eyes filled with tears. "Oh, God," she said, her voice choking, "I just don't know."

"It's very hard for you."

"Yes," she agreed without hesitation. "Yes, it's very hard. My husband tells me he needs me desperately. And sometimes I believe he does. But most of the time he is so aloof and distant and cruel, as if he couldn't care less about me or the kids or anything except his job, his success. His ambition is immense. The two sides of him, his need and his arrogant coldness, just don't fit together; but I know they are both there. I've told him I want a divorce. But I can't leave him when he needs me so— and I can't stay when his need turns to hate—"

She could be exaggerating, Roger thought in spite of himself. "Sometimes things get out of perspective," he said gently. "Perhaps he looks worse to you than he really is."

"No." she said with certainty. "No, I don't think I'm exaggerating." She loved Roger for being so straightforward with her, for not pandering to her feelings without checking their accuracy. He is so thorough, she thought, so careful. But she knew her observations were correct. "I'm certain I'm not exaggerating," she repeated. "Sometimes I think he's living on the very edge of a breakdown. He's still functional at his office; but I wonder how long that can last."

"What is his job?"

"He's in charge of the international division of a large cosmetic company."

"Oh really," Roger started to say, "which—" Then all at once the obvious dawned on him. "Regina?" he asked. "*Martin Cohen?*"

"Yes. How did you know?" She looked up at his face. "Oh no," she said. "You know him, don't you?" Before he could respond she blurted out her real question. "Do you know him well? Will it change anything for us? Roger, will it change anything?"

"No," he said, answering slowly so that he had plenty of time to be sure of what he said. "No. I don't know him at all, merely of him. Jimmy Leonetti mentioned him the other day. Rather favorably. But he means nothing to me."

"Thank God," she said. "You frightened me so."

"Yes, I frightened myself too. I don't really know why. Except that I'm so fearful that something could come between us—" He hesitated. "Are we that vulnerable?" he asked.

"I don't think *we* are," she answered him after a moment. "But our circumstances are. So many things could go wrong."

"And probably will," he said morosely. "But not this evening," he added with determination. "Tonight is all ours. Perhaps Sleepy Hollow will get us and we'll wake up years later."

"I hope so."

"I hope so too," he said fervently and then, before he realized the import of the words, he added with the greatest sincerity, "I love you, Barbara."

She had known he did, and she had felt the words coming even before he said them. Even so, she was surprised. But Roger was amazed. Never before had he felt this way; never before had he wanted to tell anyone that he felt love. He had not even known he could. Yet now that he had heard himself say the phrase, so hackneyed and yet so incredibly full, he had no doubt whatsoever that he meant it completely.

"I love you," he repeated, reveling in the sound of the words. "Barbara, I love you."

"I love you too," she said, but hesitantly, full of guilt. "I shouldn't, I suppose, but—"

"Of course you should. You must. I would never forgive you if you didn't." He laughed recklessly. Then, suddenly, he was serious again. "Is it going to be very complicated, loving each other?" he asked almost like a child looking for reassurance.

"Yes," she said simply. "Very complicated."

Neither of them said a word for a long time. The restaurant was almost empty. Most of the lights in the houses across the river were out, and only the moon and stars lit up the river in cool mobile bars of light.

"Is there anything else?" the owner asked, breaking their reverie.

"No, thank you," said Roger. Then, realizing what he wanted, "Yes, may I have the check?"

The owner presented it instantly.

They drove slowly back to New York. At one point, Roger pulled to the side of the road and they kissed, first gently and then, for a moment, with rising passion.

"Yes, darling. I want to. A lot," Barbara said. "But not tonight. I have to get home this evening. And I have to think."

He kissed her again. "Yes. This isn't conducive to thinking, I must admit." He grinned at her. "I do want you, though."

"Good. So do I. Next time."

"Soon?"

"Soon."

"Very well. On that condition I'll drive you home."

As they drove on she suddenly started to worry about Roger knowing her husband. "What did Jimmy Leonetti say about Marty?" she asked.

"He told me that he was going to be made head of Regina. At least, that's what I understood. But I only talked to Jimmy briefly; he called as he was leaving API's executive committee meeting. The board will vote on it the day after tomorrow."

"But Alex Petersen has that job."

"Apparently the exec committee isn't satisfied."

"Oh, I heard he was doing well."

"I'm not sure of the whole story, but there seems to be more to it than just his performance. Something to do with problems at API. I don't know for sure."

"What will you do? Now that I've told you about Marty?"

"I don't know. It's really up to you, isn't it? What you told me is important, but it's privileged information. The question is, should Marty become president of Regina in his condition, as you see it? Would that make him better, or perhaps make him a great deal worse?"

"He's drinking, too," said Barbara, talking to herself as much as to Roger. "If he became president, he would be so proud to start with, so arrogant. But I don't know what would happen to him after a while."

"He might do a wonderful job. I still think you might be overdramatizing the situation, at least about his work. Sometimes people are half nuts at home, but perfectly okay at their business."

"Or he might go to pieces entirely," she said. "I don't know. I just don't know."

"That would be worse for us, wouldn't it?"

"Yes. Then he would need looking after."

"But why by you? If he needs psychiatric help, get him a doctor. You wouldn't fix his bones if he broke them. Why do you have to fix his head?"

"Because I'm his wife," she said simply. "If he needed me, I would have to help."

"Let's hope it doesn't come to that," Roger said fervently.

"Oh, yes, darling," she agreed. "And I think you should tell Jimmy Leonetti that Marty is not as strong as he seems. It would be unfair to ask you to hide it. Let Jimmy decide. If Marty can convince him, he can probably be strong enough to handle the presidency."

"And you'll be able to get away?" Roger was amazed at how tough she suddenly was.

"Yes, then I'll get away," she said with determination.

For the rest of the trip they drove in silence as profound as the night sky. Roger kissed her once more when they reached Manhattan, and then dropped her near a taxi stand so that she could get home without their being seen together.

"Good night," she said gently. "It was a lovely evening. I'll carry the stars with me."

"Yes," he said, moved almost beyond words. "Yes, it was." He groped for something more beautiful to say. But the only words he could find were to repeat, "I love you."

"I love you too, darling," she said and closed the door quickly.

He saw her run a few steps to a waiting cab. She turned and waved and then she was gone, leaving in Roger a joy so deep that he hardly dared move. If only it lasts, he thought, if only it will last. . . .

Chapter 27

"What d'you want?" Leonetti demanded before Alex was fully inside his office. "Molly, get Petersen here some coffee," he yelled before Alex could reply. "Sit down. Make yourself comfortable."

Alex looked for a chair but found none that was not cluttered with papers or books.

"Sit down, sit down," Leonetti commanded. "What d'you want?"

The intercom buzzed and Leonetti grabbed the phone. "Yeah?" He waved at Alex to move some books off a chair. "Okay, then sell now!" he yelled into the phone, "Why wait and take a bigger loss later? Chrissake! We've enough profits on the deal not to give a shit."

Alex placed himself on a chair, feeling slightly overwhelmed.

"Right," said Leonetti, slamming down the phone and turning back to Alex. "Kellogg said to see you. So what d'you want?"

"I've been told you're asking for my resignation as president of Regina—"

"We're firing you."

The intercom buzzed again. With instant reflex Leonetti

grabbed for the phone. "Yeah?" he demanded. "No, honey. I don't want to talk to him," he said. "Just tell him to do what I said." He hung up and turned back to Alex. "Now, what—"

But Alex had lost patience. "Why are you firing me?" he interrupted. "Regina is finally starting to do well—"

"That's not what we hear."

"Then you hear wrong." Alex began to open his briefcase. "I've got the facts here."

The buzzer sounded and for the third time Leonetti picked up the phone. "Yeah?"

Firmly Alex reclosed his briefcase. There was no point in trying to talk to this man. He started to rise.

"Where are you going?" Leonetti demanded.

"Call me when you have some time available. I'll set you straight about Regina."

"Goddamn it," Leonetti said into the phone, "I'm tied up with Petersen right now. Can't it wait?"

Alex hesitated. If he left, he would have no chance at all of holding his job.

"Okay," said Leonetti. "I'll take it."

Alex felt a wave of anger. If that's all Leonetti cared for Regina and for him, there was no point in trying to talk to the man. Without a backward glance he walked out.

"Quick meeting," said the beautiful secretary.

"He didn't have time," said Alex. "Tell him to call me if he gives a shit." He stalked towards the elevators, so furious now that he could feel the tears of rage stinging at his eyes.

The doorman caught him just as he was about to enter a taxi. "Mr. Leonetti says for you to come back upstairs."

In spite of himself, Alex was flattered. But he had no intention of returning to the office, a supplicant whose peevish show of temper had been forgiven. On the other hand, he didn't want to overreact; after all, Leonetti had made the overture.

"Tell Leonetti I'm in the coffee shop having a donut. If he wants to see me, I imagine I'll be there for ten or fifteen minutes."

Leonetti marched into the coffee shop three minutes later. "Now," he said grinning, "what d'you want?"

"I thought you'd never ask."

Both men laughed, but Alex knew that he had only seconds

to win over the tempestuous, opinionated Leonetti. "What I want is to tell you some facts about the fucked-up company you and the rest of the board acquired when you bought Regina," Alex started, realizing that his only hope with Tough Jimmy was to be equally tough. "Nineteen million dollars of obsolete inventory; four million dollars of nonexistent receivables; no new products; a demoralized management—that's what you got. That's what you paid the incredible sum of $280 million for."

Leonetti seemed about to interrupt, but Alex would not let him. "To make matters worse," he continued firmly, "Cosgrove then issued an official forecast to God and the world saying our profits would go up to twenty million dollars this year. Where he got that figure is beyond imagination."

Jimmy Leonetti had a broad smile on his face. He liked Petersen's style.

"That the board sanctioned such a forecast without any justification is beyond belief," Alex continued, knowing that unless he could convince Leonetti that he was personally involved with the success or failure of Regina, he would, in the end, make no progress. "If I were an independent shareholder, I'd sue every member of the board over that."

"You agreed—publicly," Leonetti said bristling. "You expect to be sued too?"

"Damn right I do if things go wrong. But not alone. I should never have accepted that forecast. Hell, I should never have accepted the job; I knew I was being set up as a scapegoat. But I was at a low ebb and I didn't care. Even so, when Cosgrove said twenty million bucks, I should have told you all to go fuck yourselves."

"So why didn't you?"

"Because if I had, Regina wouldn't have had a chance. Be cause I'm just dumb enough to be loyal instead of looking out only for me. So I took the risk, the *personal* risk—and now we just might pull it off." Alex was leaning forward across the coffee table almost shouting at Leonetti. "If we do pull it off, it's because of me," he said, no longer caring whether he sounded arrogant or not. This man had to hear him. He *had* to. "Lots of people helped of course. But it's been *my* neck on the line, and *my* ideas which have kept us going."

"Yeah?" said Leonetti, his voice almost menacing. Petersen's attack was beginning to nettle him. He liked his balls, but enough. . . .

"Yes! The new fragrances which will be the biggest thing propping up our sales were my idea. Licensing our name to get enough money to advertise them was too. Special sales, which I started, will do almost five million dollars this year. Our inventories are—"

"For Chrissake—"

"I know it sounds arrogant. But I'm telling you because someone has to. If I don't, no one will. Then you'll fire me. And if you do, you can just watch Regina go down the tube."

Suddenly Alex felt exhausted. Never had he fought so passionately before, believed in anything so strongly. But looking at Leonetti smiling cynically, he seemed to have made no impact at all. Fuck it, he thought, why bother? What's the point? He could feel his hands and knees, trembling. "Oh hell," he said wearily. "I can make you listen, but it seems I can't make you hear."

"Don't get smart-arse with me, kid. I heard you good."

"Then what are you going to do?"

"First thing is, I'm going back to my office. With you." He jumped up and strode out of the coffee shop, Alex almost running to keep up.

"Hey, you paid your bill?" the man at the desk called as they passed.

"Never got served," Alex shouted back over his shoulder.

"No calls," Leonetti said to his secretary as he swept into his office. "Siddown, kid." He slammed the door. "Okay, you got my attention. Now I want to know what's still wrong with the company—and don't try to bullshit me."

"I haven't so far."

"Yeah, I'll say that for you." Leonetti laughed. "For some kid from Princeton, you're okay."

"Thanks," said Alex, determined not to be patronized any more than he had been browbeaten. "But I'm no 'kid from Princeton.' My Dad was a carpenter and I worked my way through school."

"Could have fooled me." Leonetti's face showed a new respect. "Okay, I'll play straight if you do. Now tell me the problems."

For the next half hour, using the notes he had brought with him, Alex Petersen informed Leonetti precisely where Regina's business stood. Leonetti interrupted only occasionally to ask pertinent questions. To Alex's surprise, he already knew a great deal about the company.

"So we're left with only three problems big enough to sink us," Alex concluded, "the Polish exporter, international profits, and the bad receivables."

"Tell me more about them."

"Well, most of the problem is with three drug chains all controlled by the Scarpetti brothers—"

"Tony Scarpetti?"

"Yes."

"Shit." Without another word, Leonetti reached for his phone. "Get me Scarpetti," he said. "Yeah, Tony. Maybe I can help," he said to Alex. He handed Alex a phone extension. "Hello, Tony? Listen, Tony, how come you ain't paying your bills to Regina? Guy who runs it says you owe three million bucks—"

"Hello, Jimmy. How you been?" If Tony Scarpetti was surprised, his voice didn't betray it.

"Three million, Tony."

"Yeah. Is that what he says?"

"Yeah."

"Well, I don't owe him nothing. Where'd he get that crazy idea?"

"From his accounts receivable ledger. Don't act the dumb Eye-talian with me, Tony. I know you've got an MBA from some smart school."

"Wharton."

"Right."

"Well, one thing they taught me is when I owe money and when I don't. And right now, I'll tell you, I don't owe no three million dollars to Regina. Only the normal current amount."

"So why do they show you do?"

"How the hell should I know? Maybe they screwed up booking the deal I made with their sales guy Weissman."

"What deal?"

"I bought a whole load of close-outs from him at a cut price. Several times, for each of our chains. It was a deal."

"Fuck your deal," said Leonetti belligerently. "You got a

deal with Interland for your trucking. And with the Teamsters for your staff. You wanna start talking to me about deals, let's talk about those deals."

"For Chrissake, Jimmy. What do you want? This ain't some penny-ante stuff we're talking about that I can pay on as a favor."

"You're a big outfit, Tony. You can handle it."

"Now you listen to me, Leonetti." Tony Scarpetti's voice was rising. "This is over three million bucks we're talking about. And I made a perfectly legitimate deal with Weissman."

"Legitimate," said Leonetti sarcastically. "Legitimate my arse. You never made a legitimate deal in your life. You know damn well you can't make no deals that big with a goddamn crook sales manager."

"Sure, I know that. But Cohen authorized it. He was a V.P. so there was no problem. Anyway, he got me a letter from the old man saying it was okay. We're clear, Leonetti. We don't got to repay no fucking money to nobody."

"Yeah?"

"Yeah! Damn fucking right. See ya, Jimmy." He hung up.

Leonetti slammed down his phone. "What did he mean, Cohen authorized it?" he demanded.

"I don't know."

"Is Cohen in on the deal? Is that it?"

Alex realized that here was his chance to harm Cohen seriously, maybe even push him right out. All he had to do was give an equivocal answer, just damn him by faint praise. It was a tempting thought. Particularly as he would probably turn out to be justified; it certainly sounded as if Cohen were implicated. On the other hand, he was not sure. In all fairness, he should find out the facts before crucifying Cohen. "I have no reason to believe Cohen is in on any deal," Alex said firmly. "My people at Regina are a sound group. I'll find the explanation and let you know."

Leonetti was impressed by the integrity of the answer. He believed in standing by your employees and he realized how tempted Alex must have been to sell Cohen out. "Okay," he said, "that's it. Let me know when you find out more."

"Hey, wait a second. I came here because I'm going to be fired tomorrow morning. Is that still on?"

"Dunno, kid." Leonetti grinned for the first time since returning to his office. "Let you know." He punched the intercom. "Get Knight up here. And get me my broker and—"

Alex packed his papers back into his briefcase and started to leave.

"See ya," Jimmy shouted. "Hey, and listen, don't talk to Cohen about those Scarpetti kickbacks."

"Why the hell not?"

"I'm gonna have a talk with him myself. Crooks is more in my line than yours." Leonetti grinned hugely. "Ya hear?"

As he left, Alex had no idea whether his visit to Jimmy Leonetti had been successful or not.

By the time Alex returned to his office, the effort of his fight with Leonetti had taken its toll. His shoulders ached as if from hard physical labor. But Sylvie was already waiting for him anxiously.

"You've got a thousand calls," she said. "Korsakoff has been driving me crazy. He sounds really frightened."

"You'd better get him back," said Alex wearily, wondering what new crisis the Polish exporter would turn up.

"Listen, I've got to speak to you," Korsakoff started. His voice did indeed sound frightened. "Can I come and see you?"

"Tell me what you want on the phone. There's no point in meeting."

"I got this big opportunity, see, a big export deal—"

Alex could hardly believe his ears. "You've got what?" he demanded. "An opportunity for export?"

"Yeah. I wanna buy some more of your obsolete—"

"You have to be kidding," said Alex in total amazement. "I wouldn't do business with you on a bet. You're in the middle of cheating me on our last deal, remember? You're saying you'll go broke if I try to get my money back."

"This is different—"

"Listen, Korsakoff, you have to be out of your goddamn mind—"

"But this is different," Korsakoff repeated, his voice almost a wail. "I give you my guarantee—"

"When you pick up the diverted stuff from that Polish shipment I'll talk to you."

"But listen, I gotta get an export order. I borrowed some money for the last one from one of them loan sharks. I gotta pay back. An' I don' have the money yet."

Alex's surprise turned to exasperation. "For Christ's sake, Korsakoff," he said, "why should I care? Why don't you tell your loan sharks you'll go broke, just like you told me?"

"I can't," said Korsakoff almost in tears. "They won't buy it."

"I don't buy it either. What can they do?"

There was a pause, and Alex could hear Korsakoff swallowing. "Kill me," he said, "that's what. Kill me." He swallowed again. "Listen," he said, "I'll make it worth your while. We could share the profits."

"Now you listen to me," said Alex, now thoroughly annoyed, "when, and only when, you have picked up every last piece of that diverted merchandise will I even talk to you. I don't give one sweet damn what they do to you. There's no way I would even consider helping you until that merchandise is gone. And as for the gall of offering me a kickback—"

Suddenly Korsakoff's fear turned to violent anger. "Why not you?" he screamed. "Why won't you take the kickback? Not enough? Or are you some kind of holier-than-thou jerk?"

"We don't take kickbacks," said Alex coldly.

"Oh, really," said the exporter sarcastically. "Well, Weissman didn't have no scruples when he cut prices, and he's not the only one." Suddenly Korsakoff stopped. Alex could hear him panting. Then the phone clicked and went dead.

Alex, beyond being shocked, believed Korsakoff completely, particularly after hearing about Cohen earlier. But if kickbacks were involved, why had Sir Reginald authorized the special deals?

"Get me Miss Duke," Alex called to Sylvie. Clearly, Queenie was the only person who might throw some light onto that question.

"Listen," he said as soon as she was on the phone. "Can you give me some insight into why Sir Reginald authorized price cutting to special accounts like—"

"He didn't. I told you at that meeting on the winter 'look' that Reginald never cut prices." Her voice was utterly certain.

"How can you be so sure?"

"I knew him well."

"But Queenie—"

"I knew him," she repeated imperiously. "He would not have done that." She hung up.

There seemed nothing more to say. But he *had* done it. There was the authorization letter.

Perhaps Queenie had illusions about Sir Reginald and just wouldn't recognize the truth. After all, price-cutting was hardly the worst thing Sir Reginald had done in his life, Alex thought. But it was stupid, he reflected, and the path of least resistance. That certainly didn't sound like Sir Reginald. Suddenly Alex had a new thought: Had Sir Reginald authorized anything? Couldn't someone have written that letter after his death?

The telephone rang. "It's Korsakoff again," said Sylvie.

Alex picked up the phone.

"Listen, I know I diverted. Figured to make a one-time killing. But most of it's not sold yet. Couldn't unload as fast as I thought. That's one reason I'm out of money. You've got to help me." The exporter was calmer now, but the terror in his voice was quite clear. "I just talked to the loan guy. I need the money by tomorrow."

"I'll buy it back at fifty percent of what you paid."

Korsakoff became almost hysterical. "How the hell can I do that? I won't have enough money to pay back. They'll kill me, understand? They'll kill me!"

"I understand," said Alex, "but I don't care."

"You can have it back at what I paid for it," said Korsakoff, "and I'll agree to pick up the balance."

"You'll agree, but you won't do it," said Alex coldly. "Any merchandise you deliver back to my warehouse, I'll pay you fifty percent of what you paid for it. No more."

"But that won't be enough! At least make it seventy-five percent. You must make it seventy-five percent, otherwise I can't make the deal. There's no point. If I can't pay them back the lot, there's no point, you understand, there's no point."

"Very well, I'll pay you sixty-six percent," said Alex.

"Ya gotta make it seventy."

"Okay, but it has to be back in my warehouse before I pay you a penny. Our people have to check in every piece."

"It's on the trucks now. I'll send it over right away. Get your men there. You've gotta give me the money by tomorrow morning. You've got to!"

As soon as Korsakoff hung up Alex made the arrangements to have the inventory counted. With any luck the difference between the seventy percent he was paying Korsakoff and the original selling price would be enough to buy back the merchandise already sold.

For a moment Alex was elated; then he remembered. If only I can find a way to hang on, he thought grimly.

Chapter 28

Colonel Brown-Williams rushed into Alex Petersen's office, his British reserve if not abandoned, at least strained. He waved a magazine, a flush of pleasure on his face. "We did it," he cried. "I have an advance copy of La Maarten's article in *Business World,* and she's given Regina a damn good rating." He placed the magazine in front of Alex with a flourish.

At last some good news, Alex thought. About time. He glanced quickly at the article before him: "API—The Inside Story." His heart sank. He could understand George Brown-Williams' elation, but what he saw was a disaster. It was the bold type subhead that clearly spelled the beginning of the end. "API in Serious Trouble," it read. "Only Interland and Regina Strong." The last words had been circled boldly with a red felt pen.

"Yes, it is good for Regina, George," he said keeping his head bowed. "Well done." He hoped he was hiding his disappointment.

"We got a decent write-up in *Business Week* too. They reported on one of your speeches. Even Donohue was fairly positive."

"Well done."

"You don't sound terribly pleased, sir."

"It's been a hectic week. But I am pleased, George. You've done an excellent job. I appreciate it."

"Too bad API came off poorly." The colonel was beginning to understand Alex's reaction. "Will it hurt us?"

"It might."

"Oh, I see."

"Never mind, George. That's not really your problem."

"No, sir." The colonel's British manners had fully returned. "Will that be all, sir?"

"Yes, I think so. No, one more thing. Send a copy of this article over to Jimmy Leonetti right away. By messenger." Alex paused. "Hell, send one to Horace Bronsky and to Darwin Kellogg too. No harm in boasting a little."

"Very well, sir." Colonel Brown-Williams, his pleasure partly returned, marched out of the room.

Alex picked up the article again and felt a surge of pride as he saw Pamela's name on the by-line. As he read carefully what she had written he felt a sense of intimacy, almost of importance, that he could recognize the cadence of her speech; he felt like a member of the inside group who *understood*. But gradually his sense of pleasure was overwhelmed by the critical, articulate, sharp accuracy of the contents.

"Asociated Products, Inc., is almost out of cash, its liquidity dissipated by real estate adventures which give paper profits but huge cash drains," the article opened. "Interland Trucks, still closely supervised by its former owner, Jimmy Leonetti, now a director of API, makes some profits both on paper and in fact. And Regina cosmetics, with a strong new president who exudes confidence and competence"—Alex felt such a rush of pride that he could feel himself blush—"may be able to reach the ambitious, almost unreasonable profit goals promised by API management at the time of the acquisition. But the rest is dross."

Alex read the rest of the article hoping for some redeeming comment about API. But apart from more details about the soundness of the trucking and cosmetics subsidiaries, the article was wholly critical. "Our conclusion on API," it ended, "is, of course, strongly negative. The company's real estate business, while it might become profitable in the long run, seems likely to be catastrophic in the near future; its traditional food businesses are weakening; and Interland and Regina, while viable in their own right, are not large enough to keep the rest of the wallowing whale afloat. The company's cash seems desperately tight. Frankly, we question whether the corporation can expect to survive in its present form."

Oh Christ, thought Alex. Oh Christ!

At the API offices, Seymour Asquith hurried into Herman Cosgrove's office.

"I have an advance copy of the article that Maarten woman has written for *Business World*," he said, carefully eliminating all emotion from his voice. "I'm afraid it will give us problems."

"Let me see." Cosgrove's voice was equally controlled.

As he read the article, neither Cosgrove, sitting behind his desk, nor Asquith, standing in front of it, moved or uttered a sound; they seemed as lifeless as statues in a wax museum. But behind the facade of utter professional control, there raged in each man a turmoil of emotion. Cosgrove saw before him not an article in a business magazine, but a statement of the end of his career, of disgrace, perhaps of worse. The bitch, he thought with an inner violence of which he had hardly known he was capable. Oh, the awful bitch. He could feel his body trembling with the anger which was paradoxically also panic and, at the same time, deep, humiliated disappointment. He remained immobile even when he had finished reading, as if camouflaged from the marauding outer world by the size and importance of his office. Then, gradually recovering, his mind started to work again and the anger and fear he felt turned to hatred—a hatred of Pamela Maarten so potent that it overwhelmed his fear and gave him the adrenaline to act.

"How long before that bitch's article becomes public?" he demanded. "We have to protect ourselves from her lies and slander."

"It will hit most newstands Monday. So we only have tomorrow, Friday, and the weekend." Asquith felt totally beaten by the inevitability of the circumstances, numbed by the recognition that the article would probably be the death knell of API. He had been planning to borrow a further desperately needed seventeen million dollars next week, and the banks had almost agreed. But now they would back off. Without it . . . . And what would happen to him then? Asquith wondered. He had always felt so totally safe, assuming that, as a professional accountant, he would always have a job. But if API collapsed, and after those transactions in Liechtenstein, people would ask questions; ignorant questions because they would not understand, but the answers would look bad. "Only till Monday," he repeated. "There's no time—"

"Time for what?" Cosgrove snapped, totally impatient now with Asquith's tone of resignation.

"Too late for the loan. We'll never get it once the banks see this. We were so close. It's only seventeen million, but without it—"

"Can't you close this week?" Cosgrove demanded, seeing a hope after all. "Weren't you planning to close next Wednesday anyway?"

"I was. But I won't be able to now," said Asquith morosely. "If I appear to be pushy, they'll back off. And if I wait until they see this—"

"Tell them that Horace Bronsky just invited you to visit his place in Nassau this weekend," said Cosgrove with determination. "Suggest you delay the closing on the loan until you get back."

"Delay it?"

"Of course. Tell them you'd like to discuss it with Bronsky first anyway. If you play it right, they'll think you're going to switch the loan to Bronsky's bank. If you sound confident enough, *they'll* push *you* to close this week."

"It might work." Asquith was still doubtful.

It better, Cosgrove thought, his panic starting to press at his stomach once more. Pray God, it better. "Please make sure it does," he said coldly to Asquith, dismissing him with a wave of his hand. "Make certain it does."

Bronsky too, as one of the people mentioned in the Pamela Maarten article, received an advance copy. He read it very rapidly. "Please get me Mr. Leonetti on the phone." He spoke quietly but his secretary sensed the unusual urgency in his tone.

"You're quick," were Jimmy Leonetti's first words. "My girl only just gave me the article."

"Not quick enough this time. Can't sell. Nor can you, I assume."

"Berkowitz laughed at me when I asked him. Have you found a way? What about your clients?"

"No. I can't sell myself. As for my clients, my office informed them that I am an insider at API," said Bronsky drily.

"Not bad." Leonetti's voice sounded admiring.

"I have no idea what you mean," said Bronsky without inflection. "We always inform our clients where we stand. What I was calling about," he continued, "was—"

"Alex Petersen," Leonetti interrupted.

"Yes. I assume you've reconsidered our decision too?"

"Damn right, I have. He came to see me. Impressive as hell. And doing a good job."

"Also he's getting the only favorable press API's had. So you agree to keep him?"

"Yeah," said Leonetti. "The way things are going," he added facetiously, "maybe we should promote him to Cosgrove's job."

"The only person who could run that is you," said Bronsky seriously.

"Only if you and I can find some cash."

"I'm going to try," said Bronsky, but he sounded pessimistic.

"So am I," Leonetti responded, "but I'm damned if I know where."

Chapter 29

Jimmy Leonetti preferred to discuss certain matters in Central Park. Ever since he was a boy, he had felt a glow of pleasure in its trees and grass. Once he had mentioned the feeling to some friends—and been forced to fight half the area toughs to stop the taunts. He had won and, for a while, admiring the trees in Central Park had become a fad among kids from his neighborhood. But the park had the further very practical advantage that he could be certain there were no electronic bugs. His offices were "swept" every month, and rarely were any devices found—only once all last year. Once was enough.

Leonetti had asked Alex Petersen to join him in the park and they were now strolling on the meadows, looking thoroughly incongruous amidst young matrons pushing perambulators and little children playing. It was a sunny fall afternoon with a pleasant breeze and a bright blue sky.

"Bronsky and I talked about you," Leonetti said with little preamble. "We've decided to tell the executive committee we think you should stay on as Regina's president." He looked sideways at Alex to gauge his reaction. "By the way," he added, "we control the committee."

"I'm sure you do," said Alex. He bent down to pick up a twig. Strange, he thought, when I was offered the job by Cosgrove, I hardly wanted it. Then when I thought I was losing it, I was as mad as I've ever been in my life. Now that I'm getting it back, I don't feel a thing.

"Well?" demanded Leonetti.

"Not sure I want the damn job anymore." Then, seeing the other man's consternation, he laughed. "Oh, I might as well keep it if you insist."

"For Chrissake, don't joke about it. I'm scared shitless I might have to run it myself."

"Just say the word," said Alex. "Then again, maybe you'd prefer to run API. They need a strong right arm." He knew he was going rather far. Division presidents were not supposed to make even the slightest negative remarks about the parent company to a corporate director. Yet the point urgently needed making. Alex desperately hoped Leonetti knew all about the problems at API, hoped he believed Pamela's article, but he couldn't be sure. "I'd enjoy having you as a boss," he added, to lighten his words.

"Like hell you would," said Leonetti. "Anyway, they need more than a strong arm. A boot in the rear is more like it." He paused and added seriously, "I know about the problems."

Alex decided that he could risk going further. "I hope you do. I'm afraid they might be as serious as *Business World* said, perhaps worse."

Leonetti stopped as a little girl's ball rolled in front of him. He kicked it back to her absently. "Go on," he said.

"Asquith borrowed money on Regina's current assets without telling us, and when we needed the money—"

"Yeah, I know." He looked at Alex appraisingly. "But you got back what you needed."

"I had to," Alex said simply. "My point is that Asquith must be tight as hell if he had to go that far."

"I'm sure we'll work something out."

Alex looked at the older man shrewdly. "You're not really, are you?"

Leonetti hesitated. He was impressed. Petersen had already shown he had good sense and guts. Now he was demonstrating sensitivity as well. "No," he said, deciding to be straightforward, "I'm not sure. API has a massive cash problem. On top of that they're getting shitty press."

"Pamela's article certainly hurt us—Pamela Maarten."

"You know her, eh?" Leonetti, hearing the first name, was quick to look for even the smallest advantage.

"Yes. But I could easier get Mount Everest to shrink than influence her."

"One of those, eh?"

"She's brilliant." Alex found himself jumping to her defense: "I mean—"

"I know what you mean," Leonetti grinned. "The point is that with the lousy publicity and not much else going right, I'm not that sure we can find more funds."

"I assume they need a lot?"

"Yeah. I'll know exactly in a couple of days. Let's hope not too much." He paused. "How about you? Regina have enough now?"

"Not really, but I think we'll just about muddle through."

"Don't you have any reserves overseas?"

"I think so. But I'm not sure where or how much. My guess is Cohen's got them hidden. He's not too anxious to let me find them," Alex answered drily.

Leonetti chuckled.

A young couple lay intertwined on the grass and Leonetti walked up to them and inspected them with interest.

"Fuck off," said the young man.

"Is he bothering you, lady?" asked Leonetti innocently.

"Fuck off," the girl repeated.

Leonetti walked away laughing uproariously. His good humor was infectious and Alex found himself laughing too.

"Now tell me more about Cohen," said Leonetti, suddenly serious. "Last time we talked, you were gentle on him. Commendable. But we both know the fucker's a crook. He's stealing; he's trying to oust you by hiding reserves. And I'm about to kick the shit out of him."

"I gather," said Alex drily.

"But you'd better tell me everything you know or guess. If he's as tough as I hear, I'll need some real ammunition to bust his

balls. Lets start with how you guess he worked that Scarpetti
kickback scheme. And what's this about stealing out of your plant
in Uruguay?"

Feeling good, Jimmy Leonetti strode into the room where the
confrontation with Marty Cohen was to take place. There was
nothing he relished more than a brawl—and he anticipated that
this would be a good one. Cohen should be a tough opponent,
hard to bluff; and bluff was about the only weapon Leonetti had.
He was certain that Cohen was part of Weissman's scheme to sell
at ridiculously low prices, with kickbacks to himself and Weissman. But he had no proof. After his one slip in mentioning
Cohen, Scarpetti had refused to say another word. And on the
face of it, the deals made by Weissman were legitimate, covered
by Sir Reginald's authorization letter.

During the briefing in the park, Alex had told Leonetti of his
suspicion that the letter had been prepared after the old man's
death, and Leonetti had arranged for a handwriting expert to
check the signature the same day. It had turned out, however,
that the original of the letter could not be found; several people
had copies made on a poor duplicating machine, but no one
remembered ever seeing the original. From the copies the expert
could not be sure whether the signature was genuine or a good
forgery.

"Clever of Cohen, destroying the original forgery and keeping copies," Leonetti had said to Roger Knight. "So we'll just
have to find some other way to nail the bastard."

Roger's immediate reaction had been concern for Barbara.
What effect would Leonetti's attack have on her? If only it doesn't
force her to stay with him. . . . "Is it wise to attack without
hard evidence?" he had asked. "If you bluff him and he doesn't
cave in, he'll be warned and he'll cover his trail. Then we'll never
find evidence against him or the Scarpettis."

"Fuck that," Jimmy had said testily. "He's guessed we're on to
him anyway. If we wait, we'll just give him time to plan a defense. Better out-muscle the little shit before he's expecting us."

"Very well." There was no point in arguing with Jimmy in
this mood.

Today Leonetti felt invincible. He was pulsing with good
health. His eyes sparkled. The air smelled good. If there had been

a punching bag near he would have pounded it with glee.

"Well, well, well," he said, allowing his voice to boom as he walked into the room where Cohen waited. "If it isn't my old friend Martin Cohen." He had never set eyes on Cohen before.

To Leonetti's surprise, Cohen looked more desperate than tough. He had about him the air of a cornered animal, and next to Leonetti's exuberant good health, he seemed almost rat-like with fatigue. "I've never seen you before in my life, and you're not my goddamn friend," he snapped, sounding more testy than dangerous. "I've been brought here to attend some sort of inquiry without having any idea what we are all here to inquire about."

"*You*, old friend. That's what we are all here to inquire about —you. Only it's just *me* who's doing the inquiring. You aren't inquiring about shit."

"In that case, I'll leave," said Cohen angrily. "I'm not going to be at the receiving end of an inquisition." He half rose from his seat.

"Sit down and shut up," said Leonetti roughly. "I'm asking the questions."

Cohen sank back into his seat, his face white, realizing too late that he had made a mistake in trying to bluff Leonetti. By not walking out now that he had threatened to, he was admitting his vulnerability. But he couldn't leave without finding out whether these bastards had evidence against him or just suspicions.

Leonetti towered over Cohen, surveying him as if he were a safe but nasty reptile. He knew he had the upper hand at the moment, but he was not sure how to proceed. If he attacked Cohen head on, accusing him of collusion with the Scarpetti brothers, Cohen would no choice but to deny everything. If Leonetti countered the denials with the evidence he held, Cohen would see how very slim it was. Once he did, if he had any sense at all, he would keep on denying complicity—and keep the money he had stolen. On the other hand, if Leonetti tried to cross-examine and trip him rather than bully him, then Cohen, who was now terrified and therefore at a disadvantage, would probably regain his composure and become a hard man to confuse. These thoughts crowded Jimmy Leonetti's mind as he leant over the almost cringing Cohen.

The workers in the rest of the Regina offices were unaware

of any confrontation. Without concern they went about their business of developing new packages, evaluating photographs, dreaming up displays, typing letters, adding figures, or selling cosmetics. Their enthusiasm and confidence was rising almost to the point of jubilation; Regina was starting to move again.

Leonetti decided that his best chance lay in an attack from a direction Cohen would not expect. "I want to know how the hell you plan to get the money out of Uruguay." The attack was pure bluff. Leonetti had not a shred of evidence that Cohen was involved in the Uruguay scheme. He was simply playing a hunch. "You can't get cash out because of their currency restrictions, and there's nothing you can export from there except cows and gold—and the army has its eye on those. Pretty tough bunch, those military men. They shoot before they even start with the questions. So what's your trick?" He smiled benignly.

It was Leonetti's smile more than his words which frightened Cohen. "I don't know what you're talking about," he spat out. "What the fuck are you talking about?"

Leonetti's voice became as condescending as if he were talking to a recalcitrant child. "Oh, come on, Cohen. You know you've been sharing your crooked factory manager's profits. We have the amount. We know the dates. We have a sworn statement by two people involved. We even have a record of the telephone calls you made to Uruguay setting up the scheme. We know everything about it. Let's not play games, Marty." Leonetti's voice started to rise. "Let's get straight about this. I asked you a question. Now you give me a goddamn answer. I want to know how you're getting the money out."

"What difference does it make?"

"Oh, it makes a big difference. I want back good hard dollars here, not lousy pesos in Uruguay."

"You're not gonna get back anything."

"I wouldn't bet on it, Marty boy. I wouldn't bet on it." Leonetti's voice had become soft again, but menacing.

"Look, I don't know what you're talking about. If you have any other questions, ask them so I can get out of here. I'm busy. I've got better things to do than sit here."

Leonetti realized that he was losing his advantage as Cohen's terror abated. Lunging forward, he grabbed Cohen by the lapels and half hoisted him out of his seat. "Now listen here, punk," his voice grated, "I wanna know how much of the money you stole you got out."

"And if I don't tell you?"

Leonetti dropped Cohen back into the seat. "Give me that affidavit," he said to Roger, who handed him a sheet of paper with an official red seal. "This is an indictment against you brought by the Uruguay Bureau of Internal Revenue, stating that you are to be arrested on sight if you enter territorial Uruguay."

"What the hell's that?" Cohen's face showed his consternation.

Leonetti sighed. "I just said, it's an indictment—"

"What the hell does it mean? Let me see it."

"It means if you go back there they put you in jail and never let you out," said Leonetti. "Ever." He snatched away the paper. "It also means your nice little partner down there doesn't have to pay you. He and his government friends split everything you didn't get out. Now, how much did you still have down there?" It occurred to Leonetti that, judging my Cohen's reaction, he might have more at stake than they had realized. Perhaps he was using Uruguay to collect money from other countries. . . .

"Why should I tell you?" asked Cohen cagily.

Leonetti saw an opportunity. "Because I might be willing to get out the rest of your money. Without me you haven't got a chance." He paused. "I assume you can assure me that all those funds in Uruguay belong to you," he added in a businesslike tone.

"Of course they do."

It was Cohen's first admission that he had funds there. Not much use as evidence in court, thought Leonetti, but more than anything else we've got. "Sure," he said, "I always believe my friends. Matter of fact, we have some mutual friends: the Scarpetti brothers. They send you their best regards. Enjoyed your last visit." It laid an elementary trap. If Cohen were not so frightened and so angry, he would just laugh. Even given his present state, Leonetti hardly dared hope he would fall for it. "In fact, they've enjoyed all your visits, a dozen or more they told me."

"For Chrissake, I've only been there once—" Cohen stopped in mid-sentence.

Leonetti smiled at him even more benignly. "Well," he said in a soft drawl, "once is enough."

Cohen almost lost control completely. "You son-of-a-bitch," he screamed at Leonetti, "you fucking son-of-a-bitch. What do you want from me?"

"Just a little information, and a signature. That's all."

"And what do I get?" Cohen reacted like a trapped animal seeing an escape.

"Your money out of Uruguay. And immunity from prosecution. As long as you keep your nose clean. Oh, and as long as you tell me where all Regina's overseas reserves are buried."

"You can't prosecute me," Cohen started to remonstrate, but weakly.

Leonetti realized that Cohen's resistance was ebbing. It was time to strike, to overwhelm Cohen with such a bluff that he would sign anything.

"You're one goddamn miserable little bastard crook and you know it," Leonetti started in a soft monotone. "For years you've been ripping off Regina in Uruguay and other countries down there. It's a way of life with them so you figured you couldn't get caught. Now you're scared shitless that they've stolen the money you stole. And you're right—without me, you won't get out another cent. After a while you wanted more. Much more. So you started to steal real money, dollars; dollars in America." Leonetti's voice started to rise. "You made a deal with a low-life Mafia hood, Tony Scarpetti, and that stupid tub of lard Weissman, to sell the Scarpettis Regina products at a fraction of their value —with massive kickbacks to you. You thought you could cover yourself by forging a letter from Sir Reginald. You figured since you're the boss's son-in-law nobody's ever going to question you. You thought you were so damned clever, but the only clever thing you ever did do was to marry the old man's granddaughter—that and sponge off the family fortune."

"I did not sponge. I was an executive when I married her."

"Bullshit you were an executive. You were nothing, a two-bit tobacco salesman. That's a dirty enough business. You probably learned your crooked schemes while you were there. Probably learned them from Weissman who was your unit manager before he came to Regina."

"So what?"

"So you made a deal with the Scarpettis which gave you the kickbacks and left Regina with several million dollars of receivables which I can't collect because I haven't got legally binding evidence to convict Scarpetti. But I *have* got you, Marty boy, got you by the balls. I'm going to squeeze, my shithead friend, until you give me what I want. And what I want is a signed confession saying what you did with the Scarpettis. That way you won't be going to jail, at least not as long as you keep your nose clean. If you don't, you little prick, I'm gonna see to it that you never come out, never have a chance to be a free man like Tony Scarpetti. I don't have enough to convict him, but let me tell you, I've got more than enough to keep you in jail for the rest of eternity."

As Leonetti intended, Cohen was no longer listening to the individual words. Rather, he was bowed before the onslaught of Jimmy's voice booming over him.

"Roger, pass some of those exhibits," Leonetti ordered. "Not all of them; we haven't got the time."

One by one Roger handed documents to Leonetti who slammed them down onto the desk in front of Cohen.

"A list of all the times you talked to the Scarpettis." Slap went the first piece of paper. "A list of the amount of each transaction." Slap went the second before Cohen had a chance to look at the first. "A list of all the meetings you had with Weissman." Slap. "A rather interesting letter from a Swiss bank and a list of the times you visited Switzerland—"

"None of that's illegal," said Cohen controlling his fear with an enormous effort. "It's not true, but even if it were, there's nothing illegal about any of it."

"Oh, yes there is," said Leonetti with a grim smile. "I have here a copy of your income tax returns. That's how they got Jimmy Hoffa and a lot of other hoods. Kickbacks, for your information, Mr. Cohen, are taxable."

Suddenly Cohen collapsed. His eyes filled with tears and he huddled into the corner of his chair. The pressure of the last few weeks had been too much. "Oh my God," he wept. "Oh my God."

"Sign this," said Leonetti. "Sign this and sign it now."

"I'll have to read it first and clear it with my lawyer."

"Fuck your lawyer. You sign it right now or Roger Knight here will be on his way to see the IRS in precisely one minute from now. I'll read it to you. It says:

'I, Martin Cohen, of my own free will and without duress, hereby admit to having conducted certain illegal activities with the Scarpetti brothers consisting, among other things, of

'1. Selling said Scarpetti brothers Regina merchandise at a price far below its fair value and in return for this action personally accepting illegal cash payments.

'2. Not declaring this income for tax purposes.

'I also freely admit that I was aware that these activities were illegal both for the Scarpettis and for myself and that I undertook them purely for personal financial gain.

'Signed: Martin Cohen.'"

Leonetti thrust the piece of paper under Cohen's nose. "Sign this, you little shit," he said.

While Jimmy was reading, Cohen had recovered somewhat. "I'd like something in writing on the other part of our deal," he said in a more normal voice, "the Uruguay money."

"How much?"

"I have three hundred thousand dollars worth of pesos in Uruguay."

It was Leonetti's turn to be shocked. He had no idea it would be that much. But no concern showed on his face. "At the rate their inflation is going, you won't have half that much in six months," he said, playing for time.

"The money's invested. It grows faster than the inflation," said Cohen. "Don't take me for an idiot."

"I'm certainly not going to guarantee the removal of three hundred thousand dollars."

"And I'm certainly not going to sign this piece of paper unless you do."

"One hundred thousand."

"Two hundred-fifty thousand."

"I said one hundred thousand, goddamn it. You've got nothing to bargain with. When you're in an American jail what good is money in Uruguay going to do you? I cancel my offer."

For a moment Cohen almost broke down again. Then it was his anger which broke through rather than his weakness. "You can shove it," he almost screamed. "Shove it!" He wiped his forehead. "Either you give me a guarantee for two hundred-fifty thousand," he said, his voice trembling, "or there's no deal at all."

"Eighty thousand," said Leonetti in a cold flat voice.

"You bastard," said Cohen. "You lousy chintzy bastard."

Tears ran down his cheeks. He couldn't control them. "You bastard."

Leonetti turned away in disgust. "Roger, you'd better get going."

Roger Knight started for the door, convinced that Leonetti had pushed his bluff too far. There was nothing of significance on the pieces of paper Leonetti had slammed onto the table. And the document with the beautiful red seal had been manufactured in their offices the night before. If he left the room the bluff would be over. Cohen would have won. He reached the door and, trying not to hesitate, started to turn the handle.

Cohen let out a racking sob. "Okay," he said, "I'll agree to a hundred thousand."

"Very well," said Leonetti. He started to scrawl on a piece of paper lying on the desk, reading as he wrote: "I, Jimmy Leonetti, agree to guarantee the transfer of up to one hundred thousand dollars' worth of Uruguayan pesos into the United States at an exchange rate twenty percent below the bank rate current at the time of the transfer." He doubted whether he could arrange the transfer, but he would pay it out of his own pocket if he had to. It would be a cheap price to get the Scarpettis to pay up their debt. No doubt Regina would be delighted to reimburse him.

"Twenty percent below?" Cohen interrupted. "Who the hell said anything about a discount?"

"I did," said Leonetti flatly and signed the piece of paper. I'll give you this if you sign that." He shoved Cohen's confession towards him once more.

Meekly, Cohen signed.

Chapter 30

A lex awoke groggy after only five hours' sleep. His throat hurt. The day was as dank as any New York could inflict. No sooner had he opened his eyes than he remembered that this morning's *New York Times*, which he had seen late last night, had run yet another severely critical story about API.

"Christ," he muttered angrily as the telephone rang.

Pamela Maarten's voice was brisk. "Did you see the *Times*, darling?"

"Uh huh."

"It's not too good."

"Christ," he said again.

"You sound terrible. Got the jitters, or just the flu? Either way, it will probably get worse before it gets better."

"I don't quite recall whether Job was comforted by anyone with beautiful red hair or not," he said. "Where the hell are you, anyway?"

"From the nation's capital, direct to you: Will Congress pass the national Anti-Jello Coagulation Act?" Then in a softer voice she added, "I just wanted to make sure you were awake—and wish you luck."

"Yesterday Philadelphia, today Washington—"

"Tomorrow the world," she interrupted. "Actually, tomorrow it's Baltimore."

"Wish you were here," he said. "You sound sexy."

"I am sexy. What do you think the nation's capital is all about?"

"I'm happy you called."

"Love you," she said and hung up abruptly.

Alex smiled, touched that she had called, amused again by her lack of small talk. He was so pleased that he could now confide in her about his business life.

"How can we be close, if I can't talk straight about my job?" Alex had asked. "I don't want to have to think through every statement I make to you. And I certainly don't want every statement I make published."

"Do you really want us to be close?"

"Oh yes, I'm sure of that. Don't you?"

"Of course I do."

"Then we've got to be able to talk openly."

"Okay," she had said. "I'll inform my editor that I am emotionally involved with API and wish to be removed from the case. Anyway," she added drily, "I've written as much about the damn company as I care to."

Alex chuckled as he remembered, and jumped out of bed feeling better. His eyes and throat were still sore, but he could feel his energy rising with every second. As he entered the shower he started to hum, "I will succeed, I will succeed, in nothing will I fail," and then, as he felt the hot water sting his back, he raised his voice and bellowed the second part of his private anthem, "In all I do, in all I try, my efforts will prevail."

He stopped singing when he realized it made his throat more sore. Oh Lord, he thought, suddenly remembering the enormity of the task which faced him today.

Jimmy Leonetti also woke with a bad taste in his mouth, but not from flu; apart from his one heart attack, Tough Jimmy had been practically immune from disease. In his case, it was lack of sleep coupled with the frustration of losing. API seemed doomed and Regina would inevitably slide down with it. When API was forced into bankruptcy, the court would be called in to protect the creditors. No doubt Regina would be allowed to continue to operate since it appeared to be viable now that Petersen had taken hold. But the heart would go out of it. The new vitality at Regina, the new excitement, would erode. No federal judge or trustee in bankruptcy would allow the company the freedom it needed to be a fashion leader. Courts and corporation attorneys were hardly noted for showmanship and flair. The best that Regina could expect was to become another dull toilet articles firm—no fitting monument to that dramatic man, Sir Reginald.

Leonetti had, of course, known for some time that serious problems were building at API. But he had realized their full magnitude only the day of his confrontation with Cohen.

"Christ, I need a drink after that," he had said to Roger Knight as they left the meeting. "Pathetic bastard. I expected a brawler, not a poor cripple."

"At least we won."

"Yeah. Sure. We won okay. But there's no pleasure in kicking a dog."

By the time Leonetti and Roger returned to their office, it was in an uproar. Leonetti's secretary had been scouring the town for him; Bronsky had called three times insisting it was most urgent he talk to Jimmy.

"Where the hell have you been?" were Bronsky's first words when Leonetti returned his calls. Gone was all semblance of the country professor. "We've got a crisis over at API. Cosgrove tells me he's practically flat out of cash."

"Worse than we guessed?"

"Much worse. I've got Cosgrove and Asquith next door in my conference room right now. They say they need over a hundred million dollars within two, at most three weeks."

"Jesus in heaven."

"I agree. And that's about the only place you'll get that kind of money for Associated Products, Inc. I certainly can't raise that much. There's hardly an analyst left who hasn't got API on his 'sell at any price' list."

"What can they borrow against? They must have something."

"That's the biggest problem. They almost borrowed seventeen two weeks ago but they weren't quite quick enough and the bank backed out at the last second. Now Cosgrove has finally admitted that they've already hocked every asset the company has, even the assets of the subsidiaries."

"Shit."

"I'm not sure I'd want to lend them money even if I could raise it—which I can't."

"How about all that real estate?"

"Mortgage to the limit."

"Can't they sell it? Must be worth more than the mortgage value."

"It is. Eventually. But right now the real-estate market's dead. There just aren't any buyers."

"Why didn't they tell us earlier how serious it was?"

"I asked Cosgrove that. 'Error in judgment, I now realize,' was all the fool could say. Scared witless—if he had any wits to begin with. Listen, you'd better come over. Maybe there's something we can think of. I'll call Darwin; he may have some ideas."

"How about Blake Richards? He's the one who got us into the real-estate mess in the first place—"

"What about him?" Bronsky interrupted coldly.

"Forget it. I'll be right over."

The two men, joined a little later by Darwin Kellogg and, at various times, by Cosgrove, looking pallid, and Asquith and Abrams, looking like two undertakers, started to work with several of their own staff accountants on the books of the API corporation. For the next two days and nights, almost without interruption, they struggled to find a solution. Roger Knight, helped by an audit team from Bronsky's bank, scoured API's books for assets which could be sold or used as collateral. He found some hidden in various unimportant subsidiaries. But in the context of a hundred million dollar need, they were insignificant. Every major asset had already been used to support the company's borrowing base. Worse, the value of many of these assets had been severely exaggerated; and many reserves reduced to unrealistically low levels. Some of the exaggerations semed so serious to Roger that he guessed once the banks found out, they would claim fraud. Not only did API seem doomed to bankruptcy, but its chances of recovery would be almost eliminated by the need to fight huge court cases. That sort of litigation would bleed the company's operating strength and make it almost impossible to revive. In any case, additional borrowings were clearly out of the question.

Everyone involved was cooperating to keep the crisis confidential. If the news broke, nothing would stop the crash of the company. Nevertheless, rumors were starting. The stock had fallen from sixty to fifty dollars; Accounts Payable had received several worried phone calls from suppliers whose accounts were overdue; reporters and analysts besieged the corporate PR office for information. One large manufacturer of cartons demanded cash on delivery which, for a customer as large as API, was unheard of. The API buyer indignantly refused and switched the order to another company, but he had been shaken. Even the unions were calling to inquire about the rumors.

So far, however, there had only been rumors; no hard facts and no confirmation by company personnel. Most suppliers would not stop selling to a company of API's size on such slim evidence. If they refused and were wrong, they would have alienated a very large account for a long time.

Of course if the rumors were confirmed, all supplies would dry up instantly. At that point, the company would have to declare itself unable to operate and ask the courts for protection from its creditors.

On the third day, Bronsky, Leonetti, Darwin Kellogg, and Roger Knight met to discuss the matter.

"Seems to me there's nothing left to do," Bronsky declared tiredly. "We've been through every asset."

"Fuck it, there *must* be something," Leonetti insisted angrily, his fists clenched. "We can hold off for a while. At least we've found enough cash to last for a few more weeks."

"There's no point in waiting if we don't see a solution," Darwin said reasonably. "Moreover, we're legally bound to inform the stock exchange, the S.E.C., and the public if we see no way out. I don't."

"We're rechecking all our overseas companies right now to see whether we can find other assets there. I think we may still discover something, especially in Regina," Roger said.

"A hundred million?" Bronsky asked.

"Well, no. But maybe something. It would be a start."

"Then if we could build up sales," Leonetti started, "if—"

"If a frog had wings its arse wouldn't touch the ground," Bronsky interrupted. No one in the room had heard him use any vulgarity before. The impact was profound. There was a stunned silence.

"Guess you're right," said Leonetti at last. "It just seems its worth one last try."

"Let me offer a compromise," Darwin suggested. "Alex Petersen called me just before this meeting to say he has an idea which might help. He wants to meet with us tomorrow. That's Thursday. I doubt whether he can come up with anything we haven't looked at, but he's a bright guy and it's worth listening. In the meantime, you can look through your overseas assets again, Roger. Then, if nothing comes of either attempt, I agree with Horace that we should tell the world on Friday. The best day for catastrophes—gives everyone something to think about over the weekend."

Now it was Thursday morning. One more day to go before the shit hits the fan, Leonetti thought angrily. It will take a miracle to save API now. He rolled over in bed to reach for the *New York Times* which the housekeeper always put next to his bed late in the evening. He wondered what Alex Petersen wanted. Turning to the business section, he saw the latest critical article. "Christ," he muttered, "another goddamn nail in our coffin."

Queenie's private life was as well organized as her business. The maid brought her morning tea, strong and black with just the thinnest slice of lemon to modify the bitterness, at precisely seven o'clock. She sipped it as she perused the *New York Times;* first the news of the day, which she always read to be well informed even though it usually bored her; then the business section which never failed to fascinate her. This morning she noted with annoyance another negative article on API. Finally, she read the column on ballet, which was her passion.

Today, however, Queenie's ordered circumstances belied the excitement she felt. Two days ago she had heard that API was in worse trouble than most people realized. And yesterday she had heard that Alex Petersen was planning to meet with several key people to present a scheme which might save the company. Immediately she had called him to say she would attend. She was not sure precisely what she could contribute—or what she wanted to—but she had an intuitive sense that her presence might be important. She was now utterly determined that Regina should continue, perhaps even more determined than when Reg was still alive. It was his memorial. She did not much care that, if API collapsed, she would lose a great deal of money; she had never really appreciated how rich she was, so losing her wealth meant little. And she had enough money salted away in Switzerland to keep her well off. No, it was simply that she fully understood that if API fell, it would drag Regina down with it. And that she would not brook. She would fight to save Regina as she would have fought for a child had she been lucky enough to conceive one by Reginald.

She dressed and made herself up with more care than usual, making the effect seem unstudied—simple and businesslike. It's always harder, she thought ruefully, to make things look easy.

Roger Knight's first thought as he awoke was the same as his last before he fell asleep: Barbara, how warm she was making his life. He had never had daydreams of softness before. His fantasies had always been of speed and danger and, in parallel, of depression and death. These days, however, he often woke with impossible soap opera visions of Barbara dancing and laughing so that he could hardly erase his smile long enough to shave without nicking himself.

But happiness had always been a short-lived experience for Roger Knight. This morning it survived only as long as he remained half asleep; as soon as he awoke fully he remembered that API was on the verge of bankruptcy and nothing Jimmy Leonetti or he could do would cure the problem. He was totally pessimistic about today's meeting with Petersen. And he was deeply fearful that if Regina collapsed with API, Barbara would feel so obligated to Cohen that she would stay with him after all, instead of letting herself come to Roger to be cherished and loved by him the way he yearned. . . .

Darwin Kellogg was at least as unhappy as any of the people scheduled to attend the morning's meeting. He had been shocked to learn from Bronsky how desperate the situation at API was. But when he heard from Leonetti about Cohen, he was horrified. My poor little Barbara girl, he thought; she'll never leave him now.

When Barbara had confided to Darwin some months earlier her decision to leave her husband—and hinted at a new relationship—she had felt terribly guilty already. "I'm so afraid he needs me more than anyone realizes," she had kept repeating. "More than even he realizes."

"Barbara, are you sure you *are* helping him?" Darwin had asked. "Perhaps you are doing the opposite. Perhaps you are holding him down. It's impossible for you, or anyone, to take responsibility for another person's life. You're not God."

"You may be right," she had conceded reluctantly. "But I'm still afraid he needs help."

Now she'll never leave him, Darwin worried. When she finds out, she'll destroy her own life before she'll leave him. And of course Cohen will take advantage of her. Even if API does go broke, Cecil Rand will still have enough money to interest Cohen. Barbara would never ask her father for anything, Darwin thought again. She's far too independant. In fact, as Darwin knew, Barbara had never really understood or talked to her father at all; for it had been Sig Reginald who had taken on the role of her father, replacing his own son in this as in so many things. But Cohen would have no such compunction. Money seemed to be his sole objective. Poor Barbara. . . .

And poor Roger. How would he ever be able to fill the void Barbara's return to Cohen would leave?

Darwin had only gotten to know Roger well in the last few months. At first he had not realized that the relationship which Barbara hinted at was with the silent, dignified, introspective young man he had often seen around Tough Jimmy's office. He had started to suspect from several chance remarks Barbara had made. And only a few weeks ago, Barbara had shyly admitted her love for Roger.

What would happen to Roger now? Darwin knew nothing about his depressions, but he sensed a sadness in him, and a dangerously deep feeling towards Barbara. Poor Roger, he thought again. Poor Barbara. . . .

Darwin dressed and shaved abstractedly and then walked slowly, his step without resilience, towards the API building. He had absolutely no hope for the meeting.

The first part of the sale Alex Petersen planned to make to his listeners was the easiest: He had to convince them that the Regina Cosmetic Company had turned a corner and was worth every penny API had paid for it.

"I have thoroughly good news for you about Regina," he began. "I'm going to move quickly so that I don't take up unnecessary time. I am fully aware of the crisis at API.

"First of all, let me say that I can now promise a profit of at least twenty-*three* million dollars after taxes from Regina for this fiscal year. Perhaps more; certainly not less. Some months ago I had thrust upon me the forecast that we would achieve twenty million. I admit that I was terribly worried about our ability to do that. But today many things are going in our favor. Let me summarize them:

"Back then the dollar was strengthening, so that our balance sheet translation losses seemed likely to be larger than we had budgeted. Now the dollar has significantly weakened, so that we actually have a translation gain. I know it is unpatriotic, but I have to tell you that I'm damn glad the dollar isn't strong. I doubt if it will recover before year end—a sort of Christmas bonus for us."

There were limited smiles from Alex's audience.

"Next, let me show you the figures of our new fragrances, 'Parsley,' 'Sage,' 'Rosemary,' and 'Thyme.'" Alex brought out a chart. "They are runaway successes——four of the most successful new fragrances in the business. We'll sell twenty million dollars of the four combined this year if we sell a penny. Maybe much more. We're hot—"

"We certainly are," said Queenie proudly.

"I made a mistake and almost put us into a terrible position by selling three million dollars of obsolete inventory to an exporter who contracted to sell it to Poland but started to discount it in this country instead. By a stroke of luck, we got almost all of it back from him at thirty percent less than we sold it. Now that our special sales organization is in full swing, we'll be able to liquidate most of it through other channels at a second profit. I am therefore confident that, at the most, we shall have to write off only two and a half million dollars of obsolete inventory, which is more than covered by a reserve.

"A deal I have been developing with a large mail order

house, which I have mentioned to some of you, came through recently almost double what we had anticipated—"

"Good news," Kellogg interjected.

"And I'm happy to say that in the last few days Martin Cohen has uncovered almost four million dollars of what he calls 'hidden reserves' in our foreign subsidiaries."

"He's uncovering more and more lately," said Leonetti drily.

"Most important of all, our new 'Wide World of Regina' advertising is biting. We are getting favorable consumer comments and favorable trade reaction. We are winning awards. Above all, we are getting sales. You can feel them coming in; you can feel our business trembling at the starting gate like a greyhound. Our business is healthy, it's starting to grow, it's going to accelerate."

He's impressive now, Bronsky was thinking. When he took over, he was hardly more than a bright young marketing man. Now he's a good president.

"We have problems too," Alex continued in a more somber tone. "Certain major accounts, notably the Scarpetti brothers, owe us—"

"That's taken care of," Leonetti interrupted. "You'll get your money from the Scarpettis."

Alex's face lit up with pleasure. "Great! How did you manage it?"

"I managed."

Alex decided not to pursue the matter for the moment. "Then that's no longer a problem. Others remain: There are factory delays; many formulas are wrong; some of our people are still inadequate. But these are solvable problems. Overall, there is nothing to interfere with our new momentum.

"However, there is one problem we cannot survive. We are being dragged down by API. If the trade loses confidence in our parent, we cannot win."

We all know that, Leonetti was thinking impatiently.

"So it's obviously vital that we find a way to restore strength and public confidence in API, and I have a suggestion."

This was the moment of truth, Alex reflected. He could feel his shoulder muscles contract. It's outrageous, he thought. A carpenter's boy like me to be thinking of saving a company the size of API. A year ago I didn't even care whether I kept working there. If Dad could see me now. . . . Alex took a deep breath.

"I suggest that the only way to save API—and with it, Regina —is to sell the Regina Company. I recommend to you that we sell it for a mixture of cash and stock. One hundred million dollars in cash would bail out API, according to Asquith."

The silence in the room was so long that Alex began to wonder if his suggestion was simply impertinent. He felt a knot in his stomach.

It was Bronsky who broke the silence. "Who would buy?" he asked, keenly aware that, when the company had been sold previously, API had been the only serious bidder.

"Regina would be spun off as an independent company," Alex responded. "Forty-nine percent of its stock would remain with API. The balance would be bought for one hundred million dollars in cash to be raised either from an investment consortium or from a public stock offering."

Everyone in the room knew that spin-offs of major subsidiaries were not uncommon. A company forced to divest itself of a subsidiary had the choice of selling it to another corporation or of turning it loose as an independent company by selling its shares on the open market. This second course was the more complicated because it involved registering a new stock which required Securities and Exchange Commission approval and therefore necessitated a great deal of technical work. Also, the public had to be convinced that the stock was valuable, and a brokerage house had to be willing to sell the stock. All that cost money. On the other hand, this approach had the major advantage that the public was frequently willing to pay more for an interesting or glamorous company than was another large corporation.

There was another long pause in the room. "It could be done," said Bronsky finally. "At least in theory." Yet he continued to look dubious. "But frankly, I doubt if I could find private investors willing to put up that sort of cash. It's a risky situation and a lot of money."

"It's less risky for anyone who already has money tied up in API stock," Alex said. "If he puts up more money to buy Regina, he's making a sound investment—and he's protecting his investment in API at the same time. If he doesn't put up the money and API folds, he'll have nothing left at all."

Leonetti nodded in agreement. "That's true," he said, "true in theory."

"It's all theory," said Bronsky. "How can we find that kind of money to put into a cosmetics company which only a short time ago was rumored to be in difficulties itself? And how can you convince an investor to throw good money after bad? If we make too much fuss about the fact that API is going broke, we'll get such a run against the company that even a hundred million wouldn't bail it out. And if we don't use that threat to its full effect, then no one will buy out Regina."

"Then what about a public offering?" Alex asked. "The public finds Regina glamorous. I'm certain they would be delighted to share in its ownership."

"I imagine you're right," Jimmy Leonetti growled. "You could sell Regina stock to the public. But a stock offering is out of the question in the time we have left."

"Totally out of the question," Bronsky agreed. "It would take at least nine months to get an S.E.C. clearance. API will be dead long before that."

"Then so will Regina," said Alex bitterly.

"Then there's another question, which is equally doubtful," Bronsky added. "Would the majority of API shareholders agree to sell off Regina for about two hundred million dollars? After all, that's a fair bit less than API paid for it."

"I don't think we could get as much as API paid," Kellogg interjected. "After all, it would be a fire sale."

"Damn right, you couldn't," Leonetti said.

"That doesn't mean that the majority of API stockholders would be willing to sell for that amount."

"If they don't," said Alex, "API will run out of cash and go down the tube entirely."

"You're back in the same bind," said Bronsky. "If that point is made strongly enough, it becomes a self-fulfilling prophesy. And if you don't make the point that strongly, then you won't get API shareholders to vote for selling off Regina."

"I think you will," said Roger Knight quietly. Everyone except Leonetti looked at him with surprise. "Almost twenty percent of the stock is represented in this room right now," Roger explained. "And I'm pretty sure that Mr. Bronsky could persuade old Mr. Baldwin, who owns nearly ten percent, to join him. That would add to about twenty-nine percent."

"Good God!" said Bronsky. "I had no idea this group controlled that much. Who owns it?" He paused. "Clever of you to find out," he added.

Roger nodded. "The ownership breaks as follows: Old Mr. Baldwin has about 1,400,000 shares; Jimmy controls about 700,000; it's our understanding that you, Mr. Bronsky, control about 300,000; and the trust for Barbara and the Cohen children, of which Darwin is a trustee, controls about 800,000 shares—"

"I'm afraid there's a problem there," said Darwin Kellogg in his mellow voice.

"What problem?" demanded Alex.

"Sir Reginald left the trust for Barbara and the children under the joint trusteeship of Queenie, Barbara herself, and me. But some years ago, Barbara Cohen abrogated her right in favor of Martin. She felt it was only fair after all he had done to build up Regina. I'm fairly sure Martin would be against the deal."

Leonetti started to laugh. "That's a hell of a note. I've solved that one already without even knowing it. Martin Cohen will do what I say."

"The figures you gave only add to 3.2 million shares out of fourteen and a quarter million outstanding," Bronsky interrupted before Darwin could query Leonetti, "about twenty-two and a half percent. Who owns the rest?"

Roger was impressed by the speed of Bronsky's arithmetic. "Miss Duke controls 900,000 shares."

"Then it would seem that your statement is correct, Mr. Knight," said Bronsky drily. "No doubt the majority of the shareholders of API would go along with the deal if we start out with twenty-nine percent of the shares in favor."

"Yeah," said Leonetti, bringing the group back to practicalities, "but where the hell do we get a hundred million bucks? I sure as hell can't raise money like that on a high risk venture like this."

"Nor can I," said Bronsky with finality.

"Look, there must be a way," Alex insisted. "We have a

powerful, successful company in Regina which will turn up more than twenty percent of that much money in profits alone."

"You need most of your profits for working capital," said Roger Knight mildly. "And for the moment, you need to borrow more cash just to keep the business going."

"That's because it's growing. We desperately need to build a new factory, otherwise we can't keep up with our customer demand. And obviously we need cash to finance our inventories and our accounts receivable. We can't sell merchandise unless we have it to sell."

"Exactly," said Bronsky. "So you can't finance any of the whole hundred million dollars for API out of Regina's profits. In fact, on top of the hundred million, you'd need a cash advance on profits."

"We can't go public," said Leonetti. "And I'll be damned if I know how we can go private."

The discussion continued for hours and, as the room got hotter, the frustration mounted. In the late afternoon they decided to break for some hours while Leonetti and Bronsky checked to see if there was even a chance. They reconvened that night. Both men looked dejected.

"I am forced to tell you flatly that I cannot raise the money," said Horace Bronsky. "My backers consider the deal too risky without collateral. I'm sorry."

"Ditto," said Jimmy Leonetti. "I can't do a goddamned thing."

"For what it's worth, I have tried as well," Darwin Kellogg added. "The best I could do was about ten million dollars from a very rich old friend of Sir Reginald's."

Alex Petersen was on his feet instantly. "We have a strong going concern in Regina," he insisted passionately. "At least one person believes in it enough to put up money. And API could be strong again with some better management and the cash to bail it out of its current problems."

Throughout the day, Queenie had watched silently as Alex Petersen, the junior among these business giants, fought forcefully and stubbornly to save Regina. He's just out to save his own skin, she had thought critically at first. He's out for himself, trying to make a name. Then gradually, as first Bronsky and then

Leonetti admitted defeat, and only Alex continued to fight, her admiration grew. Perhaps he really cares after all, she reflected. Sure he's out for himself. But wasn't Reg all his life? Wasn't I? Is that so bad? At least Petersen has balls. Evidently the others have lost theirs somewhere on their way up. . . .

"There must be a way," Alex repeated almost violently, his fist thumping at the shiny surface of the board room table.

"I don't think there is," said Horace Bronsky. "Sorry, but it looks over."

No, Queenie thought, suddenly as angry as Alex. No, it's not over. She would not allow it to be. Let all these strong men admit defeat. That was not how Reginald would have reacted. Nor would she. At least Petersen still has some guts left, she thought. Well, so do I.

In a single flash of insight Queenie knew what she must do. There's always a way, she thought again, utterly determined.

The silence in the room lengthened, a silence of defeat in all of them except Queenie. Even Alex Petersen was about to resign himself to the inevitable. I've lost, he thought. There's no way, nothing left to be done.

But he was wrong. Softly, her voice full of emotion, Queenie broke the silence which had lasted by then an interminable four minutes. Her words were the first she had spoken in several hours. "I have a solution," she started.

None of the men were looking at her when she began to speak and they hardly realized the impact of her words. She repeated herself to attract their full attention.

"I have a solution," she said in a more powerful, certain voice.

Suddenly the atmosphere of the room changed completely. Every one of the men leant forward in his chair, his attention riveted on what she had to say. She smiled at them almost gleefully. "'There's always a way,' Reginald used to tell me. Well, there is a way now." She paused, fully aware of the drama she was causing, and reveling in it. "I would be willing," she continued, emphasizing every word, "to sell all my API stock. Even at today's prices it's worth forty-five million dollars. And I've got another five million in other savings. I'll put all of that into buying back Regina. That will bring us halfway there. Now with that to start, and ten million from Darwin's friend, we'd have sixty percent of what we need. Horace, can't you and Jimmy raise the additional forty million?" She knew they could, once they had that much. The solution seemed obvious. She could hardly imagine why they had not asked her long ago.

It was Alex who broke the silence. "I'm afraid you would depress the API stock far too much if you sold a block of that size," he said sadly. "Also you'd have to register your stock for public sale. You have a right to such a registration under the terms of the Regina sales agreement, but it would take far too long."

Queenie looked crestfallen. "But if I own the stock, I must be able to sell it. There must be a way to get my money out so that I can buy what I really want. I don't want API stock. I want Regina stock." It was the first time anyone in the room had ever heard her voice not under control.

"If you agree to sell the stock to my clients later at today's prices, I believe I can arrange for a personal loan to you of thirty million dollars using your stock as collateral," Horace Bronsky said quietly. "You would be giving us an option to buy at today's prices at any time over the next ten years. You'd have to pay interest on the loan at eight percent a year. That would be 2.4 million dollars a year. However, if Regina continues to be successful, you'd earn most of that in dividends. The rest, at least in the early years, you'd have to pay from your own funds."

"And if it's not successful, and I can't pay?"

"Then we'd call your loan and take over your shares and, if necessary, all your private assets. You'd lose everything."

"Would thirty million be enough to raise the hundred you need?" Queenie asked.

"Damned right," said Leonetti promptly. "If you put up that, my clients would match it. Like Alex said, it makes sense for them to protect their API investment. If you have that much faith, with your knowledge and reputation in the industry, I could find people to go along."

"With your thirty, Jimmy's matching amount, and ten million from Darwin's friend, we'd have seventy million subscribed," said Horace Bronsky. "I could find the remaining thirty."

Queenie will do it, Alex realized suddenly. She would take any risk to save Regina. Christ, he thought, how simple it was in the end. So simple! API will have its hundred million dollars

and Regina will become an independent company again, a growing, dynamic independent company, with style and vitality, with
fun and laughter. . . .

"I have only one condition to make," Queenie interrupted
his train of thought.

"What's that?" Bronsky asked suspiciously.

"I insist that Alex Petersen must remain president of the
Regina Cosmetics Company. Then I'd go along."

"Thank you," said Alex very quietly. Suddenly he felt close
to tears. "Now I have a condition to make too." The others looked
at him with surprise. "I would like Jimmy Leonetti to agree to
run API, at least for a while."

"Yes," said Horace Bronsky. "I would insist on that too."

"Damn right," said Leonetti and grinned broadly. "Damn
right!"

Chapter 31

M arty Cohen was totally shattered after his meeting with Leonetti. His face was so haggard, his hair so unkempt, his clothes so untidy, that even a casual observer watching him walk unsteadily down Park Avenue would have assumed that he was crazy. He hardly knew he was walking at all. Occasionally, a tear would coast down his face. At other times the flashes of anger would come so rapidly, one after the other, that he felt as if his brain were burning.

The thought that he was going mad came to his mind. "They've driven me mad," he muttered. "They're all out to get me. Everyone. Petersen, Leonetti, Knight, Kellogg, Queenie, Aunt Ruth . . ." He rolled off the names like a litany. "They're driving me mad," he repeated again and again. "Driving me mad, driving me mad . . ."

Laboriously he walked on muttering. Passersby stared at him and moved out of his way, not wishing to be involved. It took him several hours to find his way home.

When he entered the front door, the maid saw immediately that there was more wrong than simply another drunken binge.

"Mrs. Cohen," she called, "Mrs. Cohen, there's something wrong with Mr. Martin."

Barbara hurried down the stairs. The moment she saw him she ran to him and put her arms around his shoulders. "What's the matter?" she asked. "What is it?"

"They're trying to drive me mad," he said in a matter-of-fact voice. "They're trying to get me."

She put him into their bed then, and he slept for twelve hours. In the middle of the night, he snuggled close to her and she felt more caring for him than she could ever remember. If only he could have shown her this need earlier. Now all that was left was the caring she felt for all weak things. There was no love at all. I love Roger, she thought to herself, more than anything in the world, but Martin's my husband and he needs me.

All that night, Barbara wrestled with her dilemma. I love Roger, she thought again and again. I want him, I want to live with him. But each time the opposing thought intruded, destroying her fantasy: Marty is my husband and he needs me.

The next day, Cohen seemed very much recovered. He talked rationally to Barbara, apologizing for sounding strange the night before. "I was upset," he explained. But he was subdued in a way which Barbara had never seen before. Gone was his arrogance and anger.

Cohen stayed home for two days, complaining of a headache, and moped around the house like a little boy with nothing to do. The following day he went to the office, but he was home again by five and his subdued, beaten look remained. He asked her whether she thought it would be convenient if he left town the next day to visit Regina Canada. She could not remember his ever having asked her anything like that before.

Barbara was relieved when, after vacillating for a while, he did decide to go to Montreal. She had hardly slept for the last few nights as thoughts of her love for Roger battered against her sense of duty to Martin. They were like waves, those thoughts, pounding against an immutable cliff, causing an awful turmoil in her heart. With Marty gone to Canada, and the girls at school, she finally had time to think more coherently. Sadly, sometimes desperately, she paced her room. Once she sat down at her typewriter to try to calm the turmoil by putting it onto paper.

Very gradually, the crashing conflict of her thoughts did calm. In the end, just as waves pounding themselves against the cliff will eventually subside leaving calm water, her thoughts resolved themselves into the simple understanding that, for her, the only right thing was to stay with her husband—for as long as he needed her.

The tears ran down her cheeks softly as she telephoned Roger's office.

"He's at a very important meeting over at API," his secretary told her. "Shall I reach him for you?"

"Just tell him I'd like to see him. Is it possible? Same time and place."

The secretary called back within a few minutes. "Mr. Knight says he should be there by eight," she told Barbara. "He says he'll need cheering up," she laughed.

"Oh, God," Barbara groaned as she hung up. "Oh, God!"

How could she stand to meet him, see him run up to her, his face alive with love—and know it was the last time? I can't stand it, she thought again pacing the room. Her anguish was so great that she could not be still. The walls gave her claustrophobia. Was there nowhere she could run, she thought wildly, nowhere she could hide?

The children came home at one, full of laughter and stories. "Mummy, Mummy, do you know what Suzy said when Miss Margaret told her . . ."

Barbara could hardly tolerate their happiness. How could they laugh when her world was so hopeless? Eventually, the girls went to visit some friends.

"I'm leaving," she told the housekeeper abruptly. "Back tomorrow." She offered no other explanation, no cover. There would be no need for one in the future, she realized bitterly.

It was only five o'clock when Barbara arrived at the beautiful Sleepy Hollow inn where she and Roger had first dined together and where, in the last months, they had met several times and spent so many loving hours.

"This is a message for you, Mrs. Knight," the innkeeper told her in his thick Italian accent. He beamed at her. Such nice people, he thought, this pretty lady and her slim, shy lover. "Mr. Knight, he call and ask me to write."

Barbara opened the note: "The meeting on API is going to

last much longer than I thought so I won't be there until very late, three or four in the morning maybe. Sleep well. Sorry, love. See you in the morning."

"You wrote down all this?" she asked the innkeeper. "That's really very kind."

"Mr. Knight say it very important I get down the whole thing." He leant towards Barbara with a big grin. "I think what he really mean is he love you a whole lot more than he say." He grinned as Barbara blushed. She's really such a nice lady, he thought again. "Now don't look so sad," he said. "He'll come soon enough."

Barbara nodded mutely and turned away so that he should not see her tears.

The room was the one they always had, large and bright, with a quilt bedspread and chintz drapes. They used to laugh together that such a very Italian innkeeper should run such an authentic early American establishment—laugh together, and make love for hours in the four-poster bed. We were so indecently happy, she kept thinking. She couldn't help wondering whether the way she felt now wasn't some sort of punishment.

Barbara spent the evening writing Roger a forlorn poem of love lost, of farewell. It was almost unbearable for her to write and equally unbearable to leave unwritten. She wept quietly, with resignation, and wondered whether she would have the strength to tell him what she had to. Eventually, exhausted, she slept.

When Roger arrived, worn but triumphant from his long meeting, the sun was beginning to lighten the night. Already the sky was bright enough to give promise of a beautiful fall day. The colors of the maple trees would be magnificent.

Roger kissed her. "It's a beautiful morning, darling," he told her as she awakened. "Let's watch the sun come up. It should light up the maples over the stream."

She arose and hugged him. "I love you, Roger. I always will," she said.

He found her slippers and wrapped her in the comforter from the bed. Then, with his arm around her, he led her onto the balcony. Without a word they watched the sunrise.

The vision of his great red Maserati rose to Roger's mind as he saw the same red color in the maples. But for the first time ever in his fantasy, the great red racing car was standing still and beautiful behind the country barn which served as its garage. He smiled at her and saw tears in her eyes which he couldn't explain. Suddenly, horrifyingly, he sensed that his happiness was about to end as it always did.

"It's not over, is it?" he asked. "Oh, love, don't say it's over."

Her voice was too choked, her throat too full, her heart too heavy to respond. She could hardly nod.

Queenie telephoned Cecil Rand the moment she left the meeting. Her decision to help buy back Regina would please him, she knew. But he would be deeply hurt by her determination to keep Alex on as president. Cecil had never stopped scheming for that job himself. The least she could do was to tell him immediately, before he heard the news from someone else. Also, there was the question of Cohen to consider. How would he take the news? He too had been struggling to improve his position. . . .

The telephone rang a long time before a sleepy maid answered.

"I'd like to talk to Mr. Rand, please," Queenie said politely.

"I'm afraid he's asleep."

"Obviously, dear. It's after two in the morning. But I want to talk to him anyway. This is Miss Duke calling. Please wake him and get him to the phone."

"Yes, madame." The girl, even though she was new with the Rands, recognized Queenie's name, and understood quite clearly the authority in her voice.

There was a long pause. Finally, Queenie could hear the sound of someone approaching. "Yes, what on earth do you want?" Cecil Rand asked querilously. "I was fast asleep."

"I imagined you might be," said Queenie, her amusement audible, "it's after two in the morning."

"It's after two—" Cecil started. "Oh, you just said that, didn't you?"

"Cecil, I have some important news. Are you awake?"

"I'm fine." Cecil was indeed awake now; Queenie would not have called at this hour if she did not have something of extraordinary importance to say. "Is anything wrong?"

"No. It's very right. I've been able to save Regina. Save it for a very long time." Queenie proceeded to explain in detail to Cecil Rand what had happened. She was businesslike and precise, giving him all the facts without comment and without boasting.

Occasionally Cecil would interrupt with an exclamation, but otherwise he was silent, listening intently.

"And so," Queenie concluded, "Alex Petersen will be running Regina as an independent company from now on. I shall step out as rapidly as I decently can. And I think you should too." She paused. "Don't you agree?"

Cecil's only reply was a startled exclamation. Then for several minutes he said nothing coherent while Queenie at the other end of the phone listened to his deep breathing and occasional mutters with growing impatience.

"Well?" she demanded at length.

"What would I do if I were not working at Regina?" Cecil asked sadly. "Where would I go?"

Suddenly Queenie understood the complete emptiness of the man. There was nothing else in his life, it seemed, except Regina and his hopeless desire to live up to Sir Reginald's expectations.

"But there are lots of things to do," Queenie started weakly, her lack of conviction obvious in her voice.

"Are there?"

"Well, of course—"

"Nothing. Nothing at all." Cecil's voice cracked. For an instant Queenie was afraid he would break into tears. With an enormous effort he controlled himself. "Good thing too," he said with pathetic cheerfulness. "Time I had nothing to do. You're right, everyone has to retire sometime."

"Perhaps you'll have time to spend with Barbara and the kids," Queenie said, now almost as worried that she would not be able to control her own voice as she had been that he would cry.

"Maybe," he said without conviction. "But she hardly needs me."

"Her marriage is not that stable, you know. It might be breaking up."

"Everything's breaking up," Cecil said dully. "But she still wouldn't need my help."

"But Cohen does. He'll be terribly disappointed."

"Maybe," Cecil Rand repeated, but there was a little more belief in his voice. "Maybe he might need a hand."

Although Cohen had every intention of staying in Canada for several days when he left home that morning, he changed his mind as soon as he arrived. It simply didn't seem important anymore. Instead he stayed overnight and caught the first plane home in the morning. He arrived back to an empty house, the kids having left for school and the maid for shopping.

"Where are you?" Cohen shouted for Barbara as soon as he came into the house, some of his old arrogance returning. "You're never there when I need you." There was no answer. Walking upstairs, he noted that her room had not been slept in.

He walked toward the children's room. Outside was the big notice board which carried all the family messages. Carefully he inspected it. Neatly pinned on the board was a piece of paper with a telephone number and the one word, "Mommy." Angrily he ripped off the paper and took it to the telephone.

He had to ring for a long time before the telephone bell was heard over the sound of the inn's vacuum cleaner. Finally, the voice of the innkeeper answered. "Old River Inn. Hello."

"Hello," said Cohen hoarsely. "Is Barbara there?"

The innkeeper didn't understand the rough voice of his caller clearly. "Barbara?" He paused. "Yes, Barbara, Barbara Knight. Yes, sure. She's here. She still sleeping. Is it important?"

Cohen registered the fact that he knew the Inn, knew just where it was, and also that the name had been Knight and not Cohen. For a second he assumed there was simply a mistake. It was a different Barbara; but then, with growing intuition, he became sure that there was no mistake.

"It's okay," Cohen said. He hung up the phone.

Cohen had never experienced anything like his mind's gradual descent into madness, a madness in which Barbara and his Aunt Ruth and the whores in the hotel all intermingled with an awful feeling of self-pity. . . . Nor had he experienced anything like the explosion of anger which forced him to snatch his whip and run for the large red car in the garage.

Barbara wanted to tell Roger what she felt and to try to explain to him how her love and her duty were like the waves crashing in everlasting struggle. Explain that Marty meant nothing to her—not love, not warmth, not even friendship, merely a duty which would last as long as he needed her. But she could not find the strength to say what she meant. All she could do was to stare at him silently, tears rolling down her cheeks, and pray he understood. Roger, for his part, felt a despair so absolute that he was immobilized, unable even to cry.

For a long time they held each other silently, trying to protect each other from their pain, trying to prolong indefinitely the moment. The sun rose behind the red maple tree, silhouetting its leaves so that they seemed black, almost as if the tree were mourning with them.

After a long time, Roger felt her shiver and realized she was freezing, her lips blue with the cold.

"Come back to bed," he said gently. "You are so cold."

"All through me," she said simply, her eyes spilling with tears again.

They crawled under the covers and held each other tight, clung to each other in their despair, for a long time. At last, as their bodies warmed, he gently entered her, to be even closer. Gently they made love, crying in each other's arms. Their orgasm was the climax of their love and their sadness. Afterwards they rose and dressed slowly, sadly, each feeling as empty and lonely as ever they could remember.

They walked out to the parking lot side by side, not talking, each carrying an overnight bag. Then they touched briefly and turned away from each other towards their separate cars.

Cecil Rand woke early that morning. He had hardly slept at all since Queenie called. He dressed routinely, ate his breakfast, and walked out of the house.

Perhaps I can go to the office to clear things up, he thought. But the idea was too painful. How pathetic he would feel, unable even to pretend he was needed.

Instead he walked aimslessly into the park, loitering to watch the horses cantering, helping a child whose boat had capsized in the lake. It took him almost an hour of ambling before he found himself near Barbara and Marty's house and realized that this had been his real destination all along. He moved forward more briskly.

Just as Cecil Rand reached the garage entrance, he saw Cohen dash out of the building, his face distorted, his hair dishevelled.

"What is it?" Cecil called, his vague manner suddenly gone. "What's the matter?" he demanded.

Cohen stopped, looking like a man in a nightmare. "What?" he asked, dazed.

"What's the matter?" Cecil insisted again. "What is it?"

Suddenly Cohen seemed to disintegrate. "The bitch," he said softly. "The bitch. The bitch." It was all he seemed able to say. "The bitch, the bitch, the bitch . . ." His face seemed to fall apart before Cecil Rand's eyes. He staggered and would have fallen if Cecil had not caught him. "The bitch, the bitch . . ." he muttered.

"Come with me. Come inside." With care, almost with tenderness, Cecil helped Cohen back inside. He settled him into the sofa in the living room as gently as he would a small sick child. "Now tell me. Tell me what's happened."

And, like a child, Cohen told all of it: told of his Aunt Ruth and of Sir Reginald, of the whores and the whip. And then, with tears now streaming down his cheeks, told of how frightened he was of madness. "And now she's left me. Gone off to some inn with—"

"Hush. It's not so bad. It's not so bad." Cecil Rand's voice was reassuring and certain.

"But she's left me. My wife's left me."

"It's not so bad," Cecil repeated. "She was never really a wife to you, or a daughter to me either for that matter. She was just Sir Reginald's kid."

"Yes," said Cohen, calmer now. "Yes, I suppose that's true. Sir Reginald's kid. Will she come back?" Cohen sounded as plaintive as a young child.

"She might. I don't know. But you don't need her anymore now, you know," Cecil said with certainty. "You don't need any of it anymore. You're a fine businessman in your own right. A fine businessman. And I'm here to help." He felt a surge of relief in him, a sense of fulfillment greater than he could ever remember.

"Will you help me?" Cohen asked softly. For him too the relief was enormous. Never before had he asked help from anyone.

"Of course. Of course. You don't need her now. You can tell her to get lost. I'm here to help."

"But why should you?" Cohen was sudden suspicious.

"Because I want to." Cecil Rand looked at Cohen most seriously. "I haven't been much of a father to Barbara, you know. Maybe I can be a bit of a father-in-law to you." He laughed embarrassed.

"But she's left me."

"It doesn't matter. She left me years ago. We don't need her. We don't need anyone now. We won't ever let her come back. We'll go into business together and have a great time. Absolutely. I think it will be more fun than anything I've ever done. Much more fun . . ."

Afterword

Obviously, readers of this book—and especially those connected with the cosmetics industry—will look for real people lurking behind its fictitious characters. No doubt, my vehement statements that this is not a roman à clef and my repeated assurances that there is no intentional similarity between the characters in this work of fiction and people, living or dead, who work in the cosmetics industry will be ignored.

Nevertheless, I want to say once and for all, unequivocally, unambiguously, and with utter, emphatic clarity that any similarity, between any character in this book and any real company or personality, living or dead, or with anyone associated with the cosmetics industry, is purely coincidental.

In particular:
  API is *not* modeled on Colgate-Palmolive, where I was an officer from 1972 to 1978. (Colgate is financially healthy.) And Regina is *not* modeled on Helena Rubinstein, of which it is true that I was president for five exciting years through

the end of 1978. (For one thing, Helena Rubinstein did not have half the problems of Regina—thank God! For another, Rubinstein is a different type of company: It is renowned for its treatment products, which is why it is called the "Science of Beauty" company; whereas Regina is known for its fashionable colors and its fragrances.)

Marty Cohen is *not* a copy of any of my acquaintances. Alex Petersen is *not* a copy of me. (I wish I *were* like him for I admire much about him.) Herman Cosgrove, Blake Richards, Seymour Asquith, Leonard Abrams, and the many other characters in this book are *not* copies of any people in similar positions I have ever known.

Queenie is *not* a copy of Mala Rubinstein, Madame Rubinstein, Elizabeth Arden, Estée Lauder, or all of the above. And Sir Reginald is not another reincarnation of Charles Revson, nor is he a male version of Madame Rubinstein. He is his own company's tycoon, not a copy of anyone else's.

On the other hand, Sylvie, the perfect secretary, *is* like my secretary, Diane, in the sense that they are both perfect, although not in any other way.

So why is the book about business and about a cosmetic company in particular? There must be some similarities. . . .

Yes, there are. The setting is, I hope, authentic. For one purpose of this book is to convey the raw excitement of business, an excitement that pervades me almost every day of my life and that raises countless men and women out of their beds every morning, raring to hurry to another day at the office. I love business as an activity and I hope this book gives some sense of why.

I believe too that the details of what makes a cosmetic company tick are authentic. (Not all the legal or financial ramifications are intended to be accurate; this is a novel, not a treatise on company law or a financial textbook. But the overall facts about the cosmetics industry are intended to be real.)

Most importantly, the people in this book are supposed to be realistic—not copies of anyone but true to type, believable and plausible. They *could* be real people. It just so happens that they are not!

Finally, there is one aspect of the book which is authentic in every way. The book assumes that, for the most part, business is an ethical activity which employs and excites, even fascinates, competent, decent, honest people and which generally benefits its employees, its shareholders, and the society in which it operates. That assumption is totally intentional. For I believe firmly —and have written copiously—about the value of business.

The health and wealth of the people of any nation is largely dependent on the health of that nation's economy. And the health of each nation's economy *is* the health of its business. In that single respect, this book is not only a work of fiction, but a portrayal of fact as I see it.